VAL McDERMID

Val McDermid grew up in a Scottish mining community then read English at Oxford. She was a journalist for sixteen years, spending the last three years as Northern Bureau Chief of a national Sunday tabloid. Now a full-time writer, she lives in Cheshire.

Val McDermid is the highly acclaimed author of *The Mermaids Singing*, *The Wire in the Blood* and *The Last Temptation*, tense psychological thrillers featuring criminal profiler Tony Hill. *The Mermaids Singing* won the 1995 Gold Dagger Award for Best Crime Novel of the Year. *A Place of Execution*, her complex and disturbing stand-alone thriller, was awarded the 2001 *LA Times* Book of the Year Award (Mystery/Thriller category), and is now available in paperback.

She has written six crime novels featuring Manchester PI Kate Brannigan, and the latest of these, *Star Struck*, won the Grand Prix des Romans d'Aventure in France.

A further five novels feature journalist-sleuth Lindsay Gordon.

From the reviews for Killing the Shadows

'McDermid writes thrillers that snap at the heels of the genre's conventions – extending its boundaries in a way which combines the high-octane ferocity of her American cousins with the panoramic detail of a contemporary Dickens ... This is a multi-layered novel, yet one which is as hauntingly strung together as the knots on a hangman's noose. The plotting is impeccable, the atmospheric palpable, and I doubt that it will be surpassed this year'

GRAHAM CAVENEY, *Sunday Express*

'McDermid has become our leading pathologist of everyday evil, and she both thrills and scares in this tale of celebrity stalking with a difference ... The subtle orchestration of terror is masterful'   MAXIM JAKUBOWSKI, *Guardian*

'*Killing the Shadows* exerts the dangerous pull of a rip tide, drawing us towards its unsettling resolution. The psychological and procedural details convince, and there are wickedly apposite glimpses of fictional crime writers. McDermid reveals with chilling plausibility how extrinsic factors can warp the progress of a high-profile criminal investigation. Best (or worst) of all, she shows us how guilt and grief affect those who have loved a murder victim'

ANDREW TAYLOR, *Independent*

'The theme gives the author scope for some chilling descriptions of warped minds at their gruesome work ... [*Killing the Shadows*] keeps McDermid in the first rank of UK crime writing'   SUSANNA YAGER, *Sunday Telegraph*

The Last Temptation
A Place of Execution
The Wire in the Blood
The Mermaids Singing

Kate Brannigan novels

Star Struck
Blue Genes
Clean Break
Crack Down
Kick Back
Dead Beat

Lindsay Gordon novels

Booked for Murder
Union Jack
Final Edition
Common Murder
Report for Murder

Non-fiction

A Suitable Job for a Woman

VAL McDERMID

Killing
the Shadows

HarperCollins*Publishers*

HarperCollins*Publishers*
77–85 Fulham Palace Road, London W6 8JB

The HarperCollins website address is:
www.fireandwater.com

This paperback edition 2001

2

First published in Great Britain by
HarperCollins*Publishers* 2000

Typeset in Minion by
Palimpsest Book Production Limited,
Polmont, Stirlingshire

Printed and bound in Great Britain by
Clays Ltd, St Ives plc

Acknowledgements

Several people contributed their expertise in the hope it would prevent me making too many mistakes. So thanks for linguistic expertise to Dr Sandra Truscott; for sharing her knowledge of her native tongue and for helping break the logjam to Karin Slaughter; for everything I know about crime linkage and geographic profiling to Ron Mackay; for forensic expertise to Dr Sue Black; for details of police procedure to Peter N. Walker and Roger Forsdyke; for last-minute legal queries to Sue Cragg; and for the tireless efforts on my behalf, that incomparable researcher Mary Carter, and the endlessly patient Daphne Wright. Most of all, thanks to Brigid Baillie for the customary legal advice and for always being the right person in the right place at the right time.

And of course, to Lara Croft. Without whom I would certainly have gone mad.

This one's for BB. Because it takes two to jump over the rocks in the road.

i

The haar moves up from the steel-grey waters of the Firth of Forth, a solid wall of mist the colour of cumulus. It swallows the bright lights of the city's newest playground, the designer hotels and the smart restaurants. It becomes one with the spectres of the sailors from the docks who used to blow their pay on eighty-shilling ale and whores with faces as hard as their clients' hands. It climbs the hill to the New Town, where the geometric grid of Georgian elegance slices it into blocks before it slides down into the ditch of Princes Street Gardens. The few late revellers staggering home quicken their steps to escape its clammy grip.

By the time it reaches the narrow split-level streets and twisting vennels of the Old Town, the haar has lost its deadening solidity. It has metamorphosed into wraiths of pale fog that turn tourist traps into sinister looming presences. Peeling posters advertising recent Festival Fringe events flit in and out of visibility like garish ghosts. On a night like this it's easy to see what inspired Robert Louis Stevenson to create The Strange Case of Dr Jekyll and Mr Hyde. He may have set the book in London, but it's unmistakably Edinburgh that comes eerily off the page.

Behind the soot-black facades of the Royal Mile lie the old tenements surrounding their barren courts. Back in the eighteenth century, these were the equivalent of today's council-housing schemes – overcrowded with the dispossessed of the city, home to drunks and laudanum addicts, haunts of the lowest whores and street urchins. Tonight, like a tormented replay of the worst historical nightmare, a woman's body lies close to the head of a stone staircase that provides a steep short cut from High Street down the slope of The Mound. Her short dress has been pulled up, the cheap seams splitting under the strain.

If she had screamed when she was attacked, it would have been smothered by the blanket of foggy air. One thing is certain. She will never scream again. Her throat is a gaping scarlet grin. To add insult to injury, the gleaming coils of her intestines have been draped over her left shoulder.

The printer who stumbled over the body on his way home from a late shift cowers in a crouch at the mouth of the close leading to the court. He is close enough to the pool of his own vomit to gag on the rancid stench held hovering by the oppression of the haar. He has used his mobile phone to call the police, but the few minutes it is taking them to arrive feel like an eternity, his recent vision of hell stamped ineradicably on his mind's eye.

Flashing blue lights loom suddenly before him as two police cars swoop to a halt at the kerb. Running footsteps, then he has company. Two uniformed officers gently help him to his feet. They lead him towards their squad car where they hand him into the rear seat. Two others have disappeared down the close, the woolly sound of their footsteps swallowed almost

2

immediately by the clinging mist. Now the only sounds are the crackling of the police radio and the chattering of the printer's teeth.

Dr Harry Gemmell hunkers by the body, his gloved fingers probing things that Detective Inspector Campbell Grant doesn't want to think about. Rather than study what the police surgeon is doing, Grant looks instead at the scene-of-crime officers in their white overalls. They are taking advantage of the portable lights to search the area round the body. The haar is eating into Grant's very bones, making him feel like an old man.

Eventually, Gemmell grunts and pushes himself to his feet, stripping the blood-streaked latex from his hands. He studies his chunky sports watch and gives a satisfied nod. 'Aye,' he says. 'September the eighth, right enough.'

'Meaning what, Harry?' Grant asks wearily. He is already irritated by the prospect of enduring Gemmell's habit of forcing detectives to drag information out of him piecemeal.

'Your man here, he likes to play follow-my-leader. See if you can figure it out for yourself, Cam. There are marks on her neck that indicate manual strangulation, though I reckon she died from having her throat cut. But it's the mutilations that tell the story.'

'Is all this supposed to mean something to me, Harry? Apart from a good reason to lose my last meal?' Grant demands.

'Eighteen eighty-eight in Whitechapel, nineteen ninety-nine in Edinburgh.' Gemmell raises an eyebrow. 'Time to call in the profilers, Cam.'

'What the fuck are you on about, Harry?' Grant asks. He wonders if Gemmell's been drinking.

'I think you've got a copycat killer, Cam. I think you're looking for Jock the Ripper.'

Chapter 1

Dr Fiona Cameron stood on the very lip of Stanage Edge and leaned forward into the wind. The only kind of sudden death she might have to contemplate here would be her own, and then only if she was more careless than she thought she could manage. But just supposing for a moment she lost concentration on the wet millstone grit, she'd plunge down thirty or forty helter-skelter feet, her body bouncing like a plastic doll on the jutting blocks of rock, bones and skin broken and violated.

She'd end up looking like a victim.

No way, Fiona thought, letting the wind push her back from the edge just far enough to take the danger out of her position. Not here of all places. This was the place of pilgrimage, the place where she came to remind herself of all the reasons why she was who she was. Always alone, she returned here three or four times a year, whenever the need grew in her to touch the face of her memories. The company of another living, breathing human would be impossible to bear up on this bleak stretch of moorland. There was only room for the two of them; Fiona and her ghost, that other half of herself who only ever walked beside her on these moors.

It was strange, she thought. There were so many other places where she'd spent far more time with Lesley. But everywhere else was somehow marred by the consciousness of other voices, other lives. Here, though, she could sense Lesley without interference. She could see her face, open in laughter, or closed in concentration as she negotiated a tricky scramble. She could hear her voice, earnest with confidences or loud with the excitement of achievement. She almost believed she could smell the faint musk of her skin as they huddled together over a picnic.

Here, more than anywhere, Fiona recognized the light she had lost from her life. She closed her eyes and let her mind create the picture. Her mirror image, that same chestnut hair and hazel eyes, that same arc of the eyebrows, that same nose. Everyone had always marvelled at the resemblance. Only their mouths were different; Fiona's wide and full-lipped, Lesley's a small cupid's bow, her bottom lip fuller than the upper.

Here, too, the discussions had been had, the decision taken that had ultimately led to Lesley being wrenched from her life. This was the place of final reproach, the place where Fiona could never forget what her life lacked.

Fiona felt her eyes watering. She snapped them open and let the wind provide the excuse. The time for vulnerability was over. She was here, she reminded herself, to get away from victims. She looked out across the brown bracken of Hathersage Moor to the clumsy thumb of Higger Tor and beyond, turning back to watch a wedge of rain drench one end of Bamford Moor. In this wind, she had twenty minutes before it reached the Edge, she reckoned, rolling her shoulders to shift her backpack to a more comfortable position. Time to make a move.

An early train from King's Cross then a connection to a local train had brought her to Hathersage just after ten. She'd made good time on the steep hike up to High Neb, enjoying the stretch in her muscles, savouring the bunching of her calves and the tautness of her quads. The final scramble that brought her to the northern end of Stanage had left her short of breath and she'd leaned against the rock, taking a long drink from her water bottle before she set off along the flat slabs of gritstone. The connection to her past had grounded her more firmly than anything else she knew. And the wind at her back had exhilarated her, setting her thoughts loose from the jumbled knot of irritation that had woken her. She'd known then that she had to get out of London for the day or else accept that by evening her shoulders would be a tight plane sending waves of pain up her neck and across her head.

The only appointment in her diary had been a supervision meeting with one of her PhD students, and that had been easily rearranged with a phone call from the train. Up here on the moors, no tabloid hack could find her, no camera crew could thrust their equipment into her face and demand to know what Candid Cameron had to say about the day's courtroom events.

Of course, she couldn't be certain that things would turn out in line with her expectations. But when she'd heard on last night's news that the sensational trial of the Hampstead Heath Killer was still on hold after a second day of legal arguments, all her instincts told her that by the end of today, the red-top brigade would be screaming for blood. And she was the perfect weapon for them to use to draw that blood from the police. Better to keep well out of it, for all sorts of reasons.

She'd never courted publicity for the work she'd done with the police, but it had dogged her regardless. Fiona hated to see her face splashed across the newspapers nearly as much as her colleagues resented it. What was almost worse than the loss of privacy was that her notoriety had somehow diminished her as an academic. Now when she published in journals and contributed to books, she knew her work was scrutinized with more scepticism than before, simply because she had applied her skills and knowledge in a practical way that met with pursed lips of disapproval among the purists.

The silent condemnation had only grown harsher when one of the tabloids had revealed that she was living with Kit Martin. It was hard to imagine who, in the eyes of the academic establishment, could have been a less respectable partner for an academic psychologist engaged in developing scientific methods that would help police to catch repeat offenders than the country's leading writer of serial killer thrillers. If Fiona had cared enough about what her peers thought of her, she might have bothered to explain that it was not Kit's novels she was in love with but the man who wrote them, and that the very nature of his work had made her more cautious about starting the relationship than she might otherwise have been. But since no one dared challenge her to her face, she chose not to leap into the trap of self-justification.

At the thought of Kit, her sadness shifted. That she had found the one man who could save her from the prison of her introspection was a blessing she never ceased to find miraculous. The world might never see behind the tough-guy charm he turned on in public, but beyond his sharp-edged intelligence, she had discovered generosity, respect and a sensitivity she'd all but given up hope of ever finding. With Kit, she had finally arrived at a kind of peace that mostly kept the demons of Stanage Edge at bay.

As she strode on, she glanced at her watch. She'd made good time. If she kept up her pace, she'd have time for a drink in the Fox House pub before the bus that would carry her back down into Sheffield for the London train.

She'd have had five hours in the open, five hours when she had seen scarcely another human being, and that was enough to sustain her. Until the next time, she thought grimly.

The train was quieter than she'd expected. Fiona had a double seat to herself, and the man opposite her was asleep within ten minutes of leaving Sheffield, allowing her space to spread herself over the whole of the table between them. That was fine by her since she had more than enough work to occupy the journey. She had an arrangement with the landlord of a pub a few minutes' walk from the station. He looked after her mobile phone and her laptop when she was out walking in exchange for signed first editions of Kit's books. It was safer than the left-luggage facilities at the station and certainly cheaper.

Fiona flipped open her laptop and attached it to her mobile so she could collect her e-mail. A message appeared on her screen announcing she had five new pieces of mail. She downloaded them then disconnected. There were two messages from students, and one from a colleague in Princeton writing to ask if he could have access to some data she had collected on solved rape cases. Nothing there that couldn't wait till morning. She opened the fourth message, from Kit.

From: Kit Martin <KMWriter@trashnet.com>
To: Fiona Cameron
          <fcameron@psych.ulon.ac.uk>
Subject: Dinner tonight

Hope you've had a good day on the hill. I've been productive, 2,500 words by teatime.

Things turned out at the Bailey just like you said
they would. Trust that female intuition! (only
joking, I know yours was a considered judgement
based on weighing up all the scientific evidence
...) Anyway, I reckoned Steve would need cheering
up, so I've arranged to meet him for dinner. We're
going to St John's in Clerkenwell to eat lots of
dead animal so you probably don't fancy joining
us, but if you want to, that'd be great. If not, I
made a salmon and asparagus risotto for lunch,
and there's plenty left over in the fridge for you
for dinner.
Love you.

Fiona smiled. Typical Kit. As long as everyone was fed,
nothing too terrible could go wrong with the world. She
wasn't surprised Steve needed cheering up. No police officer
relished watching a case fall apart, especially one that had
such a high public profile as the Hampstead Heath murder.
But for Detective Superintendent Steve Preston, the collapse
of this particular case would have left a more bitter taste than
most. Fiona knew only too well how much had been at stake
in this prosecution, and while she felt personal sympathy for
Steve, all she felt for the Metropolitan Police was that it served
them bloody well right.

She clicked open the next message, having saved the most
intriguing for last.

From: Salvador Berrocal <Sberroc@cnp.mad.es>
To: Dr Fiona Cameron
          <fcameron@psych.ulon.ac.uk>
Subject: Consultation request

Dear Dr Cameron

I am a Major in the plain-clothes division of the Cuerpo Nacional de Policia based in Madrid. I am in charge of many homicide inquiries. Your name has been given to me by a colleague at New Scotland Yard as an expert in crime linkage and geographic profiling. Please forgive the intrusion of contacting you so directly. I am writing to ask if you would do us the courtesy of providing your services to consult in a matter of great urgency. In Spain we have a little experience with serial killers and so we have no psychological experts to work with policemen.

In Toledo have been two murders inside three weeks and we think they are the crimes of one man. But it is wholly not obvious that they are connected and we need a different expertise to assist us with the analysis of these crimes. I understand that you have experience in the area of crime analysis and linkage, and this would be of great use to us, I think.

I wish to know if in principle you are willing to help us with resolving these murders. You may be assured of proper remuneration for this consultation if you will be our assistant.

I look forward to hearing your response.

Respectfully

Major Salvador Berrocal

Cuerpo Nacional de Policia

Fiona folded her arms and stared at the screen. She knew that behind this cautious request lay a pair of bodies that had almost certainly been mutilated and probably tortured before death. There was likely to be some element of sexual violation in the attacks. She could assume this with some degree of certainty, for police forces were well capable of dealing with routine murders without calling on the specialist help that only she and a handful of others could be relied on to provide. When new acquaintances discovered this aspect of Fiona's work, they usually shuddered and asked how she could bear to be involved in such appalling cases.

Her typical response was to shrug and say, 'Somebody has to do it. Better it's somebody like me who knows what she's doing. Nobody can bring back the dead but sometimes it's possible to prevent more of the living joining them.'

It was, she knew, a glib riposte, carefully calculated to deflect further questioning. The truth was she hated the inevitable confrontation with violent death that her work with various police forces had brought into her life, not least because of the memories it stirred in her. She knew more about what could be inflicted on the human body, more about the sufferings the spirit could sustain than she had ever wished to. But such exposure was inescapable and because it always exacted a heavy toll from her, she only ever accepted a new assignment when she felt sufficiently recovered from her last direct encounter with the victims of a serial killer.

It had been almost four months since Fiona had worked a murder series. A man had killed four prostitutes in Merseyside over a period of eighteen months. Thanks in part to the data analysis that Fiona and one of her graduate students had completed, the police had been able to narrow down their pool of suspects to the point where forensic detection could be applied. Now they had a man in custody charged with three of the four killings, and thanks to DNA matches they were reasonably sure of a conviction.

Since then, her only police consultation project had been a long-term study of recidivist burglars with the Swedish Police. It was, she thought, time to get her hands dirty again. She hit the <reply> key.

From: Fiona Cameron
          <fcameron@psych.ulon.ac.uk>
To: Salvador Berrocal <sberroc@cnp.mad.es>
Subject: Re: Consultation request

Dear Major Berrocal
Thank you for your invitation to act as
consultant to the Cuerpo Nacional de Policia.
In principle, I am willing to consider your
request favourably. However, before I can
be certain that I can be of use to you, I need
more detail than you have provided in your
e-mail. Ideally, I would like to see an outline
of the circumstances of both murders, a digest
of the pathology reports and any witness
statements. I am reasonably competent in
written Spanish, so in the interests of speed,
you need not have these documents translated
for my benefit. Of course, any communications
I receive from you will be treated in complete
confidence.
    For the sake of security, I suggest you fax these
documents to my home.

Fiona typed in the details of her home fax and phone then sent the e-mail. At best, she'd be able to contribute to the prevention of more murders and acquire useful data for her researches in the process. At worst, she'd have a valid excuse for staying out of the way of the fallout from the Hampstead Heath trial collapse. Someone – or rather a couple of Spanish someones – had paid a high price to keep Candid Cameron out of the headlines.

Chapter 2

Fiona walked through the door to the sound of REM telling her that nobody loved a sad professor. As usual, Kit had stacked up half a dozen CDs in the player in his study, hit the random button and walked out the door while there were still hours of playing time left. He couldn't abide silence. She had learned this early on in their relationship, when she'd taken him walking in her beloved Derbyshire and had been horrified to watch him filling his backpack with cassettes for his Walkman. More than once, she'd come home to an empty house where music spilled out of Kit's study, the TV in the living room blared like a bull and the radio in the kitchen added a mad counterpoint to the racket. The louder the din, the easier he seemed to find it to escape into his own imagined universe. For Fiona, who needed silence in order to concentrate on anything vaguely creative, it was an incomprehensible paradox.

When they'd first talked about living together, Fiona had insisted that whatever property they bought, it had to be capable of providing her with a quiet space to work in. They'd ended up with a tall thin house in Dartmouth Park whose previous owner had been a rock musician. He'd converted the attic into a soundproof studio that provided Fiona with the perfect eyrie to escape Kit's background racket. It was even big enough to allow her to install a futon for those nights when Kit was up against a deadline and needed to write into the early hours of the morning. Sometimes she felt deeply sorry for their long-suffering neighbours. They must dread February when, invariably, the end of a book and late-night Radiohead loomed.

Fiona dropped her bags and went into Kit's ground-floor study to turn off the music. Blessed silence fell like balm on her head. She continued upstairs, stopping off in their bedroom to shuck off her walking gear and pull on her house clothes She trudged up the remaining two flights to her office, feeling the hills in the pull of her leg muscles. The first thing she registered was the flashing light of the answering machine. Fifteen messages. She'd put money on them all being from journalists, and she wasn't in the mood to listen to them, never mind to respond. This was one occasion where she was absolute in her determination not to provide a single quote that could be twisted to suit someone else's agenda.

Leaving her laptop by the desk, Fiona noticed that Major Berrocal hadn't wasted any time. A pile of paper lay accusingly in the fax tray. That she couldn't ignore. Stifling a sigh, she picked it up, automatically straightening the edges, and headed back downstairs.

As Kit had promised, her dinner sat in the fridge. She wondered fleetingly how many of his fans would credit that the man who created scenes of graphic violence that gave critics nightmares was the same creature whose idea of relaxation after a hard day's writing was to cook gourmet food for his lover. They'd probably prefer to believe he spent his evenings on Hampstead Heath, biting the heads off small furry animals. Smiling at the thought, Fiona poured herself a glass of cold Sauvignon while she waited for the risotto to heat up, then settled down at the kitchen table with the Spanish fax and a pencil. Glancing at the clock, she decided to catch the news headlines before she began the chore of deciphering foreign police reports.

The theme music of the late evening news thundered out its familiar fanfare. The camera zoomed in on the solemn face of the newsreader. 'Good evening. The headlines tonight. The man accused of the Hampstead Heath murder walks free after a judge accuses the police of entrapment.' Top item, Fiona noted without surprise. 'Middle East peace talks are on the verge of breakdown in spite of a personal intervention by the US President. And the rouble tumbles as fresh scandal hits Russia's banking system.'

The screen behind the newsreader's head changed from the programme logo to a shot of the exterior of the Central Criminal Court. 'At the Old Bailey today, the man accused of the savage rape and murder of Susan Blanchard was freed on the order of the trial judge. Mrs Justice Mary Delancey said there was no doubt that the Metropolitan Police had entrapped Francis Blake in an operation which she described as "little short of a witch-hunt". In spite of the lack of any solid evidence against Mr Blake, she said, they had decided that he was the killer. Over to our Home Affairs Correspondent, Danielle Rutherford, who was in court today.'

A woman in her thirties with mouse-brown hair tangled by the wind gazed earnestly at the camera. 'There were angry scenes in court today as Mrs Justice Delancey ordered the release of Francis Blake. The family of Susan Blanchard, who was raped and murdered as she walked on Hampstead Heath with her twin babies, were outraged at the judge's decision and at Blake's obvious jubilation in the dock.

'But the judge was unmoved by their protests, saving her condemnation for the Metropolitan Police whose methods she described as an affront to civilized democracy. Acting on the advice of a psychological profiler, the police had set up a sting using an attractive female detective in an attempt to win Mr Blake's affections and to lure him into confessing to the murder. The sting, which cost hundreds of thousands of pounds of the police operations budget and lasted for almost three months, did not lead to a direct confession, but police believed they had obtained sufficient evidence to bring Mr Blake to trial.

'The defence argued that whatever Mr Blake had said had been at the instigation of the female detective and had been calculated to impress the personality she had falsely projected. And this view was upheld by the judge. After his release, Mr Blake, who has spent eight months in prison on remand, announced he would be seeking compensation.'

The picture changed, revealing a stocky man in his late twenties with cropped black hair and deep-set dark eyes. A forest of microphones and hand-held tape recorders blossomed in front of his white shirt and charcoal suit. His voice was surprisingly cultivated and he glanced down frequently at a piece of paper in his hands. 'I have always protested my innocence of the murder of Susan Blanchard, and today I have been vindicated by a court of law. But I have paid a terrible price. I have lost my job, my home, my girlfriend and my reputation. I am an innocent man, but I have spent eight months behind bars. I will be suing the Metropolitan Police for false imprisonment and for compensation. And I sincerely hope they will think twice before they set about framing another innocent man.' Then he looked up, his eyes blazing anger and hatred. Fiona shivered involuntarily.

The picture changed again. A tall man in a crumpled grey suit flanked by a pair of stony-faced men in raincoats walked towards the camera, head down, mouth drawn into a thin line. The reporter's voice said, 'The police officer in charge of the case, Detective Superintendent Steve Preston, refused to comment on Blake's release. In a later statement, New Scotland Yard announced they were not actively seeking anyone else in connection with Susan Blanchard's murder. This is Danielle Rutherford at the Old Bailey.'

Back in the studio, the newsreader announced that there would be an in-depth look at the background to the case after the break. Fiona turned off the TV. She had no need of their potted version of the facts. There were powerful reasons why she would never forget the rape and murder of Susan Blanchard. It wasn't the graphic police photographs of the body or the pathologist's report or her knowledge as a local resident of the scene of the crime, a mere twenty-minute walk from her own front door, although all of these had been terrible enough. Nor was it the brutality of a killer who had violated and stabbed a young mother in full view of her eighteen-month-old twin sons.

What made the Hampstead Heath murder so significant for Fiona was that it had marked the end of her association with the Met. She and Steve Preston had been close since their undergraduate days when they'd both read psychology at Manchester. Unlike most student friendships, it had persisted in spite of their very different career paths. And when British police forces had first started to consider the potential advantages of working with psychologists to improve their chances of catching repeat offenders, it had seemed the most natural thing in the world for Steve to consult Fiona. It had been the start of a fruitful relationship, with Fiona's rigorous approach to data analysis complementing the experience and instincts of the detectives she had worked with.

Within hours of the discovery of Susan Blanchard's body, it had been clear to Steve Preston that this was precisely the kind of case where Fiona's talents could be used to best advantage. A man who could kill like this was no beginner. Steve had learned enough from listening to Fiona, supplemented by his own reading, to know that such a killer would already have cast his shadow over the criminal justice system. With her expertise, Fiona would be able to suggest at the very least what sort of record their suspect would have. Depending on the circumstances, she might well be able to indicate the geographical area he'd be likely to live in. She would look at the same things that detectives saw, but for her they would have different meanings.

Early in the investigation, Francis Blake had emerged as a possible suspect. He had been seen on the Heath around the time of the murder, running away from the direction of the dense undergrowth that shielded the small clearing where Susan Blanchard's body had been found by a dog-walker who heard the children crying. Blake was branch manager for a firm of undertakers, which suggested to detectives that he had an unhealthy preoccupation with the dead. He had also worked in a butcher's shop as a teenager, which the police decided meant he was comfortable with the sight of blood. He had no adult criminal record, although he had been cautioned twice as a juvenile, once for setting fire to a rubbish bin and the second time for an assault on a younger boy. And he was evasive about what he'd been doing on the Heath that morning.

There was only one problem. Fiona didn't think Francis Blake was the killer. She said so to Steve and she kept on saying so to anyone who would listen. But her suggestions for alternative lines of inquiry had apparently led nowhere. Under the glare of an outraged media, Steve was under pressure to make an arrest.

One morning he'd turned up at her office at the university.

She'd taken one look at the hard set of his features and said, 'I'm not going to like this, am I?'

He shook his head and dropped into the chair facing her. 'You're not the only one. I've argued till I was blue in the face, but sometimes you just can't buck the politics. The Commander's gone over my head. He's brought in Andrew Horsforth.'

Neither of them needed to comment. Andrew Horsforth was a clinical psychologist. He had worked for years in a secure mental hospital whose reputation had slumped with every independent report ever made into it. He relied on what Fiona contemptuously referred to as the 'touchy-feely' approach to profiling, priding himself on the quality of insights gained from years of hands-on experience. 'Which would be fine if he could ever see past his own ego,' she'd once commented sarcastically after listening to him lecture. He'd had what she privately referred to as a lucky break on the first major case where he'd produced a profile and he'd traded on it ever since, never failing to provide the media with all the quotes and interviews they could desire. When police made an arrest on a case where he'd produced an offender profile, he was always quick to claim the credit; when they failed, it was never his fault. Faced with Francis Blake as a suspect, Fiona felt certain Horsforth could make the profile fit the man.

'I'm out of it, then,' she said with an air of finality.

'Believe me, you're well out of it,' Steve said bitterly. 'They've decided to ignore your professional advice and my personal opinion. They're going ahead with the sting. Orchestrated by Horsforth.'

Fiona shook her head in exasperation. 'Oh, for fuck's sake,' she exploded. 'It's a terrible idea. Even if I thought Blake was your man, it would still be a terrible idea. You might just get

21

something that would stand up in court if you used a trained psychologist with years of experience of therapeutic work to do the entrapment, but with the best will in the world, setting some young copper loose with an idiot like Horsforth briefing her is a recipe for disaster.'

Steve ran his hands through his thinning dark hair, pushing it back from his forehead. 'You think I haven't told them that?' His mouth clamped shut in a frustrated line.

'I'm sure you have. And I know you're as pissed off about it as I am.' Fiona got to her feet and turned to look out of the window. She couldn't bear to show her humiliation, even to someone as close as Steve. 'That's it, then,' she said. 'I'm finished with the Met. I'm never going to work with you and your colleagues again.'

Steve knew her well enough to realize there was little point in trying to argue when she was in this frame of mind. He'd been so angry at the dismissal of his own professional judgement that the thought of resignation had briefly flashed across his mind. But unlike Fiona, he had no alternative career where his expertise could make a difference, so he'd tossed the notion aside impatiently as the self-indulgence of hurt pride. He hoped Fiona would do the same, given time. But this wasn't the moment to suggest that. 'I can't blame you, Fi,' he said sadly. 'I'll be sorry to lose you.'

Composed again, she faced him. 'I'm not the only one you'll be saying sorry to before this is over,' she'd said mildly. Even then, she'd understood how badly things could turn out. Police officers desperate for an arrest, shored up by the seeming respectability of a psychologist who told them what they wanted to hear, would not be satisfied till they had their man behind bars.

It gave her no pleasure at all to see how right she'd been.

Chapter 3

The medieval stronghold of Toledo was built on a rocky outcropping almost completely enclosed by an ox-bow gorge in the River Tagus. The deep river and the steep cliffs provided natural defences for most of the city, leaving only a narrow neck of land to fortify against the enemy. Now a scenic road ran round the far bank of the Tagus, providing panoramic views of a tumble of buildings the colour of honey in the sun, descending precipitously from the ornate cathedral and the severe lines of the Alcazar. This much Fiona remembered from a hot dusty day thirteen years before when she'd explored the city with three friends.

They'd been celebrating the completion of their doctorates by touring Spain in a battered Volkswagen camper, ticking off the major sights and cities as they went. Toledo had meant El Greco, Fernando and Isabella, shop windows filled with armour and swords, and a particularly delicious way of serving quail, she recalled. If anyone had suggested to that young academic psychologist that she'd be returning one day as a consultant to the Spanish police, she'd have wondered what hallucinogenics they'd been on.

The first body had been found in a deep wooded gorge running down to the River Tagus about a mile from the city gates. According to local custom, the gorge boasted the revolting name of La Degollada – the woman with her throat slit, according to Fiona's Spanish dictionary. The original corpse in La Degollada was said to have been a gypsy woman who seduced one of the guard, allowing a sneak attack to take place on the city. Her punishment for losing her head over a soldier was literally to lose her head. Her throat was cut so severely that she was virtually decapitated. Fiona noted with weary lack of surprise that Major Berrocal's brief did not record the fate of the soldier.

The contemporary victim was a twenty-five-year-old German citizen, Martina Albrecht. Martina worked as a freelance tour guide, leading organized German-speaking parties round Toledo. According to friends and neighbours, she had a married lover, a junior officer in the Spanish Army who was attached to the Ministry of Defence in Madrid. He had been at an official dinner in the capital forty-odd miles away on the night of the murder. They were still drinking coffee and brandy at the time Martina's body had been discovered, so there was no question of him coming under suspicion. Besides, Martina's friends reported that she was perfectly happy with the part-time nature of their relationship and had said nothing to indicate there were any problems between them.

The body had been found just before midnight by a teenage courting couple who had parked their motorbike by the road and climbed down into the gorge to escape from prying eyes. There was also no question of any suspicion attaching to them, although the girl's father had reportedly accused the boyfriend of being perfectly capable of murder on the grounds that he was planning to debauch an innocent young girl.

According to the crime-scene reports, Martina had been sprawled on her back in the moonlight, arms thrown wide, legs spread. The pathologist revealed that her throat had been cut from left to right, probably from behind, by a long and very sharp blade, possibly a bayonet. It was hard to be precise, however, and since Toledo is famous for its steel, the purchase of razor-edged knives was an everyday occurrence in each of the dozens of tourist shops that lined the main streets. Death had been swift, blood pumping forwards from the severed carotid arteries in a pair of gushing fountains. Her clothing was drenched in blood, indicating that she had been standing rather than lying when the wound had been inflicted.

Further examination revealed that a broken wine bottle had been thrust repeatedly into her vagina, shredding the tissue. The relative absence of blood at the site indicated that Martina had been mercifully dead by then. The bottle had once contained a cheap Manchegan red wine, available in almost any local shop. The only other item of interest at the scene was a bloodstained guide to Toledo in German. Martina's name, address and phone number were scribbled on the inside cover in her own handwriting.

There were no significant forensic traces, nor any indication of how Martina had been brought to La Degollada. It was not a difficult place to access; the panoramic route round the Tagus actually crossed the gorge, and there were plenty of places nearby where a car could be tucked off the road. According to the woman with whom she shared an apartment near the station, Martina had come in from work around seven. They'd eaten a snack of bread, cheese and salad together, then the flatmate had left to meet a group of friends. Martina had had no firm plans, saying only that she might go out for a drink later. Officers had canvassed the cafés and bars she usually visited, but nobody had admitted seeing her that evening. The members of the tour she had led the previous day had been questioned when they'd arrived in Aranjuez the following day, but none of them had been aware of any of their fellow tourists taking any particular notice of their young guide. Besides, they'd all spent the evening together at a flamenco fiesta. Everyone was vouched for by at least three other members of the party.

In the absence of any firm leads, the investigation had ground to a halt. It was, Fiona thought, the sort of frustrating inquiry typically provoked by the first crime in a series where the offender was intelligent enough to know how to cover his tracks and had no ambivalence about being caught. Without any obvious connection between victim and killer it was always difficult to identify worthwhile avenues of investigation.

Then, two weeks later, a second body had turned up. A relatively short interval, Fiona noted. This time, the scene of the crime was the vast monastery church of San Juan de los Reyes. She remembered the cloisters, a massive quadrangle festooned with absurd gargoyles. It was there, she reminded herself, that one of their group had spotted the bizarre image of a reverse gargoyle – instead of a grotesque face adorning the water spout, this statue consisted of a body from the waist down, as if its owner had been rammed head first into the wall.

The unique feature of the church itself was the array of manacles and shackles that hung along its facade. They were the very shackles the Moorish conquerors used to chain up the Christian prisoners taken at Granada, and when Fernando and Isabella's vast army captured Granada from the Moors, the monarchs decreed the chains should be hung on the church as a memorial. Fiona remembered vividly how bizarre they had looked, hanging black in the sunlight against the golden stone of the ornamented facade.

The second victim was an American graduate student of religious art, James Paul Palango. His body had been discovered at dawn by a street cleaner who had been sweeping alongside the monastery cloisters of San Juan de los Reyes. He'd turned the corner on the paved area in front of the church when his eye had been caught by something above his head. Palango was hanging suspended from two sets of manacles. In the puffy flesh of his neck, something glinted in the early morning light. When the body was lowered to the ground, it became clear that he'd been strangled with a dog's choke chain then attached to the manacles with two pairs of handcuffs. The pathologist also reported that Palango's corpse had been repeatedly sodomized with the broken neck of a wine bottle, which remained inside his torn rectum. Again, there appeared to be no significant forensic traces. Interestingly, in Palango's pocket there was a guide to Toledo.

Police inquiries revealed that Palango was an evangelical Christian from a wealthy Georgia family. He had been staying at the parador which perched on a high bluff looking across the river to the city. According to the hotel, Palango had eaten an early dinner then gone out in his hired car sometime around nine o'clock. The car was later discovered in a parking garage opposite the Alcazar. Extensive questioning in the neighbourhood revealed that the American had taken coffee in the Plaza de Zocodover at the heart of the old town, but in the general melee of the evening *paseo* no one had noticed when he had left the café or whether he'd been alone. No one had come forward to say they'd seen him since.

Fiona leaned back in her seat and rubbed her eyes. No wonder Major Berrocal was so keen to enlist her help. The only significant information the police had gleaned from the second murder was that the killer was physically powerful enough to carry a ten-stone man up a ladder, and that he was bold enough to display his victim in a public place. In

27

a handwritten note, Major Berrocal had pointed out that once the nearby café had closed in the early hours of the morning, the area around the church was quiet and although it was overlooked by several houses, the killer had chosen the farthest point of the facade for his exhibition, where he would be least likely to be spotted.

She leaned back in her chair and stretched her arms above her head while she contemplated the information she'd laboriously worked her way through. It was professionally intriguing, no question of that. What she needed to consider was whether she could offer anything constructive to the investigation. She had worked with European police forces on several occasions, and had sometimes felt handicapped by her lack of visceral understanding of how their societies worked. On the other hand, she already felt the faint stirrings of an idea of how this killer operated and where the police might start their search for him.

One thing was certain. While she dithered, he would be planning his next murder. Fiona refilled her glass and made her decision.

Chapter 4

Fiona was halfway downstairs with the *Rough Guide to Spain* when she heard the front door opening. 'Hello,' she called out.

'I brought Steve home with me,' Kit replied, his voice relaxed into broad Mancunian by alcohol.

Fiona was too tired to welcome the prospect of late-night drinking and chat. But at least it was only Steve. He was part of the family, too well-rooted in their company to mind if she took herself off to bed and left them to it. She rounded the final turn in the stairs and looked down at them. The most important men in her life, they were an oddly contrasting pair. Steve, tall, wirily thin and dark; Kit, with his broad, heavily muscled torso making him look shorter than he was, his shaved head gleaming in the light. It was Steve, with his darting eyes and long fingers, who looked like the intellectual, while Kit looked more like a beat bobby who worked as a nightclub bouncer on the side. Now, they looked up at her, identical sheepish small-boy grins on their flushed faces.

'Good dinner, I see,' Fiona said dryly, running down the rest of the stairs. She stood on tiptoe to kiss Steve's cheek, then allowed Kit to engulf her in a hug.

He gave her a smacking kiss on the lips. 'Missed you,' he said, releasing her and crossing to the kitchen.

'No you didn't,' Fiona contradicted him. 'You've had a

great boys' night out, eaten lots of unspeakable bits of dead animals, drunk' – she paused and cocked her head, assessing them both – 'three bottles of red wine . . .'

'She's never wrong,' Kit interjected.

'. . . and put the world to rights,' Fiona concluded. 'You were much better off without me.'

Steve folded himself into a kitchen chair and accepted the brandy glass Kit proffered. He had the air of a man embattled who warily senses he might finally have arrived in a place of safety. He raised his glass in a sardonic toast. 'Confusion to our enemies. You're right, Fi, but for the wrong reasons,' he said.

Fiona sat down opposite him and pulled her wine glass towards her, intrigued. 'I find that hard to believe,' she said, a tease in her voice.

'Fi, I was only glad you weren't there because you're big-headed enough without listening to me ranting on about how I'd never have had to endure today's humiliations if I'd been working with you instead of that arsehole Horsforth.' Steve held up a hand to indicate to Kit that an inch of brandy was more than enough.

Kit leaned against the kitchen units, cupping his glass in both his broad hands to warm the spirit. 'You're right about the big-headed bit,' he chuckled, his pride in her obvious in his affectionate grin.

'Takes one to know one,' Fiona said. 'I'm sorry you had a shit day, Steve.'

Before Steve could reply, Kit cut in. 'It was bound to happen. That operation was doomed from day one. Apart from anything else, you were never going to get away with a sting like that in a trial, even if Blake had swallowed the honey-trap and coughed chapter and verse. British juries just can't get their heads round entrapment. Your average man in the pub thinks it's cheating to set people up when you haven't got your evidence the straight way.'

'Don't mince your words, Kit, tell us what you really think,' Steve said sarcastically.

'I'd hoped you two would already have had the postmortem,' Fiona protested mildly.

'Oh, we have,' Steve said. 'I feel like I've been wearing a hair shirt all day.'

'Hey, I've not been saying it was your fault,' Kit reminded him. 'We all know you got stamped on from above. If anyone should be flagellating himself, it's your commander. But you can bet your pension that Teflon Telford will be washing his hands like Pontius Pilate with a tin of Swarfega tonight. It'll be, "Well, of course, you have to let your junior officers have their head sometimes, but I thought Steve Preston would have handled matters better than this,"' he said, dropping his voice to the basso profundo of Steve's boss.

Steve stared into his brandy. Kit wasn't telling him anything he didn't already know, but hearing it from someone else didn't make failure taste any less sour. And tomorrow, he'd have to face his colleagues knowing that he was the one appointed to carry the can. Some of them would have sufficient grasp of the politics to understand he was nothing more than the designated scapegoat, but there were plenty of others who would relish the chance to snigger behind their hands at him. That was the price of his past successes. And in the competitive environment of the higher echelons of the Met, you were only ever as good as your last success.

'Are you really not looking for anyone else?' Fiona asked, registering Steve's depression and trying to move the conversation in a more positive direction.

Steve looked mutinous. 'That's the official line. To say anything else makes us look even bigger dickheads than we do already. But I'm not happy with that. Somebody murdered Susan Blanchard and you know better than I do that this kind of killer probably won't stop at one.'

'So what are you going to do about it?' Fiona asked.

Kit gave her a speculative look. 'I think the question might be what are *you* going to do about it?'

Fiona shook her head, trying not to show her irritation. 'Oh no, you don't guilt-trip me like that. I said I'd never work for the Met again after this debacle, and I meant it.'

Steve spread his hands in a gesture of appeasement. 'Hey, even if I had the budget, I wouldn't insult you like that.'

Kit grabbed one of the chairs and straddled it. 'Yeah, but she loves me. I get to insult her. Come on, Fiona, it wouldn't hurt if you took a look at the entrapment material, would it? Purely as an academic exercise.'

Fiona groaned. 'You just want it lying round the house so you can poke your nose in,' she said, trying another diversionary tactic. 'It's all grist to your grisly little mill, isn't it?'

'That's not fair! You know I never read confidential case material,' Kit said, his expression outraged.

Fiona grinned. 'Gotcha.'

Kit laughed. 'It's a fair cop, guv.'

Steve leaned back in his chair and looked pensive. 'On the other hand . . .'

'Oh, grow up, the pair of you,' Fiona grumbled. 'I have better things to do with my life than pawing over Andrew Horsforth's grubby little operation.'

Steve studied Fiona. He knew her well enough to understand the kind of challenge that might overcome her stubborn resistance, and he was desperate enough to try it. 'The trouble is, Fi, the trail's really cold. It's over a year since Susan Blanchard was butchered, and it's getting on for ten months since we were paying attention to anybody other than Francis Blake. I don't want to leave things unresolved. I don't want her kids growing up with their lives full of unanswered questions. You know the kind of emotional pain the absence of knowledge brings. Now, I really want the bastard who did this. But we need fresh leads,' he said. 'And like Kit says, at the very least it might be a useful resource for you professionally.'

Fiona shut the fridge door with more than necessary force. 'You really are a manipulative sod,' she complained. But knowing he was deliberately pushing her buttons didn't shield her from the stab of recognition. Stung, she tried a final line of defence. 'Steve, I'm not a clinician. I don't spend my days listening to people droning on about their sad little lives. I'm a number-cruncher. I deal in facts, not impressions. Even if I did sit down and stifle my disgust long enough to plough through the entrapment files, I don't know that I'd have anything useful to say at the end of it.'

'It wouldn't hurt, though, would it?' Kit chipped in. 'It's not like you'd be going back on your word and working for the Met. You'd just be doing Steve a personal favour. I mean, look at him. He's gutted. He's supposed to be your best mate. Don't you want to help him out?'

Fiona sat down, leaning forward so her shoulder-length chestnut hair curtained her face. Steve opened his mouth to speak but Kit urgently waved him to silence, mouthing, 'No!' at him. Steve raised one shoulder in a half-shrug.

Eventually, Fiona sighed deeply and pushed her hair back with both hands. 'Fuck it, I'll do it,' she said. Catching Steve's delighted grin, she added, 'No promises, remember. Bike the stuff round to me first thing in the morning and I'll take a look.'

'Thanks, Fi,' Steve said. 'Even if it's a long shot, I need all the help I can get. I appreciate it.'

'Good. So you should,' she said severely. 'Now, can we talk about something else?'

It was after midnight by the time Fiona and the *Rough Guide* finally made it to bed. When Kit came through from the bathroom, he eyed her reading material with a curious frown. 'Is that a subtle way of telling me it's about time we started planning a holiday?' he asked, slipping under the duvet and snuggling up to her.

'I should be so lucky. It's work, I'm afraid. I got a request today from the Spanish Police for a consultation. Two murders in Toledo that look like the start of a series.'

'I take it you've decided to go, then?'

Fiona waggled the book under his nose. 'Looks like it. I'll have to speak to them in the morning about the practicalities, but I should be able to get away at the end of the week for a few days without too much difficulty.'

Kit rolled on to his back and folded his arms above his head. 'And there was me thinking you were planning a romantic break to Torremolinos.'

Fiona put her book down and turned to face Kit, her fingers curling the soft dark hairs on his chest. 'You could come along for the ride if you like. Toledo's a beautiful town. It's not like there would be nothing to occupy you while I'm working. It wouldn't do you any harm to have a break.'

He dropped one arm to her shoulder, pulling her closer to him. 'I'm way behind with the book, and if you're not around over the weekend, that'll be a good excuse for me to lock myself away and work straight through.'

'You could work in Toledo.' Her hand strayed down his stomach.

'With you to distract me?'

'I'd be working all day. And probably half the night, if past experience is anything to go by.' She settled herself more comfortably into his side.

'I might as well be at home, by the sound of it.'

'You'd like it.' Fiona yawned. 'It's an interesting city. You never know, it might inspire you.'

'Yeah, right, I can see myself writing the definitive Spanish serial killer thriller.'

'Why not? It's a dirty job, but somebody's got to do it. I just thought you might like a bit of a break somewhere that does spectacular gourmet food . . .' Fiona's voice tailed off sleepily.

'I do think of other things than my stomach,' he protested. 'Isn't it Toledo that has all the El Grecos?'

'That's right,' Fiona said. 'And his house.' Her eyes were closed and her voice was a mumble as she slithered down the dreamy slope towards sleep.

'Now, that does sound worth the trip. Maybe I will come after all,' Kit said. There was no reply. An early rise and ten miles of Derbyshire moorland had finally taken their toll. Kit grinned and reached out with his free arm for the James Sallis paperback on his night table. Unlike Fiona, he could never sleep without supping his fill of horrors. But then, he reasoned, he knew that what he was reading was fiction. It didn't matter if he hadn't solved the crime when it was time to turn the light out. The killers he was interested in wouldn't be killing again until he was ready for them.

Chapter 5

The flight to Madrid was half-empty. Without having to be asked, Kit left Fiona with a double seat to herself and moved across the aisle, where he flipped up the screen of his laptop and started work as soon as they were in the air, his Walkman rendering him oblivious to any outside distractions. On the way to the airport, he'd nagged her about making a start on the thick bundle Steve had had delivered to the house, which Fiona had been studiously ignoring for the past two days. She'd been hiding behind the necessity of familiarizing herself with the material from Toledo, but if she was honest, she'd been as thorough with that as she could be. Now she had no excuse, and the flight was just long enough to get a flavour of what she had to digest.

The first section began with a page of personal ads from *Time Out*. During the course of his lengthy police interviews, Blake had admitted that although he had a long-term relationship with an air hostess, he also replied to women who advertised in the lonely hearts column. He'd said that he went for the ones who seemed insecure, because they were always grateful to meet a good-looking bloke like him. He'd admitted he was interested principally in sex, but insisted that he didn't want to waste his time on brainless bimbos. From what Fiona remembered of the original interview transcripts, Blake had seemed confident, even arrogant about his capacity to attract women; a man who knew what he wanted and didn't doubt he could get it. He certainly hadn't come over as weak or inadequate.

Based on his interpretation of the interviews, Horsforth had constructed several ads that he felt would appeal to their suspect. The first attempts had produced plenty of responses, though none was from Blake. 'So much for getting inside the head of the killer,' Fiona muttered under her breath. But the second round snared their target. He had responded to: 'SWF, 26, slim, new to N. London, seeks male guide for conversation, meals, movies and an introduction to the bright lights and good times. GSOH. Pictures please.'

Blake had described himself as a professional man of twenty-nine with an interest in cinema, reading, walking in London's parks, and enjoying female company. Under Andrew Horsforth's guidance, Detective Constable Erin Richards had written the reply.

'Dear Francis,' it read. *'Thanks for your letter, it was easily the most charming of all the ones I've received. I must confess I'm a little nervous about this because it's not the sort of thing I normally do. Would it be OK with you if we exchanged a couple more letters before we actually meet?*

'Like you, I'm interested in going to the cinema. What kind of films do you like best? Although I know it's probably not what women are supposed to enjoy, I love all those wonderful dark thrillers like Seven, Eight Millimetre *and* Fargo, *and Hitchcock films like* Psycho. *But they've got to have a good plot to keep me going. As for reading, I don't get to read as much as I should. I like Patricia Cornwell, Kit Martin and Thomas Harris best, and I sometimes read true crime too.*

'I don't really know London well enough to know where it's safe to go walking. You read about such terrible things sometimes

in the papers, people being mugged and raped in parks, that it makes me a bit nervous because I'm a stranger. Perhaps you could show me some of your favourite walks sometime?

'I work in the civil service. Nothing very exciting, I'm afraid. I'm a clerk at the Ministry of Agriculture. I moved here from Beccles in Suffolk after my mother died. There was nothing to keep me there, because my father passed away a couple of years before her, and I've no brothers or sisters, so I thought I'd come looking for adventure in London!

'I'd love to hear from you again if you think we might have enough in common to enjoy each other's company. You can write to the box office number because I'm keeping it on for a couple of weeks longer.

'Yours sincerely,
'Eileen Rogers.'

Blake had replied by return of post. 'Dear Eileen,' he'd written. 'Thanks for your lovely letter. Yes, it does sound as if we'd have a lot in common. We seem to go for the same kind of books and films for a start.

'I can understand why you might feel a bit nervous walking around London on your own. I've lived here all my life but there are many parts of the city I don't know at all, and if I have to go there for work I sometimes feel a little anxious because it's so easy to end up somewhere that can feel threatening just because it's unfamiliar. It must be so much harder for a woman on her own. I'd be happy to show you around. I know Hampstead Heath and Regent's Park and Hyde Park well, I go there often.

'I realize you must be a bit nervous about meeting a stranger like me, but I'd like to talk face to face. I can't help thinking we would have a lot to say to each other. We could meet somewhere public, like they recommend you should for a first time. I could meet you on Saturday afternoon and we could have coffee together. I thought we could meet outside the Hard

Rock Café at Hyde Park Corner at three o'clock. You can phone me to confirm the arrangements if you like.

'Please say yes. You sound just the kind of woman I want to meet.

> *'Best wishes,*
> *'Francis Blake.'*

The fish had swallowed the bait remarkably easily, Fiona thought. It wasn't so much that Horsforth had been particularly clever or subtle in the way he'd orchestrated the approach, as that Blake had been surprisingly eager to make the contact, in spite of having been the subject of such close police attention. Perhaps that was why he'd been so keen; he was desperately in need of a respite with someone who knew nothing of what he'd been through at the hands of the law. For a man who apparently liked to be in control, it must have been infuriating to be surrounded by people who thought they knew more about him than they really did. A stranger who knew nothing of his role as a suspect would allow him to feel relaxed.

Whatever the reasons, it had provided the opportunity for the operation to go ahead. DC Richards had phoned Blake and arranged to meet. The call had lasted for about ten minutes, Fiona noted. They'd chatted without much awkwardness, mostly about films they'd seen recently, then made arrangements to meet. At their first encounter, as on every subsequent one, Richards was wired for sound, transmitting the conversation to a back-up radio van that kept discreet tabs on the pair of them throughout.

Richards had played her role well, striking an appropriate balance between edgy nervousness and eager friendliness. They'd gone for coffee, then Blake had suggested a short walk through the park before they parted. As they'd walked, he'd pointed out to her the sort of places she could go safely on her own and the ones she should avoid. He seemed to know exactly which areas were open and well-lit and which were gloomy, dotted with shrubbery that could provide hiding places for anyone with dubious intentions. It wasn't the sort of analysis that the average park stroller would make of his environment, Fiona thought. Just as someone who has almost been trapped in a fire takes an unnatural interest in fire exits forever afterwards, so only someone who imagined using a park for something other than fresh air and exercise would view their surroundings as Francis Blake viewed his. He looked at his world like a predator, not a victim.

That didn't make him a killer, however. He might be a mugger, a voyeur, a flasher or a rapist and still exhibit a similar response. But Horsforth had allowed himself to be persuaded that Blake was a killer, and he had interpreted his behaviour accordingly. That much was clear from the clinical psychologist's notes on the meeting. The conversation had been innocuous enough, but Horsforth had still managed to see what he wanted to see.

It was a realization that profoundly depressed Fiona. Any kind of objective analysis of the material was already compromised, because Horsforth's early decisions about what Blake's actions implied had dictated everything in the interaction that followed.

The meetings had continued two or three times a week. On the fourth meeting, Richards introduced the subject of Susan Blanchard's murder, in the context of terrifying things that happened to women in the city. Blake had immediately said, 'I was there that day. On the Heath. I must have walked past at almost the exact time she was being raped and murdered.'

Richards had pretended shock. 'My God! That must have been awful.'

'I didn't realize anything at the time. Well, obviously I

didn't or I would have raised the alarm. But I can't help thinking if I'd chosen a slightly different route that day, if I'd gone over the rise behind the shrubbery instead of walking along the path, I'd have stumbled over her killer,' he'd boasted.

It was a significant exchange, Fiona knew. But again, it was capable of a different interpretation from the conclusion Horsforth had jumped to. What it told him was that Blake was a killer desperate to talk about his crime, however obliquely. What it told Fiona was something else altogether. She made a note on her pad and continued.

By the end of the third week, Blake was beginning to turn the conversation towards sex. It was, he indicated, time to take their relationship to the next stage, beyond cinema visits and walks and meals. Richards backed off slightly, as she'd been told to do, saying she wanted to be sure they'd be compatible before she took the ultimate step of sleeping with him. It was the planned route into talk of sexual fantasy. Fiona had to concede that this had been a shrewd move on Horsforth's part, though she might have approached it in a more indirect way. But then, she wasn't a clinician. In matters like this, she had to concede her instinct was probably not the most rigorous guide.

Now it was Richards's turn to push the direction of the conversation. And she wasted no time. It wasn't that she was sexually inexperienced, she said. But she'd found herself growing quickly bored with the men she'd slept with in the past. 'They're just so predictable, so conventional,' she complained. 'I want to be sure next time I get involved with someone, that he's got an imagination, that he'll take me places I've never been before.'

Blake immediately asked her what she meant, and presumably as Horsforth had instructed her, Richards had backed off

41

again, saying she wasn't sure she could discuss it openly in the middle of Regent's Park. She explained that she had to go out of town the next week, to a training course in Manchester, and she would write to him. 'I feel a bit exposed out here,' she'd said. 'I can put it down on paper better. Then if you're shocked or turned off me forever, I won't have to see your face, will I?'

Blake had seemed almost amused by her alternation between suggestiveness and coyness. 'I bet there's nothing you could say that would shock me,' he'd said. 'I promise you, whatever you want, Eileen, I can take you there. All the way there, whatever it is you want. You write me that letter tonight so I get it first thing on Monday morning, and I guarantee you'll be panting to get back to London by return of post.'

Somehow, Fiona doubted it. However, there was no time now to pursue her doubts to their conclusion. Kit had packed his computer into its case, the 'Fasten Seatbelts' sign was illuminated and the cabin crew were moving purposefully towards their seats for landing. Major Berrocal would be waiting for them at the arrivals gate, and a job where she was convinced she could provide useful advice was always going to take precedence over something already wrecked by someone else.

Whatever perverse fantasies Francis Blake and Erin Richards had exchanged would have to remain in the file for the time being.

Chapter 6

Major Salvador Berrocal was not waiting for them by the arrivals gate. He was actually standing impatiently tapping his foot by the door of the plane when it swung open. He had obviously arranged for a message to be transmitted ahead, for as soon as the cabin crew were back on their feet after landing, a steward was by Fiona's side, asking her to come forward to the front of the plane so she could disembark ahead of the other passengers. Kit followed in her wake, giving the steward his best smile and saying, 'We're travelling together.'

Fiona's first impression of the Spanish policeman was of tremendous energy barely held in check. He was of medium height, slender and pale-skinned, with dark-blue eyes that were never still. His charcoal-grey suit looked as if it had been freshly pressed that morning, and his black boots shone with a military gleam. Both were at odds with a shock of untidy black wavy hair, worn long enough to cover the back of his shirt collar. He acknowledged her with a polite but abrupt nod of the head, saying, 'Thank you for coming, Doctor.'

'Thank you for meeting us. Major, this is my partner, Kit Martin. I mentioned he'd be travelling with me.'

Kit extended a hand. 'Pleased to meet you. Don't worry, I won't be getting under your feet.'

Berrocal's nod was noncommittal. 'I have a car waiting,

Doctor,' he said to Fiona. He reached for her briefcase and laptop. 'Señor Martin, if you wouldn't mind going to the baggage carousel, one of my men will meet you there. He will take you and your luggage to your hotel in Toledo.' He pulled a card out of his breast pocket. 'This is my mobile number. You can reach Dr Cameron, she will be with me.' He flashed a cool smile and set off down the pier towards the main concourse.

'Mr Friendly,' Kit said.

'Mr Under Pressure, I think,' Fiona replied. She put one arm round Kit and gave him a quick squeeze. 'Ring me on my mobile, if you need me.'

They set off in Berrocal's wake, Fiona almost having to break into a trot to keep him in sight. 'Don't worry about me,' Kit said. 'I've got the guide book. I will be pursuing my own investigations into Toledo. Either that or I'll be hunched over a hotel bedside table trying to write.'

They caught up with Berrocal who was waiting by a security door. 'You must go through customs and immigration,' he said to Kit, pointing down a corridor to the left.

'Nice to meet you,' Kit said. Being pleasant was cheap, especially since Berrocal had taken the trouble to lay on a car for him. He gave Fiona a swift peck on the cheek, said, 'See you later,' and headed off without a backward glance.

'He really won't be any trouble,' Fiona said as they strode towards the customs and immigration area. 'Kit has no problem with his own company.'

Berrocal flashed his badge and steered her ahead of him past the formalities. 'I wouldn't expect you to have brought him otherwise,' he said briskly. 'I have arranged for you both to stay at the parador in Toledo, but I would prefer to go straight to the scenes of the crimes. Also, I wanted to be able to discuss the case on the way there, which would not have been possible in front of Señor Martin.'

A uniformed officer stood by an unmarked saloon car, snapping to attention as Berrocal approached. He opened the rear door, and Fiona climbed in, Berrocal walking round to the far side to slide in beside her. 'Toledo is about an hour's drive from the airport,' he told her. 'If you have any questions for me, I can answer them on the way.'

Clearly not a man for small talk, Fiona thought. None of those polite and pointless queries about her flight that usually marked her arrival in strange cities. Nor did he feel the need to make polite conversation about Kit's books, as had usually happened when he had accompanied her on foreign trips. 'What lines of inquiry have you pursued?' she asked. 'Apart from looking for witnesses, of course.'

Berrocal shifted in his seat so he could look directly at her. 'We have examined our records of violent sexual assaults. Several people have been interviewed. But either they have an alibi for the first or the second murder or both. Or else we have no reason to keep them in custody.'

'Your English is very fluent,' Fiona couldn't help remarking.

'I speak better than I write,' he said, flashing a smile for the first time since they'd met. 'My wife is Canadian. We go to Vancouver every year on holiday. So when we talked about bringing in an English expert on crime linkage and serial offenders, I was the obvious choice for the liaison officer. As I said in my e-mail, we have no local expertise in this area.'

'I don't know if any of us have what I would term expertise in crime linkage,' Fiona said dryly. 'I have some experience, but every time I do this, it seems like I'm feeling my way almost as much as the detectives. Every case is different, and sometimes the lessons of the past are not entirely helpful.'

He nodded. 'I understand. Nobody is expecting a miracle from you, Dr Cameron. But in a case like this, we need all the help we can get. It is no secret to you that when a killer

45

targets a stranger, most of our usual police procedures are useless. So we need a different kind of insight and that is what you can bring to the case.'

Fiona raised her eyebrows and turned away from his penetrating eyes, staring out of the window at the speeding motorway traffic. On one side of the motorway, she could see the city sprawling towards the centre; on the other the scarred red earth of the central Spanish plain, exposed by some sort of construction work. The terracotta soil, the almost metallic blue sky and the heavy shadows of the earth-moving equipment turned the vista into a moving De Chirico painting, resonating with heat and menace. For some reason, it reminded Fiona of the surrealism of Cervantes' imagination. Like Don Quixote, she thought, she'd be out there tilting at windmills, trying to separate the shadows from the reality, with this restless man as her Sancho Panza to mitigate her confusion.

'I read the material you sent me,' she said, pushing her fantastical thoughts to one side and turning to meet his gaze again. 'I'm not convinced your offender will have a record of sexual offences.'

Berrocal frowned. 'Why do you say that? From what I've read, I thought serial murderers generally had a history of some sort of sexual violence. And he has committed brutal sexual acts on the corpses of both of his victims.'

'That's true. But in each case, the violations were committed after death. And the penetration was with a foreign object, not the penis. Not that that necessarily discounts a sexual motive of itself,' Fiona added, almost absently. 'But I don't think the gratification sought here is primarily sexual,' she continued with more firmness. 'These crimes may appear superficially to be about sexual power but it seems to me that they are about desecration. Almost vandalism,' Fiona said.

Berrocal stirred. He looked as if he was wondering whether bringing her along had been such a good idea after all. 'If that is the case, why are the faces not mutilated also?' His chin came up in apparent challenge.

Fiona spread her hands. 'I don't know. But I imagine it was probably because the killer wanted his victims recognized quickly. They were neither of them locals, so it might have taken a little longer to identify them if their faces had been damaged beyond recognition.'

He nodded, partially satisfied by her response. He decided to reserve judgement on this woman who apparently had no difficulty in finding ways to discard the conventional wisdom. 'I think it's better if I don't ask you your theories now,' he said with another flash of his bright smile. 'Better to wait until you have seen where the crimes took place, and then perhaps we could go to the local police headquarters. I have established a control centre there for the investigation.'

'You're not based in Toledo, I think you said?'

Berrocal shook his head. 'I work in Madrid normally. But cities like Toledo have few murders in the course of a year, and most of those will be domestic situations. The result is that they have no one with experience of the more complex type of homicide and so they must bring in a specialist from Madrid. Unfortunately, we have more murders in the city and so someone like me is sent to organize the investigation.'

'That can't be easy,' Fiona observed. 'You must have to be careful of local sensibilities.'

Berrocal shrugged, his fingers drumming on the window ledge. 'In some respects. In other ways, it makes it easier for the Toledo officers. When I tread on people's feet, the local men can spread their hands and say, "Hey, it's not our fault, it's that stupid bastard from the big city, coming here and stirring things up and rubbing everybody up the wrong way." Of course, some of the detectives are a little sensitive, they see my presence as a criticism of them, but I just have to charm them.' His eyes crinkled in a wry smile. 'But you must be familiar with these responses too. Like me and my team, you are what my wife calls the visiting fireman.'

Fiona acknowledged his idiom with a half-smile. 'Sometimes that has other disadvantages too. It's possible that my unfamiliarity with a place and its local customs may lead me to place more – or less – significance on something than it should have.'

He shrugged again. 'The other side of the coin is that locals can take for granted what strikes you as an alteration in a pattern, I think.'

'Toledo is very much a tourist city, is that right?' Fiona asked.

'That is correct. It is also the seat of the archbishop, so the bureaucracy of the Church occupies a significant share of the buildings around the cathedral. Between the Church and the tourist trade, there is little room for anything else in the old city. With every year that passes, fewer people live in the old part of Toledo, fewer traditional businesses survive.'

Fiona made a mental note and continued, aiming for a tone of casual interest. 'Does that cause ill-feeling among those who are pushed out by the demands of the tourist industry?'

Berrocal grinned. 'I think most people are happy to trade a gloomy medieval apartment up five flights of narrow stairs for a building with air and light and an elevator. And a patio or a balcony where they can sit outside and enjoy the air. Not to mention constant running hot water.'

'All the same . . .' Fiona chose her words carefully. 'I grew up in a small town in the north of England. Not much more than a village, really. It's a very pretty village, right in the heart of the Derbyshire Peak District. The perfect place to go walking from, or to visit the caverns that are open to the public. Over the years, more and more tourists came. Whenever cottages went on the market, they were bought up by outsiders and turned into holiday homes. Every shop in the main street became a tearoom or a craft shop. All the pubs were more interested in catering to day-trippers than locals. You couldn't stroll down the main street or park your car near your own house in the summer months. By the time I left home, half the population would change weekly, holidaymakers who turned up with a carload of shopping. All they ever bought locally was bread and milk. The village lost its heart. It became a tourist dormitory. And the locals who were pushed out in the process weren't happy at all. At a guess, I'd say there must be some native Toledans who don't like what's happening to their city.'

Berrocal gave her a shrewd look. He was sharp enough to realize this was no idle conversation. Following on as it had from her easy dismissal of the obvious analysis of the background of the killer, he understood that she was trying to tell him something. 'You think someone is killing people because he doesn't like tourists?' He tried to keep the incredulity from his voice. This woman had, after all, come with the imprimatur of Scotland Yard.

Fiona turned away from his eyes and stared out across the rolling green fields they were now passing through. 'I don't think it's quite that simple, Major Berrocal. And really I don't want to theorize ahead of the data. But I do think your killer is motivated by something rather more out of the ordinary than sexual frustration.'

'OK. How do you want to work this?'

'What I'd like to do is precisely what you've suggested. I'd like to look at the sites where the bodies were displayed and then back at your incident room, I'd like to look at the crime-scene photographs and read the pathology reports in full. I'd also like to see the guide books that were found at the scenes of the crimes, if that would be possible. And then I would like to go back to my hotel room and think about what I've seen.'

He nodded. 'Whatever you wish.'

'I would also appreciate it if you could extract from your Toledan colleagues any reports of vandalism against tourist sites or hotels or businesses that cater to the tourist trade. And any attacks on tourists themselves. Going back, say, a couple of years. Solved and unsolved, if that's possible.' She smiled. 'I'll also need a reasonably detailed map of the city that can be scanned into a computer.'

'I will arrange it.' He inclined his head in a half-bow. 'Already you have shown me a different way of looking at these cases.'

Fiona shifted in her seat so she was staring ahead over the driver's shoulder. 'I hope so. When I look at a crime, I don't look with the same eyes as a detective. I'm searching for the psychological as well as the solid practical elements that link that one crime to others. I'm also looking for geographical clusters. But as well as that, I'm watching out for other signals that can tell me something about the criminal.'

'So then you can figure out the way his mind works?'

Fiona frowned. 'It's not so much his motivation I'm trying to get at. It's more about developing a sense of how he looks at the world. Motivation is highly individualistic. But what we all have in common is that we construct our own identities based on what we've learned of the world. So the way a criminal commits his crimes is a reflection of the way he lives the rest of his life. Where he feels comfortable, both physically and mentally. I'm looking for patterns of behaviour in the crime that give me clues to how he behaves when he's going about his ordinary business.'

She gave a wry smile and continued. 'Some of my colleagues have a different approach which you're probably more familiar with. They look at the crimes and seek a set of symptoms in an offender's past that have produced a particular way of life in the present. I've never found that very helpful. For my money, too many people share the same sort of background and don't turn out to be psychopathic serial offenders for it to be a precise diagnostic tool. I'm not saying that my methods necessarily always produce a more accurate result, but that's more because I seldom have sufficient data rather than that the methods themselves are flawed. There isn't a magic formula, Major. But my training is so divergent from that of a police officer that I'm bound to look at things from a different perspective. Between us, we see this thing in stereo, rather than in mono. I can't help believing that has to give us an advantage over the criminal.'

'That's why you're here, Doctor.' Berrocal leaned forward and said something in rapid Spanish to the driver. They were approaching a sprawl of modern suburban housing, the road lined with concrete boxes containing furniture stores, car showrooms and small businesses. He sat back and took out a packet of cigarettes, twiddling them restlessly between his fingers. 'Ten minutes more. Then I can have a cigarette and you can go to work.'

This time, Fiona's smile was grim. 'I can hardly wait.'

Extract from **Decoding of Exhibit P13/4599**

Uzqhq dftag stfyg dpqdo agxpn qeaqm ek. Upuym
suzpq ufarf qzngf uzykt qmpuf tmpnq qzyqe
ekmzp rdust fqzuz s . . .

The document in question utilizes a simple transliteration (a=m,
b=n, etc) and the arrangement of letters into groups of five
instead of the normal layout of the words. What follows is a
transcription of the coded material, with appropriate punctuation
added for sense. J. M. Arthur, Document Examiner.

*I never thought murder could be so easy. I'd imagined
it often, but in my head it had been messy and frightening. The reality is quite different. The power surge,
that's what carries you through it. Imagination really
doesn't prepare you for the real thing.*

*The other mistake I made was in thinking murder
always had to be part of something else. But the truth*

is, murder can be an end in itself. Sometimes, people have to pay for what they have done, and taking their lives is the only way to do it.

I never thought I was going to be a murderer. I had my life sorted out. But then something shifted, and I could see them laughing at me, flaunting their so-called success in my face. I'd be a poor excuse for a man if I just took provocation like that on the chin.

Nobody knows how they'll react when their life gets stolen by people who don't give a toss who gets hurt. Well, I've never been the sort who just sits back and lets things happen, and I'm going to make them pay. I'm going to change the rules. But I'm not going to be obvious. I'm going to be subtle and choose my targets carefully.

This time, they won't be able to ignore me. They won't be able to write me off. I'll be writing them off, writing their names in blood, and sending a message loud and clear. They're responsible for their own downfall, that's what I'll be saying. Live by the word, die by the word.

It's not hard to track down thriller writers. I'm used to watching people, I've been doing it for years. It doesn't hurt that they're all so vain. The Internet is clogged up with their websites and they give interviews right, left and centre. And they're always doing public appearances.

So it made sense to start with somebody who has a really high profile, to make my job as easy as it could be. I decided the best way to make my point was to give them a real taste of their own medicine. It wouldn't be enough just to kill them. I wanted it to be clear right from the word go that there was nothing accidental about what was going on. And knowing what was coming would make them suffer all the more. Satisfaction, that's what I want.

To make the punishment fit the crime, I have to get the crime right, and now I've made my list. I ranked them according to how easy I thought it would be to do them and that's how I got my candidates for execution.

1. Drew Shand
2. Jane Elias
3. Georgia Lester
4. Kit Martin
5. Enya Flannery
6. Jonathan Lewis

Now all I have to do is figure out exactly how to take them down.

They put me in this cage. But they should know that caged animals turn savage.

They've brought this on their own heads.

Chapter 7

Fiona scrambled down the narrow path, glad she'd worn flat-soled loafers to travel in. It wasn't that it was particularly steep, but the beaten ochre earth was dotted with small stones that would have been perilous to the ankles in any sort of heel. She made a mental note to check what footwear Martina Albrecht had been wearing at the time of her death. It might give her some indication as to how willingly she'd accompanied her killer to the scene of her murder.

Berrocal slowed down ahead of her and turned back, exhaling a cloud of cigarette smoke that reminded Fiona of the dried camel dung fires of the Northern Sahara. 'You OK?' he asked.

'Fine,' she answered, catching up and using the pause to scan her surroundings. They were in a narrow, flat-bottomed valley that curved away from the road. The high bluffs on either side had already cut off the line of sight to the viaduct that carried the *circunvalacion* around the southern bank of the Tagus. From here in, there would have been no chance of being caught in the headlights of a passing car. The sides of the valley were covered in scrubby vegetation, with a few small trees straggling up the gentler slopes.

'We are almost there,' Berrocal said. 'You see those bushes ahead? It's just past there.' He set off again, Fiona in his wake.

'He must have had a torch,' she observed as the tall shrubs closed around them, almost meeting over their heads. Berrocal's smoke was forced back into her face and she tried to avoid breathing through her nose until they were in the open again.

'I don't think she would have come with him otherwise,' Berrocal said. 'There's no sign of a struggle anywhere by the road or on the path.'

'What was she wearing on her feet?'

Berrocal turned and flashed her a smile, as if rewarding a bright pupil. 'Flat sandals. Yes, she probably walked into the trap without thinking twice about it.'

They emerged on the other side of the bushes in a small clearing. On the far side, a pair of gnarled olive trees flanked the path. A single uniformed officer stood in the shade at the entrance to the glade. He started forward, his hand going to his pistol butt. When he saw it was Berrocal, he snapped a salute and stepped back. The whole area was still enclosed in the familiar plastic crime-scene tapes, now looking weatherbeaten and untidy. Fiona could see the irregular reddish-brown stain on the path and the surrounding vegetation, the only obvious sign that this had been the scene of violent death. Incongruously, she could hear the twittering of birds above the distant hum of traffic. She always found herself marvelling at the way the world managed to continue apparently oblivious to the tragedy that had played itself out only yards away.

After Lesley, she had found herself walking the streets of the city where it had happened, angry and frustrated that people could carry on as if nothing had changed, as if it was nothing to do with them. Of course, in a narrow sense, it was no direct concern of theirs. But Fiona had believed then as she believed now that societies got the criminals they deserved. Brutal crimes didn't spring from nowhere; their seeds lay in the wider crimes of the community they impinged on. It wasn't a popular view among law enforcement, and when she was working with the police, Fiona kept her views to herself.

So she looked around without comment. There wasn't much to say other than the obvious. And Fiona had never liked stating the obvious.

Berrocal pointed to the bloodstained area, grinding his cigarette butt underfoot. 'She was found lying towards the rear of the blood, not in it. It adds weight to the theory that he was behind her and she was standing up when he cut her throat. Mercifully quick, the pathologist says. Then, it looks as if he stepped back and let her fall.'

'The vaginal injuries were postmortem?' Fiona asked.

'Yes. He straddled her, we think. The grass is flattened on either side of her hips, as if someone had kneeled there. He cut her panties away, probably with the same blade. There were smudges of blood on the material. Then he broke the wine bottle on the ground and' – Berrocal cleared his throat – 'he inserted the broken bottle into her vagina. With considerable force. Several times. The glass fragments are on the right-hand side of the body, which supports the idea that he was right-handed.'

Fiona crossed to the side of the clearing and looked at the crime scene from the point of view the killer would have had. 'The thing that strikes me most about this is what I mentioned earlier. The sexual mutilations are postmortem, which is unusual. There's no sign of any kind of sexual activity before the attack. He went straight for the kill. No foreplay.'

Berrocal nodded. 'You think this is significant?'

'It's a marker of someone who feels very lacking in power. There's nothing tentative about it either. It reveals a great deal of anger. So when I'm looking for linked crimes, I'll be bearing in mind that they will probably exhibit similar markers.' Fiona hitched up her trousers, crouched down and studied the ground. There was no particular reason for her to do this. In truth, she learned very little from looking at crime scenes. She had never discovered anything that wasn't covered by the files she would read later. But police officers expected her to absorb something from where the body had been found. It was almost a superstition, and so she'd long ago decided it was easier to humour them rather than start a partnership wrong-footed.

She stood up. 'Thanks for letting me see this.'

'Does it tell you anything you didn't know before?' Berrocal asked, stepping to one side and indicating she should precede him up the path.

The dreaded question. 'It confirms one hypothesis,' she said. 'Your killer knows his territory well. This isn't the sort of place that a casual visitor would know about.'

'A local man, then?'

'I think that's a safe assumption,' she said firmly. 'He doesn't just know about the existence of this place, he knows what happened here and what it means.' She heard the click of his lighter. Berrocal was clearly determined to get his blood-nicotine levels back to normal after an hour's confinement in the car.

As they rounded the curve and the road came into sight, Fiona stopped abruptly. A miniature train with a string of grubby white carriages was grinding its noisy way across the viaduct. She could hear the tinny sound of a commentary, although it was too far away to make out any of the words. 'What on earth is that?' she asked, pointing to the train and turning to Berrocal.

He raised his eyebrows in a world-weary expression. 'They

call it the *Tren Real*,' he sighed. 'The Royal Train. It takes tourists on a ride through the old city and round the *circunvalacion.*'

Fiona grinned. 'Hard to imagine the royal family riding on that.'

Berrocal's face was pained. 'It has no dignity,' he agreed. 'It's not my favourite example of Spanish tourism.'

They trudged back up to the car in silence. Fiona was oblivious to her surroundings, too busy with her thoughts for appreciation of landscape or the city vista that sprang out before them as they reached the level of the road.

'Now we'll go to the church,' Berrocal announced.

Fiona concealed her impatience. She wanted to start work properly, not waste any more time looking at crime scenes. At this rate, she'd have been as well going back to the hotel with Kit. It would have been about as useful.

A couple of hundred feet above the panoramic route Fiona was travelling back to the city, Kit was opening a heavy pair of wooden shutters with ornate iron fittings. Light flooded into the room and he whistled softly at the view. The Parador Conde de Orgaz, named after the city's most famous El Greco, sat on top of Emperor's Hill with a breathtaking panorama of Toledo laid out before it. The almost unreal vision still bore a remarkable resemblance to the background of dozens of other El Grecos, in spite of the intervening four and a half centuries. The parador was perfectly sited on the bluff opposite the city, and their room commanded a view of the whole medieval city. Kit decided to fall prey to temptation.

Twenty minutes later, a taxi deposited him by the Plaza de Zocodover, a lively square which his tour guide claimed was the heart of social life in the city. Lined with cafés and cake shops, its tall shuttered buildings had an air of slightly decayed elegance. It appeared to be a typical provincial southern European city, Kit thought. Women sturdily crossing with their heavy bags of shopping, elderly men sitting smoking and chatting, teenagers in branded leisurewear lounging in doorways and on corners, furtively eyeing the opposite gender in between posing for their benefit. But it hadn't always been like this.

Toledo, he knew from his reading, had been captured first by the Romans, then by the Visigoths, next by the Moors and finally by the Christians. Although it had become the capital of Castile and the base for the medieval military campaigns against the Moors, it had also established a reputation as a haven of cultural tolerance.

But all that had changed with the dynastic marriage of Fernando of Aragon and Isabella of Castile in 1479. Isabella's personal confessor was Cardinal Tomas de Torquemada, the man appointed by the Pope as the first Grand Inquisitor of the Spanish Inquisition.

Kit had told Fiona only that he was interested in seeing the El Grecos in Toledo. But that was merely a fragment of the truth. What had drawn him to this city was the prospect of walking the very streets Torquemada had walked, many of them virtually unchanged since the fifteenth century and earlier. He wanted to let his imagination carry him back in time to an era when the streets of Toledo were tainted with fear and hatred, when brother denounced brother, when ordained priests invented torture methods so robust they were still in use, when the state perverted a religious crusade into a means to enrich itself.

Toledo was a city that, by conquest and oppression both, was soaked in the blood of its people. The tantalizing prospect of discovering how much of that atmosphere had persisted was what attracted Kit's imagination.

It wasn't hard to erase the modern images and see the streets as they must formerly have been. The buildings were the same, tall tenements with narrow twisting passages between them, their facades alternating between patched eroded brick and pale stucco that had generally seen better days. Studded with windows shuttered against the September heat, the only thing that broke up the frontages were lines of washing strung across the alleys.

As the siesta approached, the streets emptied, and Kit found himself mostly alone as he quartered the warren of streets between the cathedral and the monastery church of San Juan de los Reyes, following his map into the old Jewish quarter, the Juderia.

He climbed a flight of steps that took him up between high blank walls and opened out in a small garden with benches that provided a spectacular vista. But contemporary panoramas were not what he was seeking. Kit let his mind wander from the present and stared down over the pale terracotta roofs, blanking out TV aerials and satellite dishes, drifting back into the past.

The Inquisition was supposed to be about establishing a pure-blooded Christian faith in Spain. But what it was really about was anti-Semitism and greed, he thought. But then, most oppressive right-wing movements had similar roots. Back then, the Spanish Jews were seen as too powerful and too wealthy. From being comfortable, safe and prosperous, their lives had been plunged overnight into a living hell.

A kind of hysteria must have swept through the cities of Castile and Aragon, as anyone with a grudge saw a way of evening the score against their enemies. Carte blanche for the inadequate, the spiteful and the self-righteous, Kit mused.

And once denounced, it was almost impossible to escape unscathed. If there were such a thing as reincarnation, Kit thought, Torquemada had probably come back as Senator Joe McCarthy. 'Are you now, or have you ever been a heretic?'

It must have poisoned the whole community. No one could have felt safe, except perhaps the Grand Inquisitor and his team of helpers. After all, they had a special dispensation from the Pope. If anyone died under torture or if some other mistake were made, they had the power to absolve one another so their hands and their souls could remain stainless.

And now, another killer was stalking the streets of Toledo, revisiting old nightmares and casting a dark shadow over this tourist playground. His tally of victims might be insignificant set beside the legalized murder of the Inquisitors, but for those touched by these deaths, the pain and bewilderment would be equally intense. That was what Fiona was staring into, and he didn't envy her one bit. She had her own ghosts, and in spite of what she told herself, he believed the work she embraced did nothing to lay them to rest. But he wouldn't push her; she'd have to reach that conclusion of her own free will, and she was a long way from there. He didn't envy her the journey either. The country of the imagination was a far easier place to inhabit.

In spite of the warmth of the sun, Kit shivered involuntarily. It was true that a place retained its spirit. In spite of the beauty that surrounded him, it was all too easy to summon up the troubled spirits of past terrors.

It was, he thought, natural territory for a serial killer.

Chapter 8

Drew Shand sat back and rotated his shoulders, grimacing as they cracked and popped. He'd tried every possible adjustment on the expensive orthopaedic chair, but he always stiffened up like this by the end of the working day, exactly the same as he had when he'd sat on a cheap kitchen chair hunched over his second-hand laptop. The electrically adjustable seat had been one of the first treats he'd bought with the famously substantial advance for his first novel. But still he got backache.

He'd thought that his debut was a pretty good read when he'd finished the first draft, but he'd struggled and failed to hide his astonishment when his agent rang him with the news that it had been sold for a mid-six-figure sum. Each of which was to the left of the decimal point. Hot on the heels of that deal, *Copycat* had been sold to TV, its adaptation winning a clutch of awards for its charismatic star, and sending Drew's paperback tie-in straight to the top of the bestseller lists on its coat-tails.

More than the acclaim, more even than the rave reviews and the Crime Writers' Association Dagger award for best first novel of the year, Drew appreciated his release from the soul-destroying job of teaching English to the over-indulged brats of the Edinburgh middle classes. The demands of keeping a roof over his head had forced him to write *Copycat* late into the night and in snatched hours at weekends over a period of eighteen months. It had been a hard grind, earning him derision from his pals, who kept telling him to get a life. But now, he was the one with the absolutely brilliant life, while they were still stuck in the nine-to-five. Drew didn't work to anybody else's schedule. He wrote when it suited him. OK, that turned out to be most days, but he was still in charge. Drew was the one who made the decisions, not some slave-driving boss acting the hardarse because his own sad wee job was on the line.

And he loved his life. He usually woke some time between ten and eleven. He'd make himself a cappuccino with his shiny new chrome Italian machine, browse the morning papers then energize his brain under the needle jets of his power shower. By noon, he'd be sitting in front of his state-of-the-art computer with a pair of bacon-and-egg rolls. He'd work his way through brunch while he reread what he'd written the day before, then he'd check out his e-mail. Round about half past one, he'd be ready to go to work.

It was only his third novel. Drew still got a helluva charge out of hammering the words down on screen, pausing momentarily to figure out the direction of the next few paragraphs before his fingers thundered across the keys with the heavy touch of a man who'd learned piano as a reluctant child. Not for him the slow composition of a sentence or the check with the word count at the end of every paragraph. Drew didn't set himself anything as mechanical as a daily word target. He just wrote and wrote till he ran out of steam. That mostly happened about five o'clock. Funnily enough, he usually found he'd written about four thousand words, give or take a couple of hundred. At first he'd reckoned it was just coincidence, then he'd decided that four thousand words was just about the limit that his brain could produce in one day without it degenerating into gibberish.

Well, it was as good an excuse as any for knocking it on the head for the day. He switched off the computer, shrugged off his dressing gown and put on his sweats. The gym was a couple of streets away from his four-roomed Georgian flat on the edge of the New Town, and he enjoyed the walk through the darkening streets, the cold air turning to smoke as it left his nostrils. Poof the Magic Dragon, he thought ironically as he turned off Broughton Street and walked up the steps to the gym.

Drew loved the gym too. He had a circuit that lasted precisely an hour. Fifteen minutes on the Nordic track, half an hour on the Nautilus machines working all the different muscle groups, ten minutes with free weights, then five minutes on the bike. The perfect mix of aerobic and strength exercises, just enough weight and reps to keep him hard without turning him into Stallone.

But it wasn't just the pleasure of feeling his thirty-one-year-old body respond to the routine that turned Drew on to the gym. It was also the opportunity it gave him to check out the other men who were there. It didn't matter if they were straight or gay. He didn't go to the gym to cruise, although he had got lucky a couple of times. Mostly, though, he just liked the chance to watch their bodies as they pushed themselves to their limits, to admire a neat bum, a taut pair of thighs, a well-defined set of shoulders. It wound his spring nice and tight for whatever the rest of the evening might hold for him.

After his work-out, Drew relaxed in the gym's sauna. Again, it wasn't the sort where sex was on offer, but it didn't hurt to eye up the talent, casting the odd sideways glance at a well-hung companion. Sometimes, the glance would be returned and they'd wait till they had the sweaty pine box to themselves before arranging to meet for a drink afterwards in one of the nearby gay bars.

That was another thing he didn't have to worry about these days. When he'd still been teaching, he'd been incredibly wary about responding to any kind of come-on anywhere that wasn't a bona fide gay establishment. Even then, he always scanned the bars as carefully as he could before he settled in for the evening. It might be OK for cabinet ministers to be out and proud, but for a teacher in Edinburgh, being a known gay out and about on the scene would still be the quickest route to the dole queue. Now, he could make eye contact anywhere he chose with anybody he chose. The biggest risk he faced was getting a punch in the face, but that hadn't happened yet. Drew prided himself on having an instinct for who was safe to come on to; he reckoned it was part of the sensibility that made him such a fucking great writer.

He smiled inwardly as he dressed. The guy he'd noticed on the rowing machine was new to the gym – or at least, new to this time of day – but he'd seen him before in the Barbary Coast bar round the corner. The Barbary was one of the newest gay bars in town and it boasted Drew's absolutely favourite place in the whole of Edinburgh. When you walked right through to the back of the bar, there was a small door set in the wall guarded by a couple of beefy leather men. If they knew your face, they simply stepped aside. If they didn't, they asked what you were looking for. If you knew you were looking for the Dark Room, they let you pass. If you didn't, they politely suggested you might want to stay in the main bar. Drew was on first-name terms with them both.

Drew had seen the guy on the rowing machine eyeing him in one of the floor-length mirrors that lined the gym. He reckoned that if he wandered into the Barbary within the next hour, he might just find him leaning on the bar. And if he knew about the upstairs room, well, that would do Drew very nicely for the evening.

God, he loved the Dark Room. There was a sense that anything could happen, and in his experience, it usually did. Several times. The people who had complained about the lovingly detailed graphic violence in *Copycat* would have a cardiac arrest if they knew a quarter of what men did to each other under cover of darkness in an upstairs room a short walk from the genteel Heart of Midlothian. He wouldn't mind betting it would shake a few real serial killers to the core as well.

Back at the flat, he took his time dressing. Tight black jeans that gave sharp definition to cock and balls, topped with a white T-shirt with the cover of his book screen-printed across it. He placed a single gold ring in one ear and threaded a studded leather belt through the hoops of his trousers. He slipped his feet into a pair of thick-soled biker boots and tightened the Velcro fastenings. He reached for his battered leather jacket and slipped his arms into the sleeves, admiring himself in the long cheval mirror. Not bad at all, he congratulated himself. Great fucking haircut, he thought, jittering his fingers through the short dark crop that he thought made him look dangerous and sexy. That new guy in the salon was worth every penny.

Drew slid open the drawer in his bedside table and took out a small silver snuffbox, a tiny silver spoon, a silver straw and an expired credit card. He flipped open the lid of the box and scooped out a generous helping of the white powder. Using the credit card, he chopped the cocaine into a pair of thick lines. He inserted the straw into his left nostril, closed his right nostril with a finger and expertly snorted one of the lines. He threw his head back and sniffed a couple of times, revelling in the numbness that spread across his soft palate. He repeated the process with his right nostril, then stood for a moment, enjoying the initial buzz as the coke hit his bloodstream. It was good stuff; he'd feel it for a while yet. And if he needed a top-up, he knew he could always score some more in the pub. It might not be up to the quality of his personal stash, but it would do the business nicely.

Finally, he snapped the steel bracelet of his chunky Tag Heuer round his wrist, taking care not to trap any of his fine dark hairs in the catch. He was ready for the time of his life.

He couldn't have known it would be the last time.

Chapter 9

Fiona pushed open the shutters and gazed across the gorge at Toledo basking in the silvery glow of a rising moon. Over on her left, she could identify the spotlit grandeur of San Juan de los Reyes, where James Palango's body had been left dangling from the shackles. From this distance, it looked far too innocuous for such a display. Certainly when they'd visited it that afternoon, it had appeared an unlikely setting for so degrading a crime. A few tourists had ambled past, reading their guide books, taking photographs and paying no attention to her and Berrocal. Fiona had to remind herself that this was the church built by the two monarchs who presided over the launch of the Inquisition. In all probability, San Juan de los Reyes had seen far worse than this latest corpse.

The visit to the church had added nothing to her knowledge, but it had given Berrocal the chance to run through the details of the crime scene and smoke another three of his execrable cigarettes. Afterwards, they had walked through the town to the police headquarters where Berrocal had made his base. 'It's easier than driving,' he had pointed out. 'So, what do you need to do now?' he asked as they set off.

'I need to familiarize myself with all the details of the cases. That way I can draw up a full list of the key correspondences between them. There's no point in trying to do a geographical profile with only two cases. There's not enough information, particularly since these two sites have been chosen for their historical significance. But what I hope to do is to be able to suggest where you should look in your criminal records for the crimes he has probably committed in the past,' Fiona explained.

'That's easily arranged. All the relevant material is in our incident room. I've set aside a desk for you there.' He took out his mobile phone and dialled. He spoke curtly into it, a brief exchange where he said little. He ended the call with a tight smile. 'The files will be waiting for you.'

'Thanks. What I'll probably do is read through it all, make some notes then go back to my hotel. I like to mull things over for a little while before I write my preliminary report, but I'll have it ready for you first thing in the morning.'

There was nothing high-tech about the incident room Salvador Berrocal had at his disposal. A dingy windowless room at the end of an airless corridor, the walls were grimy and streaked with stains that Fiona didn't want to think too closely about. It smelled of cigarette smoke, stale coffee and male sweat. Four desks had been crammed into the space, only one of which held a computer terminal. A couple of large-scale maps of the city and the surrounding suburbs were tacked to the walls, and an easel held a familiar sight – the crime board, complete with photographs of the victims and various scrawled notations. Two of the desks were staffed by harassed-looking detectives who gabbled into phones and barely looked up when Berrocal ushered her in.

He pointed to the farthest desk, where two stacks of files leaned against each other at a precarious angle. 'I thought you could work over there,' he said. 'I'm sorry our accommodation is so poor, but this was the only space available. At least the coffee is drinkable,' he added with a sardonic smile.

And at least there was a power point nearby, Fiona thought as she squeezed into the tiny gap between the chair and the desk. 'Are these the murder files?' she asked.

Berrocal nodded. 'All ready for you.'

It took her a few hours to plough through dozens of separate reports, stretching her Spanish to the limits of her dictionary and beyond. There had been a couple of occasions when she'd had to concede defeat and ask Berrocal for a translation of passages that baffled her. She had made notes as she'd gone along, working with the database painstakingly evolved by her and one of her PhD students which assigned probabilities to particular features of the two murders. The program then analysed which common features were significant in terms of attributing the crimes to one particular perpetrator. For example, most stranger killings took place after dark; that any two crimes in a series had happened at night was therefore not of much significance when it came to linking them. But it was relatively rare to commit a sexual assault on a dead body with a broken bottle, so the fact that these two crimes exhibited that particular feature was given a much higher significance by the program.

Most of the original data had come from the FBI, who had been remarkably generous with details of past cases once they had realized she was happy to have the information stripped of personal details like names of victims and perpetrators. Fiona recognized that like most statistical analyses produced by psychologists, her database was at best only a partial snapshot of the whole, but it did give her some valuable insights into the nature of the crimes she was dealing with. Perhaps more importantly, it allowed her to say with some degree of certainty whether individual crimes were part of a series or likely to be the work of separate offenders.

By the end of her afternoon's work, she had demonstrated

empirically what the police had already decided on the basis of common sense and experience: the two murders were undoubtedly the work of one man. If that had been the only service she could have provided, there wouldn't have been much point in her making the trip. But she was convinced that by analysing the data she already had, she could point the police towards other crimes the killer might have committed. With access to that information, she might finally be able to construct a useful geographical profile.

What she needed now was to get out of the police station and let her mind roam free over the nuggets of information she had extracted from the files.

She had got back to the room to find a note from Kit propped up on the desk. 'Gone down to the bar. Meet me there when you get in, and we'll have dinner.' She'd smiled then and crossed to the window to check out the view. It was strange to think that the beauty spread out before her concealed all the normal range of human ugliness. Somewhere in that honeycomb maze of buildings, a killer was probably going about his business, unsuspected by anyone. Fiona hoped that she could point the police in the right direction, so they could find him before he killed again.

But that was for later. Fiona turned away from the window and stripped off her clothes, wrinkling her nose at the smell of smoke that lingered in their fibres. A quick shower, then she changed into jeans and a ribbed silk shirt.

Fiona found Kit at a table in the corner of the bar, hunched over his laptop with a glass of inky red wine to hand and a bowl of olives pushed to one side. She put an arm across his shoulders and kissed the top of his head. 'Had a good day?' she asked, settling into the leather chair opposite him.

He looked up, startled. 'Hi. Just let me save this.' He finished what he was doing and turned off the computer.

Folding it closed, he grinned at her. 'They let you have an evening off?'

'Sort of. I've got to write a report later, but only a short one. It won't take long. I'm letting it bed down before I commit myself.' A waiter appeared and Fiona ordered a chilled *manzanilla*. 'What have you been up to?'

Kit looked faintly sheepish. 'I went for a wander this afternoon. Just to soak up the ambience, you know? This place, it's steeped in history. You can practically smell it in the air. Every corner you turn, there's something to see, something to imagine. Anyway, I got to thinking about the Inquisition, about what it must have been like here back then.'

Fiona groaned. 'Don't tell me. It gave you the idea for a book.'

Kit smiled. 'It started the wheels turning.'

'Is that what you were doing on the laptop?'

He shook his head. 'No, it's way too early to be writing stuff down. I was just doing a bit of polishing on what I've been writing this last week or so. Tickling and tidying, the boring bollocks. What about you? What kind of day have you had?'

The waiter put Fiona's drink in front of her and she took a sip. 'Routine. Going through files by the numbers. Berrocal's very organized. Very on the ball. You don't have to explain anything twice to him.'

'That makes your life a bit easier.'

'You're not kidding. The trouble is, there's not much to go at. Normally, a killer chooses a body dump for reasons that are very personal to him. But because these body dumps have particular historical significance, it complicates things. I'm not sure how much use geographical profiling will be.'

Kit shrugged. 'You can only do your best. They certainly go

in for gruesome in these parts. They've got this daft little train that takes you through the city and round the ring road on the other side of the river and the commentary is totally bizarre. It's in Spanish and German and a sort of fractured English, and they tell you all this stuff about the bloody history of the town. They've even got this place called the Gorge of the Woman with Her Throat Cut. Can you believe that?'

Fiona was surprised. 'They tell you about that on the tourist trip?'

He nodded. 'I know, it's not the sort of thing you'd normally boast about, is it?'

'That's where one of our murder victims was dumped,' Fiona said slowly. 'I was working on the assumption that only locals would be familiar with it.'

'Well, I can tell you all about it,' Kit said. 'This woman shagged one of the guards and let the enemy attack the city, so they cut her throat to make sure she wouldn't be doing that again in a hurry.'

'Did you go down to San Juan de los Reyes? The big monastery church?'

'I walked past it. I'm saving it for tomorrow.'

'Did you notice the chains on the facade?'

'It's hard to miss them. According to the guide book, Fernando and Isabella had them hung up there after the reconquest of Granada. They were used to shackle the Moors' Christian prisoners. I must say, if that's typical of Isabella's idea of decor, I can't wait to see the inside. Eat your heart out, *Home Front*,' he added with an ironic grin. 'Why do you ask?'

'That's where the second body was found. You've only been here half a day, and already you know the story behind both body dumps. It makes me wonder if I'm right in what I'm thinking.'

76

Kit patted her hand and assumed an expression of mock-patronage. 'Never mind, love, you can't be right all of the time. You leave that to me.'

Fiona snorted with laughter. 'I'm so glad I've got you to rely on. Now, are we going to eat dinner, or what?'

Fiona sipped a glass of brandy and studied the rough ideas she'd sketched out. In the background, the sound of Kit's fingers tapping the keyboard of his laptop was faintly soothing. Even the mosquito buzz of his Walkman was comforting in its familiarity. He never interfered when she had work to do, something she was eternally grateful for. She had heard too many of her friends complain that if their man wasn't working, neither were they supposed to be. Kit was always happy to occupy himself with his own work or a book, or to take himself off to a bar and make new acquaintances.

'I am convinced that the perpetrator's primary interest is not sexual satisfaction,' she read. 'However, the nature of the sexual mutilation he has performed postmortem is suggestive. I believe it is a way of demonstrating contempt for what he sees as the "weakness" of his victims, which leads me to postulate that his method of contact with his victims was one of physical or sexual appeal. At its most crude, I would suggest that he picked them up, possibly on an earlier occasion, and arranged to meet them on the nights of the murders. He may have baited his approach with the suggestion that his specialist knowledge might be of use to them in their professional lives. It is clear that he does not appear to pose a threat to those he has selected as victims. He knows the kind of places where his potential victims are to be found. This implies considerable local knowledge and suggests that he is a native of Toledo.

'These were not killings that occurred out of sexual rage

because of failure of performance or overarousal, but from a different motive entirely.'

So far, so good, she thought. She didn't think there was much to argue with there. 'These crimes demonstrate a relatively high level of sophistication and planning. It is therefore unlikely that the perpetrator is new to the world of criminal activity. He is far too comfortable with what he is doing. But if we accept that the motivation behind these murders is not primarily sexual, it therefore follows that it's unlikely his previous crimes have been sexual in their nature.

'Given that both crime scenes are significant tourist sites, and that both victims were foreigners, I believe the key to the killer's motivation is his view of visitors to his city. He sees them not as a benefit but as interlopers who are not to be welcomed. I think it most likely that his past crimes will have targeted either tourists or businesses related to tourism. He most probably began with acts of vandalism against hotels or businesses catering for tourists, such as souvenir shops. This may have escalated into attacks on tourists themselves, such as muggings.'

Fiona sat back and considered. What she was suggesting was by no means a conventional profile of a serial killer, but she had been struck from the first by the unusual nature of the crime scenes. Most killers left their bodies where they killed them or chose carefully selected body dumps that had significance only because they were unlikely to be spotted abandoning the corpse. This killer had taken a high risk with his second victim, so the sites were clearly symbolic for him at a deep level. For once, where the bodies had been found seemed at least as important as the selection of the victims. They weren't just places that symbolized violence. They would also have meaning for

78

the casual visitor to the city, as Kit's experience demonstrated.

She was pleased with the progress she had made. Now it was up to Salvador Berrocal to persuade the local police to give her the data she needed on crimes against property and persons related to tourism. Armed with that information, Fiona would be able to apply her theories of crime linkage to figure out which crimes had common offenders.

Once she had established which acts were part of series as opposed to isolated events, she would map the relevant scenes of crime on a street plan of the city that had been scanned into her computer. The powerful geographical profiling software loaded on her laptop would apply a complex series of algorithms to the points on the map. It would then chart probable areas where the perpetrator of those crimes might live or work. She could add the murder scenes to the mix, and if they didn't significantly distort the areas the computer had suggested, she might be able to indicate to Berrocal the area of the city the killer called home.

Ten years ago, Fiona mused, she'd have been laughed off the platform if she'd dared to suggest that a mixture of psychological profiling, crime linkage and geographical profiling could lead to the capture of a killer. Back then, there simply hadn't been powerful enough computer programmes to crunch the numbers fast enough, even if anyone had considered this an area worth investigating. The world of criminal investigation had changed faster than anyone could have imagined. At last, technology was outstripping the ability of criminals to keep one step ahead of it. And she was lucky enough to be part of the revolution.

And in the morning, she could put her skills to the test once more. Working with the police to capture killers was the most exciting thing she had ever done. But she never lost sight of the fact that she was dealing with real lives, not just a series of mathematical events and computer calculations. If what she did couldn't save lives, it was ultimately meaningless. And so, every case she was involved in became not only a professional challenge. It was nothing less than a measure of herself.

Chapter 10

Fiona walked into the smoky office just after eleven. Berrocal and his two detectives were all deep in telephone conversations, barely looking up at her arrival. She'd faxed her report to Berrocal at eight, knowing he'd need some time to assemble the material she needed. She'd used the three hours to have a leisurely breakfast in bed with Kit then to accompany him to see the definitive El Greco, the *Burial of the Count of Orgaz*, displayed in splendid isolation in an annex to the church of San Tomas. It had been a better start to the day than reading police files.

The stacks of folders on her desk looked the same as they had the day before. She waited for Berrocal to replace the receiver, then spoke. 'Hi. Are the reports on the vandalism and assaults not here yet?'

Berrocal nodded. 'That's them on your desk. Unsolved are on the left, the solved on the right. These are from the last twelve months.'

'Quick work.'

He shrugged. 'They knew I'd be on their backs till they came up with what you asked for. They like a quiet life. Can anyone help you with this, or is it something you must do yourself?'

'Unfortunately, I need to analyse the data myself,' Fiona told him. 'What about a map of the city?'

Berrocal raised a finger, admonishing himself. 'I have them here.' He turned to the remaining empty desk and rakcd around in the top drawer, coming up with a small tourist map and a larger, more detailed street map. 'I wasn't certain which one would meet your needs best,' he added, handing them to her.

'I don't suppose they've got a scanner here?' Fiona asked without hope.

Berrocal shrugged. 'There must be one somewhere.'

'I need the detailed map scanned in as a GIF file,' she said, opening her laptop case and fishing out a blank floppy. 'If you can have it put on the floppy, I can transfer it to my system.'

He nodded, turning to the nearer of the two detectives. He snapped something in fast Spanish. The detective quickly ended his call and gave his boss a quizzical look. Berrocal thrust the map and the floppy at him and rattled off a string of short sharp sentences. The detective gave Fiona a radiant smile and made for the door. Clearly even being a gopher for the English consultant was preferable to being cooped up in this box. '*E café con leche para dos,*' Berrocal added with a wicked grin at the disappearing back.

'Thanks,' Fiona said, reaching for the first file. She had to devise a checklist of significant factors; time of the offence, date of the offence, what form the vandalism had taken, and a dozen other particulars. Then she had painstakingly to enter the details. Where there was a known offender, she also had to input every piece of information relevant to his history and his previous crimes. There were forty-seven files to work through and the fact that everything was in Spanish slowed things down even further. It made for a long day, punctuated by regular cartons of coffee and snacks that she couldn't have itemized five minutes after she'd eaten them, so intense was her concentration.

Finally, she sat back and waited while the computer sorted the data and offered up the results of its calculations. Unsurprisingly, most of the incidents came up as discrete events. But among those, there were three groupings of crime reports that each appeared likely to have the same perpetrator. The first was a series of attacks on souvenir shops. In every case, the crimes had taken place between two and three in the morning on weekdays. The first three involved paint being thrown across the windows. But then there had been an escalation. Four further attacks had taken place where the windows had been smashed and paint thrown on to the shops' stock. All the crimes were from the unsolved pile.

A second series featured graffiti daubed on the walls of restaurants and hotels. But here, the slogans were political – right-wing rants about Spain for the Spanish, and the banishment of immigrants. Fiona immediately discounted these as the work of her killer.

A third series emerged from the unsolved pile. Within the past four months, three tourists had been attacked on their way back to their hotels in the early hours of the morning. Berrocal had already told her that Toledo was, by Spanish standards, an early-to-bed city, with most of the cafés and restaurants closed by eleven. But there were a few late-night bars, and the victims had all been in one or other of those. They had been walking back to their hotels alone when a masked man had jumped out from the mouth of an alley and attacked them. There had been no demand for money, just a silent and savage assault lasting a few minutes before their assailant ran off into the maze of narrow passages nearby.

Fiona gave a deep sigh of satisfaction. When crime linkage worked well, it was like a small miracle unfolding before her.

Now she could enter the locations of the two significant series into her geographic profiling software and see what emerged.

Kit had watched Fiona walk up the hill from San Tomas, admiring her smooth stride and the way the cut of her trousers gave emphasis to the gentle swell of her hips. *I am a lucky bastard*, he congratulated himself, luxuriating briefly in the memory of their leisurely morning in bed. Even if she did his head in sometimes with her perpetual need to analyse and dissect everything and everyone who crossed her path, he wouldn't have swapped her for any woman he'd ever met. One of the things he loved about her was her dedication to the job she did. But even when she was possessed by a case, she never lost sight of the importance of their relationship.

This morning, for example. She could have played the 'I'm indispensable' card and headed straight for the police station. But she'd assured him there would be nothing yet for her to get her teeth into and she'd taken time out to share something he'd wanted to do. He tried to do the same thing himself, but he knew he was worse at it than she was. When he was head down, going flat out for the finishing line of a book, he could think of nothing but the next chunk of text he had to get on to the screen. The only way he could show his love for her then was to cook for her and take the time to sit down and eat with her. It wasn't much, but it was better than nothing.

He spent the rest of the day being a tourist, and got back to the hotel just after six, taking a bottle of red wine up from the bar to their room. He had no idea how long Fiona would be, but that wasn't a problem. He turned the TV on to MTV Europe, poured a glass of wine, booted up his computer and collected his e-mail. The only significant message was from his agent, confirming a deal with the independent film makers who wanted to adapt his first novel for TV. Personally, he thought *The Dissection Man* was unfilmable, but if they were prepared to pay him large sums of money to find that out for themselves, he wasn't about to complain.

Not that he cared much about money. Both his parents were teachers and he and his brother had grown up in an environment where money had never really been an issue. There had always been enough and he'd never been conscious of having been deprived of anything because his parents couldn't afford it. He hadn't had much of an advance for his first or his second novel, and he reckoned no one had been more surprised than his publishers when *The Blood Painter* had become an overnight cult sensation then made the crossover to mainstream success. As a result, he guessed he'd earned more money in the previous two years than his parents had in the past ten.

And he didn't know what to do with it. A large chunk had gone on buying the house, but other than that, he and Fiona had few material desires. He didn't care about designer clothes, he had no interest in performance cars and he still preferred the kind of holiday where they'd fly somewhere, pick up a hire car and stay in cheap motels or guesthouses. His biggest expenditure was probably on music, but even there he economized by waiting till he was in the States or Canada on a book tour and indulging himself in a CD-buying spree at their lower prices.

The only real indulgence he'd craved was a retreat where he could escape to write when the book was going through that difficult middle period. Beginnings were always easy, but by the time he'd worked through the first hundred pages, depression would strike as he realized he was already falling far short of what he'd aspired to. At that stage, every interruption was a torment. Fiona was about the only person who didn't piss him off, but that was because she knew when to leave him alone.

It was Fiona who had suggested he buy a cottage in the wilds where he could go and work undisturbed for however long it took him to get over the hump of dissatisfaction. Usually, the truly terrible phase lasted for about six weeks or a hundred and fifty pages, and Fiona had informed him that she'd rather do without his company if that helped him to return more quickly to his normal cheerful self.

So he'd bought the bothy. It never ceased to amaze him that anywhere on the British mainland could feel so isolated. From the two-roomed cottage, no other human habitation was visible in any direction. To get there, he had to fly to Inverness, pick up the elderly Land Rover he garaged there, stock up with a supply of groceries, then drive for another two hours to the eastern fringe of the vast wilderness of Sutherland. His power came from a diesel generator, his water from a nearby spring, his warmth from a wood-burning stove that also heated enough water to half fill his bath. At Fiona's insistence, he'd invested in a satellite phone, but he'd only ever used it to link up his computer for e-mail.

The isolation was more than most people could have borne. But for Kit, it was a lifeline. With the only distraction an occasional excursion to shoot rabbits for the pot, he invariably found he ploughed through the hardest sections of his books in far less time than it took in London. And the quality of his work had improved as a result. He knew it, and so did his readers.

And there was no denying that absence enriched his relationship with Fiona. Even though they were in daily e-mail contact – often swapping posts that would have qualified as pornography in any other context – their reunions had all the ardour of the first days of their affair, when no amount of physical contact was too much and no demand too outrageous. Just thinking about it excited him. Who would imagine that behind Fiona's cool exterior was a sensualist who had turned the hard man of British crime fiction into a romantic fool?

She was always at her most passionate when she'd been forced to confront violent death. It was as if she needed to reaffirm her connection to life, to reassert her own vitality in defiance of a killer. Kit might deprecate the source, but he had to confess he wasn't averse to reaping the benefits.

Mentally, he shook himself. Anticipation of Fiona's return was the surest way to distract him from what he was supposed to be doing. He had decided to do one of the periodic revisions he routinely ran through to check that everything in the book was flowing smoothly. He typed in the commands to print out the last sixty pages and flicked the TV over to BBC World to check out the news headlines.

The early evening news magazine programme was in full flow, the interviewer winding up what sounded like a deeply dull item about the state of the Euro, courtesy of a junior Treasury minister. The studio anchor's voice suddenly picked up urgency. 'And news just in. Police in Edinburgh have identified the victim of a brutal murder that took place in the heart of the Scottish capital in the early hours of this morning as the international bestselling thriller writer Drew Shand.'

Kit's forehead wrinkled in an incredulous frown. 'Over to our correspondent James Donnelly in Edinburgh,' the presenter continued.

A young man with a serious expression stood in front of a grey-stone building. 'The mutilated body of Drew Shand was found by a police officer on a routine patrol of the Royal Mile just after three this morning. Police cordoned off an area behind St Giles' Cathedral which remains the scene of police activity. At a press conference earlier this afternoon, Detective Superintendent Sandy Galloway revealed that the victim's throat had been cut and his face and body mutilated with a knife. He appealed for anyone who was in the area between the hours of midnight and three a.m. to come forward.

'In the last few minutes, the identity of the victim was revealed as award-winning thriller writer Drew Shand. Thirty-one-year-old Shand was hailed as one of the new stars of British crime fiction when his first novel, *Copycat*, shot to the top of the bestseller lists on both sides of the Atlantic and won the John Creasey Memorial Dagger and the Mcvitie prize. The television adaptation of *Copycat* also went on to win several major awards and has been widely screened abroad.

'A former English teacher, Shand lived alone in the New Town area of the city. His second novel, *The Darkest Hour*, is due to be published next month. Shand, who was openly homosexual, was known to frequent several Edinburgh gay bars, including at least one believed to cater for those whose tastes run to sadomasochistic practices. At this point, police are refusing to suggest any possible motive for the killing.'

'Fucking typical, blame the victim,' Kit snarled, slamming his glass down so hard the stem broke, sending a stream of red wine across the marble floor. Ignoring it, he took a swig straight from the bottle. He scarcely registered its taste. 'Drew Shand,' he muttered, tilting the bottle to his mouth again. He shook his head in disbelief. 'Poor bugger.' He had a sudden flashback to the panel they'd done together at the last Edinburgh Book Festival, the one and only chance he'd had to appear with the rising star. He remembered Drew leaning forward, elbows on knees, hands spread open, face earnest as he struggled to make the point that the violence in *Copycat* had always been functional, never gratuitous. The audience had been won over, Kit recalled, although he'd had his doubts. Then afterwards, sitting outside the Spiegeltent, drinking Becks straight from the bottle, the pair of them had carried on the discussion, lacing their seriousness with the gallows humour beloved of police officers and crime writers alike. A vivid image of Drew throwing his handsome head back and laughing imploded behind his eyes like a terrible firework.

Kit suddenly realized how he longed for Fiona's presence. A reviewer had once remarked that Kit made his readers care so much for his fictional victims that the reader felt the shock of losing a real friend when he killed them off. At the time, he'd been proud of the comment. But back then, he'd never personally known someone who had been murdered. Sitting in a strange hotel room in an unfamiliar city, numbed with the shock of Drew Shand's death, he finally recognized the critical comment for the absurdity it had been.

Now he knew the truth.

Chapter 11

Fiona stretched extravagantly and looked at her watch. To her astonishment, it was ten past seven.

Her movements attracted the attention of Berrocal, who had been absent for most of the day but had returned a short while before. 'You are making progress?' he asked.

Fiona outlined the results of her day's work. 'I need a break now,' she concluded. 'It's easy to start making mistakes when you've been staring into the screen all day, and if I get the crime-site plotting wrong, the results are worthless.'

Berrocal crossed to her desk, peering over her shoulder at the laptop. 'This is remarkable,' he said. 'A system like this would make our job so much easier.'

'Quite a few police forces are using it now,' Fiona told him. 'The linkage program works best with crimes against property, like burglary and robbery. The version I'm using is experimental. It lets me enter my own set of variables for the checklist, so it needs a certain level of expertise to use it. But the basic version with the fixed parameters reduces burglaries wherever it's been used. It helps clear outstanding crimes from the books as well as current cases. You should get your bosses to invest in the software.'

Berrocal snorted. 'Easier said than done. My bosses don't like to spend money on anything they can avoid.'

'You did well to get them to pay for me, then,' Fiona said tartly, standing up and switching off the computer.

'When it comes to losing tourist dollars, they panic. Suddenly, we get resources that we'd never get in any other circumstances. So, what are your plans for the evening? Would you like me to take you and Kit for dinner somewhere typically Toledan?' He stepped back to allow her to escape the confines of her desk.

'That's kind of you, but I don't think I'd be very good company. I've got all this stuff buzzing round my brain, and I'd rather just go back to the hotel and have a bite to eat there with Kit. After that I'll probably feel like doing more work.'

He shrugged. 'Whatever you prefer. But you really don't have to work every minute you're here, you know.'

Fiona closed her laptop and started to pack it away. 'I think I do, Major,' she said softly. She looked up and met his eye. 'He's out there, planning the next one. He's already working on a short cycle. I hate to sound melodramatic, but when you're dealing with a killer as organized and as ruthless as this one, every day counts. I don't want his next victim's blood on my hands if I can possibly avoid it.'

Berrocal eased the car into the traffic and gave Fiona a quick glance. 'You really think the man behind the vandalism is the same man who did the muggings?'

Fiona shrugged. 'There are no certainties in what I do. And ideally, I like to work with at least five locations for each potential series. But on the basis of probability, I'd say so. The vandalism only overlaps the first mugging. After the second mugging, there's no more paint-throwing or window-breaking. So either the vandal moved away, or he found a more satisfying outlet for his anger. Everything I know about the way violent criminals escalate tells me that it's likely that, when he wasn't caught, he became more confident. He moved up a gear and started attacking the direct cause of his rage rather than hitting targets at one remove. If I'm right, it'll show up when I run the geographic profiling program.'

'You'll have proof it's the same offender?' Berrocal couldn't help sounding a little sceptical.

'Not absolute proof, no. Not even the kind of proof that will stand up in court. But if the program gives me the same likely residential locations for both series of crimes, then we're looking at a strong probability, wouldn't you say? And then your colleagues in Toledo will have an idea where to start looking for proof.' Fiona shifted in her seat, trying to unlock the tightness in her shoulders. They had turned on to the road that skirted the river opposite the bluff where Toledo glowed in the twilight. 'Amazing view,' she added.

'It's a beautiful city,' Berrocal acknowledged. 'That's why crimes like these seem so much more shocking than a routine act of violence in the back streets of Madrid. And of course, it's also why there is so much attention on this investigation. It's not just my bosses who are leaning on us for a quick solution. The newspapers and the TV stations are all over us. Luckily I've managed to keep your name out of the stories so far. I don't think it would go down well that we have had to bring in an expert from England to solve crimes so very Spanish.'

'I won't be solving your crimes, Major. I'm a consultant psychologist, not a consulting detective. All I can do is make suggestions. It's up to you to decide whether they're worth pursuing, and it's up to you to find the evidence to nail your killer.'

Berrocal grinned. 'Doctor, you know and I know that the media are not interested in the truth of the situation. If they find out about you, they will portray you as some sort of miraculous detective, a modern Sherlock Holmes who is called in because the police are too stupid to do their job.'

'Which is why we don't tell them I'm here,' she said. For a minute or so there was silence, until Berrocal turned off the main road and headed up the steep hill towards the parador, leaving the dramatic vista behind them.

'Will your geographic program tell us if the murderer lives in the same place as the mugger?' he asked.

'I don't know if there's enough data,' she answered frankly. 'On their own, the two murders won't give us anything approaching pinpoint accuracy. Not enough locations, you see. But I'll play around with various combinations and see what I come up with. I should be able to answer your question tomorrow morning.'

'Are you positive you don't want to go out to dinner?' Berrocal asked as he pulled into the car park.

'It's very kind of you. But I'd rather get through the work. The sooner I get finished, the sooner I can go home. Besides, I'm sure your family would like to see something of you.'

He gave a soft snort of laughter. 'I'm sure they would. But like you, I'll be working this evening, I'm afraid.'

'At least I'll have Kit's company for dinner. He has the knack of making me laugh, even in the middle of something as grim as this. And let's face it, Major, there aren't too many laughs in this line of work.'

He nodded gravely. 'I know what you mean. Sometimes I feel I'm dragging the sewer in behind me when I walk in from work. I almost don't want to pick up my children and hug them in case I infect them with what I've seen, what I know.' He leaned across to open the door for Fiona. 'Good hunting, Doctor.'

She nodded. 'You too, Major.'

*   *   *

93

Fiona's first reaction when she opened the door was bewilderment. The only light in the room came from the distant vista of Toledo, dramatically uplit by dozens of spotlights. Silhouetted against the light, Kit was sitting on the end of the bed, elbows on knees, head hanging. 'Kit?' she said softly, closing the door behind her. She didn't know what could be wrong, only that something clearly was.

She crossed to him with swift strides, shedding briefcase, laptop and coat on the way. Kit raised his head and turned to face her as she sat down beside him. 'What's the matter, love?' she asked, concern and anxiety in her voice. She put an arm round his shoulders and he leaned into her.

'Drew Shand's been murdered,' he said unsteadily.

'The guy who wrote *Copycat*?'

'According to BBC World, they found his body early this morning just off the Royal Mile.' Kit sounded dazed.

'That's how you found out? From the telly?' she said, dismayed at the thought.

'Yeah. I thought I'd catch the news headlines.' He gave a bleak bark of laughter. 'You don't expect to hear one of your mates has been murdered and mutilated.'

'That's terrible,' Fiona said, conscious of the inadequacy of her words. She understood only too well the shock and pain of such a discovery. Though in her case, it had been the telephone that had been the unwelcome messenger.

'Yeah, and I'll tell you what's worse. Because he was out and proud and hung in the kind of bars where the patrons indulge in the sort of sexual practices that your average Edinburger finds repulsive, he's already being trailed as the engineer of his own destruction. It's blame-the-victim time. Nothing like that approach to make the respectable citizens sleep easy in their beds, knowing it couldn't happen to them.' He sounded angry, but Fiona recognized that as a defence against the hurt.

'I'm so sorry, Kit,' she said, holding him close and letting him nestle against her.

'I've never known anybody who was murdered before. I know we've talked about Lesley, and I thought I understood how you felt about what happened to her, but now I realize I didn't really have a clue. And it's not even as if I knew Drew particularly well. But I just can't get my head around the idea that anybody would kill him. I just can't imagine why.'

Fiona had never met Drew Shand, but she knew too much of murder and its consequences not to feel the horror that lay behind the bare fact of his death. She knew only too well what murder meant to those left behind. It was the reason she had become the woman she was.

Kit had hit her with the trigger word. Lesley. If she closed her eyes, it would all come flooding back. It had been a Friday night like any other. She'd been in her first year of university teaching and had fallen into the habit of unwinding at the end of the week with the clinical staff from the institute where she was conducting a research study. They'd start in a pub in Bloomsbury, then work their way up towards Euston Station, ending up in a curry house in a side street on the far side of Euston Road. By the time she'd got back to her two-roomed flat in Camden, it had been almost midnight and the rough edges of the week had been blurred into a genial wooziness.

The light on the answering machine had been flashing crazily, indicating half a dozen messages or more. Intrigued, she'd hit the playback button and carried on walking towards the kitchenette. The first words on the tape stopped her in her tracks. 'Fiona? It's Dad. Phone me as soon as you get in.' It wasn't what was said, it was the manner of its saying. Her father's voice, normally strong and confident, had been almost a whisper, a pale quivering echo of its normal self.

A bleep, then the next message. 'Fiona, it's Dad again. I

don't care how late it is when you get this message, you've got to phone.' This time the voice cracked towards the end of the short message.

Already, she was turning, moving towards the phone. A bleep, then her father's voice again. 'Fiona, I need to talk to you. It won't wait till the morning.' All her instincts told her it was bad news. The worst kind of news. It must be her mother. A heart attack? A stroke? An accident in the car?

Fiona grabbed the phone and punched in the familiar number. Almost before it could ring, it was answered. A strange voice said, 'Hello? Who is this?'

'This is Fiona Cameron. Who are you?'

'One moment, please. I'll get your father.' There was a muffled exchange then a clatter, then her father's voice, almost as alien as the stranger's.

'Fiona,' he blurted. Then he started sobbing.

'Dad, what's wrong? Is it Mum? What's happened?' All Fiona's professionally soothing skills vanished in the face of her father's tears.

'No, no. It's Lesley. She's . . . Lesley's been . . .' He forced his ragged breathing into stillness. She heard a deep, wrenching intake of air, then he said, 'Lesley's dead.'

Fiona had no idea what he'd said next. She felt an enormous distance build between her and her surroundings, his voice a faraway echo against the ringing in her ears. Her little sister was dead. It wasn't possible. There had to be a mistake.

There was none. Lesley, a third-year student at St Andrews University, had been raped and strangled on her way back to her shared house. No one had ever been charged with the crime. The police believed the killer had raped two other students in the previous eighteen months, but they had no significant clues. A couple of footprints from a popular brand of trainers. A description so vague it could apply to half the adult males in the town. Even if they'd had DNA analysis back then, it wouldn't have been much use. He'd used a condom. All the attacks had taken place in winter and the women were wearing gloves, so they hadn't scratched their attacker.

For six months after Lesley's death, Fiona had felt as if she was walking around inside a very bad dream. Any minute now, she could force herself to wake up and none of it would have happened. Lesley would be alive. Her mother wouldn't be suicidally depressed. Her father wouldn't be drinking too much and writing endless letters to his MP, the press and the police, complaining of the failure to make an arrest. And she wouldn't be blaming herself for persuading Lesley to spread her wings and go to St Andrews when she could have joined Fiona in London.

Then one day, she'd gone to a lecture given by a visiting fellow from Canada. He'd talked about the infant science of crime analysis and how it could be applied in criminal investigations. It was like a light bulb in her head suddenly turning on. The cocoon fell away and with piercing intensity, Fiona knew what she wanted to do with her life.

An hour in a lecture theatre, and nothing would be the same again. She couldn't save Lesley. She couldn't even catch Lesley's killer. But now Fiona understood that one day she might find her redemption by saving someone else.

That prospect was enough. Most days, anyway, it was enough. But now murder had touched her life again, even if at one remove. All of this swam through her mind as she sat with Kit in her arms, doing what little she could to comfort him.

After a lengthy silence, Kit finally drew away from her. 'I'm sorry I'm being such a wet nelly,' he said. 'It's not like he was my best mate or anything.'

'You're not being a wet nelly. You knew him, you liked him, you respected his work. And it's a shock to realize he's just not here any more.'

Kit stood up and turned on a lamp. 'That's the curse of an imagination at a time like this. I keep thinking what it must have been like for him, how scared he must have been.' He took a deep breath. 'I need to do something to keep my mind occupied.' He picked up the pile of paper the printer had spewed out. 'Do you mind if we just get something sent up from room service?'

'Whatever you need.' Fiona hung up her coat and picked up her laptop. 'I've got plenty I can be getting on with if you want to work.'

Kit managed a faint smile. 'Thanks.' He settled cross-legged on the bed with his pile of manuscript and a pencil. Fiona watched him in the mirror for a few minutes until she was sure he was reading and not brooding. More than anything, she was glad he'd accompanied her to Toledo. The news of Drew's death wasn't something he should have had to face on his own.

That was something she knew all about from personal experience. And she wouldn't wish it on her worst enemy.

Extract from **Decoding of Exhibit P13/4599**

Ufime zftmd pfapa pdqie tmzp. Yqeek ngfza
ftmdp. Mrqit agdea regdr uzsft qiqnm zpuwz qiftq
pqfmu xeart uepmu xkdag fuzq.

*It wasn't hard to do Drew Shand. Messy, but not hard.
They don't realize how vulnerable they are. A few hours
of surfing the web and I knew the details of his daily
routine.*

*I didn't think it would be too difficult to pick him up.
His sort are always suckers for flattery. It was just a
matter of finding somewhere to see him off.*

*Then I found the perfect place: a boarded-up butcher's
shop. The back was tiled from floor to ceiling. There
was a butcher's block in the middle of the room and
a couple of big sinks along one wall. Judging by the
dust and cobwebs everywhere, nobody had been here*

for ages, and I didn't think anybody would be coming through any time soon. So I decided it would be safe just to leave whatever mess I made.

The next day, I parked near his flat, where I could see him come and go. He got back from the gym right on schedule, and an hour later, he was walking back towards Broughton Street. I slipped into his wake and followed him into the Barbary Coast bar. It was already quite busy, and I could see a few blokes giving me the once-over. It made me feel sweaty and uncomfortable. After all, I didn't want anybody remembering me afterwards.

Drew was at the bar and I moved up beside him. He'd ordered a drink and when it arrived, I held out a tenner and said, 'This one's on me.' He didn't argue. We moved over to a corner where it was darker, and I acted surprised when he said who he was. I said I thought the torture scenes in his book were brilliant. He went on about how the critics had complained that the violence was over the top, so I told him I thought it was great. Sexy, almost.

He gave me a funny look then. But he didn't say anything, just went to the bar and got another round in. When he came back, he asked me if that was what I was into, a bit of the rough stuff. It couldn't have gone better if I'd scripted it. Cutting a long story short, he invited me upstairs to what he called the dark room. Then I told him I had something better than that. I said I worked for a property development company, and I'd managed to get the keys to an old shop that I'd turned into a fantasy dungeon.

I couldn't believe how easy it had been. I'd thought I might actually have had to have sex with him before I could get him to come with me, and I'd been dreading that even more than what I had planned for him. But he was a pushover. The worst bit was when we pulled up in the back lane and he leaned across and started kissing me. I pushed him away, a bit roughly but that just made him all the more keen. When I was undoing the padlock, he pressed right up against me so I could feel his cock hard against my backside. If I'd been having second thoughts, that would have seen them off sharpish.

I pulled the door open, and as he reached for the switch, I smashed my heavy metal torch down on the side of his head just above his ear. He went down like a tree.

I don't want to think about the next bit. It wasn't nice. It's a lot harder to strangle somebody than it looks. Especially when you're wearing latex gloves and your hands start sweating and slipping around inside them.

Then I had to do the cutting. That was really disgusting. Horrible. Not just the blood, but the smell. I nearly threw up. I've had some shitty nights, but this beat the lot of them hands down.

Once I'd done what I had to do, I zipped his jacket back up to sort of hold things in place. Then I picked him up and carried him out to the 4 x 4. I couldn't just throw him over my shoulder or his guts would have gone everywhere.

I'd already decided where I was going to dump the body. The actual site described in Shand's book was out of the question. It was far too exposed. It would have been asking to be caught. But then, what do you expect? One hundred per cent accuracy?

I'd settled on dumping him round the side of the cathedral. When I got there, there was nobody around, so I arranged him on the steps leading up to an office building.

I undid his jacket, and displayed him by the book. God, that nearly had me throwing up all over again. Then I took off as if I had the four horsemen of the *apocalypse on my heels. Time to head back to where I was supposed to be.*

I expected it to give me nightmares. But it didn't. It's not like I enjoyed it or anything. It was a job that had to be done, and I did it well. I take pride in that. But no pleasure.

Chapter 12

The arrival of their room-service dinners forced both Fiona and Kit to surface from the salve of work. She had been entering data into her laptop and had started running various combinations through the geographic profiling software, but so mechanical a task left too much of her mind free to rerun her own memories. Trying to drown the voices in her head with alcohol was tempting. But Fiona had watched her father turn to drink, an accelerant that had plunged him into paranoid nightmares that had destroyed his life as surely as her murderer had destroyed Lesley's. If acute liver failure had not killed him four years earlier, she suspected he'd have taken his own life sooner rather than later. So the whisky bottle was, for her, no choice.

But burying herself in work wasn't doing the trick either. Sitting down with Kit to eat forced her to realize that Lesley's ghost hadn't stopped tormenting her since Kit had mentioned her name earlier. And by the looks of him, Kit was equally lost in his own thoughts. They ate their baked fish in virtual silence, neither knowing how to broach the subject that was uppermost in their minds.

Fiona finished first, pushing the remains of her meal to one side of the plate. She took a deep breath. 'I think I might be better able to settle if I could find out more about what happened to Drew. Not because I think I can help in any practical way, but . . .' She sighed. 'I know that what always helps me is information.'

Kit looked up briefly from his plate, seeing the pain of memory in Fiona's face. He knew that in the aftermath of her sister's murder what had woken Fiona screaming from her sleep night after night was ignorance. She needed to know every detail of what had happened to Lesley. Against the wishes of her mother, who was adamant in her desire to possess as little information as possible about her younger daughter's fate, Fiona had pursued all the avenues she could think of to absorb every fact relating to her sister's terrible ordeal. She had made friends of the local reporters, she had exerted every ounce of her charm to persuade the detectives to share their information with her. And gradually, as she pieced together Lesley's last hours, the nightmares had receded. Over the years, as she had learned more about the behaviour patterns of serial rapists and killers, that picture had become even clearer, giving texture and shape to her understanding, filling in the outlines of the transaction between Lesley and her killer.

While part of him felt this was an unhealthy obsession, Kit had to admit that knowledge did seem to have provided some sort of balm for Fiona. And as far as he was concerned, that was what mattered. Even though she couldn't adequately explain why it helped her to have so detailed a reconstruction in her head, neither of them could deny its force. And Kit had also come to realize that as it was with her personal relationship to murder, so it was with her professional one. The more she knew, the more secure she felt. Perhaps she was right. Perhaps the best way to make sure her sleep wasn't riven with nightmares about Lesley was to garner what she could about what had happened to Drew Shand. And it might just help him too.

'What were you thinking about doing?' he asked.

'See what they're saying on the Net,' she said. 'How do you feel about that?'

He shrugged then topped up his glass. 'It can't be worse than the movies my imagination is running for me.'

Kit gathered the dirty plates and put the trays outside the door while Fiona logged on to the Internet and connected to her favourite metasearch engine, which combed the vast virtuality of the worldwide web at her command. 'Where can I find Drew Shand?' she typed. Within seconds, she had the answer at her fingertips. Shand had had his own website, as well as a couple of fan sites dedicated to his work.

'We might as well try the fan sites first,' Kit said. 'I don't think Drew's going to be updating his own site any time now.'

The first page Fiona clicked on had a black border round the publisher's jacket photograph of the dead novelist. Beneath it were the dates of his birth and death and the atmospheric opening paragraph of *Copycat*.

The haar moves up from the steel-grey waters of the Firth of Forth, a solid wall of mist the colour of cumulus. It swallows the bright lights of the city's newest playground, the designer hotels and the smart restaurants. It becomes one with the spectres of the sailors from the docks who used to blow their pay on eighty-shilling ale and whores with faces as hard as their clients' hands. It climbs the hill to the New Town, where the geometric grid of Georgian elegance slices it into blocks before it slides down into the ditch of Princes Street Gardens. The few late revellers staggering home quicken their steps to escape its clammy grip.

Fiona shivered. 'It makes the hairs on the back of your neck stand up, doesn't it?' Kit observed. 'Bloody great opening paragraph. The kid really had something special. Did you read *Copycat*?'

'It was one of the pile you gave me for Christmas.'

'Oh yeah, I'd forgotten.'

Fiona grinned. 'There were so many.' Ever since they'd first been together, Kit had given Fiona his personal pick of the year's crime fiction for Christmas. It was a genre she'd scarcely ever read before they'd become lovers. Now, she enjoyed keeping up with her partner's competition, as long as it was a guided trip and not a random harvest of the crime section of the bookshops.

Scrolling down, Fiona ignored the hagiography and focused on any details of the crime. Nothing they didn't already know. The second fan site had little more to offer, except a rumour that Shand had frequented a pub in Edinburgh where gay sadomasochistic group sex allegedly took place in an upstairs room. 'See what I mean?' Kit said angrily. 'It's starting already. The deserving-victim syndrome. You can see it now. He was murdered because he asked for it. He enjoyed the kind of sex that could turn nasty, and it killed him.'

'It'll get worse before it gets better,' said Fiona. 'Unless they pick someone up quickly and it turns out to be nothing to do with the gay scene.'

'Yeah, right. If AIDS doesn't get you, the bogeyman will.'

Fiona called up the menu of her favourite sites on the web and ran her cursor down the list. Kit leaned into her, reading over her shoulder.

'I wonder how many people's favourite places list includes the RCMP, the FBI, various serial killer sites and a forensic pathology discussion group?' Kit asked.

'More than is healthy, I suspect,' Fiona muttered. Towards

the bottom of the list was a site that she knew infuriated most of the law enforcement officers she knew. Officially, *Murder Behind the Headlines* was run jointly by a journalist in Detroit, a private eye in Vancouver who was reported to have had a murky past in the CIA, and a postgraduate in criminology in Liverpool. Given the depth of detail they managed to come up with on sensational murder cases, Fiona suspected there were a few serious hackers involved in putting together the site. Not to mention a very large base of anonymous contributors who enjoyed the prospect of sharing whatever privileged information or hearsay they encountered. Several attempts had been made to close them down on the basis that they were making public information that allowed scope both for copycat killings and for false confessions, but somehow they always seemed to resurface with ever more sophisticated graphics and gossip. Fiona sincerely hoped that the more faint-hearted relatives of the victims never logged on to *Murder Behind the Headlines.*

Seeing where her cursor had paused, Kit groaned. 'Gossip central,' he complained.

'You'd be surprised how often they get it right,' she said mildly.

'Maybe so, but they always leave me feeling like I need a bath. And they can't write for toffee.'

Fiona couldn't resist a smile as she connected to the site. 'Never mind the morality, feel the semicolons,' she said ironically. When she was prompted for her area of interest, she typed, 'Drew Shand'. In the top left-hand corner of the page that unfurled before them, the same photograph of Drew brooding handsomely into the camera appeared. This time, however, the text was very different.

Scottish thriller writer Drew Shand has been

found murdered in the historic heart of the city he lived in and used as the background to his first gruesome novel, the award-winning *Copycat*. His mutilated body was found just behind St Giles Cathedral, only feet away from the pavements pounded daily by millions of tourists. So far, no suspects have been arrested.

MBTH hears from a source inside the investigation that there are some very spooky coincidences connecting Shand's own death and the graphic violence he turned to good commercial effect in *Copycat*. The plot of his serial killer novel centres round a contemporary re-creation of the celebrated Whitechapel Murders – a sort of Jock the Ripper gorefest.

The original Jack the Ripper's fourth victim was found by a policeman on his beat. So was Shand's fourth victim. And so too was Shand.

The police surgeon at the time of the Whitechapel Murders, Dr Frederick Brown, reported that: *<The body was on its back, the head turned to the left shoulder. The arms by the side of the body as if they had fallen there. Both palms upwards, the fingers slightly bent ... Left leg extended in a line with the body. The abdomen was exposed. Right leg bent at thigh and knee. The throat cut across. The intestines were drawn out to a large extent and placed over the right shoulder ... A piece of about two feet was quite detached from the body and placed between the body and left arm.*

<The lobe and auricle of the right ear was cut right through ... There was a cut ... through the lower left eyelid dividing the structures completely

through . . . The right eyelid was cut through to about half an inch.

<There was a deep cut over the bridge of the nose . . . This cut went into the bone and divided all the structures of the cheek except the mucous membrane of the mouth. The tip of the nose was quite detached . . . There was on each side of the cheek a cut which peeled up the skin, forming a triangular flap of about an inch and a half.> The actual cause of death was haemorrhage from the left carotid artery.

Each of these grim facts was annexed by Shand for his novel. And according to our source, they were all present in the murder of the writer himself. Apparently one of the murder squad detectives called to the scene of the crime had read *Copycat* and was immediately struck by the similarities. It was only when the police surgeon itemized the injuries and the detective went back and checked both with Shand's book and accounts of the original Ripper case that the police became convinced that they were dealing with a *Copycat* copycat.

Apparently the theory doing the rounds at police HQ is that Shand was into hardcore S&M sex. They reckon that made him vulnerable to a perp who had fixated on his book and wanted to try it out for real. Shand was apparently a creature of habit – his daily routine is outlined on his website for all to see. So it wouldn't have been too hard for the hunter to track him down and, providing the killer was Shand's type, it would all fall into place. And of course, the easy thing about killing somebody who's into S&M is they think you're only playing when you tie them up. Doesn't matter that, like Shand, your victim works out down the gym every day, because he's trussed up like a chicken all ready for you.

One other detail – the cops think he was killed somewhere else then brought to the body dump, unlike both the Whitechapel Murders and the slayings in *Copycat*. But Shand's flat was clean, so they've no idea as yet where the murder actually took place. One thing they can be pretty sure of, though – somebody's got a helluva cleaning job on his hands.

REMEMBER YOU READ IT FIRST ON
MURDER BEHIND THE HEADLINES

Kit whistled softly. 'That is seriously creepy shit.'
Fiona logged off. 'You're not kidding.'
'So what's your take on it?'
'Probably much the same as yours,' Fiona said. 'He clearly planned his crime to mirror the circumstances of one of the murders in Shand's book. Which in turn mirrors one of the original Ripper murders, apart from the gender of the victim. That he's succeeded so accurately indicates a high degree of control and organization. His intelligence therefore is likely to be significantly above average. He has a highly developed fantasy life and would probably use violent pornography to support that. He would be unlikely to respond well to authority, so if he had a job it wouldn't be commensurate with his intelligence, which in turn would be a source of irritation to him.' She pulled a face. 'But saying that is simply a matter of playing the probabilities.'

'But what about his relationship to Drew? Is he a stalker, a jilted lover, or some sort of fucked-up wannabe acolyte? What do you think?'

She dropped into one of the chairs by the window and stared out at the city. When her answer came, she spoke slowly, feeling her way from sentence to sentence. 'That is without doubt the most interesting question, Kit.' She gave him a quick smile. 'Hardly surprising that it was you who asked it. That the murderer fixated on the book and copied its crimes isn't particularly remarkable. Often killers who display their victims' bodies ritualistically are replicating images they've seen in pornography or in some situation that was particularly meaningful to them. But most sexually motivated killers would be satisfied with wreaking their havoc on any victim who broadly fitted their fantasy. To have chosen to hunt and destroy the creator of the very fiction that fuelled his desire to kill is curiously personal. And in a crime where depersonalizing the victim is often crucial to the process, it's distinctly unusual.'

Kit ran his hands over his scalp, his face a mixture of amusement and exasperation. 'It's always got to be a lecture with you, hasn't it? You still didn't answer the question.'

Fiona grinned. 'I sort of hoped you hadn't noticed. If you pushed me on it, I'd probably plump for a stalker who has become obsessed with *Copycat*. But that's purely speculation.'

'So is *Murder Behind the Headlines*, but it doesn't stop you reading that,' Kit pointed out. He got up and wandered round the room. 'It's a bit freaky, isn't it? The thought of somebody following Drew around like a shadow, invisible till the last moment when he shows himself. You never think of anything like that when you're writing. That some nutter is going to read their life story into your words.'

'You'd probably never write another book if you give that possibility space in your head,' Fiona said. 'Other people's madness is not your responsibility. Come here, give me a hug.'

He crossed to her and gently pulled her to her feet, wrapping his arms around her. She turned her face up to his. 'There are other ways of taking your mind off things, Kit,' she said softly as his lips came down to meet hers.

Inside the city walls of Toledo, the evening *paseo* was in full swing. Around the Plaza de Zodocover, people strolled in couples, families and groups, taking the evening air and catching up on the business of the day as they moved between pools of yellow light. Restaurants, many half-empty now the height of the tourist season was past, served dinner to tourists and locals, greeting their regular customers with smiles and the small change of social intercourse. The bars were doing a thriving trade, their tables full inside and out as older clients enjoyed a *digestif* with their coffee and the young men checked out the women gossiping and giggling in their separate groups. It was a sharp contrast to the dimly lit alleys and narrow streets that radiated out from the plaza, linking it with the rest of the city.

In one of the cafés on the edge of the square, Miguel Delgado smiled across at the Englishwoman who worked behind the reservation desk at the Hotel Alfonso VI. Two nights before, he'd engineered an encounter where he'd tripped over her handbag and knocked over her drink. She'd been with friends, so she'd suspected no ulterior motive when he bought her a drink to replace the one he'd spilled. Tonight, though, her friends were absent. For the price of another drink, he could make the down payment on his next act of revenge.

He swallowed the last of his *café solo* and folded up his newspaper. Careful not to draw attention to himself, he crossed to her table, inclined his head in a small bow and smiled. '*Buenas tardes,*' he said.

The woman returned his smile, without a trace of uncertainty. Minutes later, they were deep in conversation. Delgado was back in business.

Chapter 13

. . . On a professional note, I heard last night that
Blake has done a deal with one of the Sunday
tabloids. You know the kind of thing – my life of
hell as the falsely accused Hampstead Heath killer.
And on the strength of that, he's gone off to
Spain, allegedly to get away from all the pressure.
Of course, we've been keeping tabs on him, albeit
at arms' length, and according to the travel agent,
Blake has rented a villa outside Fuengirola for the
next month. At least you're far enough away in
Toledo not to stand any chance of walking into a
neighbourhood café and finding him propping up
the bar. Let me know when you're coming back
and we'll get together for dinner.
Love
Steve

Fiona cleared Steve's e-mail from the screen. She'd get
round to replying later. It was thoughtful of him to pass on
the news about Drew, but she didn't want to be distracted
from the task in hand by thinking about Francis Blake right
now. While she waited for Berrocal to arrive, she double-
checked that she had plotted her crime scenes correctly on

the map. Just as she finished, Berrocal strode through the door, full of apologies for keeping her waiting. 'So, what do you have to show me?'

The map of Toledo was monochrome on the screen, the streets and alleys black lines over the off-grey background. 'This is how it works,' Fiona explained. 'I started off with the street grid. Last night I entered the locations of the events that interest me.' She omitted to mention the news from England that had stirred memories, turning her sleep into exhausting restlessness. She wasn't looking for Berrocal's sympathy, nor, more importantly, did she want to give ammunition to anyone who might suggest her work failed to come up to the required standard. So she mainlined the cartons of industrial-strength coffee that the junior detectives had deposited on her desk and tried to keep the weariness out of her voice. 'First of all, the vandalism cluster.'

She tapped a couple of keys and the screen came alive in an irregular spread of radiant neon colours, from sea-green, grading through blues and purples to red. There were only two small blocks of red, both to the west of the cathedral and the Plaza Mayor. 'The program assigns different colours to different degrees of probability. The perpetrator of the acts of vandalism I've identified as a cluster is most likely to live within the boundaries of those red blocks,' she told him, pointing to them with her pencil.

'Very interesting,' Berrocal said softly.

'Don't ask me how it works. The maths is way beyond me. I leave that to the techies. All I know is that it does have a frighteningly high degree of accuracy.' She cleared the colours from the screen. 'Now, this is the picture we get from the muggings.' Again, the screen pulsed with vibrant colours. This time, there were three red blocks. One of them appeared almost identical to the larger of the two on the previous display, while the other two were more northerly.

'I think the reason for these two is that the location of the crimes was circumscribed by where our mugger knew there were likely to be late-night victims,' she continued, pointing to the aberrant blocks of crimson. 'But look what happens when I amalgamate both sets of results and we look at the vandalism and the mugging together.'

Fiona clicked the mouse a couple of times. Now the larger of the original two red blocks was the only bright-scarlet patch on the screen, the others fading to deep purple. 'If I were a Toledo police officer looking to clear up these instances of vandalism and mugging, I'd focus my attention on people who live right there, around the bottom end of Calle Alfonso the Tenth.'

'Fascinating,' Berrocal acknowledged. 'But what happens when you consider the murders too?'

'It's far from clear cut,' she admitted. 'We're looking at two instances, which is a very small base to work with. And, as I said to you before, because these crime scenes have historical rather than specifically personal significance, that could distort our results.' Again she cleared the screen. 'On their own, they don't provide us with anything like pinpoint accuracy.' This time, there was no small red block, just a jagged purple mass that covered most of the west of the old city and spread like a port-wine birthmark out towards the suburbs.

'However, I'm working on the principle that my theories of crime linkage and the escalation of violence are correct. Now, if I've got it right and these three groups of crimes have all been committed by the same person, then when I add the murder sites to the other two series, I should still have my red block in more or less the same place. But if I'm wrong, then the resulting picture will show a significant distortion.' She looked up at Berrocal and gave a wicked grin. 'Ready?'

'The suspense is killing me,' he said.

Fiona hit a couple of keys and the screen reconfigured itself. The red block was still there, though not in quite such a strong shade. But the purple areas had spread and become noticeably more blue. Fiona circled the red block with the end of her pencil. 'It doesn't significantly distort the key area. Which indicates that the person who committed the murders could well be the same person as the vandal and the mugger. But you see this purple zone?'

Berrocal nodded. 'That's the fallback zone, is it? If he's not in the red zone, he might be in the purple?'

'That's right. Now, the way that has changed with the murder input may not mean much in itself, given how specific he is about the body dumps and given that the places where he displays his victims are central to the nature of his crimes. But I'm tempted to go out on a limb here and suggest that he might possibly have moved house in between the muggings and the first murder.'

Berrocal frowned. 'Why do you say that?'

'It doesn't matter how high-tech a system is, there's still room for gut instinct when it comes to interpretation. I'd defend myself by saying that I've used this geographic profiler a lot now, and I've developed a sense of what the pictures mean that goes beyond what's in the manual. And there's something about the shape of this that makes me wonder if we're looking at a change of address. I'm sorry, I can't be more scientific than that.'

'So what we have learned is useless.'

'No, far from it. If he *has* moved, it's been relatively recent. Between the last of the muggings and the first of the murders. There must be civic records that would reveal who lives there and if anybody's gone in the last couple of months. I could be wrong, he could still be living there. But if I was the investigating officer here, I'd make it my first priority to look at residents inside the red block who have moved out.'

'You think he moved to make it harder for us to find him?' Berrocal asked.

'No, I don't think he was planning that far ahead. And he may not have left his home from choice. He may have been forced out because the building was being developed for some tourist-related business. He'll have seen this as a terrible provocation. If that's what happened, it could have been the factor that tipped him over the edge into murder. He's been nursing his hatred for a while now, judging by the length of time these earlier offences cover. Perhaps this tourist development has been on the cards for a long time and he'd been fighting it. Then finally, he lost. And he decided to take revenge on the people he thought were to blame.' Fiona leaned back in her seat. 'I know it might sound far-fetched, but as psychopathic motives for murder go, it's as coherent as any. And it makes sense of these events in a way that conventional theories of sexual homicide don't.'

'The way you explain it is certainly logical,' Berrocal acknowledged. 'Can you print these maps out for us? I'd like to get started on this line of inquiry as soon as possible.'

Fiona nodded. 'No problem. I'm also in the process of writing a full report for you that incorporates all my reasoning. I'll include a basic behavioural profile of the perpetrator.'

Berrocal frowned. 'I thought you didn't approve of behavioural analysis?'

'Taken on its own, I think it has limited value. But when you incorporate it with crime linkage and geographical profiling, it can be helpful.'

Berrocal looked dubious. 'So, when will your report be ready?'

'I should finish it today.'

'Good. Then I can distribute it among the investigation team. First thing tomorrow, I'd like you to attend a briefing with them to answer any questions and deal with any objections?'

Fiona nodded. 'I'd be happy to.'

Berrocal got to his feet. 'And then I presume you will want to return to England?'

Fiona smiled. 'You presume correctly. There's nothing more I can usefully do for you right now, so I may as well go home.'

He nodded. 'I'll let you get on with your report,' he said. 'Thank you.'

'You're welcome,' she said absently, her mind already on the next task. The sooner she finished this, the sooner she could start to think seriously about going home.

ii

He never knew how long it would last. That was why he had to savor every moment of it, like a kid opening Christmas presents, unsure which garishly wrapped parcel held the gift that really mattered. The trick was to arrange it so that everything built to a climax. But sometimes it didn't, and he hated that loss of absolute control, hated the rage that boiled through him when those sluts let him down, when they failed to hold out long enough for him to extract each single possible drop of pleasure from their pain. Death should be the final moment in the crescendo, not a sad diminuendo leaving the spirit dissatisfied.

That was why he worked with such dedication towards perfection. Experience had taught him that every stage released its own particular flavor, from the first moment he chose her to the final moment when he abandoned her. The secret was to plan. The taste of anticipation was almost as good as the spectrum of sensuality supplied by the execution of his perfect scheme. So too was the satisfaction of watching the small minds pitted against him as they struggled through their skirmishes with his handiwork into ultimate failure.

At first, his opponents had been as insignificant as the

crickets that chirped the night away outside this safest of safe houses. Dumb sheriff's officers who'd never investigated anything more complicated than a fucked-up raid on the local Seven Eleven had no chance of coming anywhere near him. He knew the chances of them even managing to complete a VICAP report and file it with the FBI were remote. All that paperwork, interfering with the consumption of Dairy Queen hamburgers and brewskis – no chance.

So puny a challenge couldn't last forever. He'd known that. He'd bargained on that. He'd set himself up right from the start to beat the finest, so there was no real satisfaction in running rings round the morons who'd gone into small-town law enforcement because they didn't have the stones to make something of their lives. They thought they knew their turf so well, but that hadn't stopped him moving into their territory and stealing a woman from under their noses. His greatest triumph this far had come with number five. La Quinta was the daughter of the local sheriff in a small Nebraska town.

As usual, he'd removed her from her own home. Saturday night, and her parents had gone out to a benefit dinner for the local Republican candidate for the Senate race. The girl had opened the front door without a second thought as soon as she saw the Highway Patrol uniform. It had been laughably easy to knock her to the floor with a single blow to the face. Hog-tied, she'd spent the night in the trunk while he drove the interstate, fueled by adrenaline and nicotine.

By mid-morning, he'd been home. Surrounded by dense woodland, away from the possibility of prying eyes, he'd carried her indoors and gotten down to making her his slave. Shackled to a bench in his workroom, La

Quinta had learned that pain takes many shapes and forms. The delayed sting of the razor cut. The blossoming of a burn from a smart to a roar of pain that spread inwards as the smell of barbecued flesh drifted outwards. The searing agony of flesh forced to accommodate more than it has room for. The sickening pain of a broken bone never allowed time to knit. The dull distress of a blow strategically aimed at the organs nestling beneath the skin. It took her days to die.

He'd enjoyed every waking moment.

Then he'd taken her back home. Not all the way home, of course. That would have been reckless. He drove her as far as the first bend over the county line on a quiet back road, then left her body sprawled across the blacktop for the next passing driver to crush beneath his unsuspecting wheels.

La Quinta had made them sit up and pay attention at last. He'd read enough to know what would have happened next. An urgent request to the Feebies, then a computerized search of the country to find matches. As soon as they realized he meant business, the machine would have kicked in. True to his prediction, the suits had arrived. And then, finally, she had flown in to face a flurry of cameras at the airport.

Now at last, the game was on.

Jay Schumann was in town. Dr Jay Schumann, the forensic psychologist who had turned her back on a lucrative private practice to become the FBI's celebrity mindhunter. Jay Schumann, who had single-handedly restored the tarnished image of psychological profiling with a string of spectacular successes. Jay Schumann with those intense dark eyes that contrasted so sharply with her bright blonde hair, a photo opportunity who gave the suits a human face. Jay Schumann, whose glamor had persuaded her bosses that they should use her skills on the media as well as on the criminals.

In the twenty years since she'd so heedlessly and needlessly humiliated him on the night of the senior prom, they'd both traveled a long way from the small New England town. But he had never forgotten nor forgiven the whiplash of her scorn that had branded him and distorted his life forever.

The first five had been his apprenticeship. The next fifteen would perfect his art. One for every wasted year. And then, only then, would he allow Jay Schumann to come face to face with her personal and professional nemesis.

There was a long way to go before then. But now Jay Schumann was on the case. At last the revenge proper could begin.

Chapter 14

Fiona gave a final glance at her notes then looked out across the half-empty lecture theatre. 'To sum up. That dreadful old misogynist St Paul says, "When I was a child, I spake as a child, I understood as a child, I thought as a child; but when I became a man, I put away childish things." As do most of us.

'But the sociopath is different. Most of us come to comprehend that we are not the centre of the universe, and that other people can share centre stage in the narrative of our lives. The sociopathic personality never makes that adjustment. In his limited world view, others exist at a less than human level. Their only valuable function is to meet the needs and satisfy the desires of the sociopath himself.' She gave a sly grin. 'That's why they make such good captains of industry.' Depressingly few answering smiles, she thought ruefully. Probably because half of them had their hearts already set on such a career. So serious, the modern student.

'So if we are to develop any sort of empathetic understanding of the criminal psychopath,' Fiona continued, 'we must learn to step back in time. I leave you with this thought, also from that fascinating psychological text, the Bible. "Except ye become as little children, ye shall not enter the kingdom of heaven." Or, as we so often find in our line of work, the kingdom of hell.' She gave a brief, courteous nod. 'Thank you, ladies and gentlemen. Same time, next week.'

Head down, Fiona gathered her papers together as the students shuffled out, their muted mumblings drifting back towards her. She wondered how much she disappointed them. She was certain a significant proportion of them signed up for her courses on the Criminal Mind because their imaginations had been fired by *The Silence of the Lambs*. Expecting some Jodie Foster fuelled by instinct and intuition, instead they were confronted with seminars on statistics and required to produce essays driven by intellectual rigour. The drop-out rate disturbed her departmental administrator, but not Fiona. She'd never been interested in woolly minds.

Some sixth sense made her look up and an unself-conscious smile spread across her face as she took in Kit's burly frame strolling down the aisle between the ranks of seats. He returned her smile and leaned his forearms on the edge of the platform while she finished tidying her lecture notes into her briefcase. 'Nice close,' he said. 'I like the image of the sociopathic killer as Peter Pan. The boy who never grew up.'

'Now, that's an interesting comparison. With a bit of work, I could make something of that. Captain Hook and the Lost Boys. Wendy as mother figure ... Thanks, Kit, I think I'll steal that. So, to what do I owe this pleasure?' Fiona asked, descending to his level and brushing his cheek with a kiss.

'I've been going like a train today, and I ran out of steam about an hour ago. And I remembered that there's a launch party for Adam Chester's new book at Crime in Store at six. I thought I'd swing by on the off-chance that you fancied joining me there.' Kit fell into step beside her.

'You haven't forgotten we're having dinner at Steve's tonight?' Fiona asked.

'We're not due there till eight. I thought we could swag a few glasses of publisher's plonk on the way. Show my face and remind everybody that I'm still a contender. Up to you, love. If you've got too much on, I'll meet you at Steve's later.' Kit put his arm round her waist and gave her a quick squeeze before they emerged in the atrium of the psychology faculty building.

Fiona considered for a moment. Nothing more pressing than marking essays should lie in store for her, and those could wait until morning. 'Let me check my office, and if nothing urgent's come up in the last hour, you're on.'

The mystery bookshop was crowded with a mixture of authors, collectors and fans of Adam Chester's complex and beautifully written 1950s police procedural novels. For this, the tenth in the series, his publishers had reprinted all his previous paperbacks with new jackets, the misty photographs evoking the dark and brooding ambience of the books. His editor and publicist stood proudly beside a display of the covers, flashing encouraging smiles at the potential buyers.

As soon as he walked in the door, Kit was immediately surrounded by an enthusiastic trio of women who turned up at every crime fiction event in the capital and who apparently adored him above all other writers. Fiona left him to it, edging through the crowd and helping herself to a glass of white wine. Kit was a professional; he'd give the women enough of his time to reinforce their view of him as approachable and amusing before disentangling himself and settling in for a good gossip with friends and colleagues. For herself, she was happy enough to take a back seat and watch him work the room.

'He's such a pro,' an admiring voice murmured in her ear. Fiona immediately recognized the genteel Edinburgh tones of Mary Helen Margolyes and turned to greet her with a kiss.

'Mary Helen, what a delightful surprise,' she said, meaning it. In spite of hating her melodramatic Jacobite historical mysteries featuring Flora Macdonald's younger sister, Fiona had a soft spot for Mary Helen, not least because of her acerbic tongue. 'What drags you away from the Highlands?'

'Oh, I had to come down to talk to some dreadful wee man at the BBC who's making a TV series out of the Morag Macdonald books.'

'But that's good news, isn't it?'

Mary Helen's face puckered as if she'd bitten a sour apple. 'You wouldn't say that if you knew who they've cast as Morag.'

'Tell me the worst.' Fiona had spent enough time around writers to know exactly what was required.

'Rachel Trilling.' Mary Helen's voice was fat with disapproval.

'Isn't she . . . ?' Fiona struggled to make sense of the name. 'She's the lead singer with Dead Souls, isn't she?'

Mary Helen's eyebrows rose. 'My God!' she exclaimed. 'At last I've found somebody who's heard of her. But then, what can you expect from a producer who thinks a white cockade is a tropical bird?'

'Oh, Mary Helen, I am sorry,' Fiona said.

'I'll just have to follow Kit's perennial advice and take the money and crawl,' Mary Helen said with a grim little smile.

'Apart from that, how's life treating you?'

'It would be infinitely better if you'd pass me another glass of wine,' Mary Helen said. Fiona obliged, but before they could say more, the shop manager began his introduction to Adam Chester. Adam spoke briefly and wittily about his new book, then read a fifteen-minute extract. A few questions from the floor followed, then it was time for the signing.

As the purchasers formed a queue by Adam's chair, Kit glanced across the room. 'Uh-oh,' he said to Nigel Southern, the twenty-something writer of comic *noir* short stories he'd been talking to. 'I better go and rescue Fiona from the clutches of Mad Mary Helen.'

Nigel raised his perfectly groomed eyebrows. 'I'd have thought your lady was more than a match for the Highland Harpie. What's it like, anyway, living with somebody who spends her days poking around the perverted fantasies of psychopaths?'

'Funnily enough, we don't talk about it that much. We've got a life,' Kit said. 'Anyway, that's not what she does. She uses computer analysis, not psychoanalysis.'

Nigel shook his head pityingly. 'I couldn't be doing with that. I mean, it must be like living with the control freaks' control freak. Isn't she always telling you you've got it wrong?'

Kit gave him a good-humoured punch on the shoulder. 'You haven't got a fucking clue how the grown-ups live, have you? Listen, Nigel, if you are ever lucky enough to meet a woman with half the brains, the wit and the looks of Fiona, do yourself a favour. Go on a training course before you ask her out.' Without waiting for a reply, Kit squeezed through the crowd and enveloped Mary Helen in a bear hug. 'How's the queen of the glens?' he demanded, landing a resounding kiss on her cheek.

'All the better for seeing you and Fiona. If I'm honest, the main reason I came to this do tonight was in the hope of seeing a few cheerful faces. This business with Drew Shand has cast a terrible pall over the Scottish crime-writing community. We've all been phoning each other every day for the last two weeks, making sure we're still alive.'

'You're such a drama queen, Mary Helen,' Kit teased her.

'I'm serious, Kit,' Mary Helen protested. 'It came as a terrible shock to all of us.'

'But surely there's no threat to any of the rest of you?' Fiona asked. 'I thought the police were pretty much convinced he'd been killed by somebody he picked up that night in the gay bar, what's it called?'

'The Barbary Coast,' Kit supplied. 'So unless you've got a secret life in sadomasochistic society that we know nothing about, the chances are you're safe,' he continued, putting a reassuring arm round Mary Helen's shoulders.

'Would that I could lay claim to anything so exciting,' Mary Helen said dryly. 'But it's not that straightforward, is it? I mean, Drew was killed in the precise manner in which he'd murdered one of his fictional victims. It's hard to avoid the conclusion that whoever killed him had some sort of morbid fascination with the genre. You know about these things, Fiona. Wouldn't you agree with me?'

Put on the spot by Mary Helen's sharp blue stare, Fiona shrugged. 'Hard to say. I know no more about the case than anybody else who's read the papers and surfed the Net.'

'You must have some sort of theory,' Mary Helen pressed her. 'After all, this is your field. Come on, don't be shy, you're among friends here.'

Fiona pulled a face. 'To my mind, it has all the hallmarks of a stalker murder. Someone who became obsessed with Drew and his work to the point where the only way he could resolve his compulsion was to destroy its object. And the fact that Drew had provided him with the perfect script was simply the most unfortunate element in the whole scenario. If I'm right, then the rest of you are as safe as you ever were before

Drew died. Stalkers don't by and large transfer their obsession to another target.'

'There, Mary Helen. Now you can sleep safe in your bed at night,' Kit said.

'You're a patronizing wee shite, Kit Martin,' Mary Helen said, giving him a mock-punch on the shoulder. 'Thank you, Fiona. I do feel better for hearing that, and I'll pass it round my colleagues north of the border.'

'Wait a minute, Mary Helen,' Fiona protested. 'I don't know anything for sure. What I said was nothing more than guesswork.'

Mary Helen beamed at her. 'Maybe so, but it makes more sense than the platitudes we've been getting from the police. Now, I'm going to love you and leave you because I need to go into a huddle with my publicist, if she can tear herself away from Adam for a minute.'

They watched her go, Fiona shaking her head in exasperation. 'I fall for it every time. She just fixes me with the twinkle and the dimple and twists me round her little finger.'

'Don't beat yourself up. She does it to everybody,' Kit said, reaching past her for a fresh glass of wine. 'We're all suckers for Mary Helen's "little old lady" routine. Anyway, I think she really needed the reassurance. She's not joking about people being wound up by Drew's death. Adam's editor has just been telling me that Georgia is refusing to go out on her book tour next month unless her publisher provides her with a bodyguard.'

Fiona snorted. 'The only way Georgia Lester would miss an opportunity for blatant self-promotion is if someone sewed her mouth shut. You know that. Don't you remember her turning up at Waterstone's in Hampstead with a sniffer dog in tow after the Docklands IRA bomb?'

Kit grinned. 'You've always got the knife into Georgia, haven't you?'

'That's because I don't get the benefit of the charm like you do. I'm the wrong gender.'

He spread his hands. 'She can't help herself, love. You know Georgia. She gets an idea in her head and she gets carried away. Anyway, according to Adam's editor, she's giving them hell. Threatening to move her next book to another house, threatening to tell the press that she's in fear of her life because her publisher won't protect her.'

'I know she's your mate, but if she devoted half as much energy to writing as she does to self-promotion, her books would have got better instead of worse over the years,' Fiona said cynically.

Kit put a finger to his lips. 'Ssh. Don't say that so loudly. You might give her publisher ideas. After all, there's nothing like a dramatic death to boost your sales figures. I hear the advance orders on Drew's new book have more than doubled since his murder.'

'Why am I not surprised?' Fiona sighed. 'Maybe you should mention that to the cops. For all we know, Drew might have been planning to move publishers. An editor who was going to lose him anyway might well have considered giving her balance sheet one final hike.'

Kit shook his head sorrowfully. 'Such a low opinion of the publishing trade. I can't imagine where you got that from.'

'I've been hanging out with writers too long. It sours the milk of human kindness.'

Kit acknowledged her barb with a faint smile. 'So, you really think Drew's killer won't strike again? Or were you just being kind to Mary Helen?'

Fiona shrugged. 'If I could predict the future that well, we'd have won the lottery by now. I honestly don't know.

But if he does, he won't go for someone who writes cheerful cosies like Mary Helen. He'll be looking for someone on the *noir* side of the street.'

Kit's face froze. 'Someone like me, you mean?'

'Are you seriously telling me it hadn't crossed your mind?'

Ignored by those around him, the man in the tweed jacket watched Kit Martin from the other side of the room. Whatever he was talking about with his girlfriend, it had shaken him up, that much was obvious. His eyes had widened and his normally mobile face had turned into a still mask. Good, the man thought with deep satisfaction. He liked the idea of Martin's discomfiture.

If everything had gone according to plan, Martin should have had good reason to be worried. The man's lip twitched in a tiny sneer, hidden from view behind his beard and moustache. He watched Martin take his girlfriend by the elbow and steer her through the crowded bookshop to the door. He'd barely paused to say farewell to his cronies, the man observed. The woman's words had clearly made him very uncomfortable.

With the principal object of his hatred gone, the man slipped through the press of bodies to the table that held the wine. He held his glass out for a refill, nodded his thanks and faded into the background. There were a few authors left, but they were beneath contempt, unworthy of his attentions. His opinion of himself was such that he was only interested in the very best. That, of course, had been the problem all along. He saw that now. They were the ones under pressure to come up with the goods, which explained why they'd done what they had to him.

But that was history. What he was interested in now was retribution.

Chapter 15

In the cab they took to Steve's, Kit was uncharacteristically quiet. Fiona knew better than to try to force him to talk about what was on his mind. That would simply lead to a sullen and mean-tempered denial that anything was troubling him. Like most men, a sense of his own vulnerability made him uncomfortable. Rather than make him even more uneasy by pushing him, she placed her hand on one of his and said nothing. Halfway up Pentonville Road, he finally spoke.

'I know it's hard to credit, but it really hadn't crossed my mind that Drew's killer might come after me,' he said, leaning his head against the back of the seat and sighing. 'Dumbshit or what?'

'That's the healthy response,' Fiona said. 'Why should you imagine you're going to be the next victim of a murderer who struck four hundred miles away? If – and it's still a big if – Drew Shand's death is the first in a series, we don't know what it was about him that made him an attractive target. Was it that he was gay? Was it his work? Was it something in his past that we don't know anything about? Was it his attraction to the dark side of his sexuality? All of those are imponderables and only one of them could apply to you. Statistically, your risk of becoming the victim of a serial killer is somewhere around vanishing point.'

'Even so, you'd think it would have occurred to me in passing that I might just be on some nutter's hit list,' Kit said sharply. 'After all, I'm supposed to be the one with the imagination. You thought of it, after all.'

Fiona squeezed his arm. 'Yeah, but my way of looking at the world is even more fucked up than yours. Besides, I'm your lover. I'm legally entitled to worry unreasonably about you.'

Kit grunted, putting an arm round her and pulling her close. 'Doesn't it ever piss you off, being right all the time?'

She grinned. 'Find out what you're good at and stick to it, that's what I say. And since you've just admitted I have a right to worry, you have to promise me you won't talk to strangers.'

Kit snorted. 'That's an easy promise to keep. At least until the new book comes out.'

The cab juddered to a halt outside the four-storey Islington town house where Steve occupied the garden flat. He could have afforded somewhere bigger, but he spent so little time at home that he couldn't see the point of moving from somewhere that met his needs perfectly. Two bedrooms – one of which doubled as a study – a dining-kitchen whose french windows opened out on to the garden and a living room big enough to accommodate two sofas and an armchair was all he needed. He kept the decor simple. Fiona loved the economy of style, but Kit hated its clinical purity. Both suspected Steve barely noticed his surroundings. As long as they were functional, he was content.

Fiona's low heels clattered on the stone stairs down to the basement entry. Kit, following her, marvelled at her hair as the streetlights caught it, burnishing it to a rich chestnut-brown. She was, he thought, more beautiful than he could ever deserve. Catching up with her as she rang the bell, he put his arms round her and kissed her neck. 'I love you, Fiona,' he said gruffly.

Fiona gave a low chuckle. 'Don't I know it.'

Steve opened the door and grinned down from his superior height. 'Keep it decent,' he advised. 'Some of us have to live here.'

They followed him down the narrow hall into the dining room, where the table was laid with an assortment of breads, cheeses, pâtés and salads. The air was thick with the aroma of leek and potatoes. Steve lived on soup. There was always a pan of some concoction on the stove, next to the stockpot containing the makings of the next brew. Soup was the only thing he ever cooked. Kit enjoyed mocking Steve's culinary limitations, but when cornered, he was forced to admit that Steve made the best soup he'd ever tasted and, far from having a restricted repertoire, Steve probably experimented more with combinations of flavours than Kit himself.

'It's just that it always comes with a bowl and spoon,' he had once complained. 'It's so predictable.'

'At least my guests don't need a degree in civil engineering to eat their dinner,' Steve had growled. 'I remember my first globe artichoke round your house. Besides, given the life I lead, I need something instant when I come in the door, and my soup's a damn sight healthier than a bacon butty.'

But tonight, no one was interested in arguments about the menu. In the two weeks since she'd returned from Toledo, Fiona had finally found the time to give proper attention to the case file on the sting the Met had mounted against Francis Blake. Since she insisted her input was to remain informal, she had suggested outlining her conclusions round the dinner table. So for once there was an air of tense anticipation among them as they sat down and Steve poured a robust red into their glasses.

'Soup first, then we'll cut to the chase,' Fiona decreed.

Steve gave a wry smile. 'Whatever you say, Doctor.' He filled their bowls with steaming, creamy vichyssoise. 'So what small talk shall we indulge in?'

'How about your love life?' Kit suggested.

'That should occupy all of ten seconds,' Steve said. He picked up his spoon and examined it critically. 'My love life is like the Loch Ness Monster – rumours of its existence are greatly exaggerated.'

'What happened to that CPS lawyer you took to dinner the other week?' Fiona asked.

'She was more interested in the rules on disclosure of evidence than she was in me,' Steve said. 'I'd have had a more interesting night out with the Commander and his wife.'

Kit whistled. 'That good, eh?'

'Hell, I don't suppose I was much more interesting to her,' Steve said, lifting a spoonful of soup to his lips.

'The trouble with the three of us is that in our own ways we all have a morbid fascination with violent death,' Fiona said. 'Maybe Kit should fix you up with a sexy crime writer.'

Kit spluttered. 'Easier said than done. When you cross off the ones who are already attached, the ones who have a serious interest in recreational drugs and the dykes, there's not a lot left over.'

'Besides, you couldn't stand the competition,' Steve added.

The first course over, Steve cleared the bowls away and Fiona took a couple of pages of notes from her briefcase. 'I must say, the material you gave me made for very interesting reading,' she said. 'Not least the interpretations that Andrew Horsforth placed on the interaction. It was an object lesson in what happens when you push the theory ahead of the facts. In one sense, the conclusions he drew were valid. If, that is, you concentrate on the margins and ignore the central core of the material. If you look at a series of conclusions as a continuum from most likely to least likely, he's opted more often than not for the least likely, because that's what backed up the view he started with, namely that Francis Blake was the killer.'

'But, cleverly, you started from the opposite premise,' Kit said with affectionate sarcasm. 'Nobody loves a smartarse, you know.'

Fiona stuck her tongue out at him. 'Wrong. I started from the neutral position. I tried to ignore my own half-formed opinion that Francis Blake wasn't the killer. I was concerned with achieving as much objectivity as I could.'

'Not something anyone could ever accuse Horsforth of,' Steve said. 'You'll be pleased to hear that he's been dropped from the list of Home Office-approved consultants after our debacle at the Bailey.'

'That's a bit decisive for the Home Office, isn't it?' Kit asked through a mouthful of salad.

'Horsforth's an easier scapegoat than senior police officers,' Steve said. 'We're as much to blame as him for what happened, but heaven forbid that any more mud should be slung at the Met right now.'

'Deputy heads will roll,' Fiona observed cynically. 'Before I tell you what I think, Steve, I need you to answer one question for me. Although obviously I know more or less where the murder took place, I didn't actually visit the scene of crime, so I wasn't sure about this. Is there anywhere on the Heath where someone could have watched the murder without being seen by Susan Blanchard's killer?'

Steve frowned, his eyes focusing on the corner of the ceiling as he recalled the setting for the murder. When he spoke, his voice was slow, considering. 'We found the body in a sort of hollow. There was a line of rhododendrons between Susan and the path. Then the clearing where she was found. Beyond that, the ground rose slightly to another line of shrubs. I suppose someone hidden in those bushes could have escaped observation by a killer who was intent on what he was doing. SOCO will have done a fingertip search of the whole area, though, and I don't recall anything in the forensics to indicate the presence of a third person.'

'You think Blake saw it?' Kit broke in, unable to keep quiet.

'You're doing a Horsforth,' Steve said. 'Theorizing without the data. It could just as easily have been someone else altogether who told Blake about it. Let's hear what Fiona's got to say.'

Kit cast his eyes upwards. 'I forgot. We have to have the whole lecture. No skipping to the back page to see whodunnit.' He shook his head in tolerant amusement.

'Why change the habit of a lifetime?' Fiona said sweetly. 'OK, here's what I think. Right from the start, we know we're looking for a confident criminal. We know this because Hampstead Heath is a public place, and the risk of alerting passers-by to such a violent crime in broad daylight is high. Also, the way the body is displayed indicates a man who is, at least in criminal terms, a mature offender. Blake's record, on the other hand, is trivial and shows little sign of escalation towards this sort of crime. That was the first thing that made me a little uneasy about him as prime suspect.'

'Hang on a minute, though,' Kit objected. 'You can't say that just because he doesn't have a criminal record he'd not done the sort of crimes that lead to sexual murder. It might be that he's either been clever enough or lucky enough to get away with it.'

'That's true,' Fiona acknowledged. 'And so I wouldn't write Blake off on those grounds alone. Nor would I dismiss him on the basis that the pornography the police found in his flat, although sadomasochistic in content, contained no photographs or descriptions that fit the way the body was displayed. But again, that detail gives me pause for thought, because the killer had to form that image somehow. If it didn't come from his pornography, it came from some incident in his past, around the time he was forming his sexual identity. And none of Steve's researches came up with anything comparable in Blake's history. So as far as I'm concerned, that's another question mark over Blake.'

Steve was leaning forward now, elbows on the table, an intent frown on his face. So far, Fiona had said nothing he didn't already believe himself. But he always found her cogent way of stringing things together clarified things, sometimes rearranging details so they formed a different picture. He sensed where she was heading, and he wondered if Kit had been right about what was coming.

'Another thing I would expect from this killer is that he'd have poor heterosocial skills,' Fiona continued. 'But again, that doesn't fit Blake. He had a girlfriend, but as well as that he was comfortable with contacting strange women through personal ads. We know from some of the women who have come forward that he managed to have sex with them, even if most of them found him too domineering a partner to want to continue the relationship. So here we have a man who is good at making social and sexual connections with women.'

'Better than me,' Steve pointed out. 'You're right, though. That was one of the main reasons I never liked Blake for this job. He wasn't some frustrated virgin or someone whose head was wired for beating women up as the best means of achieving sexual satisfaction.'

'I knew all that before I read the entrapment transcripts,' Fiona continued. 'As I'm sure you did too, Steve. However, it became clear from reading what passed between Blake and

Erin Richards that he knew more about Susan Blanchard's murder than he could have gleaned from the press reports. He knew, for example, that her hands were arranged as if in prayer, the fingers linked rather than having the fingertips propped against each other. Blake always maintained after his arrest that he'd heard that in the pub, but he couldn't identify the person he claimed had told him. I'll come back to that later, though.'

Kit nodded. In spite of himself, he was as fascinated by Fiona's dissection as Steve. He was sure he'd guessed where she was heading, but that didn't mean he wasn't interested in seeing how she justified reaching that conclusion. Even after all this time, he was still intrigued by the way her mind worked, so analytical in contrast to his own intuitive approach. 'Consider our breath well and truly bated,' he said.

Refusing to be thrown off her stride, Fiona ignored him and carried on. 'What I want to deal with next is the fantasies that Blake outlined in his letters and conversations with DC Richards. Based on my experience, I would expect the killer to have very specific fantasies. I would expect the object of his fantasies to be a teenage girl or a woman in her early twenties, as Susan Blanchard was. They're easier to manipulate, both in fantasy and reality. In the scenarios he plays out in his head, this killer will objectify women. He'll fantasize about control, submission, violent activity that causes the object of his attention to show extreme fear. He'll imagine threatening her with a knife, tying her up, causing her pain, cutting her, making her beg for mercy.' Fiona paused and took a long draught of her wine. 'And because he killed her out of doors, I'd expect the setting for those imaginary sexual encounters to be in a park or in woodland.

'But that's not what we find in Blake's fantasies at all.

143

Almost everything he outlined to DC Richards involves voyeurism. He talks and writes about a third person watching their sex games, being turned on by them, often joining in. Admittedly, there are some strong elements of submission and domination in there too, but they're much more in the realm of playfulness rather than the real infliction of pain. But the clincher for me is that in all of the scenarios he outlines for this woman he's aiming to bed, this woman he's been taking on walks through the parks of London – in each and every scene he describes, where they are going to have sex is indoors. At the undertaker's where he works, at the office where she works, in a deserted warehouse, in his flat. Not a single one of these elaborately detailed, pornographically described situations is out of doors.

'And finally, there's the question of the pornography that your officers found in Blake's flat. It's true there was a lot of it, both magazines and videos. And it's true that most of it was what would be classified as hardcore, mostly involving young women or teenage girls. But if the catalogue in the file is accurate, surprisingly little of it focuses on rape or S&M. What there was a lot of was threesomes and voyeurism. Plus a bit of bondage.'

'You're saying Blake doesn't match the crime,' Steve said flatly.

'Based on the product of your operation, I think any qualified psychologist with an open mind would come to that conclusion,' Fiona agreed.

'There's more, though, isn't there?' Kit chipped in. 'You think you know what really happened, don't you, Fiona?'

Steve paused halfway through spreading pâté on a piece of bread. 'You do?'

Fiona fiddled with her napkin. 'That's not what I'm saying, Kit. I don't know who did kill Susan Blanchard. But I'd stake my reputation that Francis Blake didn't.' She took a deep breath. 'However, I believe he saw the man who did. Blake's a voyeur. That's why he looks at parks the way he does. He likes to watch. I think this is what happened that morning on Hampstead Heath. He was lurking in the shrubbery hoping he'd see a couple making love. What he actually saw was very different. Francis Blake stood and watched while somebody else raped and murdered Susan Blanchard. And it was the most exciting thing he'd ever seen in his life.'

Chapter 16

The silence that followed Fiona's conclusion had the quality of empty air after the shock wave of a bomb blast. Even though Kit had guessed where she was heading right at the start of her exposition, the certainty of her judgement chilled him into stillness. Steve closed his eyes and dropped his head on to one hand, massaging the bridge of his nose between thumb and forefinger. 'That's a bit of a leap, Fi,' he said softly.

'It makes sense of all the information in a way nothing else does,' she said, reaching for the bottle and refilling her glass, as if girding her loins for a challenge to her reasoning.

Steve raised his head and met her eyes. He wanted to believe her, not least because it might give him fresh avenues to explore. But he was aware that his own feelings for her had always made him willing to give her the benefit of any doubt. He'd stuck his neck out to defend her reports to his bosses, and it had paid off in the past. This time, though, his very future hung on what he did with the Susan Blanchard case. If he screwed it up even more than it already had been his career was effectively over. No one would criticize him if he let the case slide into the unsolved regions; the public assumption would remain that they'd got the right man but had wrecked the case against him. But if he took a chance and pursued the possibilities thrown up by Fiona's theorizing, he'd better be damn sure he got it right. He cleared his throat. 'Or maybe Blake is entirely innocent,' he said.

Fiona shook her head. 'Too many coincidences.' She ticked off the points on her fingers. 'We know he was on the Heath that day. We know he fantasizes about being a voyeur. And we know he knew things about the murder victim that were never in the public domain. It's stretching credibility too far to suggest that the one man who happened to be on the Heath that morning was also the one man who happened to be told in a pub by an unidentifiable stranger precisely how Susan's body was arranged. All the reasons why Blake was a suspect in the first place have another interpretation, and only one interpretation – that he saw what happened.'

'If you're right – and it sounds reasonable to me – the irony is that Francis Blake could genuinely have helped the police with their inquiries,' Kit said. 'He knows more about this killer than anyone.'

'If you'd treated him as a witness instead of a prime suspect the very first time you interviewed him, the day after the murder, it's possible that things might have turned out very differently. But . . .' Fiona shrugged. 'Probably not.'

Steve sighed. 'One way or another, we blew it. I have to say, Fi, I think you might be right. I'm not totally convinced, but I'm going to have to take it into account.'

Fiona gave him a long, considering stare. She was used to Steve grasping her ideas more firmly than this. His very caution made her realize how much pressure he was under in this case. She hadn't wanted to become involved, but now she was glad she had done what little she could to help. 'I hope it's useful,' she said, with more humility than she usually felt when she had offered her professional opinion.

'What I don't understand,' Kit said, 'is why Blake didn't come out with the truth when he was interrogated after you finally arrested him. I mean, it's the obvious get-out for him, isn't it? "It wasn't me, guv, but I saw the bloke who did it."'

'Not if you were supremely confident that the court would throw out the case against you. Not if you knew there could be no forensic evidence tying you to a crime you didn't commit,' Fiona said. 'He had a solicitor with him, didn't he, Steve?'

'Right from the off. The first interview he did after the arrest was a "no comment". Then when we laid out the evidence, his brief asked for an adjournment. When they came back, all Blake would say was that he'd been on the Heath that morning, he'd lost track of time and realized he was going to be late for work, and that's why he was running when the witnesses saw him. As for what he wrote and said during the undercover operation, he was adamant that it was total fantasy, nothing more.'

'So when they had their little chat, the brief will have told him you'd never make it stand up in court,' Kit said, understanding dawning. 'And that little shit sat there smug as a bug knowing that he knew more than you would ever know about what happened to Susan Blanchard, and that you'd never find out what that was. What a total scumbag.'

Fiona nodded. 'He probably thought the whole thing would be thrown out in the magistrates' court. Instead of which, he ended up spending eight months on remand. And by that stage, he had no way out. He couldn't recant at that point and admit what he'd seen, because you would have been so furious that he'd jerked you around, you'd have charged him with being an accessory. He must have so much festering rage inside him for the police now.'

Kit leaned back in his chair. 'Not a bit of it. Didn't you see him on the TV? He's revelling in it. He's been having the time of his life. Not only does he have these powerful memories to relive any time he wants to. He also has the supreme satisfaction of knowing he's left the police and the CPS looking like idiots.'

'More than that, he's going to be paid for it,' Steve growled. 'Massive compensation from the Home Office for wrongful imprisonment, not to mention what he's screwed out of the newspapers.' He let out a deep breath. 'Sometimes this job would make you fucking weep.' In the soft lighting of the dining room, the planes of his face seemed even starker than usual following the bitter confirmation Fiona had brought him.

There was a long pause. Suddenly no one felt much like eating. Kit reached for the bottle and topped up everyone's glass. 'So where can you go from here?' he asked Steve.

'Back to square one? Since it wasn't Francis Blake, someone else was on the Heath that morning killing Susan Blanchard. We'll have to go back and look at every single witness statement and reinterview them all.'

Kit gave a snort of laughter. 'Yeah, right. It's not like Blake's going to be coming across with what he saw.'

'There is one thing you might like to consider,' Fiona said slowly.

Steve looked up, his eyes alert. 'And that is?'

'It's possible that Blake has managed to identify the killer. He may have recognized him, he may subsequently have seen him. He may even have seen the killer make his getaway in a car and managed to get the number. I'd say that given his moment of triumph, it's conceivable that Blake has become confident enough to try blackmailing the real murderer. I don't know if you've got the resources for this, since the investigation is officially dead, but when he comes back from his jolly to Spain, I'd watch him very carefully. Tap his phone, open his mail, carry out very discreet surveillance, monitor his bank account. It's a slim chance, but Blake might just lead you straight to your man.'

Steve shook his head dubiously. 'It's reaching a bit, Fi. Besides, I'll never get a warrant for a phone tap on the basis of this. The best I can manage is probably a loose surveillance.'

'It's better than nothing. What else have you got?' Kit demanded. 'Sure, you can go back and talk to all your witnesses again, like you suggested. But how much more are you realistically going to get out of them now so much time has passed? Plus, anything they have to say is going to be tainted by the media blitz surrounding the arrest and the trial. They're going to lean even heavier on the idea that Blake's your man. It's only human. Seems to me a slim chance is better than no chance at all. You want to redeem yourselves on Susan Blanchard's murder, I'd say you've got no choice.'

'I've also got no budget,' Steve said bitterly. 'I'm supposed to be pursuing a discreet, deniable investigation here, which means I've got hardly any bodies to speak of and even fewer resources. There's no way I can mount the sort of operation you're suggesting, even if I thought I could justify it.'

'Maybe it's time to call in your markers,' Kit said. 'There's got to be some of your team that owe you big time. Or feel like they owe Susan Blanchard and her family. Not to mention all those coppers that are smarting at what the judge had to say. I bet a few of them wouldn't mind giving you the odd bit of unofficial unpaid overtime. Fuck it, if all you need is somebody to sit outside his house in a car, I'm up for it.' He grinned. 'Never say die, Stevie.'

Steve shook his head. 'You put me to shame, you two. Fiona spends hours analysing Horsforth's shitty operation, and you offer to doorstep the number one scumbag in the capital. And all I can do is sit and whinge about how hard it's all going to be.' He straightened his shoulders unconsciously. 'Thanks, both of you. At least now I've got a new line of inquiry to get people energized.'

Kit raised his glass. 'To a result,' he said.

Steve gave a wry smile. 'To the right result.'

It was after midnight when they got home. Kit announced he was too wired to sleep and too mellowed on Steve's wine to write so he was going on line to see if any of his international playmates were around on one of the several multi-user computer games he treated as a way of winding down. 'Seven o'clock on the East Coast,' he mumbled as he wandered through to his office. 'Should be somebody out there ready to be killed.'

Fiona climbed the stairs to her attic. She'd drop off her papers in her office, then head for bed and a blissful seven hours of sleep. The winking red eye of the answering machine gave her a moment's pause as she turned to leave. Ignore it or hear it out? Duty won over desire, not least because there was obviously only one message.

It was Salvador Berrocal, his confident tones deadened by the soundproofing. 'I thought you'd like to know that we have identified a suspect in the two Toledo murders,' he said. 'I am sending you the details via e-mail, but I wanted to let you know as soon as possible that we have made progress.'

'Yes!' Fiona clenched her right hand and punched the palm of her left. Now she was as restlessly awake as Kit. Two swift strides took her to the computer where she accessed her e-mail. There were half a dozen messages, but only one that interested her. She downloaded it and opened it immediately.

From: Salvador Berrocal <Sberroc@cnp.mad.es>
To: Dr Fiona Cameron
          <fcameron@psych.ulon.ac.uk>
Subject: Toledo consultation

Dear Dr Cameron,
Finally we have managed to procure the details
that we needed to make progress.
And so we now have developed what we believe
will be a viable suspect. His name is Miguel José
Delgado. He is a bachelor and is twenty-nine years
old. Until two months ago, he was the owner of a
small general store. The shop sold mostly groceries
to local people. The business was failing, which
Delgado believed was a result of the city-centre
residents being forced out into the suburbs.
He lived in a small apartment behind the shop.
The owners of the building wanted to sell it to an
American hotel chain. The resistance was led by
Delgado. According to locals, he spoke with great
violence against the proposed development. He
claimed that tourists were a cancer eating away
the real life of Toledo. Interestingly, one witness
said he was saying often that he wasn't going
to 'bend down to be fucked in the ass' by the
Americans.
So, two months ago, the landlord found out that
Delgado was going away overnight. When Delgado
came back, his shop was boarded up and he could
not gain access to his apartment. The landlord
had moved all his possessions and the stock of
the shop into a new apartment about three miles
south of the city. They gave Delgado the keys to

his new apartment and 'a large sum in cash' and told him he could no longer run his business from their building. Delgado was not much liked by his neighbours or his customers and that probably has more to do with why his business was doing badly. They describe him as 'sometimes surly and unwilling to be helpful', although some say he could be charming enough if he wanted to, especially if he got on to his pet subject, which was the history of Toledo. He lived alone and had no girlfriend that we can discover. So, you will see that he is a close fit on the profile but also that he is appropriate to the geographical profile as well as the psychological one.

We have only one problem. We are unable to discover where Delgado is living. He has never been seen near his new apartment. In fact, two weeks after he was to move in, the neighbours called the landlord about the smell. When the landlord's men let themselves in, they found that all the perishable goods from the shop had gone bad.

The one good thing is that in spite of our failure to track him down, the killer has not yet attacked another victim.

Once again, I must thank you for your help. Without it, we would still have no idea who we are looking for. I will keep you informed of the progress of our search.

With best wishes

Salvador Berrocal

Fiona reached the end of the message and smiled. At least

one police officer looked like he was headed for the right result. She'd been nervous that the next time she'd hear from Berrocal would be when he reported that another foreigner had been killed. But for some reason, Delgado – if he was indeed the killer – had temporarily stopped.

Either that or they just hadn't found the body yet.

Whatever, there was nothing she could do about it. Fiona switched off her computer and headed downstairs. As she turned the last corner in the stairs, she saw Kit standing in the doorway of his office, a sheet of paper in his hand and a worried look on his face.

'What's the matter?' she asked.

He looked up, his eyes wide and troubled. When he spoke, his voice was uncharacteristically high in pitch. 'I've got a death threat.'

Chapter 17

Kit held the sheet of paper out to Fiona. Gingerly, she took it by the top left-hand corner. It was a single sheet of A4 paper, folded twice to fit a standard business envelope. There was nothing to distinguish it from any other computer-generated document. Standard font, nothing complicated about the layout. All of this Fiona took in first, bracing herself before she read the words.

'Kit Martin, you are a thief of other people's creative endeavour and a traducer of other people's reputations. You steal what you cannot yourself make. And your lies deprive others of what is rightfully theirs.

'Your work is a feeble reflection of other people's light. You have striven to ensure that competition is driven from the field. You take, you destroy, you are a vampire who sucks the blood of those whose gifts you envy. You know this to be true. Search your pathetic grimy soul and you will not be able to deny what you have deprived me of.

'The time has come for you to pay. You deserve nothing from me but my contempt and my hatred. If killing you is what it takes to grant what is rightfully mine, then so be it.

'The hour and the day will be of my choosing. I trust you will not sleep easy; you do not deserve so to do.

I will enjoy your funeral. From your ashes, I will rise like a phoenix.'

Fiona read the poisonous letter twice. Then she carefully put it down on the hall table and stepped forward to hug Kit. 'Poor you. What a horrible thing.' She could feel his tension as he buried his face in her shoulder.

'I can't get my head round it,' he said, his voice muffled. 'It makes no sense.'

Fiona said nothing. She just held on tight to him until she felt his body start to relax against her. 'Where did it come from?' she asked eventually.

'It was in the post. I was busy when the second delivery came; I didn't bother picking it off the mat till I was going out. I stuck it in the office. I wasn't expecting anything urgent.'

'Have you got the envelope?'

He nodded. 'It's in the bin, I just chucked it automatically.' He went into his office. Fiona followed him into the chaos of books and papers that covered all of the available surfaces and half of the floor. Not for the first time, she marvelled that anyone could work in such a clutter. But Kit not only worked here, he also seemed to have total recall when it came to the site of any particular book, file or letter. He went straight to the wastepaper bin by the desk and fished out a plain-white self-sealing envelope. He studied it with a frown. Fiona put an arm round his waist and looked at it with him. The address had been printed in the same anonymous typeface.

'West London postmark. Posted two days ago with a second-class stamp,' he said. He gave a snort of nervous laughter. 'Well, it's obviously not an urgent death threat. I suppose that should be some sort of consolation.'

'You should report this to the police,' Fiona said decisively.

Kit dropped the envelope on top of his keyboard. 'You think so?' He sounded sceptical.

'I do, yes. It's a really nasty letter. It's a death threat, for God's sake!'

Kit dropped into his chair, swinging round to face her. 'I get nasty letters all the time, love. Not death threats, admittedly, but in among the fan mail, I regularly get letters slagging off me and my books. Disgusted of Tunbridge Wells is horrified by the torture scenes in *The Dissection Man*. Ms Censor of Lambeth is appalled that teenagers have access to the depraved sexual fantasies in *The Blade King*. And then there are the ones who accuse me of being gutless for not writing about grotesque mutilation and sexual perversion in more detail. It's not all fan mail, you know.'

'How do they get your address?' Fiona demanded, suddenly struck with an uncomfortable vision of mentally unstable readers beating a path to her front door.

Kit shrugged. 'I don't know. Mostly, they come via my publisher. Some on e-mail. One or two of the more obsessive types have probably trawled the voters' roll for Dartmouth Park. I'm not that hard to find, love.'

Fiona shivered. 'That letter was bad enough. But now you're really scaring me. Honestly, Kit, I think you should take this to the police.'

He picked up a pencil and fiddled with it restlessly. 'They'd laugh at me, Fiona. It's just a crank letter. There's nothing specific in it. All it says is that I nick other people's ideas. Which is bullshit. It's just some nutter with a bee in his bonnet.'

Fiona looked unconvinced. 'I don't think you should be taking this so lightly, Kit. I really don't.' She turned away and crossed to the window, where, as usual, the blind was raised. Impatiently, she tugged the cord to shut them off from the outside world. Anything to avoid saying what was uppermost in her mind.

'It's not that *I'm* taking it lightly. It's the police that would think I was wasting their time. Anyway, why should I react to this, any more than the rest of the offensive mail I've had in the past? I've been getting letters from nutters ever since I was first published. It's no big deal. Honestly. It was a shock, that's all. You don't often get them so vitriolic. But nothing's ever come of a letter before, so I don't see why this should be any different.' He was, he knew, protesting too much. But he didn't want to be scared. He wanted this letter to be in the same class as every other piece of hate mail that had ever dropped on the doormat. Any other response opened a door he wanted to keep firmly closed.

But Fiona was determined to articulate what was in both their minds, however unpalatable it might be. 'After what happened to Drew, I don't think you can afford to ignore this,' she said quietly.

'I knew you were going to say that,' Kit said irritably. 'I knew I should never have let you see it. Christ, Fiona, you always have to analyse things, to connect them. Well, sometimes things just don't connect. They are separate. They just are. OK?'

'No, it's not OK.' Fiona raised her voice, her cheeks flushing. 'Why are you so resistant to this? Two weeks ago, one of your colleagues was murdered in a horrible, ritualistic way. Now you get a death threat, and you don't think the two might be connected? Reality check, Kit!'

He slammed the pencil down on the desk. 'The only connection between this letter and what happened to Drew is that some fuckwit thinks it would be clever to take advantage of his murder to put the shits up me. You read the letter, Fiona. That wasn't written by the person who killed Drew.

There's no specifics in it, no boasting, none of that, "You'll get what's coming to you, like Drew Shand did."'

'That doesn't prove a thing,' Fiona stormed. 'That letter was written by somebody who is off the scale of normal. So was Drew's killer.'

Kit got to his feet and hit the wall with the side of his fist. 'So were Fred and Rosemary West, but I'm pretty sure it wasn't them that wrote this. Look, Fiona. If I go to the police with something as flaky as this, you know what they're going to say.'

She folded her arms tight across her chest. 'Enlighten me.'

'They're going to say I'm doing a Georgia. They'll write it off as bandwagon-jumping. Publicity-seeking. They're not going to take it seriously. What can they do anyway? Send it off to the labs on the off-chance that my correspondent has conveniently left fingerprints and DNA all over it? I don't think so.'

Fiona couldn't resist the truth in what he said. She knew he was probably right. But that knowledge did nothing to assuage the chilly lump of apprehension in her stomach. That someone hated Kit – or his work – enough to pour out such venom on the page was unnerving. To fear that poison might escalate into real violence was, in her opinion, an entirely reasonable reaction.

She pushed past him and into the hall. In the doorway, she turned. 'It's your decision. It's your letter. But I think you're wrong.'

'So what's new?' He turned his back on her. 'I'll live with it.'

Extract from **Decoding of Exhibit P13/4599**

Tqsaf mxafa ruzwp dqiet mzp. Mxxah qdftq bmbqd etqim e. Ngfft qkpup zfsqf uf. Qhqdk napkt mpftq udaiz ftqad kmzpz afazq arftq yomyq oxaeq.

He got a lot of ink, Drew Shand. But they didn't get it. Everybody had their own theory and not one of them came close. They soon will, though. Me, I've been keeping my head down, being a good little boy, not attracting any attention. Not that anybody is paying any attention.

Which means I had no interference with the next stage of my plan. Jane Elias. She's American, but lives in Ireland; probably because writers don't pay any tax there. The bitch wasn't satisfied with earning more money than God, she wanted to keep it all.

It wasn't hard to find where she was living. You can

maybe get away with being a recluse somewhere the size of America, but not in Ireland. I knew she had a big estate in County Wicklow, on the shores of a lake. I knew it was about an hour's drive from Dublin. One of the fan sites on the web had a picture of the house. So I just drove around for a day with a large-scale map and a pair of binoculars till I found it.

The next morning, I went back down to Elias's estate. I cut down to the shoreline of the lake when I saw what I was looking for - a sailing club with lots of little dinghies pulled up on the concrete ramp. There was nobody about. It couldn't have been better. I hunkered down among the boats and checked out Elias's property on the other side of the water. I could just make out a landing stage with a couple of boats tied up alongside. If my information was right, she would come down to the lake sometime in the afternoon and go sailing.

Sure enough she appeared just after two. She got on one of the boats and went sailing off across the lake. I waited till it got dark and she'd gone back, then I dragged one of the dinghies down to the water's edge and climbed aboard. I'd sussed a hiding place earlier, further up the lake where the trees came right down to the water's edge.

I was feeling really edgy again with the prospect of what I was going to have to do the next day. There were so many mistakes I could make that would blow it. And then I had to do the killing again. I decided I wasn't going to stick to the book as closely this time. There was no way I was going to torture somebody for hours. I knew I didn't have the stomach for it. And besides, I didn't have the time or the place for something so elaborate.

What I would do, I decided, was to kill her quickly with a knife. Then I could do the things to her body that would make it look like the body in the book. It's the appearance that's important. I'm not some fetishistic killer who has to obsess about all the details. What I'm doing is sending a message, not satisfying some weird urge inside myself. If there was another way of showing those bastards that they can't get away with discounting me and my life, I'd have chosen it.

I'm trying not to think about what I'll have to do to her. My stomach's queasy enough without making it worse. I just have to keep telling myself it won't take long, and then I'll be on the road home.

They'll have to pay attention this time.

163

Chapter 18

The early morning light was pearl-grey, a thin curtain of cloud hanging just above the tops of the Wicklow Hills across the steely waters of Lough Killargan. The spectacular autumn colours of the trees were beginning to emerge against the soft green of the hillsides, transforming the landscape from chill to warmth.

Jane Elias stood on the flagged patio and gave a long, low whistle. From a stand of green, ochre and brown sycamores a few hundred yards away, two streaks of black and tan emerged, their shapes resolving into a pair of lean Dobermans as they bounded across the grass towards her. Jane held her hands out to the dogs as they skidded to a halt at her feet and luxuriated in the sensuous warmth of their wet tongues on her skin.

'Enough,' she said after a few moments. The dogs, obedient to their morning ritual, lay at her feet while she went through a series of stretches to loosen up muscles still half-frozen from sleep. Then, as Jane moved off in a slow jog, the dogs scrambled to their feet and raced ahead of her. This was the best part of the day, she thought. No promises broken, no sentences written, no phone calls taken. Everything was still possible.

Gradually, she picked up speed, heading out towards the perimeter wall that ringed her property. Five and a half miles, the perfect length for a morning run. She could beat the bounds of her domain in absolute privacy, secure from prying eyes and free from fear.

She didn't count the guard monitoring the closed-circuit TV cameras as having prying eyes. After all, she was paying him to make sure she was safe. She didn't mind him watching her run. They occupied separate universes, he in his windowless office, his bulk crammed into khaki shirt and navy trousers, his walkie-talkie at his hip, his small life somewhere else; she in the fresh air of her personal fiefdom, her streaked blonde hair fastened in a headband, her lean muscled limbs enclosed in lightweight sweats, her feet pounding out a regular rhythm as she thought about the morning's work that lay ahead of her.

After the run, she let the dogs into the mud room where she fed them on chopped steak and vitamin-enriched dried biscuit. While they were still snuffling down their food, she was already on her way through the kitchen of the Georgian mansion, heading for the private bathroom that no one else was permitted to use, not even her lover Pierce Finnegan. Five precise minutes under the hot shower, then a blast of freezing water to close her pores, and Jane was on to the next stage of her daily routine. A brisk towelling, then an application of expensive aromatherapy body milk from chin to toe. Facial moisturizer, eye gel, dark-red lipstick.

Dressed in jeans and a silk and wool plaid shirt, she headed back to the kitchen for fresh fruit salad, a slice of wholewheat toast with organic peanut butter and a tall glass of tomato juice. Once, she'd been twenty-five pounds overweight. That was one of many things that was never going to happen again.

She was in her office by seven-thirty, the day's work arrayed on one of the two large desks that stood against the walls.

Today, the task was to correct the proofs of her forthcoming novel. For the next five hours, she focused on the printed pages, scanning each line for errors, making the occasional change to a sentence she now found clumsy, sometimes reaching for the dictionary to double-check a spelling that looked odd.

At half past noon precisely, Jane pushed her chair away from the desk and stretched her arms above her head. She returned through the silent house to the kitchen, switched on the radio tuned to a classical music station and took a portion of frozen vegetable soup out of the freezer. While it microwaved, she opened the morning's post, delivered by the security staff while she was at work. After the soup and a couple of slices of bread, she returned to her office, where she dictated replies to the day's letters.

She left the tape on the kitchen counter, where the security staff would collect it and deliver it to the woman in the nearby town who acted as her secretary. The letters would return on a disk that evening, ready for Jane to print out and sign. The two women met only rarely at social occasions in town, but it was an arrangement that worked well nevertheless.

Jane walked out into the mud room and picked up a fleece jacket, letting the dogs back out into the grounds. She walked down the path to the jetty, head up as she savoured the fresh afternoon air and tested the breeze. The cloud layer had lifted, leaving a blue sky smudged with occasional puffs of cumulus. She reckoned the wind was somewhere around force five, just right for a brisk sail in the 21-foot Beneteau First Classic, currently her favourite of the three boats she kept moored at her small private marina. It was perfect for single-handed sailing, unlike the bigger Moody that she preferred when she and Pierce went out on the lough together.

She checked the boat over, then cast off, allowing it to drift out from the jetty before she raised the mainsail. Leaving a single reef in it, she headed out towards the centre of the lough, planning her afternoon cruise in her head without bothering to consult her charts. She knew this part of the lake better than she knew her own face in the mirror. Three days out of four, she sailed more or less the same route, depending on the winds. It was, she had decided, best for views across the water to the hills as well as having no treacherous snags to trip her if she grew forgetful, her mind on her work rather than her helm.

Soon she had left the shore behind, moving across the water at a sharp forty-five-degree angle, the only sounds the hiss of the water against the hull and the crack of the wind in the sails. Jane gloried in the feel of the air against her skin, loving the sense of release that sailing the lake always brought her. Who cared if people thought she was weird, a slave to routines and patterns, a paranoid recluse? She knew different. There was nothing routine about what she did on the water every afternoon she could, pitting herself and her craft against the weather and the wildness of the lake. Out here, she was Queen of Freedom Hill. Fuck them. They could call her anal as much as they liked. All that proved was how little they knew of her. They knew nothing of her life at the tiller. Nor did they know about the fierce passion of her relationship with Pierce, kept secret by both of them for so long they had forgotten there was any other way to live.

He visited when he could, which, given the schedule of a member of the Garda Siochana's undercover drug squad, was not often. They had met when he'd attended an FBI course at Quantico. One of the instructors, an old college friend of Jane's, had invited them both to dinner and the spark had been instant. Within weeks, she had sold her estate in New England and bought the property in Ireland. It was only after she'd made the move that she discovered the unexpected bonus of the tax exemption the Irish state extended to writers. Now she was as settled here as she'd ever been anywhere.

And when Pierce was travelling undercover, she would sometimes take a room in the same hotel. Being a recluse had its advantages. No one recognized her the way they might with other bestselling authors who appeared on chat shows and full-colour jacket photographs. Producing ID for Margaret J. Elias, her given name, had never raised so much as an eyebrow with hotel clerks. In two days, proofs finished and sent off to New York, she'd be flying out to Morocco to meet him. She could hardly wait.

After a long tack, she went about and cut a course at right angles to her previous direction. It would bring her nicely round the headland and into the bay, where she'd lose some of the wind, allowing her plenty of leeway to alter her heading to take the boat back out towards the centre of the lake.

Coming into the bay, she noticed a dinghy tacking erratically back and forth across the line she planned to take. With a touch on the tiller, Jane adjusted her heading, hoping the dinghy sailor would respond accordingly. But suddenly, the small boat heeled over in a capsize, catapulting the man at the helm into the water. Within seconds, the wind had carried the dinghy in one direction, the current had swept the man in the other.

Calling down the wrath of the gods against fools who didn't know what they were doing on the water, Jane started her engine then hurried forward to lower the sail. Inside a minute, she was motoring slowly towards the bobbing orange lifejacket that was all she could see clearly of the idiot who obviously didn't know how to handle his boat.

Coming alongside him, she set the engine to idle and

dropped the swim ladder at the stern. The man swam clumsily round to the back of the boat and hauled himself out of the lake, icy water streaming from him. 'Thanks,' he gasped, unfastening his lifejacket and slipping one hand inside it.

'I guess you don't know these waters,' Jane snapped, turning away to put the engine back in gear.

She never saw the cosh as it arced through the air towards the base of her skull.

Chapter 19

From below, the two women on the sheer side of the hill looked like a pair of cursors moving diagonally across a muted green screen. They had climbed swiftly from the Wye Valley at Litton Mill through the trees that lined the old railway, then out on to the bare hillside where even sheep preferred not to scramble among the limestone outcroppings. They reached the highest point of the climb and Fiona, who was quicker on her feet over the familiar terrain, chose a boulder with enough of an edge to perch on while she waited for Caroline to pant her way up the last twenty yards. She looked down at her companion with an affectionate smile.

When Fiona's sister Lesley had been an undergraduate at St Andrews, she'd learned as much about herself as she had about her studies. One of the things she'd discovered was the direction of her heart. At the time of her murder, she'd been tight in the grip of first love. The revelation of its nature had been another aspect of her death that her parents had found difficult to cope with. For Fiona, though, it had come as no surprise that the person who was sharing her sister's bed was another woman. Lesley hadn't actually told her in so many words, but Fiona had understood the meaning of the way she spoke about her friend Caroline Matthews.

Because their relationship had been clandestine, Fiona was

also the only person with whom Caroline could properly grieve. It was no surprise that out of grief, the bond of friendship had been forged. Now, twelve years later, Fiona and Caroline met whenever Caroline was in London, and they communicated irregularly by phone and e-mail. And at least three times a year, they met to walk in the Peak District.

Caroline had remained in St Andrews and was now a lecturer in mathematics. She had moved on, as Fiona had. But for both of them, the loss of Lesley was an undercurrent that would forever inform the tenor of their emotional relationships. And the debt of guilt that both bore about Lesley meant they would never let each other down.

Caroline reached the crest, scarlet and panting. She collapsed on a boulder near Fiona, her breath ragged and shallow. 'Oh God,' she gasped. 'I am so out of condition. The summer was such a washout, we hardly got out on the hills at all.'

'Sounds like you've not been to the gym either,' Fiona commented.

Caroline pulled a face. 'Julia's started going to a step class in her lunch hour, so she's knocked the gym on the head. And we both have so many work commitments, she gets pissed off with me if I spend our two free evenings a week down the gym. I keep telling myself I'll get up early and go before work. But somehow, I never manage it.'

'You'd feel better if you fitted it in.' Fiona opened her rucksack and took out her water bottle.

'Fiona . . .' There was a warning in Caroline's voice.

Fiona laughed. 'I'm sorry, you're right. I'm not your mother. Shut up, Fiona.' She extended a hand and Caroline gave her a gentle smack on the wrist. It was an old routine, born of the early days of their common grief, when Fiona had fussed around Caroline as a substitute for the caring she could no longer offer her sister.

Fiona took a swig of her water, offering it to Caroline, who shook her head. 'If I start drinking in these temperatures, I'll want to pee within five minutes. And I can't see a single bit of shelter for the next half-mile.'

'As long as you don't get dehydrated.'

'Fiona!' This time it was a shout. 'You are *not* my mother. Behave.'

'Sorry. It's living with a man that does it. Especially one who spends half his time inhabiting a parallel universe.'

'Presumably one where somebody else always remembers to pick up the dry cleaning and puts food in front of him at regular hours?'

Fiona grinned. 'It's not that sort of thing Kit forgets. It's stuff like being so engrossed in his work that he suddenly looks at the clock and realizes he was supposed to pick me up ten minutes ago. Or missing his stop on the tube because he's busy having a conversation with himself and coming round to find he's in Kennington when he should be in Leicester Square.'

'How is he, anyway?'

Fiona got to her feet, stuffing her water bottle into her backpack and shouldering it. 'Bloody-minded as ever.'

Caroline, now breathing normally, stood up, giving Fiona a speculative look. Fiona wasn't given to bad-mouthing Kit. And besides, if she had to divide the bloody-mindedness in that relationship between them, she'd have to award Fiona the lion's share. As far as Caroline had observed, Kit was pretty laid back. In debate, he was quick and decisive, but never attacked the way Fiona could if she sensed weakness in the opposition that could be bulldozed aside. 'Sounds like he's rattled your cage,' she said cautiously as she fell into step behind Fiona on the narrow track that cut across the shoulder of the hill above the spectacular curve of Water-cum-Jolly Dale.

'You could say that.' Fiona clamped her mouth shut, her eyes on the ground in front of her.

'Do you want to talk about it?'

'I'm so cross with him,' Fiona said fiercely. 'We had a blazing row the other night. He got this death threat in the post, and he refuses point blank to take it to the police. He says it's just a routine crank letter, but I'm not so sure. It felt very unpleasant to me. And after what happened to Drew Shand . . .'

'But surely that was a one-off?' Caroline said. 'According to all the reports I've seen in the Scottish media, they reckon it was a pick-up for S&M sex that went wrong. There's been no suggestion that anybody outside the gay community could be at risk.'

Fiona scowled at the horizon. 'That's only one possibility. And we don't know if Drew Shand had any death threats, because all we know is what the police are telling us. I know it's a long shot to suggest that the killing might have more to do with Drew's writing than his life, but it's a possibility, and while it's a possibility, I think Kit should be taking this more seriously.'

'And that's what you had a fight about?'

'We've hardly spoken since.'

'Presumably Kit understands why you're so wound up about this?' Caroline said, taking advantage of the path splitting into two parallel tracks to catch up with Fiona.

'I think he's got the message that I'm concerned about him,' Fiona said frostily.

'But that's not really what it's about, is it?'

Fiona said nothing, simply ploughing on resolutely and making great play of looking down at the river as it widened into the still expanse of water created by the dam for the Georgian mill at Cressbrook.

'This isn't just about Kit, Fiona. It's about Lesley.'

Fiona stopped in her tracks. 'It's nothing to do with Lesley.' Her jaw was set in a stubborn line.

Caroline came to a halt a few feet ahead of her and turned to put a gloved hand on her arm. 'You don't have to pretend with me, Fiona. You can't bear the thought of losing him because you've already lost Lesley and you know what it feels like when someone you love is murdered. And that fear magnifies the slightest danger into something life-threatening, turning you into a one-woman nanny state.' Caroline paused. Fiona said nothing, so she pressed on. 'I understand the phenomenon, because I do it myself. It drives Julia crazy. If she's in town without the car, I always pick her up. She says it makes her feel like a teenager whose mother doesn't trust her not to be snogging the local ruffian behind the bike shed.'

Caroline gave a weak laugh. 'One time, early on in our relationship, she insisted that I not pick her up after a parents' evening. So I hung around outside the school and waited till she came out. I followed her home. And I nearly gave her a heart attack because when she was cutting through one of the alleys in the town centre, she heard footsteps behind her and thought she was going to be mugged. That was when she realized that my insistence on picking her up was more about my fears than about her capabilities. So now she goes along with me, in spite of how it irritates her deep down. Fiona, you need to tell Kit why you've let this threatening letter take on such huge proportions. If he says it's nothing, he's probably right. He knows what his post is like. But he needs to know that you're not just fussing. That there's a valid reason for the way you're behaving.'

Fiona glared at the limestone cliffs on the other side of the dale. 'I thought I was the psychologist around here.' Her voice shook slightly.

'Yeah, well, psychologist, analyse yourself.'

Fiona studied the scuffed toes of her walking boots. 'You're probably right. I should explain myself better.' She met Caroline's steady gaze. 'I couldn't live with myself if anything happened to him.' Her eyes sparkled with unshed tears.

Caroline pulled Fiona into a tight hug. 'I know.'

Fiona drew back and managed a frail smile. 'I'll talk to him when I get home. Promise. Now, are we going to stand here till we get hypothermia, or are we going to the Monsal Head pub?'

Caroline pretended to consider. 'I think, on balance, I'm going to go for the pub.'

'Race you to the dam,' Fiona said, setting off across the hillside at a killer pace.

'You win,' Caroline muttered, following at a more reasonable speed. Twelve years on, and still Lesley's death was the defining event in both their lives. No matter how much they tried to put it behind them, it was there, ready to ambush them, she thought. Sometimes she wondered if they would ever be free of its embracing shadow. Or even if they actually wanted to be.

Fiona marched up Dartmouth Park Hill from the tube station, determined to set things straight with Kit. Caroline was right; she just hadn't allowed herself to accept what was driving her determination that he take the letter seriously. Head down, she scuffed through fallen leaves, easily outpacing the late commuters coming home from the office. She reached the left turn into their street in record time, gathering speed as she headed downhill. She was eager now, more than ready to apologize and explain.

So her heart sank when she opened the door and heard Kit call, 'We're upstairs.' Whoever the other component of 'we' was, she wasn't in the mood for their company.

'Just taking my boots off,' she shouted. Backpack on the floor, jacket tossed over the newel post, Fiona undid her laces and stepped free. She wiggled her toes at the pleasure of release. Comfortable as her well-worn boots were, they still caged her feet. She stopped in the kitchen to pick up a glass, reckoning that if Kit had company, the wine would already be open, then she made her way up to the first-floor living room.

The lamps were on, casting scattered pools of warm light through the wide room. Kit was in his favourite armchair, glass in hand. That would have been perfect if he'd been alone. But his companion was the last person Fiona felt like seeing.

Curled up on the sofa, her strappy sandals kicked off on the rug below her, was Georgia Lester. A legend in her own lifetime, Georgia had published over thirty novels in a twenty-five-year career that had seen her rise to challenge P. D. James and Ruth Rendell to the title of Queen of Crime. She'd been one of the first crime writers to have her work successfully adapted for TV, and that had guaranteed her a slot in the bestseller lists ever since. She was a darling of the media, shamelessly exploiting every possible opportunity to appear in print, on the radio or on TV. Men fell for her flirtatious flattery and her undeniable generosity; most women, including Fiona, cheerfully loathed her. 'She's the Barbara Cartland of crime fiction,' Fiona had once remarked to Mary Helen Margolyes, who had choked on her drink and then promptly passed the remark around the bush telegraph. Without attribution, of course.

The soft illumination flattered Georgia, softening the tautness of cosmetically tightened skin, minimizing the elaborate make-up that Georgia skilfully employed to keep the years further at bay. In this light, she could pass for early forties, which Fiona regarded as nothing short of miraculous for a woman who couldn't be a day under fifty-seven. 'Fiona, darling,' Georgia purred, tilting her head upwards in a gesture that demanded an air kiss.

Fiona obliged, conscious of her wind-burnt skin, her unbrushed hair, and that her fleece probably smelled of sweat. Georgia, naturally, was fragrant with Chanel N°5 and dressed immaculately in a flowing midnight-blue garment that clung only to the strategic points of breasts and hips. Her hair, an improbable but convincing ash-blonde, appeared to have come straight from the salon. 'I wasn't expecting to see you, Georgia,' Fiona said as she turned away and helped herself to a glass of wine. She crossed to Kit and kissed his cheek. 'Hello, love,' she said, hoping the action would combine with her tone of voice to indicate that she was offering a truce.

He caught her round the waist with his free arm and hugged her, relieved that a day in the hills with Caroline seemed to have broken down her hostility. It unsettled Kit when things were scratchy between them, but he'd realized early on that he would either have to get used to that or learn to apologize even when he didn't believe he was in the wrong. Now, he mostly gave in, for the sake of a quiet life. But sometimes, he dug his heels in, tolerating the edgy atmosphere for as long as it took for Fiona to acknowledge she might possibly have been less than right. 'Did you have a good day, then?' he asked.

'We were lucky with the weather,' Fiona said, perching on the arm of his chair. 'We did about ten miles; great views.'

Georgia shuddered. 'Ten miles? I don't know how you do it, Fiona, I really don't. Wouldn't you rather be tucked up somewhere warm and cosy with this delicious man?'

'The two are not mutually exclusive, Georgia,' Fiona said. 'I enjoy the exercise.'

Georgia's smile was the equivalent of a teacher patting a small child on the head. 'I've always preferred to take my exercise indoors,' she said.

Fiona refused to rise. 'So, how are you, Georgia? I hear you're feeling a bit nervous about your safety.'

Georgia immediately switched on an expression of tragedy. 'Poor, poor Drew. Such a terrible fate, and such a dreadful loss to us all.'

'I didn't realize you knew Drew,' Fiona said, trying not to sound as bitchy as she felt.

'I meant his work, Fiona, dear. To see such talent snuffed out so young is indescribably tragic.'

Fiona resisted the impulse to gag. 'But surely, Drew's death is no reason for you to feel under threat?' she asked.

'That's why Georgia's here,' Kit interrupted. He didn't want the sparring between the two women to drive Fiona from the room. It had happened before; rather than allow it to develop into all-out hostility that might damage the unlikely friendship between Kit and Georgia, Fiona would invariably remove herself from the fray. Tonight, however, he wanted her to stay.

'Absolutely, my dear. When Kit told me about the terrible letter he'd had, I knew at once I had to come. He was taking it so lightly, you see. And when he told me your reaction, I knew I had an ally in you, my dear.' She gave Fiona the benefit of the full radiance of her cosmetically enhanced smile.

179

'Georgia's had a letter like mine,' Kit said. 'Show it to Fiona – it must be from the same person.'

Georgia picked up a folded piece of paper from the occasional table by the sofa. She held it out, forcing Fiona to get up and collect it from her. Fiona crossed to the other armchair before she opened it and studied it. The paper and the typeface looked the same as Kit's letter. And the style was similar. As far as she could recall, whole sentences were identical.

'Georgia Lester,' she read, 'you call yourself a Queen of Crime, but all you are monarch of is plagiarism and protectionism. Your fame is based on what you have stolen from others. You give no credit where it is due and your lies deprive others of what is rightfully theirs.

'Your work is a feeble reflection of other people's light. You would be nothing without the ideas of others to feed on. You have striven to ensure that competition is driven from the field. When you could have offered help, you have trampled the faces of those who are greater than you will ever be. You are a vampire who sucks the blood of those whose gifts you envy. You know this to be true. Search your sluttish soul and you will not be able to deny what you have deprived me of.

'The time has come for you to pay. You deserve nothing from me but my contempt and my hatred. If killing you is what it takes to grant what is rightfully mine, then so be it.

'The hour and the day will be of my choosing. I trust you will not sleep easy; you do not deserve so to do. I will enjoy your funeral. From your ashes, I will rise like a phoenix.'

Fiona carefully folded the letter closed. She had no doubt it had come from the same source as the one that had so disturbed her a couple of nights before. 'When did you get this, Georgia?'

Georgia waved one hand negligently. 'A fortnight ago? I can't be sure. I came back from Dorset last Tuesday and it was among the mail waiting for me.'

'Did you do anything about it?'

Georgia stroked the hair over her right temple. 'To be honest, I thought it must be one of those crank letters Kit tells me he gets regularly. It's not something I've ever had much experience of – the letters I get are invariably from admirers. My work is so much less provocative than Kit's, you see. But when Kit told me he'd had so similar a letter, I felt sure we shouldn't ignore them. In the light of Drew's murder, I mean.'

'Georgia thinks we should take them to the police,' Kit said. 'Like you.'

Fiona looked at him in dismay. She was caught on the horns of a dilemma of her own making. While she found the letters profoundly disturbing, she was also loath to take any course of action that would link Kit with Georgia in the eyes of both police and public. If they took these letters to the police, then within twenty-four hours, a media circus would descend upon them. Whatever Georgia might promise here and now, Fiona knew the lure of publicity would be far too strong for her to resist. It would be a nightmare.

Not only would the invasion of her and Kit's privacy be hideous. But if he didn't have a stalker before, he soon would have. Photographs of their house would appear in the tabloids, an easily identifiable target for any of the seriously strange who found something in his books that tapped into their own mental frailties. She knew she wasn't being paranoid; they knew at least one crime writer whose life had been rendered so intolerable by a stalker that the family had been forced to move house and to change their children's schools.

But she was the one who had pushed so hard for action when Kit had received his death threat. If she was going to change her tune now, she'd better have a good reason lined up. 'I agree you should take them seriously,' she said cautiously. 'But I'm not convinced that anything would be gained by taking these letters to the police. As you said yourself, Kit, there's little they could do with them. It's not likely there will be any forensics on the letters, they offer no clues to the sender's identity, and the police don't have the resources to protect either of you. All it would do would be to attract unwelcome attention to the pair of you from the very kind of person you're nervous of.'

Kit looked faintly baffled. 'That's not what you said the other night.'

Fiona gave an embarrassed smile and half-shrug. 'I've been giving it some thought today. I realized I was overreacting and that you were right.'

Kit's eyebrows rose. 'Can I have that in writing?' he said.

'That's all very well,' Georgia said, her mouth drooping in petulance. 'But we could be at serious risk here. Are you seriously suggesting that we forget all about this, Fiona?'

Fiona shook her head. 'Of course not, Georgia. You and Kit must take every care.' She forced an artificial smile. 'I understand you wanted your publisher to provide you with bodyguards for your book tour? That would be a good place to start.'

Kit stared at them, open-mouthed. He couldn't believe Fiona had kept a straight face. 'You want me to get a minder?' he asked, incredulous.

'Not if you take sensible precautions. Don't be out on the street at night alone. Don't strike up conversations with strangers when you're on your own.' She grinned. 'And don't go to gay S&M bars.'

'I don't think this is a joking matter, Fiona,' Georgia said huffily.

'No, sorry, you're right, Georgia. But what you must bear in mind is that it's unlikely the person who sent these letters is the same person who killed Drew.'

'How can you be so sure?'

It was Fiona's turn to adopt an air of patronage. 'There's a saying in law enforcement. "Killers don't call and callers don't kill." Psychologically speaking, people who write threatening letters seldom carry out their threats. What they want is to cause fear without getting their hands dirty. And people who murder generally fail to advertise their intentions ahead of time. It would make their plans much harder to carry out, for one thing. If you like, I'll take both of these letters and subject them to professional psycholinguistic analysis. If, after that, I think there is some substantive reason to be genuinely worried, I'll come to the police with you. Is that a deal?'

Georgia pursed her lips. If she could have seen how it revealed the fine lines around her mouth, she'd never have done it again. 'I'll allow myself to be guided by your professional judgement, Fiona. But I'm not entirely happy, I have to say. And I will be speaking to my publisher about providing me with a bodyguard.'

'Wise move,' said Fiona, struggling to stifle the giggle that threatened to erupt.

'And now,' Georgia said, gathering her dress around her and elegantly slipping her feet into her shoes, 'I must away. Dear Anthony and I are dining with the culture minister and his partner, and I'm already fashionably late.'

While Kit saw Georgia to her car, Fiona reclaimed the sofa and stretched out full length, letting her muscles relax. The letters were disturbing. But now she had recognized what was really eating at her, she was able to put them into perspective. They contained, she believed, no credible threat.

She heard Kit running upstairs, and he collapsed on the sofa beside her, cuddling her close. 'You are a very wicked woman,' he said, laughter in his voice.

'I don't know what you mean.'

'Bodyguards would be a good place to start,' he mimicked.

'Well, she deserves it. Honestly, Kit, I don't know how you can put up with all that archness.'

'I've always had a weakness for high camp,' he confessed. 'She's good fun, Fiona. And generous to a fault.'

'Only if you're a chap, darling,' Fiona said, in a parody of Georgia's grand manner.

'And they say men are bitches.' He slid his arms around her, pressing his body against hers. 'Have we stopped fighting now?'

Fiona sighed. 'I overreacted. I always have Lesley at the back of my mind. Even when I don't know it myself.'

'Thank you, Caroline.' He buried his face in her hair and kissed her neck. Then he pulled away. 'Oh, and by the way. I just wanted to say, I've never heard a bigger load of bullshit in all my time with you. "I'll subject the letters to professional psycholinguistic analysis." Honestly, Fiona.'

'Georgia seemed to think it was a good idea.'

'Yeah, but Georgia's grasp on reality is shot to fuck. Let's not forget she actually believes our policemen are wonderful. And that accusations of racism and corruption against the Metropolitan Police are wicked lies spread by left-wing conspirators.'

'They're not?' Fiona's eyes widened in mock-horror.

'I don't know how to tell you this, Fiona, but there's no Father Christmas either.'

She pulled his head down towards her. 'I'll just have to see what you've got in your sack for me, then.'

Chapter 20

The following evening, as usual, Fiona picked up a copy of the *Evening Standard* at the tube station on her way home from work. The lead story on page three so astonished her that she made no attempt to board her train when it pulled into the station. Instead, she carried on reading, transfixed.

Queen of Crime Found Murdered

Bestselling American thriller writer Jane Elias has been brutally murdered in a horrific crime that mirrors the gruesome violence of her own work, police in County Wicklow revealed today.

Her mutilated body was discovered by a local forestry worker in the early hours of yesterday morning on a back road near the country estate that had been her home in the Republic of Ireland for the past four years. She had been so badly mauled by her killer that identification was impossible except by a distinctive scar she sustained after back surgery three years ago.

A police spokesman said, 'Experienced officers were shocked when they saw what had been done to the victim.

'Miss Elias had lived in this area for four years and was very popular with local residents. We are pursuing various lines of inquiry, but at this stage, it's hard to imagine why anyone would want to do this to her.'

Her British literary agent, Jeremy Devonshire, expressed deep shock at the news. 'It's appalling,' he said. 'I can't take it in. Jane was the most charming of women. We worked together for the past five years and I can honestly say we never had a cross word.'

A spokesman for her publishers, Turnhouse Bachelor, said, 'We are deeply shocked by this news. Jane was not only a shining talent but also a delight to work with. The whole company is grieving today.'

Psychopaths

Jane Elias leapt to the top of the bestseller lists on both sides of the Atlantic seven years ago with her first novel, *Death on Arrival*, which introduced forensic psychologist Dr Jay Schumann, an FBI serial killer profiler.

There followed an award-winning series of novels, three of which have been filmed by Hollywood, including her debut novel. The adaptation of *Death on Arrival*, starring Michelle Pfeiffer, won an Oscar.

Jane Elias was notable for her reclusive lifestyle. Unlike most top-selling writers, she shunned publicity, only rarely emerging from her seclusion to talk to the press.

She explained her move to Ireland as a desire for peace and quiet which she could no longer find in her native New England.

Security at her Georgian mansion on the shores of Lough Killargan was notoriously tight, with permanent guards and closed-circuit TV monitoring the five-mile perimeter fence.

In spite of that, she played an active role in her local community, most recently writing a play for the local church dramatic group to help raise funds for a children's playgroup.

A keen sailor, Jane Elias maintained several boats at her private marina. This morning, there was speculation that she may have been attacked while she was sailing one of her yachts on the lake.

Shocked, Fiona read the story again, half expecting that this time the words would rearrange themselves in a different order. But the news remained the same. A woman she had sat opposite at dinner less than three months before was now a murder victim. No amount of familiarity with the business of homicide investigation could lessen the immediacy of the cold horror that swept through her.

Fiona had no recollection of the journey home, her mind entirely occupied with memories of Jane Elias in life and the images her informed mind conjured up of the writer's body in death. They had met on Jane's last trip to London, on the publication of her seventh Jay Schumann novel, *Double Take*. Jane and Kit shared a publisher, and because of Jane's reluctance to make public appearances, Turnhouse Bachelor had arranged a series of private dinners for senior buyers in the book trade and key reviewers. To maximize their benefit, they had also invited a couple of their other crime authors to each of the dinners, which was how Kit and Fiona had come to meet the American. Of course, as soon as Jane had discovered Fiona's professional interest in crime, she had been far more interested in talking to her than any of the other guests, and the two women had spent a large part of the evening deep in gruesome discussion of murder and its motivations.

Fiona had been drawn to Jane, first because of her intellectual incisiveness but also because of her acerbic wit. She could see why Jane had prevailed against the understandable demands of her publishers for her to take a more active role in promoting her work. Anyone who had once been on the receiving end of that caustic tongue wouldn't want to repeat the experience in a hurry.

But now that voice was stilled forever. It was, Fiona thought as she plodded up Dartmouth Park Hill, a loss she felt more keenly than she would have expected. And now she would probably have to break the news to Kit.

She walked through the front door to the clear voice of Tracey Thorn revealing that she was out among the walking wounded. Fiona knew just how she felt. She walked into Kit's study, finding him hunched over the keyboard, fingers flying. She put a hand on his shoulder and kissed the top of his gleaming head.

'Gimme five minutes,' he said abstractedly.

Fiona left him to it. Bad news always came too soon. Better that he finished what he was focused on than she interrupted his flow with something so momentous that he would always connect it to that chapter, that paragraph. In the kitchen, she poured them both a glass of cold white wine and sat down at the table to wait. The five minutes turned into twelve, but Fiona felt no impatience. There was nothing either of them could do for Jane now.

At last, Kit appeared, grinning a greeting that faded to uncertainty when he saw her sombre face. 'What's the matter?' he asked, concern furrowing his forehead.

Fiona pushed a glass towards him. 'Bad news.' There was no way to sugar-coat it, so she didn't even try. 'Jane Elias has been murdered.'

Kit's hand froze halfway to his drink. 'Jane?' he said,

incredulous. 'Murdered? Where? When? What happened?'

Fiona pushed the paper across the table. 'That's as much as I know.'

Kit dropped heavily into a chair, reaching for his wine and scanning the paper. 'This is terrible,' he said, shaking his head. 'Poor Jane. Shit, I can't believe it.'

'I couldn't take it in either. She was such a strong personality. It's hard to imagine her as a victim.'

'It's a fucking nightmare.' Kit ran his hand over his head in a gesture of consternation. 'And it's only two or three weeks since Drew was killed.' He stopped dead in mid-gesture. 'You don't suppose they're connected? Somebody going after thriller writers?'

'No, I don't,' Fiona said firmly, reaching across the table and putting a hand on his arm. 'There's no reason to think that, Kit. Different countries, different gender, different body dumps. The fact that they both wrote psychological thrillers is just a horrible coincidence.'

'You always say there's no such thing as coincidence.'

'OK, maybe not quite coincidence. It's possible that somebody who was as obsessed with Jane as Drew's killer was with him saw the stories about his murder and decided that was the best way to deal with the object of his desire. But to decide on the basis of these two cases that there's a killer out there targeting people who write crime fiction is a nonsense.'

Kit shook his head and sighed. 'Yeah, I know. It's just that I live in a world where conspiracy theory always seems more attractive than cock-up. It's like, it would be easier to believe that there's a serial killer on a spree than that there are two seriously fucked-up individuals out there who get their rocks off murdering writers. And when you factor in the letters . . . well, it just seems like there's a fuck of a lot of crazies out there with an interest in people like me.'

'I can see why it feels like that. But I don't think it's anything more than bad timing, I really don't.' Fiona felt the hollowness of her words even as she spoke them. There was nothing she could say to help, and she hated that feeling.

Kit pulled away and slammed his hands palm-down on the table. 'I mean, how could this have happened to Jane? Of all people? She guarded her privacy so closely. Everybody knew that place of hers was like a fortress.'

'Maybe that was the challenge,' Fiona mused, unable to ignore the professional wheels going round. It was always her refuge of choice when she didn't know how else to respond. She wasn't proud of it, but she didn't know how to change it. Or even if she wanted to. Some of her best ideas had come out of work as displacement activity.

'Why would anybody have it in for her?' Kit demanded. 'I mean, sure, she generated a lot of envy from other writers. But people who say they'd kill for Jane Elias's sales figures, that's just talk. Writers don't take out the competition like the Mafia. But outside the business – why would she be a target?'

Fiona shrugged. 'The usual reasons. Love, hate, greed, fear. Was she involved with anyone?'

Kit shook his head. 'I've no idea. I never heard any gossip about her personal life. Which is unusual in itself. You know what a rumour mill the book world is. Everybody knows everybody else's business. I could tell you what her last advance was . . .'

'Which was?'

'Eighteen million dollars for a three-book deal. But I've never heard anything about who she was shagging. If there was anybody. Maybe she was just one of those people that aren't bothered about sex. I certainly didn't get any vibe off her. Did you?'

'No,' Fiona said. 'Nothing flirtatious, either with the women or the men at that dinner.'

'That's right. Dead cool, kept her distance. The only time she really got animated was when the two of you got stuck into that stuff about the compliant victims of the sexual sadist.' He got to his feet and headed for the fridge, where he started methodically removing vegetables from the chiller. 'Couscous and roast vegetables,' he said, half to himself.

'When in doubt, cook,' Fiona said affectionately. 'You want to talk about it?'

'Nope. I'm going to chop the hell out of these vegetables and then I'm going back to work while they cook. Best therapy I know.'

She finished her drink and stood up. 'I'll be upstairs if you need me.'

Kit nodded. 'You going to check it out on the Net?'

'You know me too well. You don't think I'm being a ghoul?'

Kit half turned and grinned. 'The bells are ringing for me and my ghoul,' he sang in his bass voice. 'Go and dig the dirt. You can serve it up with supper and calm my irrational fears.'

Fiona returned his smile. Unbidden, the thought came to her that if Jane Elias had had a lover, someone was in unbearable pain tonight. 'Call me when it's ready,' was all she said. It felt too much like tempting fate to tell him how much she loved him.

***Extract from* Decoding of Exhibit P13/4599**

Uimef afmxx ketmf fqdqp mrfqd vmzqq xume.
Mxxui mzfqp fapai meexq qb. Upupz fzqqp mzkbu
xxefa wzaow yqagf quftqd . . .

*I was totally shattered after Jane Elias. All I wanted to
do was sleep. It was as if I wanted to wipe the memory
of it from my brain, and sleep was the best way to do
it. I couldn't even pick up a pen and keep the record
straight until today.*

*Of course, I couldn't kill her on the boat, because I didn't
want to get blood everywhere. That would have been
completely wrong, in the context of the book. So once
I'd got her unconscious, I had to sail over to the sailing
club landing ramp, get her out of the boat and finish
her off in the shallows there.*

But my luck held. I let her bleed out a bit in the water,

then I got her in the back of the 4 x 4 and set her boat adrift on the lake. Let them work that one out, I thought.

Then I did what I had to do. I don't know why, but it felt worse than doing Drew Shand. Maybe because she was a woman. Or maybe because I had to strip her and she looked much more vulnerable than she did with her clothes on.

Everything went according to plan. And from what I read in the papers, it sounds like the message is starting to trickle through. Not before time.

Now, it's time to start thinking about number three. Georgia Lester. I've been reading her book again, and why anybody would publish it, never mind turn it into a film, is beyond me. It's unfortunate that my plan will help sell more copies of her pitiful book. But that can't be helped. I've got to keep thinking about the bigger picture.

I've done a recce on her cottage in Dorset, and it's perfect for what I want to do. It's finding when she's going to be there that's the difficult bit.

I know she's in London this week, and looking at her

engagements on the website, I think she'll go down to Dorset at the weekend and come back on Tuesday or Wednesday.

I'm not looking forward to this one little bit. It's the worst prospect so far. What I'm going to have to do to her is so horrible. I keep rereading the bit of the book that describes it, and it turns my stomach to think I'm going to have to copy that. But I can't stop now. That would make everything I've done so far completely pointless.

When I feel like this, I look around me and see what I've been reduced to because of what they did to me. I don't get any pleasure out of doing this, but it does give me back my self-respect. I haven't taken everything they've thrown at me lying down, and that's worth something.

So I just have to grit my teeth and do what has to be done. Two down, four to go. They should have got the point by then.

Chapter 21

Like police officers, fire fighters and journalists, Fiona had discovered that the fastest and most effective tool for putting emotional distance between herself and the terrible things her job forced her to confront was black humour. So when entering Jane Elias's name on her metasearch engine threw up a website called *Laughing With the Dead Celebs*, she couldn't resist.

Jane Elias's death had been in the public domain for less than a day, but already she merited her own cartoon tombstone. Fiona clicked on Jane's name. The screen dissolved into a coffin-shaped frame. 'Jane Elias killed somewhere around forty-seven people in her seven novels. Some would say it's about time she discovered what it feels like. Not us, of course. If jokes about death offend you, don't scroll down this page.'

Fiona, naturally, carried on scrolling. So far, there were only four contributions.

> *Why did Jane Elias have to die?*
> *So she could finally get her hands on a good plot.*
>
> *Do writers know when they start out how it's going to end?*
> *Jane Elias obviously didn't!*

197

What did St Peter say to Jane Elias at the pearly gates?
'So, Jane, whodunnit?'

What was the motive for Jane Elias's murder?
Sales figures to die for.

Only the first was worth a smile, and a pretty thin one at that, Fiona decided, closing the site and heading for a more conventional tribute web page. The first site she checked out was one that had been created by a fan. It simply said, under that day's date, *'Jane Elias was found murdered today. This site is closed as a mark of respect.'*

She had more luck with her second choice, also an act of devotion from one of Jane's readers. The bare details of the murder were reported and below them were a series of boxes offering hyperlinks to other areas of the site. Offered a choice of *Her Life, Photo Album, The Investigation, Condolence Book* and *Related Links,* she opted for the photographic record first, curious to see what the site's creator had been able to assemble, given Jane's notorious camera-shyness.

First came the jacket photograph that had only ever appeared on her first novel. It was an unremarkable face, the sort it would be hard to describe in terms that would differentiate it from a million others. Mid-brown hair in a jaw-length bob, parted on the right; straight brows, dark eyes, an absolutely average nose and full lips that curved in a faint smile, giving nothing away. She was wearing an open-necked shirt, revealing a thin gold chain round her neck. Apart from the blonde highlights and a few more lines etched into the corners of her eyes, she looked exactly the same as she had on the night Fiona had met her.

Next came her high-school yearbook picture. The hair was longer here, hanging straight to the top of small breasts, but still with the same parting. At eighteen, Jane had worn unfashionably heavy-framed spectacles that made her eyes look unfocused. Her face too was fuller, almost plump. If all Fiona had had to go on was this, she doubted she'd have picked Jane out of a crowd.

A third photograph showed Jane accepting the first of her two Edgar awards at a Mystery Writers of America dinner. Her smile was broad and unself-conscious and she looked surprisingly elegant in a figure-hugging black dress that shimmered with sequins.

The final shot in the gallery showed a completely different side of Jane Elias. Taken at the finishing line of a charity half-marathon in Dublin, it revealed Jane in mid-stride, her running shorts and vest showing off the smooth planes of well-developed muscle that covered legs and arms. The camera had caught her in a candid moment, her expression exposing the blissed-out altered state of the athlete who has gone through the pain barrier. She looked more attractive here than anywhere else, Fiona noticed with detachment.

From studying the photographs, Fiona moved to the condolence book. If she'd been involved with the investigation, she'd have suggested the police take a look at the messages posted by fans. Given the tendency of psychopaths to attempt to insert themselves into the inquiry into their crimes, it was an obvious place for Jane's killer to go. The dozen messages Fiona scrolled through seemed innocuous enough, but there was plenty of time for the strange and bizarre to show up. She bookmarked the page, resolving to return in a day or two to see if anything resembling Kit and Georgia's letters showed up.

There was nothing else on the fan site that interested her, so, like a child saving its favourite part of the meal for the last, she directed her web browser to *Murder Behind the Headlines*. She typed in 'Jane Elias' in the search box and hit the <return> key.

Queen of the serial killer thriller Jane Elias has finally found out what it's like to suffer what she handed out to dozens of victims in her books. Unfortunately, she won't be able to put her experiences to good commercial effect because the man – or woman – who abducted her made sure she wouldn't live to tell the tale.

Elias's body was found on a back road in the early hours of the morning by a forestry worker whose truck ran into the body, strategically placed in the middle of the road just round a blind bend near the novelist's estate in County Wicklow, Ireland. This shows striking similarities to one of the body dumps in *Death on Arrival*, Elias's first novel which was turned into an Oscar-winning vehicle for the luscious Michelle Pfeiffer.

And according to MBTH's sources in the County Wicklow coroner's office, Elias suffered injuries that have much in common with the description of what happened to the victims in that novel, only in her case they were postmortem, rather than while she was still alive. Maybe her killer was more squeamish than his victim. Here's the template from the book:

<The delayed sting of the razor cut. The blossoming of a burn from a smart to a roar of pain that spread inwards as the smell of barbecued

flesh drifted outwards. *The searing agony of flesh forced to accommodate more than it has room for. The sickening pain of a broken bone never allowed time to knit. The dull distress of a blow strategically aimed at the organs nestling beneath the skin.>*

Creepy, huh? Especially after the recent copycat murder of *Copycat* writer Drew Shand in Edinburgh, Scotland. Unlikely though it may sound, conspiracy theorists are already speculating that somebody is taking out serial killer thriller writers. Now that's taking criticism a little too far.

But the truth may lie in a different direction.

MBTH can exclusively reveal that Jane Elias's greatest secret was that for the last five years, she had been involved in an affair with undercover drugs cop Pierce Finnegan, one of the key figures in the Irish Republic's police force, the Garda Siochana's fight against drug dealers. Finnegan was instrumental in the cracking of a major heroin supply route last year, and the word is that there's a price on his head from senior gangland figures still awaiting trial. He is reportedly liaising with Europol presently, and has high connections with the US drug enforcement authorities. Frankly, his affair with Elias was a far better kept secret than anything in the leaky Garda files.

Elias met Finnegan when he was attending an International convention of criminal intelligence personnel at Quantico. Friends claim she was visiting the convention anonymously, under the wing of a software company in Florida who were pioneering a computer photofit program. During the convention, she was able to sneak into several closed sessions, where she heard Finnegan speak. Later, friends introduced them and the two immediately formed a close personal bond. Not even his Garda bosses knew about the affair.

As a result, Elias moved to Ireland, where Finnegan was a regular visitor to her high-security compound in County Wicklow, though among locals, it's doubtful if even Elias's security staff knew his true identity. Elias often had secret liaisons with her lover when he was on the road. She would check into the same hotel and the two would share clandestine nights of love. So, no mystery about where her plotlines came from.

Now speculation is rife that whoever killed Elias was either taking revenge on Finnegan or sending him a warning to back off and compromise his trial evidence. The death of Drew Shand could have provided the killer with the perfect blueprint for a killing that would send the desired message to Finnegan without necessarily being connected to any of the Garda agent's cases. Of course, that would only work if the affair remained a secret.

Sorry, Pierce. Sorry, Mr Murderer. We just blew your cover.

REMEMBER YOU READ IT FIRST ON
MURDER BEHIND THE HEADLINES

Fiona took a deep breath. This was dynamite if it was true. Having a lover who was an undercover drugs investigator provided a far more credible motive for so violent a murder than the notion that a serial killer was targeting writers. Knowing how law enforcement agencies worked against their own, Fiona seriously doubted that the relationship was a secret to Finnegan's bosses, but the pair had certainly done a good job of keeping it out of the public eye.

She couldn't help feeling relief. Although her logical self had been reluctant to accept the possibility of a murderer who wanted to rid the world of thriller writers, her emotional self had known nothing but the gnaw of fear ever since she'd read the newspaper headline. Fiona knew far too much about the relentless capabilities of serial offenders; the notion that Kit might be a name on a hit list had been rattling round her head for the past hour and she was selfishly grateful that there was a logical explanation for Jane's death that could not touch her own lover.

She closed down the computer and made her way downstairs. Kit was back in the kitchen, tipping couscous into a pan of boiling water. He looked round and forced a crooked smile. 'Ten minutes,' he said.

'Did you manage any work?' Fiona asked, topping up his glass and refilling her own.

'Nothing like other people's tragedies to get the words flowing,' he said, a sharp edge to his voice. 'It's like a defence mechanism. My brain uses writing to block out the static. As long as I'm staring at the screen and getting stuff down, I can't be thinking about the hell Jane had to go through before this bastard let her die.'

'That's the trouble with having an imagination,' Fiona said. 'Especially one like yours. You don't even have to try to come up with a hundred harrowing scenarios.' She crossed the room and he turned to accept her hug. 'Her injuries were postmortem. She wasn't tortured.'

'I suppose we should be grateful for that,' Kit mumbled

into her hair. He pulled away gently. 'So what did you dig up?'

'Bottom line? You shouldn't be worried on your own account.' She sat down at the table and outlined her researches in detail.

'You know what I think about those muckrakers,' Kit protested. 'How can you be sure they've got it right about her relationship with the undercover guard? Maybe they were just mates. Maybe he was just a contact that she milked for ideas and deep background.'

Fiona shrugged. 'I can't be certain. But they've obviously got some very high-level sources and they exploit them to the hilt. So unless we hear otherwise, I'd take what they say at face value.'

'Easier said than done,' he muttered.

'One thing that might help set your mind at rest – when you're ringing round to see if anybody else has had threatening letters, see if anybody knows whether Jane had one. If she didn't, then it's even more evidence to support my theory that people who write death threats aren't the ones who kill.'

'Maybe I should just ring the local police and ask them.'

'Yeah, right. Like they're going to tell you.'

'They might tell Steve.'

Fiona acknowledged the sense of his statement with a dip of her head.

'And I'm meeting him tomorrow night anyway,' Kit continued, taking the roasting dish of vegetables out of the oven and tipping them into the couscous. He placed the food on the table with a flourish and sat down facing Fiona. 'I'm going to ask Steve if he can find out about whether Jane got any death threat letters,' he said. 'If she didn't, then you're probably right, and Georgia and I are in the clear. And in the meantime, I promise to be careful without being paranoid. Will that do you?'

Fiona smiled. 'That'll do me fine. But if somebody does come after you with a knife, no heroics. Just leg it.'

'What? You don't want me to stand my ground and be a man?' Kit teased.

'God, no. I'm far too busy to take time off to organize a funeral.' Fiona tasted her dinner. 'Mmm. Wonderful. Take care of yourself, darling, I could never afford to replace you in the kitchen.'

Kit pretended to look hurt. 'Only in the kitchen?'

'If I don't eat every day, I die,' she said. 'I'd miss shagging you, but it wouldn't kill me.'

'You think not?' he said dangerously.

'Let's not put it to the test.'

He grinned. 'Right answer, Doctor. So, do you fancy a quiet night in?'

'Kit, we've never had a quiet night in. Why would we start now?' She raised her eyebrows provocatively. 'But I wouldn't say no to fucking your brains out.'

'You talked me into it, you smooth bastard.' Kit's grin promised to take no prisoners.

Jane Elias would soon be cold in earth. Neither of them had forgotten that for a moment. Keeping the ghosts at bay was the most important thing they could do for each other, and they knew it. It was, as so often in the past, their unspoken contract.

Chapter 22

Georgia Lester sat at the kitchen table, hands cradling a china cup of weak Earl Grey tea, staring unseeingly down past autumn-bedraggled herbaceous borders to the skeleton apple trees at the bottom of her cottage garden. She didn't register the perennials that were due to be cut back, the roses that would be pruned when next the gardener came. That was neither her interest nor her job. She only ever noticed the garden when it was beautiful. Ugliness she preferred to tune out. There was enough of that in her head without adding to it from outside.

What she enjoyed about her cottage was the peace. Being Georgia Lester was a tiring business. It was a constant effort to maintain the image of sophisticated beauty and elegance that the world expected from her. Of course, she had created that expectation herself, a conscious invention of a persona and style that would mark her out from the herd. But that didn't make it any easier, and these days, whenever she looked in the mirror in the morning, it seemed as if the mountain was looming higher every day. Perhaps it was time for another visit to that charming man in Harley Street who had done such a good job with that loose skin around her jawline.

But here at the cottage, she could absolve herself from the need to maintain the facade. Well, she could when she was here alone, she amended, a sly smile of reminiscence lifting the corners of her mouth. A girl did need distraction now and again, and devoted as Anthony was, he couldn't quite provide the stimulus of a taut young body with all the sexual energy that accompanied it. None of her flirtations lasted long, she made sure of that. Nor did they mean anything more to her than a kind of blood transfusion – something necessary but somehow impersonal.

This weekend, however, Georgia had a different agenda. No dressing up for lovers, just working on her rewrites. Unlike most of the writers she knew, Georgia loved the revision process. It allowed her to step back from the nuts and bolts of getting her first draft on paper and focus on the quality of the writing itself. She'd established a reputation for finely crafted prose, and she always maintained that came from her attention to the detailed sentence-on-sentence shape of her book. She had three clear days of her favourite work ahead now, and she was looking forward to it.

Already, her mind was racing onwards to the section of the book she would be working on that day. The typescript was already sitting on her desk, next to the Mont Blanc Meisterstück fountain pen she always used to make the revisions her secretary would later transfer to the computer. She wasn't even going to bother dressing yet. She'd slob around in her fluffy dressing gown, hair hidden in a silk turban, until lunchtime. Then she'd soak in the bath while she listened to *The World At One*. A snack for lunch, then she'd have to venture out into Dorchester. There was plenty of food in the freezer, but she'd inexplicably run out of white wine, and dinner without a glass of chilled Chablis was unthinkable. She firmly believed that writers needed the discipline of routine. And that included the small pleasures of life as well as the habits of mind that made it possible for her to turn out a book a year.

Georgia finished her tea and poured a fresh cup. She planned to make the most of these three days. When they were over, she would be plunged into an author tour to promote her latest hardback. Thinking of it reminded her that she still hadn't persuaded her publisher to foot the bill for the handsome bodyguard she'd hired before leaving London. She didn't really think anyone was after her, in spite of her protestations to dear, sweet Kit that they should take those tiresome letters to the police. But she had no objections to cashing in on the possibility. It never hurt to keep one's name firmly in the public eye. The notion that she was sufficiently significant a writer to attract the attention of a stalker would inevitably draw new readers to her, curious to discover what it was about her that was so special. And once drawn to her, Georgia was utterly convinced they would remain to devour her backlist in its entirety.

Thanks to astute planning like that, she had climbed to the top of the heap. She was well aware that her activities earned her disapproval from many of her fellows. It bothered her not a whit. They could pretend all they liked that they were too high-minded to stoop to her tactics. The reality was that they were jealous of the column inches she gathered.

Unaware that she was about to generate the greatest publicity of her career, Georgia sipped her tea and felt very, very contented.

Chapter 23

Fiona was running late. Literally. Dodging students, she swerved into her secretary's office. 'Bloody Northern Line,' she gasped, trying to wrestle her coat off and open her office door at the same time. She crossed the threshold, shedding jacket and briefcase and reaching for the folder of notes for the departmental meeting that had been due to start five minutes earlier, her secretary following her.

'There's a Spanish policeman been trying to get you,' she said. She consulted a message sheet in her hand. 'A Major Salvador Berrocal. He's been ringing every ten minutes for the last half-hour.'

'Shit, shit shit!' Fiona muttered savagely.

'He said would you call him back as soon as possible,' her secretary added helpfully as Fiona dithered between desk and doorway. 'It sounded urgent.'

'I've got to go to this meeting,' she said. 'Barnard's been trying to dump half his seminars and I don't want to be landed with them.' She ran a hand through her hair. 'OK. Call Berrocal and tell him I'm unavoidably detained but I'll get back to him as soon as I can. Sorry, Lizzie, I've got to run.'

She raced down the corridor and skidded to a halt outside the meeting room, attracting curious looks from those who had only ever seen Fiona in cool and elegant mode. She paused for a moment, smoothing her hair and taking a deep breath to regain her composure, then swept in with an apologetic smile. 'Sorry, tube,' she muttered, taking her place halfway down one side of the conference table. Professor Barnard neither faltered in his convoluted sentence nor graced her with a glance.

It felt like the longest meeting in history, and Fiona had to force herself not to fidget restlessly as they ploughed through seemingly endless departmental minutiae. She managed to contain her impatience, refusing to allow Barnard's domineering presence to fluster her into accepting more than one additional seminar group. But even as she argued her case, half her mind was on Berrocal's urgent message. He must have a suspect in custody. Or so she hoped.

At the end of the meeting, Fiona scooped up her papers and swept out, earning raised eyebrows and an exchange of meaningful looks between those of her colleagues who preferred to dismiss her as being too arrogant by half. Back in her office, she asked Lizzie to hold her calls and started to dial Berrocal's number before she was even seated.

'Major Berrocal?' she asked when the phone was answered on the second ring.

'Si. Dr Cameron?' His tone gave no clue to the nature of his news.

'I'm sorry not to have called back before this, but I couldn't get away,' she gabbled. 'You have a development?'

He sighed. 'Not the sort I had hoped for. I am afraid we have another murder.'

Fiona's heart sank. This was the news she had been dreading so much she had refused to consider it a serious possibility. 'I'm sorry to hear that,' she said inadequately.

'I am calling to ask if it is possible for you to come back to Toledo and consult further with us. Perhaps the information generated by this latest murder might help you pinpoint where we should be looking for our suspect now.'

Fiona closed her eyes. 'I'm sorry,' she said, hoping he could hear the genuine regret in her voice. 'It's impossible at present. I have too many commitments here that I can't avoid.'

There was a ponderous silence. Then Berrocal said, 'I was afraid you would say that.'

'There's no reason why I can't examine the evidence if you can fax the details to me,' she said, her sense of duty kicking in ahead of her common sense.

'That would be possible?'

'I've got a very heavy schedule, but I'm sure I could make time to analyse the material,' she assured him, already wondering how she would fit it in.

'Thank you,' he said, his relief palpable even over the phone.

'Perhaps you could give me the bare bones now?' Fiona asked, pulling a blank pad towards her and tucking the phone between ear and shoulder.

'The body was found inside the courtyard of the Alcazar.' Berrocal's voice was clipped and clinical now. 'An Englishwoman, Jenny Sheriff. Twenty-two years old, from Guildford.' He split the unfamiliar place name into two words. 'She was working as a receptionist at the Hotel Alfonso the Sixth on a year-long exchange to improve her Spanish. Her shift ended at ten last night and she told a colleague that she was meeting a man for coffee in the square. She said he was fascinating, he knew all there was to know about Toledo.'

'Did she mention his name?' Fiona asked.

'No. We have a barman who says he served her and a man with coffee and brandy just after ten. He remembers because he had noticed her several times before, drinking there with friends. But he didn't notice the man she was with because he was sitting with his back to the bar. The barman doesn't remember them leaving, because a group of tourists came in for drinks shortly after that.'

'When was she found?'

'This morning, the custodian who opens up for the rest of the staff at the Alcazar found the staff entrance unlocked. When he walked into the courtyard, he saw her lying there. She had been stabbed several times in the stomach. Our preliminary report indicates that the murder weapon was probably a military bayonet. The death matches those of many of the Republicans killed by Franco's forces when they relieved the siege of the Alcazar in the Civil War. This ties in with the theme you identified of tourist scenes associated with violent death. And there is a further connection. Like Martina Albrecht, her vagina had been mutilated after death by repeated insertions of a broken bottle. And finally, there was also a city tourist map from the hotel in her pocket. So, I think there is little doubt that we are dealing with the same man. Delgado or whoever.' His voice was edgy with frustration.

'No signs of forced entry?' she asked.

'No. It looks as if he must have had keys. We are working on that angle. He may have a friend who has access to the keys, or he may have somehow acquired his own set. We'll be checking all the keyholders' home addresses. It's possible that wherever he's hiding out might be near one of them. He could have made an illegal entry and got his hands on their keys that way.'

Fiona sighed. 'I'm really sorry about this, Major. When you told me you had a suspect, I hoped that would be an end to it.'

'Me too. But Delgado seems to have disappeared into the landscape. Every police officer in the city has his name and his picture, but we don't have a single sighting of him to follow up.'

'It must be very frustrating for you.' She frowned as she spoke, trying to snag something at the edge of her consciousness.

'It is. But we will keep on trying. I will fax the material over to you as soon as it becomes available.'

After she put the phone down, Fiona stared at the wall, waiting for her subconscious to throw up whatever was lurking there. Nothing came. Then the phone rang again, pulling her back to the immediate demands of the work she was supposed to be doing.

In spite of her best efforts to concentrate, only part of her mind was focused on her seminar group that morning. Berrocal's problem niggled in the corner of her brain. Frustrated by her inability to drag to the surface whatever nugget was lurking just out of reach, she spent her lunch break in the nearby swimming baths, ploughing up and down mindlessly, trying to reach the semi-trance state that exercise could produce. But still it eluded her grasp.

Walking back to the department, she summoned up the image of the Alcazar in her mind's eye. Perhaps that would help her unlock the puzzle. The imposing building stood on the highest point of the old town, the perfect position for a fortress, a situation that had been exploited by every occupying power since the Romans. It dominated the city, bigger than anything else in the line of sight, its four-square geometry a reproach to the higgledy-piggledy appearance of the rest of the buildings that rambled down the slopes towards the Tagus.

But it had never been a lucky building. It had burned down several times and been seriously damaged in the Civil War, when Franco's men had bombarded it for months. From a distance, it was a forbidding sight, its walls apparently lacking the ornate decoration of its skyline rivals, the cathedral and San Juan de los Reyes. The only breaks in its severity were the four circular turrets that adorned the corners, each with a Disneyland flourish of roof.

Inside the high walls, it was a different matter. Each of the exterior facades was decorated in a different architectural style. Fiona had never toured the Alcazar, but she had seen photographs, and she'd found it almost absurd that so elaborately stylized a building should have ended up as Army offices with a museum tacked on to them.

Even so, it had still managed to acquire a new layer to its bloody history. Now it was a crime scene. The resting place for the latest victim of a ruthless killer she was supposed to help catch. An objective she was apparently some distance from achieving.

In spite of her mental nagging, still her mind refused to release its inspiration, and by mid afternoon Fiona had given up. She decided to work late, dealing with the correspondence that had piled up to dangerous levels in her in-tray. Kit was out for the evening, doing an event at a bookshop then going for a drink with Steve, so there was no urgency about getting home. When she finally left her office, she ran into a couple of part-time lecturers from the anthropology school who persuaded her to come for a drink at the staff club.

She was on her second glass of wine when the conversation veered off at a tangent. Two of her colleagues were pouring scorn on the notions of a third about funerary customs in West Africa. Some electrical current sparked in Fiona's brain and suddenly she knew what she needed to tell Berrocal. With a mumbled apology, she jumped to her feet and hurried back to her office.

Of course, when she got through to the Spanish police,

Berrocal was out of the office. She didn't want to leave her hunch as a message with a minion, because she was aware how bizarre it would sound. Equally, she didn't want to wait until morning. She switched on the computer and went straight to her e-mail program.

From: Fiona Cameron
                   <fcameron@psych.ulon.ac.uk>
To: Salvador Berrocal <Sberroc@cnp.mad.es>
Subject: Re: Toledo murders

Dear Major Berrocal,
A thought has occurred to me about where your suspect may be hiding out, although it is probably grasping at straws.
As we know, he is obsessed with the history of Toledo, which is now linked in his mind with the business of death. Where do death and history intersect? In graveyards. I wondered if there was the kind of cemetery in or near Toledo where there are large tombs or funerary vaults. If so, he could be camping out there.
He obviously has some sort of shelter, since he is managing to remain well enough groomed not to attract adverse attention to his appearance. I think he could possibly have broken into a mausoleum or family vault which he is now using as a base of operations.
If you have no other leads, it might be worth examining this possibility.
I will be at home later this evening, where I

intend to go through the material you promised me.
Good hunting!
Best wishes
Fiona Cameron

Chapter 24

Kit closed the last of the books with a flourish and put down his pen. 'Thanks, pal,' he said to the bookseller who moved the pile of hardbacks to one side.

'Do you mind doing some of the paperbacks as well?' the woman asked.

'Happy to.' He glanced across to Steve, who was browsing the true crime section. 'I'll not be long,' he called.

'No problem,' Steve said, pulling a book about forensic anthropology from the shelf.

'I thought it went well,' he said absently as he signed.

'It was great,' the bookseller enthused. 'It's the first time we've done a whole week of themed events, and it's been terrific. We've really put on sales, not just at the events but during the day as well.'

'That's because you've promoted it so well in the store,' Kit said. 'The windows look the business, and that pulls the punters in. It was a good audience tonight.'

The woman pulled a face. 'Apart from the nutter in the front row.'

'You always get one.'

'Oh, I know, but the way he kept going on about poor Drew Shand and Jane Elias . . . what a sicko. Doesn't it worry you that weirdos like that are reading your books?'

Kit stood up and shrugged. 'Not really. It's the ones who keep their mouths shut you have to worry about. Isn't that right, Steve?'

Steve looked up, startled. 'Sorry, you speaking to me, Kit?'

'Yeah, I was saying it's not the nutters who mouth off that want watching. It's the ones that don't let on that they're candidates for the locked ward that really cause the problems.'

Steve snapped the book shut. 'That's right. The perfect murders are committed by people who are smart enough to make them look like accidents and strong enough to keep their mouths shut afterwards.'

Kit snorted. 'Unlike that bloke in Sheffield who cut his wife's head off and brought it round to show the girlfriend how much he loved her.'

The bookseller shuddered. 'You're making that up.'

'I wish he was. Truth is usually much more horrible than even *his* fiction,' Steve said. 'You done, Kit?'

They walked down the hill from the bookshop in companionable silence. By unspoken consent, they turned into the first pub with beer that Kit classified as decent, an establishment where no expense had been spared to make it look like a 1930s public bar, all bare floorboards and wooden chairs. All it lacked was sawdust on the floor. As they elbowed their way to the bar, Kit finally spoke. 'You don't think there's any connection between Drew Shand and Jane Elias being murdered, do you?' he asked.

'I don't know enough about either case even to speculate,' Steve responded. He pushed through the drinkers and caught the barmaid's eye. 'Two pints of bitter, love.'

Kit grinned. 'Lack of knowledge never stopped Fiona. She reckons it's about as likely as Man United getting relegated from the Premiership. But she might just be saying that to stop me worrying.'

Steve took a mouthful of his beer then grinned. 'And you think I'm going to contradict her? And risk bringing down the wrath of God on my head?'

'You know what your trouble is, Stevie? You let Fiona get away with far too much. You defer to her like you do to nobody else I've ever seen you with. But with a woman like Fiona, you can't afford to roll over. Give her an inch and before you know it, her flag's flying over the whole world.'

'Old habits die hard,' Steve said, aware that Kit was marking his territory as obviously as an undoctored tomcat. He knew his friend was right. When the shape of his relationship with Fiona had been forged, he hadn't understood that she needed someone who would stand up to her and challenge her. Now, it was too late to change. Worse still, it had become the established pattern of his personal relationships with women. He could be tough with female colleagues and subordinates, never making any allowance for their gender. But as soon as the possibility of romance entered, Steve reverted to the wimp who had failed to win Fiona. He didn't like it, but he didn't have sufficient time or motivation to change it. Even supposing he could. Steve snapped out of his thoughts and tuned back into what Kit was saying.

'I don't need humouring. I just need to know whether you think I should be watching my back, with these threatening letters going the rounds.'

They made their way to a table in the corner that they knew from experience was in one of the dead spots of the sound system. They could have a conversation there without risking laryngitis or eavesdroppers. Steve took a cigar from his breast pocket and lit up. 'Run that past me again, Kit. I couldn't hear you over the racket at the bar.'

Kit shook his head. 'You weren't listening. You were

thinking about women. I was telling you about these death-threat letters that seem to be going the rounds among some of us crime writers. I've had one, Georgia Lester's had one. Fiona suggested I ask around to see if anybody else has had one, and I sent out some e-mails today about it. So far, I've got three others admitting to it. Jonathan Lewis, Adam Chester and Enya Flannery. And my agent's had one too. And they all sound like they've been written by the same person. Plus, Enya and Jonathan both said they'd had similar messages on their answering machines. Though the voice was too muffled to recognize, even if they'd know the person.'

'And you're wondering if there's a connection to these two murders? If there's somebody out there with a grudge against crime writers?' Steve tried not to look as incredulous as he felt. He knew Kit had a healthy ego about his own work, but he hadn't realized that he and his fellow writers actually thought they were important enough to provoke someone to serial murder.

'Well, it had crossed my mind,' Kit said. 'I don't think that's unreasonable in the circumstances. One crank letter is easy to dismiss, but six makes me a bit uneasy. And I wondered if you could maybe put a call in to your oppos on the other side of the Irish Sea and maybe check out if Jane Elias got one of these death threat letters.'

'Kit, the papers are full of Jane Elias's affair with this Garda Siochana officer. Frankly, I'd have thought that had a lot more to do with her murder than anything else. From what I hear, Pierce Finnegan made plenty of enemies over the years, inside the tent as well as outside. There's no better way of getting to someone in law enforcement than going for the people they love. So no, I don't think you should be losing sleep over the idea that somebody might be coming after you.'

'But you'll make the call? To put my mind and Fiona's at rest?' Kit eyed Steve over the rim of his glass. If he wouldn't do it for friendship, he'd do it for his quaint notion of courtly love. Kit would have put money on it.

'I'll see what I can find out,' Steve said. He knew he was being manipulated, but it was more effort to fight it than he could be bothered expending.

Kit nodded, satisfied. 'That's all I wanted to hear. Fiona's saying she doesn't think there's likely to be a connection, but I'm not sure if she really thinks that or if she's only saying it to keep me happy. I sometimes feel like Fiona thinks I'm some fragile little flower that needs protecting from the wind and rain.'

Steve spluttered a mouthful of beer over the table. 'Fuck's sake, Kit,' he got out. 'You're about as fragile as the Forth Bridge.'

Before Kit could respond, their peace was shattered by an announcement that a live Irish band was about to start playing. Kit drained his pint and stood up. 'Let's get out of here. Come back to ours, it's only ten minutes' walk.'

Neither of them noticed the bearded man who had sat at the back of the bookshop event abandoning his half-drunk pint of Guinness and following them out of the pub at a cautious distance. He'd left the shop before the signing and waited patiently in a nearby doorway until Kit and Steve had left. He'd walked down the hill in their wake and when they entered the bar, he'd loitered outside for long enough to allow them to buy their drinks and settle down. Then he'd attached himself to three other men heading for the bar, bought himself a drink and found a seat where he could see the back of Kit's head and Steve's profile.

Now, he pursued them through the night streets, careful to keep well back. He smiled to himself. His caution was a waste of time, really. The stupid fools didn't have a clue. When they turned into a gateway, he stopped in his tracks, pretending to tie his shoelace. Then he continued down the street, glancing to one side as he passed the house they'd gone into. He couldn't help a spasm of jealous anger as he took in its elegant proportions. If he had his way, Kit Martin wouldn't be enjoying his smug and cosy life for much longer. He had plans to make things much less comfortable for Mr bloody Martin.

They arrived to find Fiona in the kitchen finishing the penne puttanesca that Kit had left for her. 'You're back early,' she said.

'We thought we'd try and catch you with your secret lover,' Steve teased.

Fiona poked her tongue out at him. 'Too late. She's just left.'

'The Paddies invaded the pub,' Kit said. 'You know how I hate that bloody bogus bogtrotter music.' He snagged two bottles of Sam Smith's Organic Bitter from the drinks cupboard. 'So we thought we'd come back and spoil your evening.'

'You're too late for that as well. Salvador Berrocal called earlier to tell me there's been another body in Toledo, so I've been ploughing through Spanish scene-of-crime reports and entering data on the computer instead of indulging myself with a long hot bath.'

Kit pulled a face. 'Bummer,' he said.

'How was the gig?' Fiona asked.

'Not a bad turnout, considering I didn't have a new book to promote. Sold a fair few books and signed every bit of stock I could lay hands on.'

'He's being modest again, Fi. He had them in the palm of

his hand. They loved him. All the women wanted to take him home and all the blokes wanted to take him for a pint,' Steve said as he sat down opposite her.

'And you two got to be the lucky ones,' Kit said. 'Somewhere in your youth, or childhood . . .'

'We must have done something ferociously wicked,' Fiona responded. 'How's things with you, Steve?'

He made a gesture with the flat of his hand to indicate, so-so. 'We got a lucky break on a serious racist attack down in Brick Lane, three lads in custody and one of them singing like a diva. That's about the best of it. Blake hasn't come back from Spain, but we've had a look through his finances and there's nothing to indicate any blackmail proceeds. The only large payment into his account is the money he made from selling his story to the papers. He took a chunk of that out in cash, which is presumably what he's spending in Spain.'

'Scumbag tabloids. Makes you sick,' Kit commented.

Fiona sighed. 'He's technically an innocent man. There's nothing to stop them paying him.'

'He's not innocent if he watched Susan Blanchard get killed and said nothing,' Kit protested.

'We don't *know* that, though. It's only my theory,' she reminded him.

Seeing she'd pushed her plate away, Steve took out a cigar and lit up. 'I did take my own advice about a second trawl through the eyewitnesses, however.'

'Any joy?' Fiona asked.

'Well, it's early days yet, but there might be something. I read through the original statements again, and I noticed that one person mentioned seeing a cyclist coming from that general direction. She was walking her dog, and she remembered this cyclist because he was going much faster than people on bikes generally do on the Heath. We didn't follow it up at the time because Blake emerged as such a strong suspect so soon.'

Fiona frowned. 'You know, I remember making a note of that when I was on the case officially. I think I might even have mentioned it in my preliminary report,' she said thoughtfully.

'So have you interviewed her again?' Kit asked.

'I went to see her personally,' Steve admitted. He held his hands up as if to stem a protest from Fiona. 'I know it's pathetic, a detective of my rank going out and taking witness statements, and I know I should be able to delegate, but if we screw up again and I'm left carrying the can, at least this time it'll be my can.'

'What did she have to say?' Fiona asked.

'She didn't have a lot to add. Her walk had already taken her past the shrubbery where the murder took place, and she's still racked with guilt because she was wearing a Walkman. She's convinced that if she hadn't been listening to the Mozart Requiem, she'd have heard something and been able to raise the alarm. Anyway, about ten minutes later, a bike came up behind her and raced past. She took notice partly because cycling isn't really permitted on that part of the Heath at that time of the day, although some people ignore the rules. But mostly she remembered him because of his speed. He was going like the clappers, she said.'

Fiona sighed. 'Not much chance of a decent description, then.'

Steve shook his head. 'I'm afraid not. She only saw him from behind and she doesn't know anything about bikes so we don't know whether it was a racing bike or a mountain bike. She remembers he was wearing a helmet and proper lycra cycling gear. Black trousers, she thinks, and a dark top. Maybe purple or dark-blue or even maroon.'

'Like that narrows it down,' Kit said.

'However ...' Steve held up one finger and smiled. 'She has agreed to be hypnotized to see if there's anything else lurking in her subconscious about this cyclist. And, when we reinterviewed the other witnesses who came forward and asked specifically if they'd seen anyone cycling that morning, we got one other hit. A nanny was sitting on a bench at the bottom of the hill when he went past her. She said he was going so fast she thought he wouldn't be able to make it round the bend, but he cleared it and headed for the exit on to Heath Road.'

'How come you didn't pick that up first time round?' Kit asked, never reluctant to put Steve on the spot in spite of their friendship.

Steve looked embarrassed. 'She's Filipino. Her English is pretty good, but it isn't her first language. When we spoke to her before, we didn't have an interpreter. The DC who did the preliminary interview decided she had nothing useful to tell us, so he didn't bother setting up a second interview with an interpreter. This time, we did it properly.'

'And did you get some useful product?' Fiona asked.

Steve took a long pull from his bottle of beer and nodded. 'Sort of. She reckons he was wearing goggles and a helmet and a dark outfit. She thought it was a mountain bike. She reckoned it looked like the one her employer has. We've identified the make and model, though of course she might be wrong about that.'

'That's pretty good recollection after all this time,' Fiona said thoughtfully. 'How much prompting did it take?'

'Almost none,' Steve said with a hint of bitterness. 'As soon as she was asked about a cyclist, she started nodding and got quite excited. She said she'd tried to tell the policeman who came before, but once he'd established she hadn't seen Blake, he'd lost interest. In our defence, I have to say we didn't get her on the first appeal for witnesses. It was about ten days or so later that she came forward. Her employers had been away the week of the murder and she was nervous about coming to the police without their permission. So by the time she made herself known to us, Blake was already our prime suspect.'

'Not much of a defence,' Kit commented. 'And you have the nerve to get pissed off when I put the occasional dozy detective in my books. So where do you go from here?'

Steve fiddled with his cigar. 'I'm tempted to bring Blake in and ask him to make a witness statement.'

Kit snorted in derision. 'I can imagine the statement you'd get from Blake. I'd lay money that it would contain the words "fuck" and "off".'

Steve threw a mock-punch at Kit's shoulder. 'Don't mince your words, Kit, tell us what you really think.'

Ignoring them, Fiona said slowly, 'You'd have to handle it very carefully. You've taken the public position that you're not actively seeking anyone else in connection with this. If you pull Blake in for questioning, it would be very easy for him to shout harassment since, by your own admission, the investigation is closed. If you defend yourselves by saying the inquiry is still ongoing, then you alert the real killer to the fact that you're looking for him more actively than you ever were.'

'But we'd have to balance that against what Blake might tell us,' Steve argued.

'I think Kit's right. I don't think he'll tell you anything useful,' she said, shaking her head. 'He's got too much to lose if he really did witness the murder.' She counted off the points on her fingers. 'One, he risks prosecution for obstruction of justice for not revealing what he has known all along. Two, he loses the edge he might have if he knows the killer's identity and wants to blackmail him. Three, he loses the power of his secret fantasy. And four, he loses the public protestation of innocence that's already earned him a lot of money from the newspapers and will net him much more in compensation from the Home Office.'

'So if it was up to you, you'd leave him alone,' Steve said baldly.

Fiona raised her eyebrows. 'I didn't say that. I just said I wouldn't question him about the murder.'

Steve smiled. 'On the other hand, if the traffic division know that when he drives through King's Cross at thirty-one miles an hour, they should check he hasn't been drinking . . .'

Kit shook his head, pretending sorrow. 'That would be harassment,' he observed.

'Only if we're clumsy about it. And I intend to keep tabs on him when he does come home.'

Fiona gave a nod of approval. 'It's an outside chance, but he still might lead you straight to a killer.'

Steve's face was grim. 'I've seen slimmer chances pay off. Believe me, if Francis Blake has anything to hide, I'm going to find out what it is.'

Chapter 25

Steve replaced the handset of the phone and made a note on his pad. He'd spoken to the Garda officer running the inquiry into Jane Elias's murder earlier in the day, and he'd hung on to wait and see if the man would get back to him. The guard had promised a response as soon as possible, but had pointed out that Elias's office alone contained hundreds of letters and thousands of sheets of paper. However, he'd already had a team working on it, and he'd eventually called to pass on the information that so far, no letter resembling those received by Kit or Georgia or their colleagues had been found among Jane Elias's papers.

It wasn't conclusive, of course. She could have thrown it straight in the bin or burned it on the open fire in her drawing room. But no letter had been found with the body nor had the Garda had any written communication from a purported killer. There was nothing to indicate any connection between the letter-writer and Jane Elias's murderer. Steve was glad he had good news for someone; he wished someone had the same for him.

He yawned and stretched his arms out so wide his shoulders cracked. He was far from the only officer still at his desk in New Scotland Yard at nine in the evening. Most of those remaining not actually on night shift, however, were well below the rank of detective superintendent. But then, he reminded himself with regret unmixed with self-pity, most of them had families to go home to. He'd accepted long ago that he would probably never reach that happy position. The ferocity of his undeclared – because he knew it to be unreciprocated – love for Fiona Cameron had put him involuntarily out of the running in the crucial years of his twenties when all his friends had been settling down first time around.

He'd sublimated his unrequited passion in his work and when one day he had realized that the strong bond of friendship that locked him to Fiona was, after all, enough, he had understood that he had arranged his life in such a way that he would never again have time, energy or opportunity to form the sort of relationship that would satisfy him. But lately, he had begun to wonder.

So many of those friends who had become established couples a dozen or more years ago were single again. Few of them seemed to remain that way for too long. Maybe at thirty-eight, it wasn't too late. Perhaps the time had come when he could plug into a network of single life again. Certainly, if Francis Blake persisted in his declared intent to sue the Home Office, it wasn't beyond the bounds of possibility that a high-profile scapegoat would have to be found. The debacle of the sting could still mean that he'd end up with lots more time on his hands. He knew if his bosses decided he should be the one to shoulder the blame publicly, he risked at the very least being sidelined, shunted into areas where his public profile would be nonexistent, the professional challenges minimal. Without a demanding job, he would have time to fill. Time not to kill, but to grow.

On the other hand, he might yet find the key to unlock the mystery of Susan Blanchard's killer. And while the idea of life with a partner, life perhaps even with children, was a haunting dream, the satisfaction of a job well done was something he craved more actively because he had experienced its intoxication so many times, he knew it could be a reality again and he never grew tired of it.

With a sigh, Steve closed the file on Francis Blake. He'd re-read it a dozen times over the previous week, but he had no niggling sense of having missed something, no gut intuition that told him where the next lead might lie. He wished Fiona's advice hadn't chimed with his own instincts about how Blake would react. At least pushing a suntanned and contemptuous Francis Blake for a witness statement would give him something to attack. But he knew she was right. The only reason he wanted to talk to Blake was the desire to make a man he despised uncomfortable.

Thinking of Fiona in the context of this case set anger burning slow inside him. If only they'd been able to continue working together, he wouldn't be in this mess now. The thought stirred a buried memory. Steve jumped to his feet and crossed to his filing cabinet. Right at the very beginning of the case, Fiona had drafted a bare-bones profile with some suggested avenues of inquiry. In the general chaos that had supervened, Steve had entirely forgotten about its existence until she had mentioned it in passing the previous evening when they'd been talking about the cyclist.

His fingers flurried through the folders as he tried to remember where he'd put it. On the second pass, he found what he was looking for. 'FC prelim' was scrawled in black marker pen on the top right-hand corner of a pale manila file. Steve smiled and pulled it out. It was painfully slender, which was why he'd missed it the first time. He flicked it open and started to read Fiona's precise and familiar prose. As usual, she had not identified the case by name, not entirely trusting the security of her university computer.

Case SP/35/FC

The victim and the crime scene were both categorizable as low risk. She was a 'respectable' married woman, accompanied by her twin children, with no evidence of criminal involvement by anyone in her immediate circle. The crime scene is a public place, reasonably populated by passers-by with little to divert their attention from what is going on in their immediate vicinity. The crime took place in broad daylight, yards from a well-used thoroughfare. Hampstead Heath is generally regarded as one of the safer park spaces by day in the capital, relatively well-policed and lacking a reputation for either serious assaults or drug-related activities.

This means conversely that the perpetrator took a high level of risk to carry out his crime. This indicates either a relatively high level of maturity and sophistication or a reckless disregard for the consequences of his action.

If however we examine the nature of the crime itself, it is clear that this was not an opportunistic attack born of spur-of-the-moment rashness. The weapon used in the crime – a long-bladed knife – must have been brought by the perpetrator to the scene; the attack took place in one of the few easily accessible yet largely invisible areas of the Heath, indicating a degree of premeditation; and it is possible, given witness statement 1276/98/STP, that he came equipped with the means of his escape, viz a bicycle. I would therefore incline to the view that we are looking for a man who has a high degree of confidence in his abilities.

Such criminal maturity comes only with experience. While he may not have killed before, there is a high probability that he has previously committed serious sexual attacks. If he has a criminal record, the likelihood is that it will have begun with incidences of voyeurism and possibly flashing, escalating through minor sexual assault to rape. However, it is entirely possible that he has avoided establishing an arrest and conviction record.

I would therefore recommend a thorough trawl of both solved and unsolved rapes and serious sexual assaults over the last five years in an attempt to establish crime linkage and develop a suspect. The key factors to look for are:

1. *Offences that have occurred out of doors – research indicates that rapists tend either to commit their offences indoors or in the open, seldom mixing the two.*
2. *Most rapists tend to offend against members of the same ethnic group, although this is not invariable. Since the victim here is white and blonde, the chances are high that his previous victims share similar characteristics.*
3. *He was not disconcerted by the presence of small children. It may even be that this provides an element of his satisfaction. Therefore any incidents which include the element of child witnesses and which fit the above patterns are even more likely to be among his previous crimes.*
4. *Offences where the perpetrator has made his escape on a bicycle. If this has worked well for him in the past, he is more likely to have repeated it.*
5. *Offences where the offender has used or has threatened to use a knife. It is clear that he must have brought the knife to the Heath with him, so it is likely that it forms part of his previous activities.*

With the results of such a trawl, it may be possible to establish escalation through crime linkage and thus to develop a geographical profile that could lead to the identification of a valid suspect.

As always, he thought, Fiona was succinct and to the point. And, as she had generously failed to remind him the previous evening, she had picked up on the possible significance of the bicycle straightaway. At the end of the formal report, she had attached a Post-it note in her small, neat writing. *I know,* it read, *that you have a couple of witnesses describing a running man near the scene of the crime. I don't think this is your killer. Whoever committed this murder was together enough to make his escape in a much less attention-grabbing way. If I had to stick my neck out, I'd say the mysterious cyclist – who hasn't, as far as I can see from the statements, come forward to admit being on the Heath at the crucial time – is a far more likely suspect. Let's talk soon. F.*

Although the case of Susan Blanchard's murder was officially closed, Steve had managed to shame his boss into allowing him a small staff to continue the inquiry that none of them would publicly admit to until and unless it produced a culprit who could credibly replace Francis Blake in the eyes of the public as well as the Crown Prosecution Service. He had one detective sergeant and two detective constables assigned full-time under his command, as well as a pool of goodwill among most of the officers who had worked with him on the original inquiry.

Mentally reviewing what the members of his team were doing, he decided to use DC Joanne Gibb for the records trawl. Joanne was a meticulous researcher and she was also skilled in developing relationships with officers both in other divisions and outside the Met. He'd seen her soothe and cajole hostile case officers in other forces, making them forget their resentment at having the big boots of the Met trampling over their patches. Nobody would be more dogged in tracking down cases with similar MOs to those suggested by Fiona; nobody would be better at extracting details from investigating officers.

Steve carefully copied out the parameters Fiona had laid

down and left a note for Joanne to start on the job first thing in the morning. He stretched luxuriously, both relieved and energized by having put something positive in train. Tonight, he might actually sleep properly, instead of the ragged hours of tossing and turning that had been his recent lot.

He unfolded his long lean body from the chair and took his jacket off the hanger depending from the hook he'd superglued to the side of the filing cabinet immediately behind his desk. Functional, not aesthetic, like so much of his life, as Fiona had pointed out more than once from the earliest days of their friendship. Perhaps if he'd had Kit's style, things might have worked out otherwise, he mused as he patted his pocket to check he had his keys. Pointless to speculate, he decided. To have had Kit's style, he would have had to be a different man. And a different man might not have reaped the rewards of a constant friendship with Fiona as he had done.

Two strides away from the door, the phone on his desk rang. Steve dithered briefly, then turned back. 'Steve Preston,' he said.

'Superintendent Preston? It's Sergeant Wilson on the duty desk here. We've just had a fax from the Spanish Police. Francis Blake's booked on a flight tomorrow morning from Alicante to Stansted. He's due to land at eleven-forty-five. I thought you'd want to know as soon as possible.'

'Thanks, Sergeant. Do we have the flight details?'

'It's all on the fax. I'll get someone to bring it up.'

'Don't bother, I'll pick it up on my way out.' Steve replaced the phone and allowed himself to smile. Now there would be two lines of inquiry running tomorrow. While Joanne searched for the tracks of a killer, Detective Sergeant John Robson and Detective Constable Neil McCartney would be on the tail of someone who might lead them to the same man.

Definitely a turn for the better, Steve thought, his shoulders noticeably squarer as he headed for the door for the second time.

iii

This was the only place that mattered. This was the sacred place, the sacrificial grove where morality became concrete. Everything in it was chosen. Nothing was accidental except for the shape of the room, about which he could do nothing. There had been a window, but he had covered it with a sheet of plywood then carefully plastered over it so that the wall was entirely smooth. Only the door interrupted the perfect balance of the room. That, however, was acceptable. It rendered the room symmetrical in the way that the human body was symmetrical about the axis of the spine.

He had papered the walls with lining paper. The wallpaper he wanted had been discontinued years ago, but that was of no consequence. He'd made a stencil of the stylized leaf pattern that had run down it in stripes, had paint specially mixed to replicate the exact hues of green he remembered, and meticulously made a perfect copy. Then he'd covered it in a light coat of colourless yacht varnish, so that any splashes or smudges could be readily cleaned off without damage. That, he felt, was one improvement he could comfortably make.

The floor had been easy. He'd bought the old parquet tiles from an architectural salvage yard. Maple, the man had told him. From the offices of an old woollen mill down Exeter way. It had taken a few evenings to lay them in the closest possible approximation to the remembered arrangement, but it had been a task more boring than truly challenging.

The light fitting had come from a junk shop out on the Taunton road. It had been the very first thing he'd bought, the item that had in fact given him the idea for this magical place. It could have been the original, so closely did its three frosted bowls match his memory. As he gazed at it in wonder in the dingy shop, it came to him that he could make the place live again, reassemble it just as it had been, and make of it a temple to the dark desires it had bred in him.

The furniture was simple. A plain pine table, though the scars on this surface were different from the ones he recalled. Four balloon-backed pine chairs, worn dark along the top from the regular wear of hands pulling them out and pushing them in. A small card table covered in faded green baize, where the tools of his vocation were arrayed, their shining steel glittering in the lamplight. Surgical dissection knives, a butcher's cleaver, a small handsaw and an oilstone to make sure they were always laser-sharp. Beneath the table was a stack of polystyrene meat trays of various sizes and an industrial-sized roll of clingfilm.

The killing took place elsewhere, of course. It didn't matter where. That was irrelevant to the meaning of the ritual. The method was always the same. Strangulation by ligature was the technical term, he knew that. More reliable than hands, which could slip and slither on skin slick with the sweat of fear. The crucial reason for this choice of means was that it did least traumatic damage to the body. Stabbing and gunshot wounds created such havoc, destroying the perfection he craved.

Then came the cleansing. Naked to match his sacrifice, he lowered the stripped body into the warm water and opened the veins to allow as much blood as possible to seep out, to prevent the ugly stains of lividity from spoiling the appearance of his oblation. Then he would drain the bath and refill it. The body would be carefully purified with unscented soap, the nails scrubbed, the effluents of sudden death washed away, the body purged of every defilement.

Finally, he could set about his task. Once the process had begun, he could afford to waste no time. Rigor would start within five or six hours of death, making his job both more difficult and less precise. The body, laid out on the table, pale as a statue, was his votive offering to the strange gods of obsession that he had learned must be placated all those years ago.

First, the head. He sliced through the sinews and complex structures of the throat and neck with a blade so fine that it left a trace no thicker than a pencil line when he removed the knife to exchange it for a cleaver to separate the skull from the first vertebra. He put the head to one side for later attention. Then he made a Y-incision like a pathologist. He peeled the epidermis back, carefully rolling the body so he could remove the skin from neck to toe, stripping it off like a wetsuit till he had revealed a cadaver that resembled an anatomy illustration. The shucked skin went into a bucket at his feet.

Then he plunged his hands into the still-warm mass of the abdominal cavity, gently lifting the intestines and internal organs clear before slicing them free and placing them in a pile to one side. Next he broke the diaphragm and carefully removed the heart and lungs, putting them symmetrically on the other side of the torso.

He moved down to the wrists. He severed both neatly, the disarticulation causing him no problem. His career in the butchery trade had provided him with all the basic skills, which he'd refined to an art, he confidently believed. Never had the human body been so perfectly dissected nor so reverently.

The feet were next. The elbows and knees succeeded them, followed by the separation of the remaining upper limbs at hips and shoulders. Now he was working swiftly and surely, jointing the torso with the efficient movements of an expert at home in his specialism. Time flew by as his hands worked methodically, until all that remained was a mound of jointed meat, the head facing outwards at the top of the table.

Now, his excitement was at a peak, his heart pounding and his mouth dry. With a soft moan, he took his penis in his blood-slicked hands and carefully slid it into the open mouth that sat like a totem in front of him. Holding the head by the hair, he thrust into the slack-jawed orifice, his body shuddering with his ecstasy.

All passion spent, he stood with his fists on the table, leaning forward and breathing as heavily as a marathon runner at the finishing tape. The sacrament was over. Nothing remained but the disposal.

For most killers, that would have presented insurmountable problems. If Dennis Nilsen had managed to develop a more practical way of getting rid of his victims, he would probably have been reducing the homeless statistics of London for years.

But for a man who owned a wholesale butchery

company, it was a simple matter. He possessed dozens of freezers filled with packs of meat. Even if anyone ever made it through the padlocks of the freezer that his staff knew was his own private cache, they would see nothing more suspicious than dozens of freezer packs. Human flesh, fortunately, looked much like any other kind once it was slaughtered.

Chapter 26

Dusk on Hampstead Heath had never lost its magic for Fiona, especially at this time of year. By early October after a hot summer, full daylight exposed the dust dulling the turning leaves, the faded tones of the grass, the parched grey of the earth. But as the sky purpled in a hazy sunset, the colours resumed their depth and richness, providing maximum contrast with the city spread out below her.

Unlike the Heath, the London streets lost all definition in the gathering twilight. The dying sun dazzled off occasional windows in the taller office buildings, flashes of fire studding the amorphous grey mass like synapses sparking in a brain. It wasn't the wild and varied landscape of the Derbyshire hills, not by any stretch of her imagination, but it reminded her that such places not only existed but were part of her mental map, there to be regained at need. It was a refreshment, of sorts. In the week since she'd read the news of Jane Elias's death, Fiona had made her way to the Heath at least once a day. Now she settled on a bench at the top of Parliament Hill, content to do nothing more demanding than people-watching for a while.

Some of the passers-by were familiar from her walks on the Heath; dog-walkers; joggers; a gaggle of skate-boarding boys about to broach their teens; two elderly women from her own street who strode briskly past with a nod of acknowledgement;

the bookshop assistant practising her race-walking. Others she'd never seen before. Some were obvious locals, often deep in conversation with partners or children, feet automatic at every junction on the path. Some were obvious tourists, clutching maps and frowning over their struggles to identify landmarks in the dim vista below. Some refused to fit neatly into any category, their pace anywhere between an aimless stroll and an intent hike.

Which category had Susan Blanchard's killer fallen into, Fiona wondered? Suddenly alert, she asked herself what had prompted that thought. It wasn't as if she hadn't visited the Heath regularly since the murder, although she had tended to avoid the path that passed the crime scene. But why had that thought popped into her head now?

Fiona scanned the path in both directions, convinced she had registered someone or something that had subconsciously triggered thoughts of the murder. It couldn't have been the thirty-something couple, the man with their baby strapped to his chest. Nor the middle-aged man with his black Labrador. Nor the two roller-blading teenage girls giggling over some anecdote. Puzzled, she looked around.

He was hunkered down in a hollow about fifty yards away, perhaps twenty feet from the path. At first glance, he looked like a jogger. Lightweight sweat pants and a T-shirt, training shoes. But he didn't appear to be breathing hard, as someone who had toiled up the slope would inevitably be. Nor was he staring out at the view. No, he was watching the two girls on the roller blades as they swooped in circles round a wide junction of paths, their voices shrieking laughter and insults at each other.

When the girls moved off, their bodies hidden from his line of sight by a clump of bushes, he stood up, gazing back along the path to see who else was coming. For a few minutes, no one seemed to capture his attention. Then a pair of adolescents strolled into view, arms entwined, the girl with her head on the boy's chest. At once, the man's pose became more alert. His hands thrust into his pockets and he dropped back into his crouch.

Fiona watched the boy and girl out of sight, then got to her feet and took several paces in the direction of the man. She ostentatiously stared across at him and took out her mobile phone. As soon as he realized what she was doing, he straightened up and started running down the slope towards a path that wound through dense shrubbery.

Fiona put her phone away. She'd had no intention of calling the police, but it was enough that he thought she might be going to. What could she have reported, after all? A man who appeared to have an interest in watching teenage girls. He had done nothing threatening, nothing particularly out of the ordinary, nothing that couldn't be explained in tones of outraged protest. Even his sudden departure could be easily justified; he'd paused in his run and was sufficiently rested to continue.

Innocuous though his behaviour could be made to sound, it had been enough to set Fiona's antennae jangling. It wasn't that she suspected the strange man of being anything more than a rather timid voyeur. But it reminded her that Susan Blanchard's killer must have scouted his killing zone thoroughly before he had struck. He would have walked the ground, not cycled it, taking in every detail of landscape, plotting his escape routes, selecting his victim. He might have been sophisticated enough to disguise his interests entirely, but Fiona doubted it.

She wondered where he was this evening. The urge to kill again would be strong in him, she reckoned. Where would he be walking now? What reconnaissance would he be making? How would he choose his next location? Would he come back to the Heath? Or would he try another nearby site? Highgate Cemetery? Alexandra Palace? Or did he know his city well enough to move further afield? Where were the borders of his mental map? She knew the limits imposed by his psychology; they were evident in his actions. But where did his geographical boundaries lie?

Questions she couldn't answer crowded into her head, shattering the peace she had come to the Heath to find after a trying day at work. Time to walk back home through streets of substantial houses with their grubby stucco and grimy yellow London brickwork turned gloomy by the dirty orange of sodium streetlights. Time to enjoy her own voyeuristic pleasure by glancing in at the lit windows she would pass, savouring glimpses of people's lives played out in brief snatches caught in her peripheral vision. And of course, the feeling of superiority she couldn't stifle when she noted some particularly tasteless interior.

'You should get a life, you sad girl,' she muttered as she spotted a newly decorated living room that incorporated three clashing wallpaper patterns, and made a mental note to share it with Kit later.

As she pushed open the front door, the phone began to ring. Fiona hurried through to the kitchen and grabbed it on the fourth ring. 'Hello?' she said.

'Dr Cameron?' The voice had the tinny echo that mobile phones sometimes produce.

'Is that Major Berrocal?' Fiona asked uncertainly.

'*Si*. I am sorry to trouble you at home, but we have some developments here I thought you would want to know.'

'No, that's fine, it's no trouble. Have you found Delgado?' As she spoke, Fiona shrugged out of her jacket and reached for the pad and pen kept by the phone.

'Not exactly. But we have found where we think he has been hiding out.'

'That sounds like progress.'

'*Si*. And it is thanks to your idea.'

'He was living in a mausoleum? . . . A tomb?' Fiona felt a quickening of gratified pride.

'Not exactly, no. There is a big cemetery to the north of the city that fitted the suggestion you made, so we persuaded the local police to make a search of it. There were no signs that any of the tombs had been opened, so the officers decided we were truly crazy and Delgado was not to be found there. But one of my officers, he is what my wife calls a bulldog, and he went back there today.'

'And he found something?' Fiona urged.

'*Si*. There is a small shed that used to be used by the workmen to store their tools. It has been empty for some years now, but my officer discovered that the boards nailed over the window had been loosened. He went inside and he found what we think is Delgado's camp. There was food, water, a sleeping bag and some clothes. We compared fingerprints we found with the ones on Delgado's possessions in the apartment, and the match was perfect.'

'So, you know he's been there.'

'*Si*. I have men watching the cemetery now, but I fear he will not return. The fruit in the shed was starting to rot, and so I think he must have seen the local police searching and now he will not go back there.'

'What a disappointment for you,' Fiona said. 'So near, and yet so far.'

'Close, but no cigar, huh? I think he will be dangerous on the run, no?'

Fiona thought for a brief moment. 'I don't think he'll panic. So far, his reactions have been quite controlled. He knows the city and the surrounding area well. He probably has a fallback position in mind.'

Berrocal grunted noncommittally. 'What I am afraid of is that he will feel cornered and he will decide to go out in a blaze of glory. Something spectacular. He has nothing to lose now. He knows we know he is the killer. Maybe the best he can hope for is to make his point in one final dramatic way.'

'You're thinking a spree killing? A massacre?' Fiona asked.

'It's what I fear,' Berrocal acknowledged.

Fiona sighed. 'I can't think offhand of another case where a serial killer has moved on to a spree killing. But then, most serial killings are primarily sexual homicides, and I've felt from the start that these murders stemmed from a different motive. I honestly don't know what to say, Major. I have to say your reading of the situation seems plausible to me.'

There was a long pause between them. Then Berrocal said, 'I will make sure the city is on full alert. It's not a big place. We should be able to find him.'

Whistling in the dark, Fiona thought. Everyone who deals with serial offenders ends up doing it. 'Sit down with someone who has an intimate knowledge of Toledan history,' she advised. 'Ask them about sites in the city connected with violent death. If he's going to strike again, either with a single murder or a spree, that's what he'll focus on. And that's probably where you'll catch him.'

'Thank you for the advice.'

'You're welcome. I'm sure you must have worked it out for yourself, though. Let me know how you go on.'

'Of course. Good night, Doctor.'

'Good night, Major. And good luck.' As Fiona replaced the phone with heavy heart, she heard the click of the front door opening. 'Kit?' she called, surprised.

The door closed and her lover's familiar voice replied, 'Hi, babe, I'm home.'

He walked into the kitchen and enveloped her in the suffocating hug she had come to find comfort in. Fiona tilted her head back to kiss him, her hazel eyes bright with pleasure. 'I wasn't expecting you till late. I thought you were all going out for supper with Georgia after her event.'

Kit let her go and crossed to the fridge. 'That was the plan. Only, no show without Punch.'

'What? Georgia decided she needed her beauty sleep more than a night of drunken revelry with reprobate crime writers?' Fiona teased, taking down a couple of glasses for the wine Kit was opening.

'Who knows? She didn't show.'

'You mean she cancelled?' Fiona's incredulity was obvious. The notion of publicity-hungry Georgia Lester missing the chance of delivering a lecture at the British Film Institute was almost beyond belief.

'No. I mean she didn't show. No message, no word to the BFI or to her publicist. No answer from her home phone or her mobile, according to said publicist.' Kit drew the cork and poured the wine.

'So what happened?'

'Nothing much. The audience hung around like lemons for about half an hour then the guy who was supposed to be introducing her got up and said that Ms Lester was indisposed and they could obtain a refund from the box office. We all went for a quick drink then I came home.'

'So, a mystery, then,' Fiona said lightly. 'What's the theory, Sherlock?'

'The drinking team ended up with two schools of thought.' Kit settled into a chair and prepared for narrative. 'The charitable one goes like this. Georgia has a cottage down in Dorset where she goes allegedly to write, but in reality, I happen to know, to shag senseless the latest Italian waiter she's got her claws into. Well away from Anthony, the boring but doting husband, right? So, there she is, having her wicked way with Super Mario, she loses track of the time and ends up leaving at the last minute, only to run out of petrol miles from anywhere. And the battery on her phone has died.'

'That's the charitable version?'

'Come on, Fiona, you know Georgia. Most people who only see the public face find it hard to say much about her that doesn't involve a certain degree of bitching.'

'I can't wait for the uncharitable alternative,' Fiona murmured.

'That goes like this. After Drew's murder, Georgia was bleating that she wanted Carnegie House to provide her with bodyguards. She took the line that she was a high-profile Queen of Crime who needed protection from the nutters out there, and that was the duty of her publisher. Of course, several of my colleagues thought it was just a way of getting Carnegie to pimp for her . . .'

'Oh, cruel.'

'But possibly true. Anyway, as you know, she was threatening that she wasn't going to tour with the new book if they didn't give her some protection with a bit more muscle than a publicist and a sales rep. And of course, this lecture was technically the first event of the tour. So several of my colleagues reckon that Georgia decided to do a no-show to put the frighteners on her publishers. After all, it's not like the BFI is a bookshop. Not turning up there would hit the headlines without costing her too many sales,' he added cynically.

'The intention being that tomorrow morning her publishers will be calling her with promises of a pair of thugs to escort her round the bookshops of Britain?' Fiona asked, trying not to sound as bemused as she felt.

'Yup. She'll be ringing them up doing the pitiful, "Poor little me, I was so terrified that when it came to it, all I wanted to do was run away and hide." Not to mention how heartbroken she is to have let down her legion of devoted fans. So, if Carnegie House really value their top-selling crime author, they will of course be laying on a bulletproof limo and a team of minders for her . . .'

'Which in turn will generate even more publicity.'

'A point which everyone is sure never crossed Georgia's mind,' Kit said with affectionate sarcasm.

'That really is the most disgustingly cynical analysis I have heard in a very long time. You guys should be ashamed of yourselves.'

Kit gave a grim smile. 'A fiver hopes they're right. Because what they don't know is that Georgia's had a death threat. And that Georgia really did think she might be on a killer's hit list.'

'You didn't tell them?'

'What would have been the point? Someone would have blabbed. When I started asking around to see who else had had letters, I was careful not to mention Georgia by name. With her name in the frame, somebody would have sold the story to one of the newspaper diary columns. So everybody was being very entertaining at Georgia's expense this evening.'

'And you? Knowing what you know, what do *you* think?'

Kit ran his hands over his face and his scalp. 'There are far worse things that could have happened to Georgia. I just hope everybody's right. That she's at the wind-up. Because if she's not, then I think it's about time I started to get seriously scared.'

Chapter 27

'What did I tell you?' Kit demanded, brandishing the *Guardian* under Fiona's nose at breakfast two days later. 'If it says it in The Loafer, it must be true.' He pointed to the item in the literary gossip column and read, '"The word on the mean streets is that crime writer Georgia Lester has gone to ground in fear of her life. Bestseller Lester failed to turn up for a prestigious lecture at the British Film Institute on contemporary *noir* films-of-books and has not been heard from since.

'"Lester has apparently fallen out with publishers Carnegie House over their failure to provide her with minders on her upcoming book tour to promote her latest psychological thriller, *Terminal Identity*. Her demand followed hot on the heels of the shocking murder of Edinburgh-based wunder-kind Drew Shand last month, which police believe may be stalker-related, and the equally bizarre murder of American recluse Jane Elias near her Irish estate, a supposed gangland killing connected to her lover, an undercover drugs cop.

'"Now open season has apparently been declared on crime writers, a friend claimed that Lester was outraged by what she saw as a lack of concern for her welfare and reportedly said she'd make Carnegie pay for it. Whether in pain or in cash wasn't clear.

'"That Lester, noted for her willingness to accommodate

the media, has turned her back on a major platform to express her views will surely have sent a strong message to her publishers that she isn't going to be fobbed off, however paranoid her demands." Well, that's what the world's saying. So maybe I should stop worrying?'

Fiona shook her head. 'I don't think so. Not until you hear it from Georgia herself. What's in The Loafer was probably leaked by one of your drinking cronies from the other night.' She was more worried than she was willing to acknowledge, however, so she searched for something more reassuring. All she could come up with was the line she'd been using ever since she'd seen Georgia's death threat. 'Whatever is going on, I don't think the person who wrote your letter is responsible. Of course, it makes sense to be cautious. But I don't think you should be living in fear.'

Kit grumbled indistinctly through a mouthful of Weetabix. The silence that followed was broken only by the sounds of breakfast being consumed and the turning of pages as they both read their sections of the paper.

Suddenly, Fiona rallied. This was far better reassurance than any platitude she could come out with. 'Now, that is what I call much more interesting than the spreading of unsubstantiated rumour,' Fiona said, folding the news section over and passing it to Kit.

Suspect held in
Elias murder

A man has been arrested in connection with the brutal murder of American thriller writer Jane Elias, the Garda Siochana in County Wicklow have confirmed.

The suspect is John Patrick Regan, a 35-year-old house builder from Kildenny, a small town fifteen miles from Ms Elias's estate on the shores of Lough Killargan.

Ms Elias was found dead on a country road ten days ago. She was last seen by security guards at her estate leaving her private dock in a 21ft yacht twelve hours earlier.

Regan is believed to be a cousin and business associate of Thomas Donaghy, who is currently awaiting trial on charges of heroin smuggling. He was arrested during a major operation by the Garda last year, which was the result of an undercover sting operation and led to the confiscation of heroin with a street value of £1.2m.

Pierce Finnegan, the Garda officer responsible for the operation, is believed to have been Jane Elias's lover and there was speculation last night that her murder was intended to discourage Finnegan from giving evidence when the case against Donaghy and his co-accused comes to court next month.

A Garda spokesman said, 'We have a suspect in custody who is being questioned about the death of Jane Elias. At this moment, no charges have been laid.'

Jane Elias's death shocked the quiet Irish community where the reclusive writer was highly respected.

cont. p3

Kit scanned the newsprint quickly then looked up at Fiona with a half-smile. 'I suppose that counts as good news,' he said.

'As good as it gets in a murder inquiry, I think.'

He shook his head, his mouth pursing in bitterness. 'What a stupid bloody reason to die, though. I mean, to be killed not for anything you are or anything you've done. To be murdered because of the person you love.'

'It happens all the time when you think about it,' Fiona said. 'Women murdered by ex-husbands who can't accept they've chosen someone else to be with. People murdered because the person they sleep with is the wrong religion or the wrong colour. Or the wrong gender.'

'No, that's different. There, you've got an element of choice. At some level it's a conscious decision, you know what you're getting into. But you can't know when you get involved with someone in law enforcement that it's going to rebound on you like that.'

Fiona shook her head. 'It *is* the same thing. It's all very well, you saying there's an element of choice in the examples I cited. But you know it's not entirely true. If we lived in Northern Ireland and I was a Protestant vicar and you were a high-ranking Republican, could you have walked away from loving me because it might cost either of us our lives?'

Kit glared at her across the table. 'Don't be bloody silly. Of course I couldn't have.'

'Well, then. I don't suppose Jane Elias was blind to the potential risks of loving Pierce Finnegan. She was far too smart for that. And I'd guess that she accepted the risk because taking a chance on being with him was infinitely preferable to playing safe and doing without him. Just as it must have crossed your mind that living with a woman who has helped the police to put away serial offenders has its attendant risks,' Fiona added, softening her voice to take the challenge out of her words.

'I won't pretend I haven't had my moments. Thing is, Fiona, I never once thought that your job might put me on the line. It's always been you I've been worried for. I suppose I was projecting what I feel on to Jane. I reckon she must have had her sleepless nights over Pierce, but maybe, like me, she never thought she'd be the one catching the rebound.' He spread his hands wide, smiling at her.

Fiona reached across the table for his hand. He met her halfway. 'I love you, you know,' she said.

'By heck, that's a bit soft for the breakfast table,' he teased.

'Oh please, don't come the hard man of British *noir* with me,' Fiona protested. 'You're forgetting, I know the truth.'

'You could ruin my reputation with a word,' he said ruefully.

'So make a fresh pot of tea and my lips will remain sealed.' She retrieved the paper and shook it out. 'There is one very good thing about this arrest.'

'What's that?'

'It means there's no connection between the murder of Jane Elias and the murder of Drew Shand. So we can all stop worrying about a serial killer stalking the world's best thriller writers,' Fiona pointed out.

The water rushed noisily into the kettle, drowning Kit's muttered reply.

'What?' Fiona asked.

Kit turned to face her. 'I said, always supposing the Irish cops have got it right.'

Fiona shook her head, laughing. 'What is it with you? You *want* to feel like your life's under threat? You getting into method writing?'

This time, there was no deprecating smile. 'No. I don't want to live my life looking over my shoulder. But you have to admit, it wouldn't be the first time the cops have arrested the wrong person.'

'But there's no reason to suppose they have in this case.'

Kit shrugged. 'There's no reason to suppose they haven't.'

Fiona frowned. 'It's not like you to be the pessimist in this kitchen.'

'I'd call it realism, not pessimism.' Kit's tone indicated he wouldn't readily be persuaded otherwise.

Fiona pushed back her chair. 'Fine,' she said calmly. 'Leave it with me.'

Jane Elias Arrest – Latest Breaking News

You can always rely on the cops for the obvious line of inquiry. And so John Patrick Regan is behind bars tonight, accused of a crime that has shocked the bestseller buyers of Middle America.

Readers of this site will remember we broke exclusively the identity of Elias's long-term lover, Garda Siochana undercover cop Pierce Finnegan. And since law enforcement officers scan this site as avidly as our most devoted fans, they decided they'd better make a trawl through Finnegan's recent cases.

And bingo! They hit on Tommy Donaghy and his team of major-league drug runners. Donaghy and three of his lieutenants are currently awaiting trial on charges of heroin smuggling, thanks in no small part to Finnegan's talents at mounting an undercover sting. Although Donaghy is based north of Dublin, the Garda did a trawl of his known associates and came up with his cousin, John Regan, who lives a mere fifteen miles from Elias's estate in the Wicklow Hills. And, by strange coincidence, Regan's building firm did some of the restoration work on the Georgian mansion where Elias lived.

Regan is a small-time jobbing builder, divorced with two kids, who lives in the sleepy Irish town of Kildenny. He also owns a motor launch and on the afternoon Elias disappeared, he was out fishing. All on his ownsome. So he's a man with means, motive and opportunity and not an alibi in sight. Looks good to the Garda, especially since they have no other leads to speak of.

It's unfortunate for them that Regan has no criminal record. Word is that so far forensics have come up blank, but they're still looking. Expect charges before bedtime. Or sooner, if Regan decides to confess. Which, given the shoot-themselves-in-the-foot tendencies of the Irish, is probably pretty much a given. Let's just hope for John Regan's sake that Pierce Finnegan isn't in charge of the interrogation.

REMEMBER YOU READ IT FIRST ON
MURDER BEHIND THE HEADLINES

Fiona stood up and waited impatiently for the printer to finish. She grabbed the sheet of paper from the tray and ran down the three flights of stairs to Kit's office. She knew he'd abandoned the kitchen for the womb of his desk; Classic FM on the radio had given way to Gomez cheerfully singing that there weren't enough hours in a day. She knew the feeling.

Kit was staring gloomily at the screen, reading through the last pages he'd written. Fiona dropped the paper on the keyboard in front of him. He ran a hand over his smooth scalp as he read, massaging the soft skin into ridges and furrows. 'Sounds a bit flip to me,' he said dubiously.

'That's just the tone they use. Believe me, if there were good reasons for thinking this arrest isn't kosher, they'd be shouting it from the rooftops, not dropping vague hints. I've told you; they pride themselves on getting the stuff that nobody else knows or is willing to publish. And like most of us, they like to cover their backs just in case they've got it wrong. Trust me, I'm a doctor . . .' Fiona leaned over and kissed the tender skin where earlobe joined jawline.

Kit swivelled in his chair and pulled her into his arms. Now, there was nothing half-hearted about his smile. 'Thank you,' he said. 'You've put my mind at rest.'

'Good. Does that mean we get to go out and play like normal people do on a Saturday?'

'You want to be normal? What's brought that on?'

'I thought we could maybe give it a whirl, see what we've been missing all these years?'

'All right. Just this once. But only if we get to come home and be seriously abnormal later.'

'I'll hold you to that.'

He grinned. 'I can hardly wait.'

Extract from **Decoding of Exhibit P13/4599**

Gznqx uqhmn xq. Ftqkh qmddq efqpe ayqna pkrad vmzqq xumee ygdpd q. Mooad puzsf aitmf udqmp.

Unbelievable. They've arrested somebody for Jane Elias's murder. According to what I read, Elias was sleeping with an Irish cop who went undercover to put away some serious drug dealers last year. And they reckon this was a revenge killing. Well, they're right about that, at least!

They're mad, those Paddies. Gangland executioners don't go to such elaborate lengths to take somebody out, but I suppose the upside is that it means my targets won't be on their guard. I was beginning to worry that I might not be able to con Kit Martin if he was on the look-out for somebody after him.

Mind you, I'd expected Georgia Lester to be a bit more

cautious. I'd interfered with her fuel line so her car would break down, and I was right behind, all ready to be the knight of the road. She was standing by the side of her Jag looking helpless when I pulled up behind her. I offered to have a look at it, but she said she was going to call the AA. I whacked her when she bent down to get her mobile. Then I dragged her into the back seat. It took me about five minutes to get her back to her cottage. It's got an outhouse down the bottom of the garden, which I'd settled on. I left her tied up and gagged there while I dumped the Jag. By the time I got back it was well dark. All the better, really.

It's the only one I've done that's given me nightmares. I dream I'm suffocating under a mountain of meat and I can't get free. And then I see her eyes. She'd come round by the time I got back. Her eyes were popping out of her head, like a horse when it gets frightened. I could see the whites all round the irises. It nearly freaked me out. I had to hit her again, which I didn't want to do. But I couldn't face strangling her while she was still conscious.

I really don't like the killing. I like the way I feel afterwards, that sense of power that floods through me when I think how well I'm getting my own back. I wish there was an easier way of doing it. But I've got to stick to the plan.

I wonder how long it will take them to work it out this time?

Chapter 28

Joanne Gibb remembered a doctor friend once talking about the abbreviations the medical profession scribble on notes. Not the ones about blood pressure and pulse rate – the ones like FLK for 'Funny Looking Kid'. What came to mind that Monday morning was NFRH – 'Normal For Round Here'. Working serious cases in CID produced similar effects in every dedicated officer. Pale skin, hair that was lank within an hour of showering, black smudges under the eyes, frown lines across the forehead and around the mouth, shoulders held unnaturally stiff. Yup, definitely NFRH. She scowled at herself in the mirror of the women's toilet. It was cosmetic surgery she needed, not cosmetics.

Given how she'd aged externally in three years working for Steve Preston, she shuddered to think about the condition of her internal organs. She poked her tongue out at her reflection, noting it already had its coating of yellowish fur only an hour after the alarm clock had ended the four hours' unconsciousness she'd managed the previous night. Too much coffee and too little sleep was giving her ulcers, she was convinced of it. The cigarettes were wrecking what remained of her aerobic fitness and she didn't even want to think about what the drink was doing to her liver. Now her boyfriend was muttering about settling down and starting a family. Judging by the state of the rest of her, all she could expect from her reproductive system was a three-headed monkey.

Men, she decided, had it easy. They mostly managed somehow to look attractively wrecked or admirably haunted like Steve Preston, making women want to take them home and mother them. Women, on the other hand, ended up labelled dog-rough, deserted by their men for next year's model. Well, it had been her choice, joining the Met. She could have got a job in a bank or in retail management and hung on to what looks she had for a bit longer. And been bored shitless, she reminded herself as she dragged a brush through her jaw-length brown bob. Maybe if she had her hair cut? Something a bit more lively instead of the heavy curtain that hung lifeless round a face she'd once thought of as heart-shaped.

Joanne closed her eyes and sighed. Enough of this self-pitying vanity. She should remember what was important and take her pride in that, not in what she looked like in the mirror. She stuffed her make-up back in its pouch and then into her bag. Picking up the bundle of folders that represented her weekend's work, she managed to find a spare finger to pull the door open and headed down the corridor to brief the boss.

She found Steve Preston behind his desk with his usual mug of Earl Grey tea, the smoke from the first slim cigar of the day pooling under the low ceiling. 'Morning, Joanne,' he said. He looked to her familiar scrutiny like he'd had about the same amount of sleep as her.

'Boss,' she acknowledged, dumping her files on the edge of his desk and subsiding into the chair opposite him.

'You didn't log off till half past two this morning,' he observed.

Joanne excavated her cigarettes from her bag and lit up. 'I was chasing.'

'Catch anything?'

Joanne waved her hand at the files, trailing a thin ribbon of smoke. 'I concentrated on the Met, the City boys and the Home Counties. I can do a wider trawl if you think it's worth it. You know, it would make this sort of job so much easier if we had some sort of central reporting system for serious offences,' she said with the tired bitterness of those who have to work against inadequate systems.

'It'll come,' Steve said. 'Too late for our sanity, probably, but it'll come. The Bramshill boys are playing around with the Canadian system, VICLAS. It's supposed to be more sophisticated than anything the FBI have got, but it's anybody's guess when they'll actually start using it to benefit field operations, especially the ones as far down the pecking order as this has become. So till then, we're stuck with phone calls and faxes and calling in favours. How did you do?'

'Depressingly well. I can't say it's been fun to be reminded of just how many rapes and serious sexual assaults get reported in any given year. But I think I've dug up some interesting stuff. I've done a digest for you. That's what I was doing at half past two this morning.' Joanne opened the top file and took out two sheets of paper. 'There you go.'

Steve glanced at the carefully collated information. 'Nice job, Joanne. Want to take me through it?'

Joanne grabbed her own copy of the digest and pulled the top file on to her lap. She took a pair of reading glasses out of the breast pocket of her shirt and perched them on her nose. 'How I did it, I asked for cases that matched all five criteria that you asked about,' she began, relishing as she always did the process of report and discussion that frequently stimulated new ideas. 'Then I asked them to include any other cases that matched three or more of the criteria. What I was looking for was cases where the assault took place out of doors, where a knife was involved, where the victim was a young blonde female, where there were child witnesses to some or all of the assault and where the perpetrator may have made his escape by bike.

'To be honest, I didn't expect many hits. But we've got four rapes and two serious sexual assaults that incorporate all five points. All six took place north of the river. The first was reported two and a half years ago, in Stoke Newington. A woman sunbathing in her garden with her baby asleep in its pushchair was assaulted by a man wearing cycling gear who climbed over her garden fence. Her screams alerted a neighbour and her assailant got away.

'The second was in Camden about ten weeks later. A woman was walking along the canal towpath with her three-year-old son when a man jumped out from behind a wall and held a knife to her throat. He told her he was going to rape her, but they were disturbed by a group of students who came along the towpath. He jumped back over the wall and pedalled off on a bike before anyone could stop him.

'The third one was on the top floor of a multistorey car park in Brent. Fifteen weeks later. This time, he raped a woman shopper. She had installed her kid in the car seat and he came up from behind, pushing her down on the seat and raping her at knifepoint. According to the investigating officer, she thought he was wearing a cycle helmet.

'Nearly six months go by before the next reported rape. This time, he moved further west, to Kensal Rise. The victim was taking her new baby for a walk in the cemetery.' Here, Joanne's professional mask slipped and she glanced up at Steve. 'It's not as weird as it sounds,' she said defensively. 'These old Victorian cemeteries can be quite attractive, you know. Especially where there's not much green space around.'

Steve shook his head. 'I never said a word, Joanne. My mate Kit reckons Highgate Cemetery is the best source of inspiration he knows. Of course, he's not a copper . . .'

'Anyway, she was walking the baby in the cemetery when she was jumped by a bloke in lycra shorts and a top, with a cycle helmet and goggles and what looked to her like one of those expensive kitchen knives that are made from one solid piece of metal. She fought back pretty hard and got seventeen stitches in her arm for her pains. She saw him take off afterwards on a mountain bike. It's the best description we've got.'

'IC1 male, between five-ten and six feet, slim build, dark hair, pale complexion,' Steve read wearily. 'Well, that makes half the male members of the Metropolitan Police suspects.'

'Not half of them, boss. I reckon there's not more than ten per cent could make anything like a decent getaway on a bike.'

Steve grimaced at his cigar. 'You're probably right. What's interesting is that the description doesn't fit Francis Blake. He's too short, and I don't think anyone would describe him as slim. He's far too broad in the shoulder. OK, let's hear the rest of it.'

'Number five was a school cleaner in Crouch End. She was last out of the building one Friday night eighteen months ago. He was waiting for her. As she locked up, he came up behind her and held a knife to her throat. He dragged her into some bushes at the edge of the path and raped her. She had no kids with her, but I've included this one because it took place in a primary school playground and he was definitely on a bike. What do you think?'

'It's worth keeping in the cluster for now. And the last one?'

'Now, this one's really interesting. It was only five weeks

before Susan Blanchard's murder. And it was a bit further afield, actually in Hatfield. But it was in a park. A nanny was out with the little boy she looks after, walking in the woodland garden area. She was knocked to the ground, reckons she was actually unconscious for a few minutes. When she came round, she'd been dragged into the bushes and he was raping her. He had a knife at her throat and told her he'd stick her like a pig if she made a sound.'

'Fuck,' Steve swore softly. 'Why didn't we pick up on that when Susan Blanchard was killed?'

Joanne's mouth tightened in a prim line. 'Principally because Hertfordshire didn't tell us about it.'

'Why the hell not? It's not as if we kept the Blanchard murder a secret! It was all over the media. Didn't it occur to them that it might be the same bloke?'

'Apparently not. The reason being that they reckoned one of their own for it. They had an accused rapist out on bail and they thought this was him taking one last bite of the cherry before he went down. As the investigating officer charmingly put it to me,' Joanne added tartly. 'By the time Susan was killed, chummy was inside doing a seven stretch for three rapes, so they didn't bother telling us because it couldn't have been him, could it?' Sarcasm saturated her voice.

'Great.' Steve crushed out the stub of his cigar and sighed. 'Did their rapist admit to the nanny as well, then?'

'Apparently so. But all his other rapes were late-night backstreet jobs, and none of his other victims were blondes. Hertfordshire believed him, but I don't.'

'No, me neither. But I suppose at the time they had no good reason not to, and it cleared the books for them. They're not the only ones who snatch at the easy option.'

Joanne glowered. 'With respect, sir, Blake wasn't the easy option. He was a plausible suspect.'

'That's history, Jo. I'm more interested in the future than the past.' Steve got up and paced restlessly behind the desk. 'And these six cases are all still unsolved?'

'Apart from the Hertfordshire one, yes. He doesn't leave much in the way of evidence. He used a condom. And cycling gear doesn't leave a lot of fibre evidence. What we do have is a few pubic hairs from the Kensal Rise rape, which has given us a DNA profile. But so far there's no match with any of the DNA samples on record.' Joanne closed her file and replaced it with the others. 'There are no viable suspects in any of the outstanding cases. I don't know where we start to look, boss.'

'Me neither. But I know a woman who might.' Steve came to a halt opposite the window and stared unseeingly at the depressing view beyond.

'Dr Cameron?' Joanne asked.

Steve nodded.

'I thought she'd refused to work with the Met again?'

'She did. And she meant it.' He turned back to face her, an ironic smile on his face. 'Hand me down my grovelling shoes.'

'You'll be wanting a flak jacket as well,' Joanne said, remembering Fiona Cameron's icy stare.

'I don't doubt it, Jo. I don't doubt it for one minute.'

Chapter 29

A handful of miles away, Kit Martin was sitting in a greasy spoon, waiting for an HGV driver who should have crossed from Belgium overnight. According to a mutual friend, the trucker could fill Kit in on some of the scams that smugglers were pulling on the cross-Channel routes. The man claimed he was no smuggler himself, but he knew all the wrinkles and for a surprisingly small price, he was prepared to give Kit as much background as he could.

He hadn't mentioned the meeting to Fiona; he knew his source was vouched for, but Fiona might place the trucker in the category of the strangers Kit wasn't supposed to be meeting alone. But he needed the information this contact could provide, and besides, he felt at no risk here. Probably the most dangerous thing in the café was the heart attack on a plate disguised as the King Size All Day Breakfast. And now he'd heard from Steve that the Garda had found no evidence of death threats at Jane Elias's home, he was even less inclined to live like a recluse afraid of his own shadow.

Kit looked at his watch. The man was ten minutes late, but that was no big deal. He'd warned Kit he couldn't be sure when he'd get to their rendezvous. It would depend on the eternally unpredictable traffic on the M25. Kit stirred his mug of tea, rearranging the film on the orangey-brown surface. The two men at the table next to him scattered a handful of coins on the table to pay for their breakfasts and walked out, leaving behind a copy of the *Daily Mail*. Kit reached across and snagged the paper. He ignored the political splash on the front page and flicked forward. The story that caught his eye was the lead on page five.

Missing thriller writer's car found at beauty spot

A car belonging to missing crime writer Georgia Lester has been found abandoned in woods near a popular tourist destination several miles from the bestselling author's country cottage.

Dorset police revealed that the car was spotted by walkers yesterday near Burman's Pond, a local beauty spot near Dorchester.

The car, which was unlocked, contained an overnight bag and a distinctive Moschino jacket, both belonging to Miss Lester.

A police spokesman said, 'There is no sign of a struggle or any indication that Miss Lester met with an accident.

'If she is safe and well, we would urge her to get in touch with her nearest police station as soon as possible.

'If anyone saw Miss Lester or her car prior to Sunday evening, we would also ask them to contact Dorset police.'

He refused to say whether police were regarding Miss Lester's disappearance as suspicious.

Fears have been growing for her safety since she failed to turn up for a lecture she was due to deliver at the British Film Institute on Wednesday evening.

Her husband, Anthony Fitzgerald, said last night, 'I am very worried about Georgia. I spoke to her on Tuesday evening and she told me she was looking forward to the BFI event.

'The first I knew that she had missed her lecture was when I returned home on Wednesday evening to find several urgent messages from the organizers on our answering machine.

'I have been trying to contact her ever since, without success. I did report her missing to the police on Friday morning, but they didn't seem to be taking it very seriously.

'But I know my wife, and I know she would never let her fans down willingly. Something has happened to her, but I have no idea what.'

There has been speculation that Miss Lester has deliberately gone missing. Colleagues have suggested that she was angry with her publishers, Carnegie House, for refusing to supply her with bodyguards for an upcoming book tour.

Miss Lester claimed that following the murder of fellow thriller writer Drew Shand, she was in fear of her life.

A friend said last night, 'We all thought Georgia was overreacting, but she was adamant that her publisher was recklessly putting her at risk.

'When she didn't show up at the BFI, some people reckoned she was trying to punish them. But now we're beginning to wonder if she was right after all.'

The Lady Vanishes – p11

'Oh, shit,' Kit muttered under his breath, hastily turning the pages. What struck him most forcibly was Anthony's reaction. To have reported Georgia missing to the police suggested this was no stunt on Georgia's part. And Kit couldn't quite believe that Georgia would have kept Anthony in the dark, leaving him to worry and fret needlessly. Causing deliberate pain to those she cared about just wasn't part of Georgia's make-up.

Almost the whole of page eleven was taken up with a feature article, illustrated with a large photograph of the instantly recognizable Agatha Christie. Inset into it was a smaller shot of Georgia, looking haughtily glamorous as ever, her artfully blonde hair swept up in a convoluted arrangement on top of her head.

The Lady Vanishes

The mystery surrounding the whereabouts of contemporary Queen of Crime Georgia Lester has strange echoes of another famous disappearing act.

The most distinguished crime writer of them all, Dame Agatha Christie, went missing for eleven days in 1926 before being discovered in a hotel in Harrogate where she had registered under the assumed name of her husband's mistress.

Agatha's disappearance followed a row with her philandering husband Colonel Archibald Christie. He had packed his bags and gone to spend the weekend with his mistress, Nancy Neele.

That evening, leaving their daughter Rosalind asleep in bed, Agatha drove off from her Sunningdale mansion in her grey Morris Cowley. She left a letter for her secretary, saying her engagements should be cancelled and that she was off to Yorkshire.

But she also posted a letter to the Deputy

Chief Constable of Surrey, claiming she feared for her life and asking for his help.

Her car was found abandoned next morning. Like Georgia Lester's Jaguar, Agatha's Morris was found near a local beauty spot, Silent Pool. Inside the car was Agatha's fur coat and a small suitcase containing three dresses, two pairs of shoes and her expired driving licence.

The newspapers of the time fell upon the story, speculating on whether the missing mystery writer had been murdered or committed suicide.

This newspaper even offered a £100 reward for information leading to her discovery. Suspicion naturally fell on her unfaithful husband while the manhunt continued. Silent Pool was dredged, light aircraft flew low over the area looking for traces and a pack of Airedales and bloodhounds were tracked over the ground, all to no avail.

The police of four counties coordinated a mass search of the Downs, in which 15,000 volunteers took part.

Criminologist Edgar Lustgarten wrote a piece for the *Daily Mail*, commenting that Agatha was indulging in 'a typical case of "mental reprisal".'

Sales of her books boomed, naturally. Meanwhile, at the Hydropathic Hotel in Harrogate (now the Old Swan) a woman registered as Mrs Neele was enjoying all the facilities the hotel had to offer for seven guineas a week. She was chatting to guests, claiming to be from South Africa, taking meals in the restaurant and enjoying the ballroom dancing.

But a sharp-eyed banjo player in the hotel band recognized her from the press photographs.

Police were called in and watched her for

two days before her husband arrived and confirmed that the mysterious Mrs Neele was in fact his wife.

The press accused her of publicity-seeking, although two doctors testified that she was suffering from a genuine case of amnesia brought on by stress.

Agatha Christie carried the truth behind her vanishing act to her grave. We will never know if she really lost her memory or if she was taking public vengeance against her husband.

And today, similar questions must arise from Georgia Lester's disappearance. With her new book due out, is she simply seeking publicity? Is she taking her revenge against her publisher for not taking her fears of a stalker seriously?

Or has something more sinister happened to Britain's contemporary Queen of Crime?

Her legions of fans anxiously await the answer.

They weren't the only ones, Kit thought. He wouldn't mind some answers himself. What's more, if Georgia had indeed staged her disappearance, he felt he deserved them. They were supposed to be mates, him and Georgia. She had been one of the first crime writers he'd ever met once he was himself a published author.

He vividly remembered the first event they'd done together, at a literary festival in the Midlands. His first novel had just come out in paperback, and it was only the third public appearance he'd ever made as an author. He was overawed to find himself on the same platform as Georgia, already a bestseller, and another writer whose books had leapt to prominence on the back of a particularly classy TV adaptation. In the green room before the event, the TV-tie-in author had gleefully spotted Kit's nerves and was indulging himself in a pernicious mixture of patronizing put-downs and the sort of event-disaster anecdote calculated to trigger a fit of panic in any but the most sanguine.

Georgia had swept in on the tail end of one of these, all white silk and Chanel N°5. She'd taken one look at Kit's anxious face, then shot a shrewd glance at the other author. 'You really are a bastard, Godfrey, upsetting this poor sweet boy,' she'd said, then settled like a stylish swan on the arm of Kit's chair. She put a manicured hand on his arm. 'I've been so looking forward to meeting you, Kit. I thought *The Dissection Man* was absolutely the best thriller I read last year. I just know you are going to be a mega-star.'

He'd mumbled something awkward and complimentary in response.

'And you absolutely mustn't be nervous, darling. Just remember, those people are out there because they love what we all do. They want so very much to like you as much as they like your books. You'd have to be an utter monster for them not to take you to their bosoms. And you're clearly not that, my dear.'

It had been what he needed to hear. Thanks to Georgia, he relaxed into the event and, to his astonishment, actually began to enjoy himself. He watched and listened as she and Godfrey worked the room and by the end of the evening, he'd come to realize that he too could perform. All he'd lacked was the technique that provided the confidence to allow him to sail through.

Afterwards, he'd gone for supper with Georgia and her publicist. It had been the start of what had developed into a surprisingly close relationship. Surprising because, although one strand of Georgia's work incorporated some of the grisliness of his own serial killer thrillers, they could not have been more different in temperament, outlook and lifestyle. But their mutual respect and affection had always carried them over their differences in everything from politics to social background. The amused tolerance he sometimes felt for her more scandalous pronouncements had never even dented their friendship. His only regret was that Fiona never seemed to see beyond Georgia's public face to the warmth behind it. Somehow, Georgia always seemed to get under Fiona's skin, though he could never quite grasp the source of the friction. What seemed like an innocuous remark to him could provoke a sudden flash of irritation in Fiona's eyes, leaving him baffled. In the end, he put it down to bad chemistry and tried to keep them apart wherever possible.

Kit wished he could work out what was going on with Georgia. While she was perfectly capable of something as outrageous as staging a disappearance to embarrass her publishers, he really didn't believe she would let Anthony suffer too. In spite of Georgia's frequent indiscretions and infidelities, she relied on Anthony's dogged devotion for the stability she needed. Over the years, he had cultivated an air of studied nonchalance about her predilection for young Latin lovers, but there was no doubt in Kit's mind that however bizarre a marriage it might seem to outside eyes, theirs was a union that was built for survival.

He re-examined the notion he'd earlier dismissed out of hand. It was, of course, possible that Anthony was in on it. Hard though it was to imagine Anthony, that profoundly respectable man, leading press and police up the garden path, if anyone could cajole him into it, it would be Georgia. And if the police weren't taking her disappearance seriously, the chances of that being the case were probably stronger. It was a hope Kit clung to, not wanting to contemplate the more disturbing possibility that lurked constantly at the edge of his consciousness. If something terrible had happened, he wanted to postpone that certainty for as long as possible. He couldn't allow himself to begin to imagine that Georgia might never come back.

Kit forced himself away from such thoughts, superstitiously believing he could influence her return by visualizing it. He allowed himself a wry smile. He could just imagine the press conference when Georgia resurfaced. Would she play the amnesia card? Somehow, he doubted it. No, she'd infinitely prefer the melodramatic. She'd gone into hiding in fear of her life after what had happened to poor, dear Drew. But she had decided to re-emerge into the world because she couldn't bear the thought that uncertainty about her fate was causing pain to her friends, her fans and most of all to her dearly beloved husband Anthony.

Yes, he thought. That would be the way she'd run it. There would be howls of outrage from some quarters at such blatant manipulation of the media and wasting of police time – in that order of priority, Kit decided with a cynic's certainty. But her fans would go for it, their imaginations hypercharged with the fuel he and Georgia and the rest of them provided. And that was the crucial thing.

But his determined whistling in the dark wasn't entirely successful; the other, less entertaining possibilities still pressed close. He could immediately discount suicide. Nobody who loved herself as much as Georgia did could ever plunge so far into despair so fast. Someone would have noticed and rallied the troops round her.

As for the other, more terrifying, option, that was a route he wasn't prepared to travel without a guide. And since the best possible guide would be coming home to him that evening, he decided that he wouldn't even allow himself to consider that scenario till then. As he reached that decision, the need for it was taken out of his hands. A short, thick-set man with tattooed hands dropped into the chair opposite him.

'You'll be Kit Martin, then?' he said in a strong Geordie accent.

Kit extended a hand across the table. Salvation took many strange forms, but he was always willing to recognize it when it arrived.

Chapter 30

Fiona glared angrily across the table, the hazel of her eyes darkening. 'That,' she said with plosive precision, 'is taking the piss.'

Steve shook his head. 'You know me better than that, Fi.'

'I thought I did.' She turned away and stared unseeingly at the wall. When she spoke, her voice was calm and measured, a distillation of her fury channelled through her control. 'I thought you understood the depth of my commitment to what I do. It wasn't my pride that was wounded when you threw me out and brought in Andrew Horsforth, you know. It was my belief that people like you had begun to take seriously the value of what me and a handful of my colleagues are doing.'

'You know I do.' There was no apology in his voice.

Fiona faced him. 'Your bosses still see psychologists as nothing more than a tool they can use in whatever way suits them. And that's not good enough.'

'You think I don't know that? You think I don't want to change that?' he demanded, his own eyes dark with frustration. 'Fi, help me out here. Help me change their minds. All I'm asking is that you run these cases through your crime linkage program and see what the geographic profile comes up with. I thought you wanted Susan Blanchard's killer caught? If you won't do it for the sake of our friendship, then do it for her and her kids.'

'Oh, that's well below the belt, Steve. Look, I've already suspended my better judgement and given in to moral blackmail over this. I reviewed Horsforth's material, even though, God knows, some of it made me feel sick to my stomach. I made some suggestions about how you might continue the investigation. I offered that much out of friendship. But now I feel like you're taking advantage of that friendship. You're fresh out of favours.' Her chin came up in a challenge.

Steve held her gaze. He knew there was justice in her words but his determination to get a result in this case was stronger than his shame. 'I need this doing, Fi,' he said, laying it out for her as straightforwardly as he could. 'I've got no resources to fall back on with this case. My bosses don't want to know unless I can come up with some sort of blinding revelation. They just want the whole thing to go away. So do I, but I want it to go away because we've nailed the right person. And right now, I'm dead-ended. I've got officers who desperately want to work this case to a standstill, but I need some sort of lead to put them on. My best chance of that is what you can give me.' He clamped his mouth shut and locked stares with her, his lean face taut as sculpture.

They glowered at each other, the friendship of half a lifetime on the line. 'I won't do it,' Fiona said.

Steve's lips compressed in a thin line. He felt the high hopes he'd arrived with sliding out of reach, but he wouldn't let go. Not yet. He refused to release her eyes, willing himself to be the last one standing.

'I really won't do it, Steve,' Fiona repeated.

He recognized it for a tiny crack of weakness and leaned forward. 'I need this.'

She nodded wearily. 'I know you do. So here's the deal.

I have a PhD student who's working on crime linkage and geographical profiling. What's going to happen is that the Met is going to pay my student to analyse the material. On a consultancy basis.'

'I don't know if I can find leeway in the budget for that.'

'You better had, Steve. At least this way somebody gets some benefit from this.'

'But you'll supervise?'

Fiona shook her head. 'Terry Fowler is perfectly capable of a straightforward analysis like this. I don't insult my students by looking over their shoulders. I'm out of it, Steve. I keep telling you this and you're not hearing me.'

He ran a hand through his hair in a gesture of frustration. 'I suppose I'll have to make do with second best, then.'

'I'm not fobbing you off. Terry will do a good job for you. Steve, you've got to stop punishing yourself over this case. I know you care about what you do, but you can't let it put our friendship at risk.' Fiona reached across the table and took his hand. 'I suppose it's too late to tell you to get a life?'

Steve managed half a smile. 'Well past too late.'

'It's what saved me,' she said simply.

Steve's eyes clouded over. 'He did, didn't he?' He wanted to say that he'd wished they could have been each other's saviours, but he never would now. Either she already knew and had made her own accommodation with his feelings; or else the fresh knowledge would swirl through their lives as a disruptive current, threatening the balance that had evolved between them. Whatever, it would be pointless.

As if on cue, the front door opened. 'Hi, Fiona, I'm home,' echoed down the hall. They heard the thump of Kit's satchel hitting the floor as he tossed it into his office in passing. Then he was in the doorway, grinning at the sight of them, oblivious to the tension in the room. 'Hey, Stevie, I wasn't expecting to see you tonight.'

'I came to see just how overdrawn I was at the bank,' Steve said wryly.

Kit crossed to Fiona and gave her a hug. 'Steve wants more work done on the Susan Blanchard case,' she said.

Kit looked over the top of her head at Steve, his eyebrows raised in mild interrogation. 'She blew you out, then.'

'In a manner of speaking,' Steve said.

'The Met are going to pay Terry Fowler to do the job,' Fiona said firmly.

'I hope,' said Steve. He got to his feet. 'I'll call you in the morning about the arrangements.'

'Don't go, Steve,' Fiona urged. 'Stay for dinner. We could have a Scrabble challenge match afterwards.'

It was an olive branch, he knew. The part of him that had hated to beg wanted to carry on walking, but he was uncertain what that would mean for the future of their relationship. His pride was a small sacrifice for the healing of the breach that had opened between them. Steve looked at Kit. 'Depends what's for dinner,' he said.

Kit frowned. 'Lemme see.' He opened the fridge and stared into it. 'I've got chicken breasts, shallots, fresh tarragon, fennel ... What about chicken and tarragon pilaff?' He looked round.

Steve pretended to consider for a moment. 'Pudding?'

'You don't ask much, do you?' Kit complained. 'There's some home-made chocolate ice-cream in the freezer, a few strawberries and half a jar of mango coulis in the fridge. That do you?'

'OK, you talked me into it.'

Kit shrugged off his jacket and tossed it over a chair then set to work. 'How was your day?' Fiona asked as she watched him chopping and dicing.

'Very productive,' Kit said. 'I went to see a contact. But I better not go into details in front of the law,' he added, grinning over his shoulder at Steve. 'Tell you what, though. Georgia's kicking up a storm in the papers. You seen the tabloids today? The *Mail* did a big piece comparing her disappearance with Agatha Christie's vanishing act back in the twenties.'

'She's still not shown up, then?' Fiona asked. She turned to Steve. 'Georgia Lester, the crime writer? Have you been following the story?'

'I've seen it in the papers, yes. Didn't you say she'd had a letter like yours, Kit? What do you think? Has she gone underground out of pique or out of fear?'

'The letter didn't really scare her until she found out I'd had one too. She was edgy about it, definitely. I know she was pitching her publisher to send her out on the tour with a pair of minders, but I reckoned that was just Georgia trying it on. She can be a bit of a grandstander,' he added affectionately, reaching for a heavy cast-iron skillet hanging beside the cooker.

'One thing's for sure,' Fiona said dryly. 'The suicide option is a nonstarter with Georgia.'

'Why do you say that?' Steve asked.

'Suicides have low self-esteem. Georgia, on the other hand, is a woman entirely devoid of the slightest shred of self-doubt. On a scale of one to ten, the health of her ego would be somewhere around eleven.'

'She's right,' Kit confirmed. 'Most of us, we get a bad review, we kick the cat, we swear at the computer screen, we hurt. Even if we pretend we're far too manly for that.

But Georgia, she gets a bad review, she sends the reviewer flowers and a note saying she hopes they'll be better soon.'

Steve snorted with laughter. 'You're making that up.'

'Swear to God, it's a true story. Georgia could no more top herself than wear a shell suit.'

'So there's only one alternative, is that what you're saying? If she hasn't staged this disappearance as a publicity stunt, then she's been abducted?' Steve put into words what Kit and Fiona had been avoiding.

There was a long moment of silence. Then Kit tipped the diced chicken into the pan with the shallots. Steam rose in the air, carrying the cooking smells across the room. 'I suppose that's what we're carefully not saying,' Fiona said.

'Which doesn't mean you're not thinking it. I would be, in your shoes. After Drew Shand and Jane Elias, it's got to be in the front of your mind,' Steve said.

'But there's no connection between those two murders,' Kit protested. 'The Garda have arrested a local man for Jane. And you told me they haven't found any threatening letters among her papers, which put the damper on my nerves a bit.'

'It doesn't matter that there's no connection,' Fiona said. 'Psychologically speaking, that is. What we know is that two thriller writers have been murdered. So when a third goes missing, it's inevitable that we start wondering if the same thing has happened to her. It's the mind playing tricks, Kit. Subconsciously we always look for sequences. Even when they're not there. So although your conscious mind is denying that Drew and Jane's deaths could have any connection to Georgia, at a lower level, you can't help picturing it as a sequence and worrying about it.'

'Nevertheless,' Steve interrupted, 'and speaking purely as a copper, I couldn't rule out the possibility that Georgia has been abducted.'

'And of course, if she has been, and there's been a ransom note, then the police would have made sure that was kept quiet,' Fiona said thoughtfully. 'They would be playing it exactly as they are. Making out they're not unduly worried, acting like they're treating it as nothing more than possibly suspicious.'

'I'd say so, yes,' Steve confirmed.

'So what you're both saying is that it's pointless to speculate,' Kit said.

'Pretty much, yes.' Steve inhaled deeply. 'This smells wonderful, Kit.'

'It will be,' he said confidently. 'I hope wherever Georgia is, she's getting something half as good.'

Fiona smiled ironically. 'I hope so too. Because if this turns out to be a put-up job, she's going to be on bread and water for a very long time to come.'

Chapter 31

The clock read 3:24. Fiona had no idea what had woken her, but her eyes had snapped wide open, her brain firing on all cylinders. No point in trying to get back to sleep, she knew that. Insomnia seldom afflicted her, but when it struck, she knew the only answer was to get up and keep her mind occupied until sleep felled her again.

She slipped out of bed. Kit grunted, turned over and began breathing rhythmically again. Fiona padded across the carpet, taking her dressing gown off its peg and moving out on to the landing. The distant hum of traffic was the only sound. She had no sense of another presence besides her and Kit. As she mounted the stairs, she looked out of the window to the garden below. The dim light of a three-quarter moon turned it into an eerie conglomeration of monochrome shapes. But none were unfamiliar. Whatever had disturbed her sleep, it wasn't a stranger in either house or garden.

In her office, Fiona turned on the desk lamp and took a can of Perrier out of the tiny fridge by her desk, one of Kit's more bizarre birthday presents. She'd been less than thrilled at the time – though she hoped she'd disguised her disappointment – but she'd come to appreciate its benefits since. He was good at that, coming up with things she'd never have imagined she needed. She popped the top of the can. It was so still in the soundproofed attic that she could hear the bubbles ping as they broke against the metal.

She switched on her computer and waited for it to boot up. Then she went straight on line. America was awake; there would be plenty of people up and about in the chat rooms to keep her amused. As she logged on, she remembered it was the night once a month when *Murder Behind the Headlines* had an on-line discussion that ran from ten till midnight. She pointed her browser at their site and waited to be connected.

Fiona scrolled through the subjects up for debate and clicked on Jane Elias. She came in on the middle of what seemed to be a heated exchange about the Garda Siochana. Offered the chance by the browser to backtrack on the conversation, she opted for that.

What she read gave her a physical chill in her chest. According to three separate posts, the word locally on the Jane Elias murder was that the guards had arrested the wrong man, and they knew it. Allegedly, they'd been railroaded into bringing in John Patrick Regan by senior officials in the Serious Crimes Unit, in spite of the reluctance of local officers. Now, in the absence of any early forensic results linking Regan to the crime, it appeared that the local cops were getting jittery about the arrest and his lawyer was fighting for him to be set free. According to one post, everybody in Kildenny who knew John Regan was adamant that the man didn't have the brains to organize an abduction, never mind the balls to kill a woman and mutilate her corpse.

That was the point where the discussion had degenerated into a slanging match over the police. Fiona couldn't have cared less how good or bad the Garda Siochana were in an obscure corner of County Wicklow. She had more important things to think about.

She logged off, turned off her computer and stared at the blank screen. Regan's arrest had been a far greater reassurance than she had been prepared to admit to Kit. Without him in the frame, the picture looked very different indeed. It wasn't a matter of the subconscious forcing connections; it became a logical conclusion.

Normally, the murders of two people working in the same field on opposite sides of the Irish Sea would be so insignificant it would pass unnoticed. But when they were both public figures; both award-winning thriller writers; both writers whose work had been adapted successfully for film or TV; and both murdered in styles that followed elements in their work more or less slavishly, it stretched coincidence to a point where notice had to be taken.

Fiona weighed the elements of her knowledge in the balance of her experience. Yes, there were such things as copycat killers out there. And Jane Elias's killer was as likely to be a copycat as a serial murderer at the start of his series, given the physical distance between the victims and the apparently very different manners of their death.

Fiona, however, had never liked coincidence.

She got up from her desk and ran downstairs to the spare room, where Kit's vast library of crime fiction covered the walls from floor to ceiling. *Nothing as straightforward as alphabetical order*, Fiona sighed to herself. She scanned the shelves, looking for one of Georgia's books. The first one she found was *Last Rights*, the final part of a trilogy of legal thrillers she'd completed a couple of years before. Fiona turned to the inside back flap and read the author biography there.

Several of Georgia's books had been adapted for TV, including the legal thrillers. Only one, a stand-alone psychological suspense novel whose graphic violence had shaken many of her traditional audience to the core, had been made into a movie. *And Ever More Shall Be So* had been a low-budget British film, made with sponsorship money from Channel 4. Fiona vaguely remembered reading about its success. Something in the film had captured the attention of a mass audience and it had become a surprise hit on both sides of the Atlantic. The haunting, ethereal theme tune of an unaccompanied boy soprano singing 'Green Grow the Rushes-O' as a lament, a plangent counterpoint to the nightmares of the film, might have had something to do with it. For some reason, she'd never seen it, though Kit certainly would have done.

Now all she needed was to find the book. One among two or three thousand couldn't be so hard, could it? Methodically, Fiona made her way along the shelves, pausing whenever she encountered Georgia's name. How the hell did he ever find anything in here, she wondered? And why was he incapable of ever throwing away a book, no matter how crap he pronounced it to be?

About halfway along the second wall, Fiona found what she was looking for. The first edition of *And Ever More Shall Be So*, a personal dedication on the title page in Georgia's surprisingly neat handwriting. 'To darling Kit, already *il miglior fabbro*. With lashings of love, Georgia Lester.' How very Georgia, Fiona thought with a sardonic smile.

Fiona turned out the light and made her way back up to her attic. She settled down on the futon, pulling the throw over her legs so she wouldn't get cold. Then she began to turn the pages. But what she read there put all thought of normal comfort out of her mind.

Chapter 32

Steve thrust his arm out to prevent the lift doors closing. They opened fully and he stepped in, coming face to face with DC Joanne Gibb. 'Morning, Joanne,' he said.

'Morning, boss. Am I allowed to ask how the grovelling went?'

Steve pulled a face. 'Let's just say we're heading in the right direction. Dr Cameron is putting me in touch with one of her graduate students who will do the analysis. If I can find some money to pay for it.'

'But we could be making real progress here,' Joanne protested. 'Surely Commander Telford's going to see the sense in following up this lead?'

Steve smiled. 'I think I can persuade him to share our view.' The lift shuddered to a halt at their floor. 'Wish me luck. I'll see you and Neil in my office in fifteen minutes.'

He turned down the corridor, walking past blank-faced doors until he came to his immediate superior's office. Steve knocked and waited for the invitation to enter. Commander David Telford was sitting behind what Steve would have bet was the tidiest desk in the building. Not a single scrap of loose paper blemished its polished surface. Pens clustered in a metal holder, a pad of paper sat by the phone, and that was it. The walls were blank save for Telford's framed commendations and his business studies degree from Aston University. 'Sit down, Steve,' he said, his face stern. He was determined to obliterate from the collective memory of the Metropolitan Police the notion that anyone other than Steve Preston was to blame for the Francis Blake fiasco. Steve understood that, and knew it was the reason why Telford – or Teflon, as he was known to the lower ranks – continued to treat him as if he brought a bad smell into the office with him.

'Thank you, sir.' Sometimes playing the game was a killer, but Steve cared too much about catching criminals ever to consider seriously the alternative.

'Still no progress, then?' Telford's question implied the answer he wanted to hear. He cared more about image than justice, Steve knew. Finding Susan Blanchard's killer was not at the top of Teflon's agenda. Better that his team never found the real killer so the world could go on thinking the Met had been cheated of Francis Blake by the trial judge rather than their own maverick operation.

'On the contrary, sir. I think we've opened up a new line of inquiry.' Painstakingly, Steve went through the fresh evidence about the cyclist and what Joanne's trawl of records had produced. 'Now I need budget authorization to commission a geographic profile based on this cluster of cases so we can develop viable suspects,' he concluded.

Telford frowned. 'It's all a bit tenuous, isn't it? Nothing in the way of hard evidence, is there?'

'The problem with this case all along has been the absence of hard evidence, sir. The lack of forensics at the crime scene, the relative lack of witnesses, the lack of apparent relationship between killer and victim. It's obvious that the killer has some experience in covering his tracks, and that suggests he's committed sexually motivated attacks before. This is the most promising line of inquiry we've had since we began the investigation, sir.'

'Clutching at straws,' Telford complained.

'I think it's rather more than that, sir.' The words, 'with respect' hovered on Steve's lips, but he held back, unwilling to utter that particular lie. 'It's a valid investigative strategy. Sooner or later, we're going to come back under the spotlight over this case if we don't resolve it. When that happens, I'd like to be able to say we left no avenues unexplored.'

'I thought Dr Cameron had publicly refused ever to work with us again?' Telford was off on another tack, unsettled by Steve's subtle threat of publicity.

'It wouldn't be Dr Cameron doing the analysis, sir. We would be commissioning another member of her department.'

Telford cracked a smile. 'One in the eye for her, then.'

Steve said nothing. Perhaps malice would win where common sense had failed.

Telford swivelled in his chair and appeared to study his degree certificate. 'Oh, very well, do your analysis.' He turned abruptly back to Steve. 'Just don't screw up this time, Superintendent.'

Steve walked back to his office, his hands fists. How sweet it would be to find Susan Blanchard's killer, he thought. OK, Telford would take the public credit, but everybody inside the force would know the truth. Justice served, in every possible way.

He pushed open the door of his office, where he found DC Neil McCartney and Joanne waiting for him. Neil was a large untidy man in his mid-twenties. Steve had never seen him look anything other than mildly dishevelled and he was incapable of sitting in a chair without looking as if he was sprawling. He often wondered what the lad had looked like in uniform. His appearance alone would probably have guaranteed that he'd be booted up to CID at the earliest possible opportunity. It also hadn't hurt that he was a good policeman; shrewd, thoughtful and tenacious to the point of bloody-mindedness.

'All right. We've got the go-ahead for the geographic profile,' Steve announced as he squeezed round Neil's awkwardly arrayed legs. 'I'll take the material over to the university personally as soon as we've finished up here. So, Neil, what's Blake been up to?'

'As far as we can tell, nothing of any great interest. Sleeping late, going out for a paper and a pint of milk and a couple of videos most mornings, then back home. Down the bookies some lunchtimes, a couple of pints in the local boozer then a walk in the park. Back to the flat and apparently staying in watching TV, judging by the flickering at the window. Nothing sinister, nothing dodgy. Which is just as well, with us running minimal surveillance one-on-one. For all we know, he could be up to all sorts when we're not around. Some days when we are there, he doesn't put his nose across the door. He could have a harem in there and we'd be none the wiser.'

Steve nodded sympathetically. 'I know it's less than satisfactory. But we'll just have to keep as close an eye on our friend Mr Blake as we can. Until we come up with a better active lead, he's the only thing we've got. It might be an idea to have a discreet word with the people in the downstairs flat, see if they've seen or heard any sign of company. But only if we're sure they're not mates. I don't want to alert Blake to our continued interest. What do you think, Neil?'

Neil wrinkled his nose. He'd worked for bosses who didn't like to be told their suggestions might not work. But he'd learned enough about Steve Preston to know that speaking his mind would seldom be held against him. Especially in such close company as they were at present. 'I don't reckon it, guv,' he said. 'They're a youngish couple, mid-twenties,

I'd say. They look like the kind that think we're the bad guys, know what I mean? They'd probably think it was their bounden duty to tell Blake the pigs were sniffing round.'

It wasn't what Steve had been hoping to hear, but he trusted Neil's judgement. 'Is John on him today?' he asked.

'Yeah.' Neil yawned.

'OK. So why don't you take yourself off for the rest of the day, Neil? Get your head down.'

'You sure, guv?'

'I'm sure. Joanne can keep things ticking over here. If we need you, we'll shout.'

Neil unfurled his body from the chair and stood up, stretching luxuriously. 'I'm not going to argue. Fuck me, more than eight hours to sleep in. My body might collapse with the shock.' He slouched out of the room.

'Do you want me to hold the fort then, boss?' Joanne asked.

'Yeah. I'm going over to the university to see some bloke called Terry Fowler. Dr Cameron left a message that she's made all the arrangements. I don't know how long I'll be – depends how much I have to brief this Fowler. And I'm supposed to drop in on Dr Cameron herself when I'm done. So I'll see you when I see you.'

It felt strange walking into the psychology department and not heading straight for Fiona's office. The porter gave him directions to the cubicle on the third floor that Terry Fowler shared with another graduate student. Steve knocked on the door and was surprised to hear a woman's voice invite him to come in.

He stuck his head round the door. There were two computer desks, one vacant, the other occupied by a young woman with spiky platinum-blonde hair, scarlet lipstick and

297

glasses with heavy black frames. Her ears gleamed with silver from three sets of piercings and a pair of ear-cuffs. Steve smiled. 'Sorry to bother you. I'm looking for Terry Fowler.'

The woman cast her eyes upwards in a parody of exasperation. Then she grinned and pointed at her head. 'You found her. Theresa Fowler at your service. Fiona playing the old trick of working on your gender assumptions?'

Irritated with Fiona for setting him up as the perfect model of the prejudiced policeman, Steve walked in with an apologetic shrug. *Nothing like starting at a disadvantage*, he thought. 'What can I say? I fell for it. I apologize. I'm not usually prone to sexist assumptions.' He extended a hand. 'Steve Preston.'

'Pleased to meet you, Superintendent.' Her handshake matched his; firm, no nonsense, nothing to prove. 'Don't worry about it. Psychologists find it hard to resist playing silly games. It goes with the territory. Grab a chair and make yourself comfortable. Well, as comfortable as you can on one of those instruments of torture.'

Her smile was infectious, and he found himself returning it. 'Call me Steve, please.' He pulled up a plastic bucket chair and sat down. 'I take it Fiona has briefed you more fully than she briefed me?'

She shook her head. 'Only in the most general terms. She said you had a group of cases you wanted me to run through the crime linkage system. Then if there's a cluster, I've to do a geographical profile. And you're going to pay me, which is a major plus, I have to tell you.' Terry leaned back in her chair, unconsciously showing off a slim body in black jeans and T-shirt.

'There's a little bit more to it than that,' Steve said, opening his briefcase and taking out the file Joanne had compiled. He had added four unrelated cases, to test the accuracy of the crime linkage programme, but he wasn't going to tell Terry that. 'First of all, I have to stress that this material is highly confidential.'

'My lips are sealed,' Terry said, pushing them together in a tight pout.

'I don't doubt it,' he said stiffly, determined to keep things formal. 'But I couldn't help noticing that you share this office. So whenever you leave the office, you're going to have to take this file with you unless you can be sure it will be secure in here.'

'OK.'

'Even if you're only popping out to the loo or the coffee machine.'

'Point taken.' She smiled and raised her hands palms outwards in a placatory gesture. 'It's cool, Steve. I understand.'

'I don't mean to teach you to suck eggs.'

Terry shook her head. 'Hey, you've never worked with me before, how are you to know I'm not some ditzy blonde?' She widened her eyes, her mobile face a question.

Steve's turn to grin. 'Fiona doesn't hate me that much. OK, here's what I've got for you. Six rapes and four serious sexual assaults. As Fiona said, I want you to see if there are grounds for believing any or all of them to be linked. If you get a cluster, I'm keen to see what the geographic profile produces. If we get that far, I then want you to enter another location into the geographic profile to see what happens.'

Terry raised one eyebrow. It should have looked pretentious but somehow she avoided that. 'Is the other location in the file?'

Steve shook his head. 'I don't want to influence the way you're thinking. Once I see the results, then we'll take it from there.'

'Fine by me. How quick do you need it?'

Steve spread his hands. 'Yesterday?'

'Yesterday costs extra. But for the regular fee, you can have it tomorrow. On one condition.'

Steve tilted his head slightly, his face suspicious. 'One condition?'

'You have dinner with me tomorrow.' Her smile was the calculated flirt of a woman who expects to get her own way.

Steve felt hot blood flushing his cheeks. 'I have dinner with you?'

'Is it such a strange idea?'

He forced himself to cling on to his professional reserve. 'I just don't think it's a very good one.'

'Why? You're not married, are you?'

'No, but . . .'

'So, what's the problem?'

'I'm not in the habit of mixing business and pleasure,' he said, aware as he spoke that he sounded like the kind of stuffed shirt he'd always prayed he'd never become.

'Where else do people like us meet interesting dinner companions? We don't have to talk about work, you know,' Terry said. 'I won't quiz you about your ten greatest cases if you don't ask me to define Piagetian theory. Come on, what have you got to lose? Even if you have a totally crap time, it's only going to be for a few hours. And I won't tell if you don't.'

Pleasantly bewildered but still wary, Steve ran a hand through his dark hair. 'This is all rather sudden.'

She shrugged. 'Life's too short. You've got to seize the moment.'

'But why me?'

'God, you lot know how to ask questions, don't you?' Now she was laughing, even white teeth gleaming like the big bad

300

wolf. 'Because you've got a brain and a sense of humour, because you're a nice-looking geezer and because you're not a geeky psychologist. Four very good reasons. So, you going to have dinner with me, or what? It's OK if it's no, I can take it. I'm a big girl. And I'll still do your analysis, no hard feelings.'

Steve shook his head, entirely disorientated by the way the meeting had deviated from his expectations. 'OK, let's do it,' he found himself saying, realizing as he spoke that the idea was genuinely exciting.

'Good call, Steve. I'll ring you tomorrow when I've got something for you, OK?' She was already reaching eagerly for the file.

Understanding he was being dismissed, Steve got to his feet. 'Er . . . about dinner? Where shall I book? What sort of food do you like?'

She shrugged. 'You choose. I don't eat meat but I love fish. And I never met a cuisine I didn't like.'

'Why am I not surprised? Thanks, Terry.' He walked down the corridor to the flight of stairs that would take him to Fiona's office, grinning from ear to ear. He couldn't quite believe what had just happened. He'd been blown away by the charisma of a stranger. He'd thrown aside one of his strongest principles, and he was feeling more light-hearted than he had for months. Maybe at last his luck was on the turn.

Chapter 33

Steve's smile didn't survive his encounter with Fiona. When he walked into her office, she was staring blankly at her computer screen, hands linked behind her head. 'Isn't it a lovely day?' he said blithely, settling on her sofa.

Fiona looked at him as if he'd gone mad. 'It is?'

'I think so,' he said cheerfully. 'I've just had a very interesting encounter with Terry Fowler.'

'Oh good,' Fiona said absently. 'She's very efficient. I'm sure she'll do an excellent job for you.' Her voice tailed off and she frowned at the wall above his head.

'Earth to Fiona . . . Is there anybody home?'

'I'm sorry, Steve, I didn't sleep much last night. I'm . . . a bit distracted.'

'You wanted to see me about something?' he reminded her.

Fiona scowled and squeezed the bridge of her nose between her finger and thumb. 'I know. It all made perfect sense when I left the message, but now . . . Well, I don't know if I'm overreacting.'

Fiona this distracted was too unfamiliar an experience for Steve to take lightly. 'Let's hear it,' he said. 'Then we can both decide.'

She nodded. 'Makes as much sense as anything else. I woke up in the middle of the night. You know, the way I do sometimes. No obvious reason, but I couldn't get back to sleep. So I went upstairs to surf the web for a while, and I ended up in a chat room where people were discussing the Jane Elias murder. And the general consensus seemed to be that the Garda have arrested the wrong man.'

Fiona took a deep breath. 'Now, I know you have a fairly low opinion of the kind of people who hang around in newsgroups in the middle of the night in cyberspace, but a couple of the people who had posted actually know this guy and they're saying he just doesn't have what it takes to plan or to carry out so complex a scheme. Now, if the police do have the wrong man and if Jane's murder was nothing to do with her relationship with her Garda Siochana lover, then logic suggests that the same person might have murdered Jane Elias and Drew Shand.'

'That's reaching, Fi, and you know it. Different countries? Totally different MO and no signature that we know of?'

'There is a signature of sorts, Steve. Both Drew and Jane were award-winning authors who wrote serial killer thrillers that have been successfully adapted for TV or film. And they were both killed in ways that mirror deaths that are described in the very books that were adapted.' Fiona was focused now, her previous abstraction history.

'It's not a conventional signature,' was the only protest Steve could find.

'I know. But I've been working another case – the Spanish one – with an unconventional signature, and I suppose that's why I'm probably more open to the idea than I normally would be. So, humour me. Just for the sake of argument, let's say it's a possibility that the two crimes have the same perpetrator.'

Steve nodded. 'OK. Out of purely academic interest, let's see where that takes us.'

'Where it takes us is that Georgia Lester is missing. Having had at least one death threat letter which, when she discovered Kit had also had one, scared her more than a little. Kit, who knows her as well as anyone, seems to think the papers are right and she's gone to ground as some kind of bizarre publicity stunt. You said last night it's possible she's been abducted. Either of these may be the case. For all I know, the police are negotiating with a kidnapper as we speak. That's something I imagine you could find out with relative ease if you were minded to. But there is another possibility.'

'I have a sinking feeling I know where you're heading with this,' Steve said.

'I think Georgia could be the third victim of a serial killer. If that's the case, then for the signature to hold, it would follow that she's been murdered in the manner of one of the victims in a serial killer novel. Agreed?'

Steve decided to go along with Fiona for the time being. 'Theoretically, yes.'

'After I'd been on-line last night, I checked out Georgia's output. She's only published one strictly serial killer novel, *And Ever More Shall Be So*. Which was made into a film. She's an award winner – she's won the Crime Writers' Association Gold Dagger for best crime novel of the year twice. She fits all the criteria, Steve. So last night, I skimmed the book.' Fiona paused, pushing her hair back from her face, revealing dark smudges beneath her eyes.

She continued, her voice now the calm, dispassionate tone of the lecturer imparting information. 'The killer in *And Ever More Shall Be So* does abduct his victims. He uses the trick of pretending to have broken down in a country lane, but in broad daylight so they won't be suspicious of him. Then he takes the victims back to his lair, where he strangles them.

Finally he skins and dismembers them and wraps them up like joints of meat.'

Steve stared at Fiona for a long moment. It was a grisly prospect, but if he accepted her basic premise, it was an inevitable conclusion. 'And you think this might be what's happened to Georgia Lester?'

Fiona looked him straight in the eye. 'I'm scared shitless that this is what has happened to Georgia. Tell me I'm being paranoid here, Steve.'

'You're the psychologist, Fi. You know it's only paranoia when it's groundless. What you're telling me might be pretty far-fetched, but it's not entirely without foundation.' Steve leaned forward, his elbows on his knees, his hands clasped. However sceptical he was trying to sound, part of him was entirely convinced by Fiona's thesis. 'In the book, what does he do with the remains?'

'The killer's a wholesale butcher in the town where his victims live. He's got a big freezer that's supposedly obsolete. He keeps it padlocked shut. That's where he puts his packages of human flesh. So if I'm right, the logical place to look for Georgia Lester right now would be Smithfield Market. They live in the City, you see, her and Anthony.'

Steve closed his eyes. He wondered just how he was going to convince the detectives searching for Georgia Lester that they were going to need a search warrant for Smithfield Market. 'One more question,' he finally said. 'Do you think there's a connection with the death threat letters?'

Fiona shrugged. 'I don't know. My first reaction was that the writer of the letters wasn't a killer. There's no boasting about the murders in any of the letters I've seen, which I'd expect if the letter-writer was the killer. And generally speaking, people who write anonymous threatening letters have a different mind-set from those who actually kill. But

305

the more this goes on, the less certain I feel about trusting my judgement. If there is someone out there killing writers at the same time as someone else is sending those same people death threats, it's hard to believe it's pure coincidence.'

'We don't know whether Jane Elias or Drew Shand had any letters similar to the ones sent to Kit and the others, though, do we? And the Garda told me they hadn't found anything like that among her papers.' While he was willing to accept Fiona might have made a case for a serial killer, Steve was reluctant on a personal level to believe the letters held a direct threat. If they did, that meant his closest male friend could be the next target. And that was a prospect that chilled him to the bone.

Fiona stared numbly at him. His words washed over her, making no impression on the worm of anxiety that wriggled inside her. 'All I know is that if there is a serial killer out there, Kit is almost certainly on his list, whether or not the letter-writer and the murderer are one and the same. He fits all the criteria, just like Georgia. You've got to do something about this, Steve.'

Chapter 34

Fiona was uncharacteristically silent as they walked through the busy Holborn streets from her office to the quiet café-bar where Steve had arranged the meeting. Her mood seemed matched by grey skies and tall, dark Victorian buildings that hemmed them in as they headed down towards Farringdon Road. In an attempt to distract her, he said, 'Does your graduate student make a habit of propositioning strange men?'

'You mean Terry?'

'She asked me out to dinner.'

'I see her impulse control hasn't improved any.' Fiona sounded amused.

'She makes a habit of this kind of thing?' Steve demanded, unaccountably deflated by the thought.

'Propositioning men? I don't think so, no. But she is irrepressibly drawn to following her urges, hunches and inspirations without pause for thought.'

'Ah,' he said.

'It's just what you need, Steve. Someone to jolt you out of your rut,' she said, slipping her arm through his and giving it a squeeze.

'Is that how you see me? A man stuck in a rut?'

'You must admit, you're a creature of habit and caution. A

brief encounter with a charismatic whirlwind like Terry could be just what you need.'

'You think that's all she's in the market for, then? A brief encounter?' Steve said, trying to keep his tone light to match Fiona's.

'I have no idea. Sorry, I didn't mean to suggest she saw you as nothing more than a plaything. And it's not as if she has a reputation for playing the field. I've been working with Terry for nearly two years now, and all I've ever seen her do with blokes is put them in their place. Which is usually very firmly at arm's length. Not,' she added hastily, 'that there's anything wrong with that. I've seen too many students distracted because they're the most attractive woman in the seminar group and they can't resist the lure of other people's lust.'

'But Terry's not one of those, that's what you're saying?'

They side-stepped to allow a woman with a pushchair to pass. 'Definitely not. She's well aware of her charm, but to her credit, she doesn't trade on it. When she started her PhD, she was living with someone, but they split up . . . oh, it must be eighteen months ago. Since then, I don't know of anybody significant. So she must have really taken a liking to you.' She squeezed his arm and smiled up at him.

'You know a lot about her,' Steve observed.

'You're fishing. Which I assume means you said yes?'

'I did.'

Fiona raised her eyebrows. 'Good for you. Time to live a little, Steve. Let yourself go. And I think Terry's the perfect woman to do it with. She's bright and she's talented. And she's good fun.'

Steve smiled. 'I'd worked that much out for myself. I suspect I'm going to have to keep my wits about me with Ms Fowler.'

'Which is no bad thing in a relationship,' Fiona commented with a wicked grin.

'Hey, steady on. We're only having dinner, not moving in together.'

Fiona said nothing, merely pinning him with an inquisitive look as she let go of his arm to turn into the café-bar. It had opened on the crest of the city's coffee craze, the decor *Home Front* nineties, with every wall a different off-primary colour, tall aluminium vases crammed with exotic foliage scattered strategically around. The chairs were low wraparound armchairs that gripped the hips, the tables knee-high and stained the colour of herbal teas. The background music was generic Britpop played just loud enough to cover the hissing and spluttering of the coffee machines. It was marginally too far from the university for it to attract the student population. Mid-morning, only half a dozen tables were occupied. Steve led the way to a corner table at the rear, where they were unlikely to be overheard. From the elaborate menu of hot and cold beverages, Fiona ordered a cappuccino, Steve an Americano. He produced his cigars and lit up, blowing a perfect smoke ring towards the ceiling.

Fiona smiled. 'You only do that when you're nervous,' she said.

'I do?'

'I've noticed it before. When you're feeling twitchy, you blow smoke rings.'

'So that's all I am to you, a walking laboratory rat,' he said affectionately.

Before she could reply, a tall black woman in a caramel-coloured business suit toting a briefcase walked into the café and looked around her. Seeing Steve, the woman headed purposefully towards them. As she approached, Fiona took in the details. Low-heeled court shoes, powerful calves. Hair cut close to her head, high cheekbones, a parakeet nose and dark eyes behind fashionable oval-framed glasses. It was hard to gauge her age, but given that Fiona knew she was a Detective Chief Inspector, she had to be in her mid thirties at least. When she reached their table, the woman nodded to Steve and reached a hand out to Fiona. 'Dr Cameron? It's an honour to meet you. I'm Sarah Duvall. City of London Police.'

They shook hands and Duvall sat down opposite Fiona. 'Good to see you again, Steve,' she added with a curt nod.

'Thanks for coming, Sarah. I know you're up to your eyes at the moment,' he said.

'Aren't we all?' Duvall replied. The waiter arrived with the coffees and Duvall asked for a large espresso. Fiona wasn't in the least surprised. Something had to have fuelled this brisk no-nonsense woman through the ranks of the City police and it wouldn't have been supportive praise. 'So, Steve tells me you wanted to talk to me about the Georgia Lester inquiry,' Duvall said, giving Fiona a sharp look of appraisal.

'To be honest, the more I think about it, the more I think I'm probably wasting everybody's time,' Fiona hedged, aware she was not operating in her usual assertive mode and wondering whether she was actually feeling slightly intimidated by the other woman.

'I'm willing to be the judge of that,' Duvall said. 'So, if you'd care to lay it out for me?'

Fiona began at the beginning, with Drew Shand's murder, and outlined the hypothesis she'd already explained to Steve. Duvall listened in silence throughout, her features immobile, her body still as standing water. When Fiona came to the end of her theory, Duvall simply nodded. 'I see,' she said. She picked up her cup and sipped her coffee.

'I don't think you're wasting my time at all,' she finally said. She glanced at Steve. 'I can speak frankly here?'

'Fiona understands issues of confidentiality,' he confirmed.

Duvall picked up her teaspoon and stirred her espresso thoughtfully. 'The main investigation into Georgia Lester's disappearance is being handled by Dorset Constabulary, since that is where she was last known to be and where her car was subsequently found. My involvement has come about because her London residence is on our patch. Certain inquiries needed to be made in London, and it was decided that these should be handled at a level rather more senior than would deal with most missing persons. For reasons I'm sure you'll appreciate.' Fiona nodded, impressed with Duvall's incisive and logical manner.

'There have been suggestions, as you rightly point out, that Ms Lester has engineered her own disappearance as a publicity stunt. And to some degree, we have been allowing that assumption to run. However, I do not believe that to be the case. Apart from anything else, she had already engaged a bodyguard to accompany her on her book tour, which I don't think she'd have done if she was planning to disappear as a publicity stunt. Also, her husband's distress is clearly genuine, and I have been assured by everyone I've interviewed that she would not deliberately cause him such anxiety. We have been monitoring Mr Fitzgerald's telephone and his mail, with his full consent, and there have been no communications seeking a ransom. And there would have been by now if she had been abducted. I think we can be fairly sure of that.

'As you suggest, this leaves the unpalatable option that Ms Lester is dead, and not by her own hand. There is nothing to suggest she has met with a fatal accident. And so, I have been proceeding as if I were dealing with the early stages of a murder inquiry. I find what you have to say both disturbing and also curiously satisfying, because it chimes entirely with my own instincts about this case. I do wish someone had told me about these death threat letters before now, however.'

Fiona looked penitent. 'That's partly my fault, I'm afraid. Georgia wanted to take them to the police, but my partner, Kit, was opposed to the idea. He thought they were crank letters and he didn't want to be seen to be publicity-seeking after Drew Shand's murder. I should have been more insistent. I'm sorry.'

Duvall nodded. There was no concession in her face, no attempt to reassure Fiona. Her expression said that Fiona really should have known better, and Fiona smarted under it. 'I'll want to see them as soon as possible,' was all Duvall said, however.

'I'll get them to you later today,' Fiona promised. 'They're back in my office. I'm sorry, I wasn't thinking straight. I should have brought them with me.'

Duvall's lips tightened in silent agreement.

'So how do we proceed from here?' Steve asked, anxious to move away from the edginess between the women to more productive territory. 'I can't see you getting a warrant to search Smithfield Market on the basis of what Fiona's given you.'

Duvall took another sip of her coffee. A technique designed to give room for thought, Fiona decided. 'I can try,' she said eventually. More coffee. 'We have one or two very understanding magistrates in the City. And we do have a very good relationship with the market authorities. We actually have a squad of officers based in Smithfield itself. What might help me, Doctor, is if you could tell me a little about what sort of person you believe is committing these crimes and whether they are likely to strike again.' She gave a tiny, tight smile. 'Prevention is always a good note to strike with magistrates.'

'I'm not a behavioural psychologist,' Fiona said. 'I'm an academic. I don't do profiling based on stuff about whether your killer wet the bed or was abused by a drunken father. I leave that to the clinicians who have a range of experience to draw on.'

Duvall nodded. 'I know. Personally, I prefer a little intellectual rigour in criminal investigation,' she said wryly. 'But based on what you know of this sort of killer, is there anything you can tell me?'

'These killings are fuelled by rage. Most serial homicides are sexual in their nature, but occasionally there are other motives. For example, the missionary type, who sees his goal as ridding the world of a particular group of people who don't deserve to live. I've recently been working on such a case with the Spanish police. In that instance, I'd characterize the motivation as loss.'

'Loss?' Duvall interrupted.

'Most adults develop their sense of self as a complex matrix of interlocking factors,' Fiona explained. 'So if we lose a parent, if our lover leaves us, if the career we had worked so hard for is shattered, we feel bereft and upset but we don't lose our sense of who we are. But there are some people who never achieve that sort of integration. Their sense of self becomes entirely bound up with one aspect of their lives. If they lose that element, they are entirely cast adrift from the normal checks and balances. Some commit suicide. A smaller group turn the rage and pain outwards and seek their revenge on those they perceive to be somehow responsible.'

'I see,' Duvall said. 'And you think that's what may have come into play here?'

Fiona shrugged. 'That's what my experience would lead me to think.'

Steve leaned forward. 'So what sort of person would see serial killer thriller writers as his nemesis?'

313

'Or her nemesis,' Duvall interjected. 'We're equal opportunity coppers in the City, Steve. Unlike the Met.' Again that thin, tight smile behind the barb.

Steve shook his head. 'If it's a serial, it's a man. Drew Shand was a gay man who was last seen leaving a gay pub with another man who has not come forward as a witness. So we have to assume he was the killer.'

Duvall inclined her head in concession. 'I'll grant you that. For now, at least.' She turned to Fiona again. 'Humour us, Doctor. What sort of person would want to kill these writers?'

Fiona refused to allow herself to feel patronized or intimidated. She had a point to make and Sarah Duvall wasn't going to keep her from making it. 'Creative writing. It's a field where passions run high. I know, I live with a writer. I suppose it could be a deranged fan stalker out to make a name for himself, a Mark Chapman type of killer. But they mostly stop at one. That's enough to make the statement. And they're not usually sophisticated enough to develop so complex a killing structure.

'It could be a wannabe writer who is eaten up with resentment at the success of others. In his parallel universe he might believe they've ripped off his plots, stolen his ideas, either by conventional means or by creeping into his mind while he's asleep. I would characterize the writer of the death threat letters as being most likely to fit in that category, based on their content.

'Or it could be a writer whose career has gone into terminal decline. Maybe someone who sees those particular writers as having snatched the success he should have had.' Fiona spread her hands. 'I'm sorry, I can't be more specific than that.' Duvall, she noticed, was looking sceptical.

'I'd never have imagined that anyone could feel so threatened by writers that they'd want to kill them,' Steve said.

'Whoever is doing this has become obsessed with the notion that this particular group of writers has somehow done him a deep and destructive wrong. And this is his way of righting that wrong,' Fiona said.

Duvall frowned. 'It's not as if writing books changes anybody's life.'

'You don't think the pen is mightier than the sword, then?' Fiona asked.

'No, I don't,' Duvall insisted. 'Book are just . . . books.'

'Sticks and stones will break my bones, but words will never harm me? That's what you think?'

Duvall considered. 'I don't think I've ever read anything that changed my life. For good or ill.'

'"Poetry makes nothing happen",' Fiona said.

'I'm sorry?'

'Something W. H. Auden wrote. Do you think the same thing is true of film and TV?' Fiona asked Duvall. This was between them now, Steve sidelined as they stared intently at each other.

Duvall leaned back in her chair, considering. 'We're always being told by your colleagues that when kids watch violence on TV, they copy it.'

'There's certainly anecdotal evidence of that. But whether it influences our behaviour directly or not, I think what we read and what we watch alters our view of the world. And I can't help wondering if this killer is someone who doesn't like the way that these writers and the adaptations of their books have presented the world,' Fiona parried.

'Sounds a bit far-fetched to me.'

Fiona shrugged. 'But strange as it seems, logic seems to dictate that if Georgia is dead and if these killings are linked, the motive lies in what the victims have written.'

Duvall nodded. 'The victim as teaching aid.'

'Read the vic., learn the killer,' Steve said. 'Rule one of stranger murder.'

'And he is going to kill again,' Duvall stated baldly.

It was the issue that Fiona wished she could avoid, the question that had been haunting her since she'd found the key passages in *And Ever More Shall Be So*. 'Yes. Unless he's stopped, he'll kill again. And what you need to do now is draw up a list of potential victims and see they're protected.'

Duvall's composure slipped momentarily and she looked at Steve for guidance. This time, it was his face that remained impassive. 'I don't see how we can do that,' Duvall stalled. She clearly objected to being told how to do her job by someone she perceived as an outsider.

'I'd have thought it was pretty straightforward,' Fiona said crisply. Now she was dealing with Kit's fate, her normal assertiveness was back in the driving seat with a vengeance. 'You're looking for award-winning crime writers who have written serial killer novels that have been adapted for film or TV. Get in touch with the Crime Writers' Association. They'll be able to put you in touch with one or other of the crime buffs who will be able to give you chapter and verse.'

'But there must be dozens,' Duvall protested. 'We couldn't possibly offer them all protection.'

'At the very least, you should warn them.' Fiona's voice was as implacable as her face, her hazel eyes intense in the gloom of the café.

Duvall's face had closed down. 'That's impossible. I don't think you've thought this through, Dr Cameron. The last thing we want is to start a panic. There's enough of a media circus as it is and we don't even know yet whether Georgia

Lester is alive or dead. It would be totally irresponsible to go public at this stage.'

Fiona glared at Duvall. 'Some of these people are my friends. I *live* with one of them. If you're not going to warn them, then I certainly am.'

Duvall's narrow nostrils flared. She turned to Steve. 'I thought you said she understood confidentiality?'

Steve put a hand on Fiona's arm. She shrugged it off impatiently. 'DCI Duvall's right,' Steve said gently. 'We don't know anything for sure yet and it could seriously damage our chances of putting a stop to this man if we panic prematurely. You know that, Fi. If this didn't touch Kit, you'd be the first to say we should avoid giving this killer the oxygen of publicity.'

'Yes, Steve, I probably would,' Fiona said angrily. 'But it *does* touch Kit, and I owe him far more than I owe the City of London Police.'

There was a dangerous silence. Then Duvall said, 'By all means warn your lover to be on his guard. But I must insist that you keep it to yourselves.'

Fiona snorted derisively. 'These aren't idiots you're talking about here. These are intelligent men and women who live by the power of their imagination. Since Drew Shand died, the Scottish crime writers have formed a phone tree so they can check on each other daily. I've already had one of them on to me looking for reassurance. A lot of them know what I do for a living. If you do find Georgia in pieces in Smithfield, my phone is going to be red-hot. I'm not going to tell these people there's no cause for alarm.'

'Fi, you know there's a big difference between suggesting they should be on their guard and telling them there's a serial

317

killer on the loose who might be targeting them. And you also know that's a line you're perfectly capable of walking,' Steve said.

Fiona pushed herself out of her chair. 'You might have forgotten Lesley, Steve. But I never will. And I'm going to deal with this as I see fit, not as you think best.'

Steve watched her stride out of the café, hair flowing with the speed of her passage. 'Oh fuck,' he groaned.

'I'd appreciate knowing what the hell that was all about,' Duvall said. 'Sir,' she added more as calculated insult than an afterthought.

Steve crushed his cigar out impatiently. 'She's right, I wasn't thinking about Lesley,' he said, half to himself. He straightened up in his chair. 'Lesley was Fiona's sister. She was murdered by a serial rapist when she was a student. They never made an arrest. It's why Fiona became a criminal psychologist. She always believed that if the university had given their female students proper warning, Lesley would have been safe. She's probably wrong, but survivors have to find someone to blame. Otherwise they end up blaming the victim, and that's even less healthy.'

Duvall nodded, understanding dawning. 'No wonder she's worried about the boyfriend.'

'I'm worried about him too, Sarah. He's my best mate.' Steve's face was stern.

'You'd better go after her, calm her down. I don't want her running around like a loose cannon in the middle of my investigation. However helpful she's been.'

Steve, who liked being told what to do about as much as Duvall herself, gave her a hard stare.

Duvall held up one hand in a placatory gesture. 'And when I get back to Wood Street, I'm going straight to my guv'nor to get a full murder squad working the case. I'll be working on my search warrant application this afternoon. You can tell her that to reassure her.'

'I will, Sarah. I'm glad you're taking this seriously. Because if anything were to happen to Kit Martin, Fiona wouldn't be the only one baying for blood.'

Chapter 35

What she wanted to do was to jump in the first passing taxi and go straight home to Kit. But Fiona had always struggled against putting desire before duty, so she swept through the streets back to her office, oblivious to everyone and everything, her head buzzing with chaos, her gut knotting with fear. There was no particular reason why Kit should be the next name on the list, but equally, no strong reason why he should not be. She had to find a way to make him take her seriously without leaving him as scared as she was.

She was walking into her office when she heard someone call her name. She turned to find Steve running down the corridor towards her, a fine sheen of sweat on his face. 'Wait, Fi,' he shouted as she turned on her heel and slammed her door behind her.

She hadn't even got her jacket off when he was in the room beside her. One sleeve in and one sleeve half out, she had no way of resisting when he pulled her into his arms and hugged her close. 'I know you're scared,' Steve said.

'Fuck scared,' Fiona snarled. 'I'm furious. People are at risk, and you won't protect them.' She pulled away and dragged her jacket off, throwing it on the sofa. 'You wouldn't be keeping this under wraps if somebody was murdering police officers, Steve. Why don't Kit and his friends merit the same consideration?'

'Apples and oranges, Fi. Police officers know how to keep the lid on things. But if we start issuing blanket warnings to crime writers, it'll be a madhouse. We can't offer them protection, we don't have the bodies. So some of them will run screaming to the media about how crap the police are and the papers will whip it all up into mass hysteria. And then the cranks will start. And the stalkers. And the hoax phone calls. And then it'll be the vigilantes taking the law into their own hands, protecting their heroes. And before you know it, somebody will get hurt who is nothing to do with this whole mess.' Steve paced as he spoke, his tension evident in every movement.

'It stinks, Steve, and you know it. If Georgia has been killed – and believe me, I am praying that Sarah Duvall's team don't find anything in Smithfield apart from animal carcasses – then I think it's inescapable that there's a serial killer out there. And I won't let my lover and his friends be the stalking horses while you guys fuck around failing to catch the right person.' Fiona slammed open her desk drawer and pulled out a plastic folder, throwing it towards him. 'There're the letters. Kit's, Georgia's and the other four. You get them to Sarah Duvall.'

Steve's face tightened. 'Fine. Just promise me one thing. Promise you'll do what you have to do in a responsible manner.'

Fiona looked as if she was about to burst into tears of rage. 'Oh Steve, you should know me better than that.' Her voice was a reproach that cut like a whip.

Steve flinched, as she had intended. 'I'm sorry, Fi. But you've got to see my point. We can't afford to start a media witch hunt. Look, I'm scared too. If anything happened to Kit, I'd never, ever forgive myself.'

'So do something to make sure it doesn't.'

Steve threw the folder of letters on to a chair in frustration. 'Don't you see? I can't. It's none of my professional business. The City force are totally separate from us and I can't interfere in their case.'

'Well, there's nothing more to say, is there?' Fiona's voice seemed to come from a long way off.

Before Steve could respond, the phone rang. She reached for it automatically, saying, 'You'll have to excuse me. I have work to do.' Fiona deliberately turned her back on him. 'Hello, Fiona Cameron.'

Steve watched her shoulders slump as she registered who was calling. 'Just give me a minute, Major,' she said, covering the mouthpiece with her hand. She glanced over her shoulder. 'Goodbye, Steve.' She waited until he had picked up the letters and was walking through the door, then moved to the chair behind her desk.

Stifling a sigh, she spoke into the phone. 'Sorry about that, there was someone just leaving.'

'I'm sorry, I have called at a bad time,' he apologized.

'Right now, believe me, there's no such thing as a good time. How can I help you, Major?'

'I have very good news,' he said. 'We have Miguel Delgado in custody.'

Fiona forced herself to sound bright in spite of the headache that was starting behind her eyes. 'Congratulations. You must be very relieved.'

'*Si*, and pleased that we have succeeded. You were right, he had another line of defence in place. He had a friend with what my wife calls a Winnebago. Somebody he thought he could trust, because he knew this friend was himself a criminal. But his friend is only a small-time thief, a burglar. His friend, he had seen Delgado's face in the paper and he knew whatever Delgado had done, it must be very serious.

322

And the only really serious crimes he had heard about were the murders. He didn't want to be implicated in crimes like that, so although he let Delgado take his van, he tipped off the local police. We found him early this morning on a camp site a few miles out of the city.'

'Well done. Has he confessed?'

She could hear Berrocal sigh. 'No. He has said nothing since he was arrested.'

'Is there any solid evidence tying him to the crimes?'

'The second victim? The American? A waiter has come forward who says he remembers seeing Delgado with him a couple of days before the murder. We are hopeful that forensics will be able to match up fibres, but we won't have that for a while yet. Also, we are testing the knives that Delgado had in the van when we caught him. Again, we don't have the results yet. So, we have nothing much to put pressure on with.'

She hoped he wasn't looking for help from her. She wanted to tell him to fuck off, that she had far more important things to worry about. But the professional in her knew that putting an end to the Toledo murders was just as important as what was happening in her own life. When it came to value, she had to believe all human lives were equal. Otherwise there would be little point in her work. So she forced herself not to let her frustration and hostility loose on Salvador Berrocal. 'I'm sure you've got a very experienced team to work on him,' she said, reaching for the button to switch on her computer.

'I have never dealt with a serial killer in interrogation before. But I have a plan,' he said, sounding enthusiastic. 'I figured I would make him angry. Use one of my team to taunt him. You know the kind of thing. These stupid local cops, how could they be so dumb as to arrest a pathetic specimen like him? It's obvious that whoever did these crimes was clever enough to plan very carefully and charming enough to get his victims to go along with him willingly. And an ugly, smelly failed shopkeeper like Delgado couldn't possibly have what it takes to be the Toledo killer. My man will act as if he's disgusted to be wasting his time on such a pointless interview.'

'I think that'll make him very angry,' Fiona said. 'Which will almost certainly work to your advantage. You've obviously thought it through very carefully.' *Now go away and leave me alone,* she thought. 'Let me know how you get on.'

He was still thanking her for her profile when she put the phone down. So let him think she was a rude bitch. She was past caring. Fiona headed straight for her e-mail program and started to write a new message. Kit wouldn't answer the phone when he was writing, but she knew he checked his e-mail every hour or so.

From: Fiona Cameron
           <fcameron@psych.ulon.ac.uk>
To: Kit Martin <KMWriter@trashnet.com>
Re: Advice

Remember the message on the front of *The Hitchhiker's Guide to the Galaxy?* Well, DON'T PANIC.
I didn't want to alarm you this morning. I had an idea, but I wanted to run it past Steve first. Overnight I discovered that the locals think the Garda have arrested the wrong man for Jane Elias's murder. Taking into account Drew's death and Georgia's disappearance, I had to think about the possibility of a serial offender. So I took a look at *And Ever More Shall Be So* and was disturbed by

certain parallels I found there. I've had a meeting
with the officer in charge of the case in the City of
London Police, and the good news is that they're
taking me seriously.
The bad news of course is that if I'm right, then
Georgia is probably, as we feared, dead.
And the worst news is that there may be other
killings. And of course, the police are already
saying they don't want to issue a general warning
and start an unwarranted panic, not least because
they don't have the staffing levels to offer people
any protection . . .
There is NO REASON to suppose you're specifically
at risk (and yes, I still think the death threats are
probably unrelated to the murders), but it makes
sense to take precautions. Don't answer the door
to strangers. Don't go anywhere alone. I mean,
anywhere. Fuck bravado, I want you safe.
I'm at work if you need to talk. Departmental
meeting 2–3, seminar 3.30–5, home by 6. I hope.
I love you.
Keep safe.
F.

She hit the <send> button and watched her message
disappear into the ether. The logical part of Fiona's mind
knew that she could not save Kit if someone was determined
to kill him. But she could adopt the alarm principle. A burglar
had once told her that security systems on private houses
were no deterrent to the determined raider. If he wanted
to get into a specific house, he could and he would. Where
they were useful was in putting off the casual burglar. 'You
gotta make the house next door look like an easier option,'

he'd explained. Well, if the price of Kit's life was making someone else look like an easier option, Fiona was prepared to do that.

Afterwards, she'd live with the consequences. For now, what was important was keeping Kit alive.

In spite of what she'd said to Fiona, Sarah Duvall was conscious that she owed a duty to potential victims. She'd always been a proponent of preventative policing, but it acquired a new urgency when murder was the crime in question rather than burglary or street crime. Her first priority was the preparation of an application for a search warrant for Smithfield Market, but once that was under way, she had turned her attention to what else she could usefully achieve.

Because she'd never worked with Fiona, Duvall recognized she was probably far more sceptical of her insights than Steve Preston, who seemed to regard the psychologist as virtually infallible. So she was wary of Fiona's contention that the death threat letters were unlikely to be the work of the murderer. Duvall didn't believe in coincidence. In her book, even synchronicity was suspect. She simply couldn't believe that a serial murderer happened to be targeting thriller writers at the same time as a completely different individual was sending them death threats. Either they were one and the same person, or the letter-writer had inside knowledge. So if she could go some way towards identifying the source of the letters, she would either have uncovered the identity of the killer or at the very least, someone who might lead her to her culprit.

While she wasn't willing to take everything Fiona had said at face value, Duvall was prepared to acknowledge common sense when she heard it. And it seemed to her that it was more than likely that the letter-writer could well be either a frustrated wannabe writer or someone whose career had crashed and burned. If that were the case, then the chances were that there were authors' agents and publishers' editors who would have come into contact with the writer of the letters and who might even be able to make a guess at their creator. These people worked with words; it wasn't beyond the bounds of possibility that they might recognize the prose style of the writer.

So she had set one of her team the task of identifying appropriate authorities, including an expert in the genre of crime fiction. As a result, she had arranged a breakfast meeting for the following morning with two leading agents and three editors in the field. They had no idea what she wanted to talk to them about, though she had impressed them both with the urgency of her request and the need for confidentiality.

But that was for the morning, and she'd work out how best to handle that later. What she had to focus on now was finding out who might be the future targets of her putative serial killer.

It was a goal that had brought her to Clapham and a quiet row of terraced cottages set a couple of streets back from the Common. According to her detective constable, what Dominic Reid didn't know about contemporary crime fiction wasn't worth knowing. As the car pulled up to the kerb a couple of houses away from Reid's, Duvall switched on the interior light. 'Give me a minute,' she said to the DC who was driving her. She used the time to refresh her memory on the brief he'd prepared for her earlier.

Dominic Reid, forty-seven. He'd started off working in BBC Radio, then branched out as an independent producer. His company currently made a couple of Radio

Four quiz programmes, and he had a list of credits in radio documentary, mostly concerning one aspect or another of mystery writing. He'd written a guide to crime fiction for a major bookselling chain, reviewed the genre for a couple of magazines, and had recently published *Paging Death*, a critical study of modern British crime fiction. If anyone could tell Duvall who might be in the sights of a serial killer, it was Reid. 'Do you read this stuff?' she asked the constable. 'Crime novels?'

He shook his head. 'I tried to read one once. I counted five mistakes in the first twenty pages, so I binned it. Too much like a busman's holiday. What about you, ma'am?'

'I never read fiction of any kind.' Duvall sounded like a teetotaller talking about strong drink. She clicked off the light. 'Let's do it,' she said.

Reid opened the door almost before the twin tones of the bell had died away. He was a lean, gangling man with an engaging, bony face under a thatch of untidy greying blond hair. 'Detective Chief Inspector Duvall?' he asked, suppressed excitement obvious in his expression.

'Mr Reid,' Duvall acknowledged with a nod. 'Thank you for agreeing to see me at such short notice.'

He stepped back, gesturing that they should enter. Duvall and the DC filed into the hall. There was barely room for the three of them; stacks of books leaned against one wall, reaching above waist-height. They followed Reid into the front room, where three walls were lined with shelves crammed with more hardbacks. Apart from books, the only furnishings in the room were four battered armchairs and a couple of occasional tables. On one chair, a large black and white cat lay curled, not twitching so much as a whisker at their arrival.

'Please, sit down,' Reid said.

Duvall gave the chairs the once-over for cat hairs, and opted for the one nearest the door as being least likely to do major damage to her suit. She caught the DC's eye and nodded to the far chair.

'Can I get you anything to drink?' Reid said eagerly. 'Tea, coffee, soft drinks? Or something stronger?'

'Thanks, Mr Reid, but I don't want to eat into your time any more than necessary. Please?' Duvall waved a hand at the remaining empty chair.

Reid folded his long body into the chair. 'I've never actually met a senior police officer before,' he said. 'Seems strange, I know, since I've read about so many. But there it is.' He swallowed, and his Adam's apple bounced in the open neck of his shirt.

'I appreciate you making time for us. And I'm sorry my colleague wasn't able to explain why I needed to see you so urgently.'

'Very mysterious. But of course, you would expect that to appeal to me, wouldn't you?'

Duvall acknowledged his remark with a thin smile. When necessary, she could be as warm and confiding with a witness as anyone. But anoraks like Reid didn't need to be cosseted to part with every piece of knowledge they possessed. 'It's a highly confidential matter. Before I can lay it out for you, I have to be certain of your discretion.'

Reid sat up straight, a look of surprise on his face. 'That sounds serious.'

'It is *very* serious. Can I rely on you not to repeat this conversation to any third party?'

His head bobbed up and down several times. 'If that's what you want, yes, of course I'll keep it to myself. Is this anything to do with Georgia Lester's disappearance?' he asked.

'What makes you say that?'

He gave an awkward little shrug. 'I just assumed . . . You're from the City Police, and I know that's where Georgia lives. And with her disappearance being in the news . . .'

Duvall crossed her legs and leaned forward from the waist. 'It's true that I am the officer investigating Ms Lester's disappearance. But I have a further concern. In the light of the recent murders of Drew Shand and Jane Elias, we are considering the possibility – and I put it no stronger than that – that there might be a connection.'

Reid folded his arms across his chest in an automatic gesture of defence. 'You wonder if there's a serial killer targeting crime writers.' It was a statement, not a question. 'Yes, I can see why you might be thinking along those lines. I won't pretend it hadn't crossed my mind, but' – he inclined his head towards the bookshelves – 'I put it down to too much reading.' He gave a lopsided half-smile.

'And it may well be that we're letting our imagination run away with us too,' Duvall acknowledged. 'But we have to explore every possible avenue. And that's why I want to pick your brains. I'm anxious to try to establish who else might be at risk, if our theory proves correct.'

Reid was nodding. 'And you think I can help. Well, nobody knows more than me about the genre. Tell me what you want to know.'

Duvall allowed herself to relax slightly. She was going to get what she needed with almost no expenditure of energy. Which was just as well, because she was beginning to feel the day had gone on altogether too long. 'If there *is* a connection, there seem to be certain linking factors. All three have written serial killer novels. All three have won awards for their books. And all three have had their books successfully adapted for TV or film. I imagine there aren't too many others who fit that category?'

Reid unfolded his arms. 'More than you'd think, Chief Inspector. Obviously, you'll be thinking about thriller writers like Kit Martin, Enya Flannery, Jonathan Lewis.'

Duvall blinked quickly at the mention of Kit Martin's name, but otherwise showed no sign that his name held any more significance than any other. But if he was the first name out of the expert's hat, Fiona Cameron might well be justified in her fears, Duvall thought as she listened to what Reid was saying.

'But as well as the pure serial killer novels, some authors of police series have included serial murderers in their books. Ian Rankin and Reginald Hill, for example.' He got to his feet. 'I've got a database on my computer next door. All the factors you describe are among my criteria, so we can do a multiple search and find out exactly who fits the bill. Why don't we go and see what that comes up with?'

Duvall uncrossed her legs. 'That sounds like a very good idea. Lead on, Mr Reid.'

iv

Susannah's teeth were chattering. Uncontrollable casta-
nets rattling through her head. She didn't remember the
cottage being cold when they'd been here. But then,
the weather had been mild in September. An hour of
the gas fire in the late evenings had been enough to
take the nip off the air. That and Thomas's warm body
next to hers. Now, there was no warm body. And only
the chill of damp November air to caress her body. Her
captor clearly wasn't about to spend his money on the
gas meter just for the sake of her comfort.

Her naked skin was gooseflesh. That had as much to
do with ambient temperature as fear. Though certainly
her fear was enough to produce goose pimples in a
tropical climate. One minute she'd been working on
her monthly billing, the next minute there had been a
knock at the door. She'd looked out of the window. An
unfamiliar white van in the drive. But the man standing
on the doorstep with the package and the clipboard wore
the familiar uniform of the courier that her company
always used to send her packages of work.

She hadn't been expecting anything from head office
that afternoon. And it was late for the courier, who
usually arrived mid-morning. It must, she thought, be

something urgent. Perhaps the Brantingham contract. Phil had mentioned in that morning's e-mail that it was close to finalization. Susannah had opened the door and smiled at the courier.

She never knew what hit her. Only that something did.

The next thing she knew was excruciating pain. Pain expanded to include blackness and movement. And the low thrum of an engine. She was lying on her side, drool running from her mouth. And she couldn't move. Slowly, as if she was very drunk, she identified the pain. The principal source was her head. Like a very bad migraine, except that this originated in the back of her head, not the front.

Next in the hierarchy were her shoulders. Her arms seemed to be pinioned behind her. That was the information her screaming muscles sent her. She tried to straighten up and a new wave of pain swept up her legs. As far as she could figure out through the blitz of sensory overload, her feet were fastened together and linked to her wrists. Hog-tied, wasn't that what the Americans called it?

By keeping perfectly still, the pain diminished. Still unbearable, but at least now she could think of something else. Blackness and movement. And the rough feel of carpet under her cheek. What else could it be but the boot of a car?

That was when the fear kicked in.

She had no idea how long they'd been travelling. There was no way to measure the duration of pain.

At last, the movement stopped with a jerk. Then the engine noise ceased. She strained to hear something but nothing came. Then the boot cracked open. The shock to her eyes triggered a nauseating pain in her head. Then *they adjusted and she saw a dark silhouette against the night sky.*

Susannah opened her mouth and screamed. The man laughed. 'No one to hear you, pet,' he said. The accent was Geordie, she registered that much.

He bent over and grunted with the effort of lifting her out of the car. He staggered slightly under the weight as he walked. With her face jammed against his shoulder, Susannah could see nothing. The quality of the air changed and she realized he had taken her indoors. A few more steps, a turn to the right and suddenly they were in glaring fluorescent light. He let her fall and she screamed as she hit cold tile. Her head cracked against something cold and hard.

The next time she came round, she was naked. She was sitting on a toilet, her right arm handcuffed to a towel rail firmly bolted to the wall. Dazed, confused and in pain, she worked out that her legs were shackled, the chain passing behind the bowl so she was anchored to the toilet seat.

But at least now she knew where she was. Thomas had rented the cottage on a remote Cornish headland to celebrate their first anniversary. They'd spent a week here, walking on the cliffs, watching the birds, cooking simple meals, making love every night. It had been idyllic.

This was a nightmare.

And it had only grown worse.

When she had called out, he had reappeared. Tall and broad, with the muscles of a weightlifter. His dark hair cropped in a crew cut over a face that seemed oddly familiar. She couldn't figure out where she'd seen him before. But then, his face was unremarkable. Nondescript. If she'd written an inventory of his features,

335

it would have fitted thousands of men. Dark eyebrows, blue eyes, pale complexion, straight nose, average mouth, slightly receding chin. The only strange thing about him was that he was wearing a white lab coat and he had a stethoscope hanging round his neck like a doctor. He stood in the doorway, appraising her.

'Why are you doing this?' Susannah croaked.

'That's none of your business,' he said. He produced a second set of handcuffs. 'If you struggle, it's going to hurt a lot more.'

She lashed out with her free arm, but he was too quick for her. He gripped her wrist and snapped the cuff round it. He extended her arm and fastened the other cuff round a water pipe. Then he took a roll of elastoplast and taped her wrist and hand to the wall so her arm was immobilized.

As bemused as she was terrified, Susannah stared disbelieving as he wrapped a blood pressure cuff round her upper arm and inflated it. Then he left the room. She recognized the apparatus he came back with. She'd been a blood donor for years. 'What are you doing?' she protested as he located a vein and inserted a needle.

'Taking your blood,' he said calmly, with all the assurance of one of the nurses at the blood transfusion centre.

Incredulous, she watched mesmerized as her blood started to flow down the tube and into the container. 'You're mad!' she shouted at him.

'No. I'm just different,' he said, settling down on the edge of the bath to wait.

Susannah stared. 'What are you going to do to me?'

'I'm going to feed you and make sure you have enough to drink. And I'm going to take your blood.'

He got to his feet and started to walk out of the small bathroom.

'You're a vampire?' she said faintly.

He turned and smiled. Its very normality made it the scariest thing she'd seen so far. 'No. I'm an artist.'

When he came back, he was carrying an assortment of paintbrushes, from the finest calligraphy brush to one that was almost an inch across. Satisfied that he'd drawn almost a pint of blood, he detached the apparatus and released the blood pressure cuff, keeping his thumb over the puncture. He applied cotton wool and elastoplast to staunch the bleeding, then stripped away the restraining tape. He unlocked the handcuffs and stepped back quickly so she could not hit him.

'There, that didn't hurt a bit, did it, pet?' He placed the jar of blood in the sink and walked out of the room. He returned with a can of energy-giving electrolyte drink and a paper plate that held a stack of liver pâté sandwiches and half a dozen chocolate biscuits. He put them on the floor, within reach of Susannah's free left hand. 'There you go. That'll stop you feeling faint. And it'll help your body replace some of the blood you've lost.'

Then he turned his back, as if she had ceased to exist for him. He picked up the jar of blood and stuck the brushes in his pocket. Then he stepped into the bath and stared consideringly at the wall. There were two rows of tiles above the edge of the bath, but above that there was an area of blank plastered wall about six feet square. He selected a medium-sized brush and dipped it into the blood.

Then he began to paint.

Susannah began to sob.

Chapter 36

By the time he was on his second cup of coffee, Steve was beginning to wonder if he'd turned into a manic depressive overnight. Less than an hour out of bed and he'd already swung between the poles of nervous anticipation and deep despair more times than he could count.

But then, as he'd commented to Fiona only the day before, these were only the symptoms of mental illness if they were groundless. And he had good reasons for both sets of emotions. His optimism, tempered though it was with his natural wariness, all centred round Terry Fowler. If she was as good at her job as Fiona had promised, and if Joanne had identified the right cases, the Susan Blanchard case might take its first positive move forward in a long time. That would be reward enough. But added to that, he had the prospect of dinner with her this evening. He couldn't remember the last time he'd looked forward to a date with a woman with such conviction that it would be fun. He'd better remember to book somewhere for dinner. Not too upscale; he didn't want them to feel uncomfortable. But not too informal, either; he wanted her to realize that he was taking her seriously. Normally, he'd have asked Kit to recommend somewhere. But that was out of the question today.

For, like his optimism, his pessimism was both professional

and personal. There was no escaping the fact that he had done serious damage to his oldest friendship. Fiona had demanded more of him than was in his power to give, but she was bound to feel he'd failed her. Her and Kit both. He'd tried to phone several times the previous evening, but the answering machine had been switched on. Doubtless Fiona had decided they should monitor their calls, and he was clearly not on the approved list.

The trouble was, she was right in emotional and moral terms. But he was right in practical terms. And those two certainties were mutually incompatible. All his adult life, he'd been glad that the job he loved had never turned on him and threatened to destroy something that was important to him. He'd seen it happen with colleagues – marriages crumbled, children become enemies, friendships betrayed – and he'd always known that, but for fortune, it could have been him.

Now, he'd run out of grace. His oldest friend estranged and his best male friend at risk, and there was nothing he could do about it. It wasn't even his case. All he knew about what was going on he knew because Sarah Duvall had had the courtesy to tell him. But he had been a senior CID officer for long enough to know that this was the worst kind of case to resolve. No criminal was harder to catch than a killer who killed without apparent connection to his victim, who operated on a logic clear only to himself, who left few traces and who was smart enough to stay several steps ahead of any pursuit. When such killers were caught, it was often almost by accident. Neighbours complained about the smell of the drains; a spot check of a numberplate revealed it belonged to another car entirely; a police officer stopped a random speeder.

That Kit's life might hang by so slender and serendipitous a chance was almost more than Steve could bear to contemplate. How much worse it must be for Fiona, who had already had to live through one such apparently random loss. And now, when he should be at her side, supporting them both, he was the outsider.

Steve carried the remains of his coffee through to the bedroom and contemplated his wardrobe. He couldn't rely on being able to get home to change before the evening. He chose a lightweight navy wool suit that he knew didn't easily crease. A white shirt and a blue tie for now; a dark grey shirt, carefully folded and bagged, and a scarlet silk tie for the evening. Fiona had given him the tie, he remembered. Strange that it was the exact shade of Terry's lipstick. Even in something so basic, the two strands of his life were intertwined.

As he dressed, Steve tried to put his personal feelings far from the front of his mind. He had important things to do today, and he needed to be clear-headed. But it didn't work, and as he walked to his car, he knew that whatever broke with the Blanchard case, he wouldn't settle until he knew what Sarah Duvall was doing.

What Sarah Duvall was doing was wondering why she'd ever imagined that authors' agents and publishers' editors would be able to tell her anything about the death threat letters that Kit Martin, Georgia Lester and at least three other crime writers had received.

The five people she'd just had breakfast with had listened with rapt attention to what she had to say. Then they'd dropped their quiet bombshell. 'We get over three thousand unsolicited manuscripts a year,' one of the agents had said. 'Out of those, we might ultimately take on perhaps a maximum of three new authors. That means there are a lot of unhappy people out there, and frankly, DCI Duvall, if you'd read some of those typescripts, you'd realize we're not always dealing with the most balanced of individuals.'

'I regularly get abusive letters,' an editor said, backing up the agent. 'Usually from people I've turned down, but once or twice from authors I've dropped from my list because of poor sales. People take it very personally, because writing is a very personal thing. But it never goes beyond that. They let off steam, add you to their mental hate list, they bad-mouth you round the business, but that's all.'

They'd passed the letters round from hand to hand, commenting only that they seemed rather more hostile than usual. But they all agreed that none of them would have bothered the police, or even their company door security with them. 'We're in a very emotive business,' another of the agents had said. 'Feelings run high. But we're dealing with people who regard words as weapon enough.'

However, Duvall had extracted from each of them a promise that they would take copies of the letters back and check them against any hate mail in their own files on the off-chance that they might spot some congruence. It had been a long shot, so she wasn't unduly surprised that it hadn't paid off.

That didn't stop her feeling disappointed. She hoped it wasn't an omen for the rest of the day. She didn't want to end up with egg on her face after an operation as major as the search of Smithfield Market.

It never occurred to her that, indirectly, what she was hoping for was the murder of Georgia Lester.

Terry Fowler looked as relaxed as she had done the day before. She was wearing a thin black cardigan over a white T-shirt and what looked like the same pair of black jeans. She had pulled up a chair next to her so Steve could look over her shoulder at the computer screen. 'Interesting results,' she said, her fingers tapping the keys. He noticed her hands were surprisingly broad, with strong fingers that ended in short, blunt nails carefully trimmed, as if to remove the temptation to chew them. She wore a heavy silver ring on the third finger of her right hand. 'I was able to use a set of parameters that Fiona's already developed for serial rapes. It needed one or two modifications, but because I was working with a more or less off-the-shelf package it was a lot quicker than starting from scratch. And since you seemed to be in a bit of a hurry . . .'

'Habit, I'm afraid. Another day or two probably wouldn't have made a lot of difference.'

'Urgency's not a bad habit in your line of business, I imagine,' Terry said, half turning to give him a grin. 'You gotta try and get to the bad guys before they do worse things.'

'Something like that.' Steve sighed. 'Sometimes it's more a matter of getting things done before the bureaucrats notice how much of the budget you're draining.'

'Yeah, right. Well, this particular budget drainage ran the crime linkage program on the files you gave me.' She raised her eyebrows at him. 'Including the four that you slipped in to see whether I was doing it properly.'

'That's not why I put them in,' Steve protested. 'It's not about putting you on the spot, it's about showing my colleagues that this isn't a load of mumbo jumbo. It strengthens the value of the results if I can demonstrate that the programme weeds out the cases we know to be irrelevant.'

'Just testing,' she murmured. 'It's OK, I'm not really offended, I understand the principle of control groups . . . Anyway, having run all the cases through the computer, it appears you do have a cluster here.' Her tone became more brisk as she got into the meat of her results. 'Four of the rapes and two of the serious sexual assaults. The Hertfordshire case has a slightly lower probability than the other five, but it still comes in at eighty-seven per cent, which I would regard as a definite positive.'

Steve felt a small surge of excitement, though years of practice kept it well hidden. 'And how does that translate in terms of the geographical profile?'

'Let's take it stage by stage,' Terry said, her right hand clicking the mouse over dialog boxes. A map of North London spread out before them in monochrome. She tapped a couple of keys and the screen flooded with colour, iridescent greens, blues, yellows, purples and a patch of burgundy. 'This is what we get from the first two. Add in the third and fourth . . .' More five-finger exercises on the keyboard. Now the patch of red was more clearly defined, the colour clearer. But a second, purplish-red zone had also appeared slightly to the north of the original scarlet. Steve, who had seen Fiona do this enough times to be able to glean some meaning from what was in front of him, noted that the main highlighted area covered a dozen streets in the northern part of Kentish Town. The second patch was up towards Archway.

'Add in the fifth, and that second patch gets less significant,' Terry continued. 'But when we introduce the sixth incident, see what happens.' The original red sector changed scarcely at all, but the purple area grew noticeably more reddish in tone.

'And what do you conclude from that?' Steve asked, pretty sure he knew what was coming next.

Terry turned her head and grinned at him. 'Same as you, I expect.' She picked up a pencil and pointed to the main red zone. 'If we have correctly identified a genuine cluster, then chances are your man lives in this area here. It's possible that he lives in the other hot spot, but I'd be more inclined to think that's where he works. When an offender is at the start of his career, he tends to stick closer to home. And if we look at the first two cases, the only hit we get is this section here that simply intensifies in probability the more cases we input.'

She leaned back in her chair and swivelled it around so she was half facing Steve. Without looking at the screen, she hit a couple of keys. 'And when we add in the Susan Blanchard murder, let's see what happens.'

No amount of self-control could prevent Steve from revealing his shock. 'What did you just say?'

Terry grinned. 'You look like a stunned cod,' she said. 'I thought that would shake you.'

'Have you been discussing this with Fiona?' Steve demanded, hiding his feelings behind a sharp tone.

'Nope. I worked it out all by myself. When you said there was another case to add in to the series, I figured it had to be something pretty serious. And the only thing more serious than violent rape is sexual homicide. Also, it had to be an important case for you to be prepared to lash out on crime linkage and geographic profiling. Probably one that had stalled, because this sort of process isn't your first port of call. Since you were interested in North London cases, chances are you were looking at a rape-murder north of the river, as yet unsolved. Put it all together and it comes up with Susan Blanchard.' She spread her hands in the theatrical manner of a magician revealing the rabbit in the hat.

'I'm impressed,' Steve acknowledged. Fiona had said Terry was impulsive; she hadn't mentioned she was also intuitive.

Terry shrugged. 'It was no big deal. I'm supposed to be trained to make connections.' She smiled. 'You really shouldn't be surprised when I do it.'

Steve laughed. 'I'm surrounded by people who are supposed to be trained to make connections, and most of the time you'd never know it. You're right, of course, it is the Susan Blanchard murder I'm interested in.'

'I thought you guys had closed down the investigation after that complete fuck-up at the Bailey? Wasn't the official line that you weren't looking for another suspect?'

'Well, we couldn't exactly say anything else without making ourselves look even more foolish than we did already,' Steve said, the edge of bitterness in his voice creeping through in spite of his best intentions.

'Yeah, right. But secretly, you're still ferreting away?'

He nodded. 'I have a small team of officers working on it.'

'But not Fiona?'

There was a silence. 'I'd rather not get into that, if you don't mind,' he said. 'Maybe you should ask Fiona the history.'

'Cool.' Terry flapped one hand from the wrist in a dismissive gesture. 'It's none of my business. I'm just grateful for the cheque in the post. So, you want to see what happens when we add the Susan Blanchard murder into the mix?'

'Is Sinn Fein IRA?'

'Whoa, there speaks the detective. OK, in spite of the fact that you're a prejudiced bigot, I'll share my results with you.' Her grin took most of the sting out of Terry's words and she hit the <enter> key. The principal scarlet sector changed not at all, but the more northerly area grew less red. 'I don't have to spell it out for you, do I?'

Steve shook his head, a feeling of deep gratification surging through him. 'No. Your program thinks that whoever killed Susan Blanchard is the same man who committed four rapes and two serious sexual assaults in the course of the previous two years. And I have to tell you that from where I'm sitting, that's the best news I've heard in a long time.'

Terry gave him the grin he was beginning to recognize as

a marker that he was about to be challenged. 'Yeah right. You have a well weird take on the world, Steve. Not a lot of people think a serial rapist turned killer falls into the good-news category. You should get out more.'

'I thought you were already taking steps to rectify that,' he said, returning the smile.

'It's a dirty job, saving the filth, but somebody's got to do it,' she said flippantly. 'So where are we going?'

'There's a new brasserie opened in Clerkenwell. The chef trained with Marco Pierre White and he specializes in fish. I managed to get a cancellation for seven thirty. How does that sound?'

'Sounds cool.'

For a brief moment, Steve thought about offering to pick her up, but he knew he was unlikely to have the time. He didn't want to start letting her down so soon. If things worked out between them, his job would provide plenty of opportunities for dislocated social engagements in the future. Besides, he didn't want to appear the pushover he secretly knew himself to be. Instead, he scribbled the name and address of the restaurant on a piece of scrap paper. 'I'll see you there.' He stood up. 'I've got to get back to the Yard and get my team working on this. Can you give me a printout of the map?'

Terry turned back to her computer. 'You want a blow-up of the red areas?' she asked.

'Please.'

'You need a written report?' she asked.

'Might as well get my money's worth,' Steve said.

'Fax or e-mail?'

'Both, if you don't mind.'

'Be with you by the end of the morning.' Terry winked. 'See you tonight.'

Steve nodded and walked to the door. As he turned to leave, she blew him a kiss. The blush lasted all the way down the stairs. So did the smile. Terry Fowler had done more than waken his dormant case from its slumber. She'd wiped all his fear for Kit from his mind for as long as he'd been with her. And that was worth far, far more than the Metropolitan Police could ever imagine paying her.

Back at the Yard, Steve summoned Joanne into his office. Neil was busy watching Francis Blake, and John was off duty, so his resources were minimal, in spite of the new possibilities that Terry's study had produced.

Steve tossed the maps across the table to her, unable to keep his exultation off his face. 'Looks like we're on the way to somewhere at last. Geographic profile of your rapes. When the Susan Blanchard murder was factored into the analysis, the central red area didn't change at all.'

Joanne looked up, the excitement sparkling in her eyes. 'That's brilliant. Wow! So, what do you want me to do?'

'I'm afraid it's time for drudgery. Identify the streets outlined in red – and one street either side, for the sake of my peace of mind – and get the electoral roll.'

Joanne sighed. 'And go through the electoral roll checking it against CROs?'

'Unless you can think of a better way of doing it.'

'When I rule the world, they'll organize the criminal records database so you can search it with any one of a dozen parameters,' she said, getting to her feet. 'I'm on it.'

'Thanks, Joanne. Oh, and thanks for the restaurant tip.'

She raised her eyebrows. 'I hope you enjoy it.'

Steve grinned. 'I fully intend to.'

Joanne turned on her way out of the door. 'If you get there, of course. I mean, if I get lucky, we could all be checking out a new number one suspect this evening. Right, sir?'

'Get lucky, Jo. But try not to get lucky before tomorrow morning if you want to remain my favourite DC.'

After she left, Steve stared at the closed door, feeling the buzz in his veins that came from the knowledge that at last they might be only hours from a lucky break. Thinking of lucky breaks reminded him that there had been a message on his desk asking him to ring Sarah Duvall.

Part of him dreaded the call. If Georgia Lester had been found dead, he wanted to put off the knowledge and its implications for as long as possible. On the other hand, it was feasible that she'd turned up alive. Steve reached out and punched in Sarah's number.

Extract from **Decoding of Exhibit P13/4599**

Azoqf tqkru zpsqa dsumx qefqd edqym uzeyk
xurqe sauzs fasqf mxaft mdpqd. Ftqkx xtmhq faefm
dfeqq uzsft qbmff qdzft qzuze bufqa rftqp gynet
ufbmp pke.

*Once they find Georgia Lester's remains, my life's going
to get a lot harder. They'll have to start seeing the
pattern then. But it'll take them a day or two to go
official with it. They won't want to admit what's going
on because that'll cause a panic.*

*So I need to hit my next target fast, while he's
unsuspecting. But I've got to be careful not to rush
things. Patience, that's the secret. Never snatch at half
a chance. Never lose your cool. Just sit it out. Even when
the waiting's hard and bitter.*

*Take the courier's uniform. I knew right from the begin-
ning what I needed to get Kit Martin. But I had no idea*

how I was going to lay my hands on it. Then the gods smiled. I was in the launderette one evening, watching my clothes tumble around in the washer. There was only one other man there, and when he dragged out his damp clothes and stuffed them in the drier, I couldn't miss the logo of Capital City Couriers blazing across the dark-blue drill jacket. And there were matching trousers. Pure manna from heaven.

After he dropped some tokens in the slot, he looked at his watch and headed across the road to the local boozer. I waited a few minutes, and then loaded the courier's entire wash into my holdall. Piece of piss.

I sat and waited for my wash to finish, cool as a cucumber. Ten minutes later, I was walking back to my flat with my wet laundry on top of his. The trousers needed taking up, and the jacket's a bit tight on the shoulders, but that really doesn't matter. It's not like I'll be wearing it for long.

Just long enough to convince Kit Martin to open his front door to Postman Pat.

Chapter 37

Fiona looked at the clock on her office wall. Breakfast that morning had been tense, in spite of both their efforts to maintain something like normal life in the face of the fear that flickered below the surface. She had extracted an assurance from Kit that he wouldn't open the door to strangers, nor would he go out alone, not even for his usual lunchtime walk on the Heath. She could see he was already chafing under these restrictions, but at least he could salvage his pride by telling himself he was doing it to mollify Fiona rather than out of cowardice.

The worst part of it was the not knowing what was going on. She almost wished she had been able to be sanguine about Steve's refusal to offer Kit any formal protection. At least then they'd be in communication and she would be aware of how the investigation was progressing. But she couldn't bring herself to forgive his failure to stick his neck out for the sake of friendship. So she would somehow have to deal with her unaccustomed ignorance.

She glanced at the clock again. This was pointless. She was achieving nothing sitting here. The paper she was supposed to be revising before submitting it for publication stared accusingly at her from the computer screen, as neglected as a piece of wasteground. In her heart, Fiona knew she couldn't concentrate in the office. If she took the paper home, she could at least hope to get the work done there. Nothing would happen to Kit while they were in the house together.

The decision made, Fiona was taking her jacket off its peg when her phone rang. She resisted the temptation to ignore it and crossed the office to pick it up on the fourth ring. 'Hello, Fiona Cameron,' she said.

'Dr Cameron? This is Victoria Green from the *Mail*. I wonder if you could spare me a few minutes?'

'I don't think so.'

'If I could just explain what it's about?' The journalist's voice was warm and ingratiating.

'There's no point, because I'm not interested. If you bother to look at your cuttings library, you'll see I don't do interviews.'

'It's not an interview we want,' Green said quickly. 'We'd like you to write an article for us. I know you write articles, I've read you in *Applied Psychology Journal*.'

'You read *APJ*?' Fiona said, her surprise holding her back from putting the phone down.

'I have a degree in psychology. I've read your work on crime linkage. That's how I knew you were the best person to talk to about writing an article for us.'

'I don't think so,' Fiona reiterated.

'You see,' Green continued undaunted, 'I've got a theory that Drew Shand and Jane Elias were murdered by the same person. And I think Georgia Lester might be the next victim. I'd like you to apply your crime linkage work to these cases to see if I'm right.'

Fiona replaced the receiver without responding. The word was out. It wouldn't be long before others jumped on Victoria Green's bandwagon. If she'd had any doubts about going home to Kit, they had ended with the phone call.

*　　*　　*

The man with the face like a chicken shrugged. 'Meat's meat, innit? Once it's skinned and off the bone, your human flesh isn't going to look much different from a piece of beef or venison.'

Sarah Duvall sighed. 'I appreciate that.'

'And it's huge, the market. I can't begin to count the number of fridges and chill cabinets and freezers in that place. It's not like walking into your local butcher's shop, you know. There's twenty-three trading units in the East Building and another twenty-one in the West.' His dark eyes glittered and his beaky nose twitched in a sniff.

Sergeant Ron Daniels smiled benevolently at the small man. Working as officer in charge of the Smithfield Market policing team, he'd got to know Darren Green, the traders' representative, over a period of years. He knew that behind his aggression was a reasonable man, provided he was accorded sufficient respect. 'Nobody appreciates that more than me, Darren. We've got a big job on our hands and that's why we've come to you.'

Duvall turned to the Home Office pathologist. 'Professor Blackett, what's your take on this?'

The balding, middle-aged man sitting behind her looked up from his notebook and frowned. 'It is problematic, as Mr Green points out. But on your suggestion, I read the relevant section of Georgia Lester's book. And if we're dealing with a copycat killer, then the cuts of meat he would end up with are going to vary from the standard butchery cuts in several key details.'

'It's still just going to look like meat, though, innit?' Darren Green insisted.

Tom Blackett shook his head. 'Trust me, we can spot the difference.' He flicked his pad over to a clean page and began to draw. 'Human beings are bipeds, not quadrupeds. Our shoulders and our upper leg muscles are very different from those of a cow or a deer. Particularly the leg. If you take a transverse section through the middle of the thigh, taking off the head of the femur, which is far too obvious to leave in place . . .' He pointed to the rough sketch he'd made. Darren Green leaned over and looked suspiciously at it. 'You've got the rounded outline of the shaft of the femur here. In front of it, you've got the anterior group of muscles, the rectus femoris and the vasti. Behind it you've got the posterior group, the adductor magnus and the hamstrings. And here, on the inside, you've got the medial group of muscles, which is where most of the blood vessels and nerves are also situated. The chances are you're also going to have a lot more fat than on the average animal carcass.'

Green's face broke into a smile as understanding dawned. 'Right,' he said. 'That arrangement of meat, it's nothing like what you'd get on a leg of beef or venison.'

'And of course, a joint of human beef is going to be a lot smaller than the corresponding cut from a cow or a deer,' Blackett continued. 'Which is something any butcher would recognize at once, I presume?'

'I dare say,' Green said cautiously. 'But even if a group of us do help you out with this search, it's still going to take forever to cover the ground. We'll never get it done and dusted before the morning's trading begins. Don't forget, it's not like a shop that opens at nine o'clock. We do most of our business between four and seven in the morning.'

'If we were talking about searching the whole market, I'd have to agree with you, Mr Green,' Duvall said. 'But we do have information that will narrow the targets down considerably. We're looking for freezers that are not in everyday use. Ones that are for more long-term storage.

356

Probably ones that are locked up. That's why we need the full cooperation of your members. We don't want to have to go around breaking into their property. So what I need you to do is to contact everyone who has a unit in the market and ask them to make sure they'll have staff on the spot tonight who can give us access to all their storage. And that they'll be there all night if need be.'

'Bloody hell,' Green protested. 'That's a tall order.'

'If you don't have the resources to do it, I can second some of the market police officers to you. But it has to be done,' Duvall said, her voice adamant as her face was implacable.

'They're not going to like this,' he complained.

Daniels took over. 'We're not doing this for fun, Darren. This is a very serious matter.'

'That's right,' Duvall said grimly. 'Now, I need you and your volunteers at Snow Hill police station for nine o'clock so Professor Blackett can give you a full briefing on what you'll be looking for, and so you can be assigned to the officers you'll be assisting. I intend to commence operations at ten precisely. I have no desire to disrupt your night's trading. But that depends on you and your members. I suggest you get on with it.' The smile on her lips did nothing to diminish the force of the command. With muttered complaints, Green left the others.

'What do you think, Ron? Will it work?' Duvall asked.

The big man nodded. 'I think you'll get all the cooperation you need. I'll have a word with Darren, make sure he lets people know that the traders aren't under any suspicion at this point.'

Duvall nodded. 'You seem very confident that you can spot what we're after, Professor,' she said.

'If I'd sounded as dubious as I feel, your Mr Green would have been as obstructive as possible. It's not easy to identify

357

human flesh by sight, Chief Inspector. It's simple enough to run tests to confirm it once we have something suspicious, but whether we find anything depends entirely on how good your killer is.' Blackett paused, then raised his eyebrows. 'Always providing he exists.'

Chapter 38

Detective Constable Neil McCartney was tired. Watching Francis Blake for twelve hours a day was a killer assignment, in no small part because the man led such a bloody boring life. Sometimes he wouldn't see hide nor hair of his target for the whole shift. At least Neil had swapped over on to days, ten till ten, which was slightly less desperate than the long nights when all Blake seemed to do was watch videos and sleep. But Neil knew this was only a brief respite. With Joanne stuck in the office bashing the computer, it wouldn't be long before John was hassling to get the day shift again. It wasn't unreasonable – he had a wife and young kids who didn't want to be quiet all day because daddy was sleeping.

That could have been his life, Neil thought with an edge of sourness. If he hadn't been stupid enough to choose the wrong woman. He'd met Kim on the job. She was bouncy and vivacious, the life and soul of every party. Not the sort he'd normally have gone for, being a quiet sort of bloke, really. He'd thought the looks he got were envy. It was only a long time later that he realised they were pity. He was her alibi for her affair with one of the custody sergeants, the perfect distraction to fool the man's wife at every police function. And the best possible alibi was marriage.

At first, his bitterness had been turned on himself. But there was no point in being sour about Kim; she was the woman she was. So his search for somewhere to put the blame had ended with the job.

He could so easily have turned into another rancorous copper, taking out his spite on those he came into contact with professionally. But the transfer he'd sought had taken him into plain clothes and on to Steve Preston's team. And that had saved him. It had reminded him of why he'd joined the police in the first place. Putting villains away, that was what it was all about, and to hell with the office game-playing. That was how Steve ran his squad, and officers who couldn't live with that didn't last long.

So now Neil's loyalty, first and last, lay with his boss. That was why, however tedious the surveillance got, he was prepared to stick it out. The fiasco of Francis Blake's entrapment and subsequent trial had only stiffened his resolve. That was what happened when politics got in the way of policing, and he was as determined as his boss to set the record straight and catch Susan Blanchard's killer. So he stifled his doubts about the point of what he was doing and stuck to Blake like chewing gum.

He yawned. The rain drizzled relentlessly down his windscreen. It seemed a fitting counterpoint to the lack of excitement in his and Francis Blake's lives. If he had the kind of money that Blake had trousered over his newspaper deal, Neil was bloody sure he'd be living somewhere with a bit more class than this. No two ways about it, this was a dump.

The flat Blake had rented on his release was less than a mile from his old place in King's Cross. The new place was in a busy but faintly seedy street off the Pentonville Road, the sort of place where the locals were off-duty hookers, the hopelessly unemployed, the elderly poor and the mentally ill. The best you could say about it was that it was handy for public transport. Halfway up the road, some uninspired architect had designed a utilitarian block in grey brick that looked like it had been jerry built in the sixties. It was cut off from the neighbouring terraced houses by a service lane that ran up either side and round the back. On the ground floor were half a dozen shop units – a newsagent, an off-licence, a betting shop, a minimarket, a kebab shop and a minicab office. The two floors above were divided into flats, and it was in one of these drab boxes on the second floor that Blake had taken up residence. It depressed Neil just thinking about it.

Not only would he be living somewhere with a bit more class than this, he'd be doing something a bit more exciting than the occasional trip to the bookies or the video shop round the corner.

From what Neil could see, Blake might as well still have been locked up in the Scrubs.

A couple of miles away, Steve Preston and Terry Fowler were having a very different evening. For once, Steve had managed to drag himself away from work with time to spare, leaving Joanne ploughing her way through apparently endless criminal record searches. Neil had had nothing of significance to report, so there was no specific professional worry niggling at the back of his mind to distract him from the company.

Terry had been five minutes early, claiming pathological punctuality made it impossible for her to be fashionably late for anything. 'I'm always the one who arrives at parties while the hosts are still in the shower,' she'd said. 'Makes for an interesting start to the evening.'

Steve didn't mind in the least. He was perfectly happy with an extra five minutes in the bar to enjoy admiring her. Terry was wearing a simple knee-length black dress in some material he didn't recognize that seemed to flow and shimmer around her body whenever she moved. For someone who'd been languishing in the doldrums for what he now realized was far too long, Steve allowed himself warily to wonder if his luck had truly changed as much as it appeared. *Careful,* he cautioned himself. *You know as soon as your emotions are engaged you build too much too fast. Take it easy, don't let her see how much you need this. Just for once, treat your personal life with the same circumspection you bring to building a case.*

But nothing happened over dinner to change that feeling of overwhelming luck. He was aware of being an engaging companion, and she seemed more than willing to appreciate him. The conversation never lurched into one of those awkward silences while someone figured out what to talk about next. They'd swapped stories, made each other laugh, started to sketch the details of their lives. For a man accustomed to containing himself in a private place for most of his waking hours, Steve was pleasantly surprised to find that Terry's apparent candour had the knack of making him open up. For the first time since he'd met Fiona all those years ago at university, he recognized a woman who allowed him to relax, who made no demands other than that he be himself. Ironic, intelligent and apparently lacking all pretension, Terry seemed to Steve to be as attractive inside as she was on the outside. He couldn't for the life of him figure out what she'd seen in him. When she left him at one point to go to the toilet, he found himself watching the door, eager for her return as he hadn't been with anyone for years. *I feel like a teenager again,* he thought, bemused. *This is insane, Preston. Put the brakes on.*

All through dinner, Steve had kept waiting for the other shoe to drop. But it didn't. She didn't even demur when he insisted on paying for the meal. 'You earn a lot more than me, sugar,' she'd said with a casual shrug.

It was after ten when they emerged on Clerkenwell Green.

A thin rain had started while they'd been inside so they huddled together under the awning to wait for a vacant taxi. The white neon of the restaurant's name cast its shadow on Steve's face, turning it into a chiaroscuro of planes and angles. Terry's hair flared platinum in its glow. She snuggled into Steve and grinned up at him. 'So, handsome,' she said, 'did you put clean sheets on this morning?'

Steve laughed out loud. 'Why? Did you?'

'In spite of the fact that I figure your place will be a lot more civilized than mine, yes, I did.'

He shook his head, his smile crinkling the skin round his eyes. 'OK, I'll own up to being presumptuous. Yes, I changed the sheets this morning.' He squeezed her close.

In response, Terry shifted so that she was facing him. She stood on tiptoe and leaned into his body. She gripped his lapels and pulled his face down to hers. Then she kissed him. Long, languid and luxurious.

It was all the reply he needed. Any pretence at caution disappeared in the instantaneous heat of his desire for her. When they got back to his flat, for the first time in years, Steve unplugged the phone and turned off his pager. For tonight, there was nothing so urgent it couldn't wait until morning. Nothing except Terry, and that was more than enough.

Night in the city. A few years previously, the streets around Smithfield Market would have been deserted at this time of night. Tall grey buildings, blank-faced, turned the narrow streets into twisting canyons. The streetlights hardly seemed to cut the gloom. The market itself was closed, the vast Victorian glass, brick and iron construction under restoration.

But now, all that had changed. Bistros and brasseries, bars and restaurants had colonized the area, their bright lights spilling on to pavements and making the streets lively

363

with patrons. Old buildings had been developed into luxury apartments for the new rich and Smithfield had reinvented itself as a brave attempt at the epitome of cool.

The market halls had been restored to their former glory. Even when it was closed for business – which was how most people only ever saw it – it was an impressive sight. Tall elaborate wrought-iron railings stretched the length of the avenue dividing the East from the West Building, richly painted in grape-purple, dark-cyclamen and deep-aqua, with their details picked out in gold. From their midst, ornate cast-iron pillars sprouted, acanthus leaves flowing into cantilevered struts supporting flat canopies that sheltered the roadway from the rain.

The inside was a marriage of magnificent Victorian ironwork and relentlessly modern technology. Lorries carrying carcasses backed into special sealed loading bays to protect the meat from the elements, then the meat was loaded on to a mechanical meat rail system and delivered directly to the tailor-made trading units. Smaller boxed and crated deliveries were brought into temperature-controlled service corridors running either side of both buildings. It was a far cry from the old market system of porters rushing hither and thither with meat exposed to whatever airborne contamination came its way. It was a system that should have made the killer's job much harder.

Just before ten o'clock, Sarah Duvall's team arrived. Some came in unmarked cars, but most had walked the short distance from their briefing at Snow Hill police station. Duvall had been adamant that the operation should be kept as low-key as possible. The last thing she wanted was a squad of liveried police vans and cars lined up outside Smithfield late at night. Such a sight would inevitably alert the news media and once they had the sniff of a story, it wouldn't take them long to ferret out what was going on.

Darren Green had done his job well. The traders knew what was coming, and surprisingly few had complained about the potential disruption to the night's trading. Now the search was about to begin, it was Green's moment. His earlier irritation had given way to excitement and he was buzzing round the uniformed officers like a fly around uncovered meat, making sure they were all supplied with the overalls and headgear they needed to comply with the strict hygiene regulations.

Duvall surveyed the team before her. She'd managed to scramble together a dozen uniforms, half a dozen detectives, and four butchers who would assist the officers permanently based at the market in the search. Tom Blackett was there, along with two of his assistants from nearby Bart's. As they waited for the last stragglers to arrive, Blackett crossed to Duvall's side. 'I'm amazed you got a warrant for this,' he said. It was half a grumble.

'I called so many favours in on this that if I end up with egg on my face, I'm going to be in payback city for years.'

'I can imagine. Not many magistrates would stick their neck out on something as tenuous as this.' Blackett's smile was as cheerful as the drizzle that had just started to fall. 'Let's hope we find something.' He moved away to talk to his assistants.

Duvall cleared her throat. 'Right, everybody. You all know what you're supposed to be doing once we get inside. Professor Blackett and his assistants will wait with me under the clock in Middle Street. If anyone finds anything at all suspicious, come to us at once and the pathologists will go with you and examine whatever it is you've found. Mr Green?'

Darren stepped forward with a theatrical gesture that looked completely absurd. 'This way,' he announced.

'Good luck,' Duvall called as the team filed in. She followed them as they fanned out to their allotted sections. 'We'll need it,' she added under her breath.

Chapter 39

For once, Kit was awake first. He shifted across the bed and wrapped his arms round Fiona, kissing the back of her neck. 'Unnh,' she groaned.

'I'm getting up now,' he said. 'I'm going to make kedgeree for breakfast.'

'Oh God,' Fiona sighed. 'Must you? Couldn't we just lie here and luxuriate in the afterglow for a while?'

Kit chuckled. 'The afterglow was then. This is now. I can't think why, but I've woken up with an appetite. Get yourself out of bed, Dr Cameron. Breakfast in . . . oh, make it forty minutes.' He peeled himself away from her with another kiss and jumped out of bed, pumped with energy. When it came to displacement activity, like most writers, Kit had turned it into a fine art.

Fiona listened to his receding footsteps, then dragged herself into a sitting position. She yawned, stretched her spine and got out of bed, flexing shoulders that had stiffened in the night. Too much tension, she told herself. Far too much tension. Not knowing what was happening in Sarah Duvall's investigation was a kind of torture. And given how she'd left things with Steve, she couldn't even use him as a way in.

If Georgia was dead, she needed to know. Her fear for Kit vibrated through her constantly now, and she couldn't be with him twenty-four hours a day. At least if they found Georgia's remains in the market, they could take steps to make him safer than he was now. And if she was wrong . . . For once in her life, Fiona longed to be hopelessly, embarrassingly wrong. She wanted nothing more than to see Georgia's face smiling out of the morning papers, restored to Anthony's arms in one piece. She'd even forgive her for the anxiety she'd caused, if only it meant she could feel Kit was safe again. She didn't know how she was going to get through a normal day at work when her mind was so heavily occupied elsewhere.

Twenty minutes later she was showered, dressed and decently made up. More than that, she was awake. Over breakfast, they said little, allowing the radio to fill the silence. There were too many thoughts and fears rumbling in the background of their minds for idle chatter to be possible. Fiona finally pushed her plate away after two helpings. 'That was wonderful,' she said. 'Not only a night to remember, but a morning as well.' She stood up and reached for her briefcase.

'You're lucky to have me,' he said, grinning wolfishly, then spoiling it with a wink.

'I know. And I plan to keep it that way. You will look after yourself today, won't you?' Fiona gave a nervous smile and stepped into his arms for a hug. 'Take care,' she said softly.

'Of course I'll take care. I've got a book to finish, love. I'll talk to you later.' It was a promise he fully intended to keep.

Like a child on Christmas Eve, Steve had scarcely been able to sleep. What had happened between him and Terry thus far had left him feeling breathless and exhilarated. But the promise of what could follow had robbed him of all but the sketchiest of sleep. And yet he wasn't tired.

He leaned back on the pillows, stretching his arms over his head and arching his spine. Relaxing again, he rolled on his side to watch her. She was a sprawler, legs and arms extended like a giant starfish. Terry lay on her stomach, face turned towards him. Even with smudged make-up and sleep-distorted hair, he thought she was gorgeous. He felt dazzled and dazed in equal measure. His own body felt strange and new. He'd made more technically perfect love with a woman before, but last night technique had seemed irrelevant. He'd occupied his body entirely, not a scrap of himself available for scrutiny of what he was doing. There had been none of that sense of performing for someone else's benefit, or his own. Whatever had happened between him and Terry, it had consumed him as never before.

And it had been fun. They hadn't just burned up in the heat of passion, they'd found laughter as well. Steve had woken in the same familiar space, but he was looking at the morning with the eyes of an explorer. It was unnerving, almost frightening to find himself so thoroughly gripped by attraction. All his adult sophistication, all his professional shrewdness had left him unprepared and vulnerable, and he didn't know how to handle it.

Terry stirred, making a small indeterminate noise in the back of her throat. Her face twitched, eyebrows rising. Then she opened her eyes. A moment's disorientation, then her mouth spread in a self-satisfied grin. 'Thank fuck it wasn't a dream,' she said, gathering her limbs together and snuggling against him.

He rubbed his chin, bristled with overnight stubble, across the snarl of her hair, slipping his arms around her. 'You academics have a real way with words.'

'Ah, but actions speak louder than words, and I am definitely a woman of action,' Terry countered, running her fingers down the defined muscles of his chest and across his ribs. She could feel him hard against her, and hooked one leg over his, languorously moving her hips towards him.

Steve groaned softly. 'You're a morning person, then,' he said, his voice roughening with arousal.

She pulled her head back and pouted. 'You have a problem with that?' Her voice was as much of a tease as what her body was doing to his.

He drew her into his arms, her breasts warm against his chest. 'Not unless you have to be somewhere in the next hour.'

Sarah Duvall felt sick. She knew it had more to do with having had no sleep and too much coffee than with what she'd seen at Smithfield Market, but understanding didn't make her faint underlying nausea go away. Explaining to Anthony Fitzgerald exactly what he was going to have to identify at the morgue hadn't helped either. She almost wished that the killer had stuck more closely to the text. Then there would have been one less horror for them to face.

She sat grim-faced in the back of the car. But the immobility of her features disguised a mind that was racing. This case was messy in more ways than the obvious. It was going to produce potentially devastating media interest, which meant every move she and her team made would be under scrutiny not only from an army of hacks but also from a nervous hierarchy worried lest she should do or say the wrong thing.

And then there was Fiona Cameron. With this latest development, Fiona would no longer be the only person putting two and two together and coming up with a serial killer. It wasn't something Duvall wanted to acknowledge publicly, but she had no conviction that they could continue to maintain there was no connection between the deaths of Drew Shand, Jane Elias and Georgia Lester. Either way, it wouldn't be long before some bright and ambitious journalist remembered that Fiona lived with a crime writer. They'd be beating a path to her office, and while she believed Fiona was unlikely to go to the press off her own bat, Duvall had no idea how she would respond to a direct question from a journalist. And once the kite was in the air, there would be a stream of panicking thriller writers demanding police protection. It was a minefield. Especially if the media also found out that someone had been sending out death threats to crime writers.

And then there was the investigation itself. This morning had been a nightmare, but that was only the beginning. After the gruesome discovery just after midnight, she had tried to prevent the market from opening for trading less than four hours later. But Darren Green had argued vigorously that she was out of order. By no stretch of the imagination could she claim the whole market was a crime scene. It was obvious, he pointed out, displaying an intelligence and a steely determination she wouldn't have suspected him capable of, that whatever had been done had been done some time previously. Hundreds of people had been in and out of the market since then, and there was no chance of the police finding any traces of their quarry anywhere other than the immediate vicinity of the freezer in question.

His trump card had been to point out that the best way to make sure the police questioned every potential witness was to allow the market to function as normal. They could take names and addresses of everybody who turned up and maybe even begin their interviews.

It had been a smart suggestion, not least because it allowed Duvall to save face. So they'd sealed off the storage area and drafted in a small army of officers to make sure nobody entered Smithfield without providing contact details. Meanwhile, the SOCOs had begun the painstaking task of examining every inch of the equipment store where the grisly discovery had been made.

So far, so bad. What made it even worse was that she was going to have to continue her liaison with the local police in Dorset. Whatever had happened to Georgia Lester might have ended up on her ground, but it had started on their patch. If there were going to be eyewitnesses, the chances were far higher that they'd turn them up down there. Much more likely that someone noticed something out of the ordinary in a remote country area than that one person with a load of meat would attract attention in Smithfield Market. Always provided the officers down there knew what the hell they were doing, she added automatically. Duvall had never been good at delegating authority even to her own team, but having to rely on another force for the core of an investigation was her idea of hell on a stick. Thus far, she'd not found anything specific to complain about in the work of her Dorset colleagues, but nevertheless she felt a general unease that they weren't moving sharply enough on the case. She'd have to set up a meeting, preferably down there so she could get a feel for where the initial abduction had taken place.

But that would have to wait. First, she owed Steve Preston the courtesy of filling him in on what his steer had led to, so she'd asked her driver to detour to New Scotland Yard before returning to her offices in Wood Street. She took the lift to his floor and stalked down the corridor, earning a few apprehensive looks from those she passed. A quick tap on the door, and straight in. Her first impression was that Steve had somehow squeezed a week's holiday into the last twenty-four hours. The lines of strain round his eyes had relaxed. Instead of the pallor of the senior officer overworking on an obsession, his skin had a healthy tone. His eyes were bright and the grin he greeted her with was light years away from the careworn smile of the previous day.

'You look as if your caseload is going better than mine,' Duvall said, easing herself into the seat opposite him, aware that her suit was crumpled and she probably smelled stale as a pub ashtray.

Steve arched his eyebrows in surprise. 'Must be an optical illusion. I hear you had a long night.'

Duvall nodded, pushing her glasses up her nose. 'And it's going to be a long day. I thought you'd like to know how it worked out.'

'Appreciate it,' Steve said, dipping his head in acknowledgement.

'We went in around ten and started turning the place upside down. Butchers and bobbies searching freezers and cold cabinets for dodgy-looking meat, traders screaming about their stock being interfered with, pathologists poking around anything that looked remotely abnormal. Which there wasn't much of, I have to say. The deal was, if we found anything seriously suspicious, the pathologists would take it back to the lab and test to see if it was human or not. I'd had the whole team briefed about what they should be looking for. But when it came to it, it was all academic.'

'How do you mean?'

'Around midnight, the lads found a freezer at the back of a storage area. It was padlocked shut, and nobody would admit to having keys for it. According to the market supervisor's office, it had been put there a month ago by one of the traders who was supposed to arrange for it to be taken away. But he was adamant that it hadn't been locked, and two of his staff backed him up on that. So we took the bolt cutters to it. When they opened the door, it was full of packaged meat. Except for one shelf. All that contained was a parcel wrapped in black plastic bin liners.' Duvall paused for effect, her expression a question.

Steve closed his eyes momentarily, his angular face pained. 'The head?'

'The head. The butcher who was helping them dropped to the floor like a stunned ox. They had to take him to hospital to have the cut on his head stitched. He hit the corner of a worktop on the way down.'

'He'll be drinking off that for the rest of his life,' said Steve. 'I presume it was Georgia Lester's head?'

'No question. The husband's got to ID it later today, but there's no doubt about it.'

'When are you making the announcement?'

Duvall sighed. 'My boss wants to hold a press conference this afternoon. We're waiting for Dorset to confirm they can have someone here for it.'

'Would you have any problem with me breaking the news to Kit Martin ahead of the press conference? He and Georgia were close, and he'll know that Fiona talked to us. It seems the least I can do.'

Duvall frowned. 'I'd rather we kept it in the family for as long as possible. I know he's your friend, but we can't afford a perception that one writer is getting preferential treatment from the police.'

Steve shrugged. 'It's your case, Sarah. To be honest, I was thinking about the long-term interests of the Yard as much as being considerate to Kit. Fiona Cameron is a good operator, and we've been denied her services for a while now because of our own bloody-minded stupidity. In spite of that, she came to us with her suspicions. I'd have liked the chance to do a bit of bridge-building here, maybe mended the breach. I'm sure it could have benefits for the City force too.'

Duvall's wry smile concealed the burn of genuine annoyance. First Darren Green and now Steve Preston had out-manoeuvred her in a matter of hours. It wasn't good for the spirit, especially a spirit as normally self-confident as Duvall's. 'That's a good point, sir.'

Steve recognized the use of his title as the signal to back down. 'It's your decision, Sarah.'

'I suppose it can't do any harm. Provided you make it clear to him that he mustn't talk to the media before we do.' A last attempt to appear in control.

'I don't think it would even occur to him.' Steve stood up and reached for his jacket. 'She was his friend, Sarah. He's not that desperate for personal publicity.'

She accepted the implied rebuke in silence and got to her feet. 'I'll keep you posted,' she said. 'How's the Blanchard case going?'

Steve shrugged into his jacket and spread his hands wide. 'Chasing what might be a lead. But it's an uphill struggle. I haven't got the resources to run a proper operation.'

Duvall's smile was tight. 'Keep it deniable, huh?'

'Something like that. At least until we've got a cast-iron case.'

Duvall winced. 'And I thought I was having a bad day.'

Steve opened the door and stood back to let her precede him. 'Don't let it get you down. There's more to life than the job.'

He walked down the corridor with the loose-limbed stride of a man out for a walk in the park. Duvall stared after him, the usual impassivity of her face defeated by her astonishment. Steve Preston, claiming there was more to life than the job? It was about as likely as Bart Simpson joining the diplomatic service.

Feeling somewhat shaken, Duvall headed for her car to return to her own office in Wood Street. It was clearly a day for surprises. Maybe Dorset would turn out to be the home of a new breed of supercops. And maybe, just maybe, between them they would find Georgia Lester's killer before the media ate them alive. Stranger things could clearly happen.

Chapter 40

Fiona left the lecture theatre, heading for her office. She had no recollection of what she'd spent the last fifty minutes saying. She'd been flying on automatic pilot, looking down on her students with the distance of dissociation. Her anxiety hummed inside her like a high-tension cable, shutting her off from everything else. She wanted to be home with Kit. She wanted him where she could see him, or at the very least, sense his presence. Knowing that would be intolerable to him didn't make it any easier to be without it.

Something had to break soon, she told herself. Either they would be able to dismiss the notion of a serial killer, so they could all relax and return to something approaching normality. Or everyone would accept that Kit and a handful of others were at serious risk and take steps accordingly. If the police wouldn't protect him, then she'd arrange it herself. She knew there were agencies around who provided bodyguards and Fiona had no reservations about surrounding Kit with professional protection. He'd go ape, of course. But then, he might not have to know.

Whatever happened, their lives would never be quite the same again. Kit had been confronted with his own physical vulnerability, however much he chose to scoff at it. That would inevitably change his view of himself. And Fiona had been forced to recognize that all these years on, she was still no nearer a position where she could effectively protect those she loved. Ignorance may have been a valid excuse when it came to saving Lesley; but even now, with all the knowledge and experience in her arsenal, Fiona could not be sure of saving Kit.

It wasn't a comforting thought.

She dumped her papers on her desk and checked her e-mail. Apart from routine departmental memos, there was only a brief note from Kit, saying, 'Ten o'clock and all's well.' He'd promised to post Fiona at regular intervals after her insistence that he stay in touch. He claimed it made him feel like a wimp, but both knew it was only a token demurral.

She began to compose a short reply, but she was interrupted by a phone call from Spain. 'Hello, Major Berrocal,' she said, trying not to sound as distracted as she felt. Part of her registered with weary surprise that it wasn't like her to care so little about a case she'd been involved in.

'I thought I had better let you know what progress we have made,' he said, sounding rather dispirited himself.

'That's kind of you.'

'There is not very much to report, I'm afraid. Delgado refuses to admit his guilt. He just sits there with a face like stone, saying nothing at all. But the good news is that it seems we are starting to get some forensic evidence to back up the circumstantial evidence. We have found a former neighbour of Delgado's who works at the Alcazar and who thinks Delgado may have been able to access the keys on one of his visits to the house. And best of all, we have finally located two witnesses who saw him with the Englishwoman on the night he killed her. A husband and wife from Bilbao. They saw the story in the newspaper and got in touch with us. It turns out they were staying in the hotel where she worked and that's why they noticed her. She had checked them in, you see, so they remembered her. We have charged him with that murder for now, but I think we will eventually have enough to make him stand trial for all three killings.'

'That's good news,' she said, not really caring. 'You must be glad he's off the streets.'

'Very glad. We would never have got so close so quickly without your help. I have made sure my superior officers know this. I think this may persuade them that we need you to come and train us in crime linkage and geographical programming.'

Fiona gave a hollow laugh. 'I think you're being very optimistic, Major. But good luck with your case against Delgado.'

'Thank you. And good luck with your own work, Dr Cameron. I'm sure we'll be in touch again.'

Fiona made her farewells and replaced the phone. She knew she should be feeling triumphant, but instead she felt frustration. Her work had helped stop someone killing strangers in Toledo. But no one would let her do the same for the man she loved. Maybe she should call Sarah Duvall and offer her services.

The woman could only say no.

Kit was in the kitchen making coffee when the doorbell rang. He froze in the middle of what he was doing. He wasn't expecting anyone, and in spite of his bravado in front of Fiona, he was keenly aware that if there was indeed a killer out there with a list, his name would inevitably be near the top. Carefully, he put the spoon back in the bag and leaned it against the coffee maker. He took a deep breath and walked down the hall.

He was inches away from the door when the bell screamed again, making him twitch involuntarily. *The Postman Always*

Rings Twice. James M. Cain, a classic American *noir*. That didn't have a very happy ending either. He tiptoed the last few feet and put his ear to the door. 'Who's there?' he called.

The flap of the letterbox clattered open. A disembodied voice from the region of his groin said, 'It's Steve, Kit.'

Kit felt a dizzy relief and hastily turned the lock, pulling the door wide open. 'I'm not paranoid, honest,' he said. Then, seeing Steve's face, he stepped back. Stupid bastard, he cursed himself silently. Steve wouldn't be here in the middle of the day unless the news was the worst kind. 'It's not Fiona?' he croaked, his mouth suddenly dry, his eyes wide.

Steve put a hand on his arm and gently manoeuvred him across the threshold. He closed the door firmly behind him. 'As far as I know, Fi's fine. Come on, let's go through to the kitchen. I need to talk to you.'

Numb with anxiety, Kit led the way, almost stumbling as carpet gave way to tiled floor. 'I was making coffee,' he said, knowing it was irrelevant but wanting to preserve ignorance for as long as possible.

'Coffee would be good,' Steve said. He sat down at the table, patient while Kit completed the ritual, busying himself with frothing milk and forcing water through the packed coffee grounds. Kit carefully placed one cup in front of Steve, then sat down with his own.

'It's Georgia.' It was a statement, not a question.

Steve nodded. 'One of my colleagues found her remains in the early hours of this morning.'

'Was it where Fiona said it would be? In Smithfield?'

'She was right in every particular but one.' Steve took out a cigar and fiddled with the cellophane wrapper. 'It wasn't pretty, Kit. Whoever butchered her left us her head. So we'd be in no doubt what we'd found.'

Kit took a long shuddering breath. 'Jesus,' he exhaled

slowly. He put his hands over his face, his shoulders shaking. Steve felt helpless. He'd known Kit for years, but their relationship had never needed to encompass grief before. He had no sense of what the rules of engagement were. When policemen cried, they usually didn't want their fellow officers to acknowledge it, not even the women. They just wanted to get it over with. Steve got up and went to the cupboard where the drinks were kept. He found the brandy and poured a good two fingers into a glass. He put it in front of Kit, laid a hand on his heaving shoulders and said, 'Drink this, it'll help.'

When Kit raised his head, his eyes were red and swollen, his cheeks wet. He pushed the brandy to one side and reached for the coffee, wrapping his large hands round the cup to suck what heat from it he could. 'I kept hoping Fiona was wrong,' he said. 'I kept telling myself it was the kind of sick thing I'd make up, not the sort of thing that really happens, you know? It was the only way I could get through it. I just couldn't let myself believe there's someone out there killing us.'

Steve sighed. 'When you've seen as much as I have, Kit, you know that real life can trump fiction every time. I'm truly sorry about Georgia. I know she was a friend.'

Kit shook his head wearily. 'She was always larger than life. I'd have put Georgia down as indestructible. Underneath all that froth, she was so sharp, so strong. I know people thought we were an odd couple, but she was closer to me than almost anybody in the business. She was brilliant. She could make me laugh. And she was always there. When the writing was going to shit, she'd bring a bottle round and we'd bitch about what a hard life it was, even though we both knew what lucky buggers we were.' He drained his cup and rubbed his eyes fiercely with the back of his hands. 'Fuck, what a bastard life is.'

'They're not announcing it formally till later this afternoon,' Steve said, resorting to what he knew. 'But I didn't want you to turn on the radio and hear it that way.'

'Thanks. How's Anthony, do you know?'

Steve shook his head. 'It's not the Met's case. It's City of London, so I've not had any direct dealings with it. But I happen to know he's doing the formal identification round about now.'

'Poor bastard.' He reached for the brandy then, and swallowed hard. 'If I write him a note, will you post it for me? It's only that I promised Fiona I wouldn't go out alone. I thought she was being overprotective, but now . . .' He got to his feet. 'Gimme a minute.'

'Take your time,' Steve said, unwrapping his cigar and lighting it. While he waited for Kit to return, he couldn't help his mind gliding away from the pain and mess of Georgia's death to thoughts of Terry. Even Sarah's hideous news hadn't managed to take the gloss off the previous night, or the morning after. They were meeting again that evening. Steve's habit of caution seemed to have abandoned him along with the weariness that had infected his interior life for so long. He didn't want to play this cool, to act hard to get. He wanted to be with her, and since Terry assured him the feeling was mutual, it seemed crazy not to snatch every moment that offered itself to him. Part of him was longing to share with Kit what was happening to him. But this wasn't the time.

When Kit came back into the kitchen, he was holding an envelope. 'I didn't have a proper sympathy card, just had to make do with a postcard. I don't think Anthony will mind. I just wanted to let him know I was thinking about him. Tell him I'm here if he needs anything. You know?' He handed the card to Steve. 'I've stamped it. If you could just stick it in the box at the bottom of the road, he should get it tomorrow morning.'

'Are you going to be OK?' Steve asked, getting to his feet.

Kit took a deep breath. 'I'll be fine. You need to get off, there'll be work piling up for you.'

Impulsively, Steve stepped forward and wrapped his arms round Kit in a hug. Kit hugged him back, his arms tight round Steve's back. There was no awkwardness when they let go and moved apart. 'Thanks for telling me, Steve. You're right, it would have done my head in completely if I'd heard it on the news. Now I know, I can unplug the phone. The last people I feel like talking to right now are journos.'

'Will you tell Fi?' Steve asked. 'Or do you want me to?'

'I'll e-mail her now. I don't want to phone her when she's working, you know how it is.' Kit followed Steve to the front door. Unusually, he didn't wait till Steve was out of sight to close the door. Instead, he shut it immediately, locking both Yale and mortise. Then he walked slowly back to his desk and clicked on to his e-mail program.

From: Kit Martin <KMWriter@trashnet.com>
To: Fiona Cameron
          <fcameron@psych.ulon.ac.uk>
Subject: Bad as it gets

You were right. Georgia is dead. Cold hard words for a cold hard fact. Steve just left. He came to tell me himself, didn't want me to have it sprung on me by a phone call from a hack or a news broadcast.

They found her in Smithfield, like you said. I've read *And Ever More Shall Be So*, I can imagine only too well what it was like. Only thing different, according to Steve, is that the killer left the head with the body.

I wish you were here. Or I was there. I feel very disconnected from my life. Very disorientated.

Please don't worry about me. I have taken to heart all you said. I'm going to stay battened down until you get back, and then reconsider what's the best course of action until somebody puts this mad fucker behind bars.

Somewhere in all of this, there has to be some clue that will open it up. I presume they're going to link the investigations now, even if only unofficially. Do what you can to get included on the team. Not that I want you to be working when you could be with me. But I want this guy caught, not just for Georgia's sake but for my own peace of mind. And if anybody can make a case for linking these crimes, it's you.

I love you.
K.

Kit sent the message, then exited from the program. He took the magazine out of the CD player and emptied it. He went upstairs to the living room where Fiona's classical CDs were kept and went along the shelf. Clutching the Verdi requiem, he walked back downstairs and loaded it. He pressed play and sat down in his chair. While the music swelled, Kit leaned back, eyes closed, his mind playing movies of the friend he had lost.

Chapter 41

The conference room was packed, bright with TV lights and stuffy with the exhalations of too many excited bodies. Speculation buzzed from journalist to journalist about the nature of the announcement. The more cynical, having seen it all before, attempted to make their guesses sound like convictions. It had to be Georgia Lester, and she had to be dead. That was their flat take on the situation. It had to be Georgia because there was nothing else that important on the stocks right now. If there had been, they would have had a whisper from a contact. And she had to be dead, otherwise it would be her publishers holding the press conference. Obviously.

Besides, they all claimed inside knowledge. One of their sources said there had been a big operation last night around Smithfield Market and it had something to do with the missing writer. The more literate of them had smugly put two and two together and come up with the answer they hoped would be confirmed this afternoon. If they were right, it would be a guaranteed front page. And that was what really mattered.

It was, the more confident among them maintained, just a matter of detail now. Dotting the i's and crossing the t's. And getting one of that lesser breed of reporters, the ones who didn't have a title like Crime Correspondent or Home Affairs

Specialist, to go in search of the husband for the heartbreak photo and the tear-jerking quote.

Nevertheless, a hush descended when the police filed in. That it was serious was obvious. The Deputy Commissioner himself was there, flanked by DCI Sarah Duvall and a face none of the reporters recognized. The officers settled behind the bank of microphones, self-conscious and uneasy. The Press Liaison Chief was hovering like an anxious parent before the nativity play. When everyone was satisfied with the sound quality, the Deputy Commissioner cleared his throat. 'Thank you for coming this afternoon, ladies and gentlemen. I have a short statement to make, and then I will take questions.' He introduced his fellow officers. The stranger turned out to be a detective chief superintendent from Dorset. The DC looked down at the paper in his hand.

He cleared his throat again. 'As a result of an operation carried out by officers of the City of London Police last night in the vicinity of Smithfield Market, human remains were recovered. These have been identified as the missing crime writer, Ms Georgia Lester. As a result of this, a murder inquiry has been set up. DCI Duvall will be in operational control of the investigation. We will be liaising with our colleagues in Dorset, where Ms Lester apparently went missing last week.

'This is a particularly horrific crime, and we would appeal for anyone who saw Ms Lester after she left her cottage in Dorset last Wednesday. Her car was found abandoned on Sunday, but we have no idea how long it had been there. We would like to narrow that time frame down if possible. We are also appealing for any witnesses who may have seen anything unusual around Smithfield Market during the course of this past week.' He looked up and pursed his lips. 'I'll take questions now.'

A hubbub of voices, hands waving. The Press Liaison Chief

pointed to one. 'Corinne Thomas, BBC Radio. When you say human remains, what exactly do you mean?'

The Deputy Commissioner indicated to Duvall that she should give the prescribed answer. 'Ms Lester had been dismembered. The manner suggests someone with rudimentary anatomical or butchery skills.'

Second questioner. 'Jack O'Connor, *The Times*. One of Ms Lester's novels, which was made into a film, features a killer who kidnaps his victims then butchers them. As I recall, the bodies in the book were hidden in a wholesale butcher's. Do you believe her killer copied the book?'

'No comment,' the Deputy Commissioner said firmly.

O'Connor wasn't giving up. 'Do you believe this crime is connected to the Edinburgh killing of Drew Shand, who was murdered recently in a manner identical to one of the victims in his book?' The background agitation of his colleagues almost swamped O'Connor's voice, but there was no doubt from the grim faces looking down at him that they'd heard him.

'No comment,' the Deputy Commissioner said again.

A third questioner jumped to her feet. 'Sharon Collier, the *Mirror*. Are you refusing to deny that there's a serial killer targeting thriller writers?'

'I'm neither denying nor confirming anything of the sort, Ms Collier. At this stage, I have no evidence to allow me to offer any comment on these questions.' The DC was starting to look a little edgy. The Press Liaison Chief quickly found one of his tame hacks and prodded him into action.

'Patrick Stacey, the *Express*. Where exactly was the body found?'

Duvall took the initiative. 'We discovered Ms Lester's remains in a disused freezer in a storage area in Smithfield

Market. According to the owner, the freezer had been await-ing transport to another meat depot and had been there for about five weeks. So if anyone saw someone using that freezer during those five weeks, we are keen to hear from them.'

The questions were coming faster now. 'Do you have any suspects?'

'What leads do you have?'

'Is her husband a suspect?'

'Is there a serial killer on the loose?'

'Is an arrest imminent?'

'Have you called in the services of a profiler?'

Abruptly, the Deputy Commissioner rose to his feet. 'That's all for now, ladies and gentlemen. When we have any more to report, we will keep you informed.'

'Wait a minute!' A shout rang out across the room. A bearded man in a tweed sports jacket, check shirt and red tie was pushing his way through the ranks of journalists.

The DC looked to the Press Liaison Chief, who made a shooing motion with his hands, indicating they should leave now. The Dorset officer started to move to the side of the room, but Duvall sat still, staring at the man who was making determined progress, apparently unconcerned about the people he was shoving out of his path.

'Why don't you tell them the truth?' he shouted, his face flushed. 'Why deny what everybody knows is the truth? There's a serial killer out there and he's killing crime writers who have stolen his stories.'

By now, several uniformed officers were attempting to reach the source of the disturbance. But the floor of the press conference was in chaos as journalists tried to see and hear what was going on. There was a hubbub of voices, but still the man in the tweed jacket could be heard. 'How do I know?' he yelled at the top of his voice. 'I know because it's me. I killed them. Drew Shand. Jane Elias. Georgia Lester. They stole my stories and I made them pay.'

Duvall was on her feet now, pushing past her boss and diving down into the melee. Disregarding obstacles, she fought her way through the excited throng, driving a path to her quarry. No pause to apologize to the photographer she elbowed in the ribs, nor the radio reporter who took a crack on the jaw from her outflung arm. By now, the man in the tweed jacket had managed to free himself from the crowd around him sufficiently to start scattering sheets of paper in the air. He threw the leaflets high above his head and they fluttered in the air like albino bats unnerved by sudden light. Journalists were pushing and shoving each other, trying to grab a flyer for themselves, while others were baying questions at the man in the tweed jacket, who was grinning with the fixed rictus of a gargoyle.

Two of the uniforms grabbed him just as Duvall made it through the final rank of the press pack. Panting, her jacket ripped across one shoulder, she faced the stranger. 'Get him out of here,' she commanded. 'Custody suite. Now!'

The journalists howled in protest as the uniformed officers led the man away. Duvall noticed he put up no struggle. She stood, marooned in the middle of the media, watching the man and his escorts leave through the door she'd entered by. She became gradually aware that the Deputy Commissioner was shouting into his microphone. 'Ladies and gentlemen, this press conference is over. Please leave the building. I repeat, please leave the building.' He might as well have been singing 'Yellow Submarine', Duvall thought. At least that would have caught their attention.

Ignoring demands for her reaction, Duvall snatched one of the crumpled flyers and pushed her way back through the outraged and frustrated journalists without a word.

Approaching the platform, she gestured with a sweeping motion that they should all get out of there. The DCS from Dorset looked eager to be somewhere else, while the Deputy Commissioner looked furious. As they shuffled out, Duvall took the chance for a quick flick through the flyer.

The author, one Charles Redford, claimed to be the murderer of Drew Shand, Jane Elias and Georgia Lester. In a style that was disturbingly reminiscent of the threatening letters Duvall had already examined, Redford announced that they were being punished for stealing his ideas and preventing him being published. He had previously sent them all manuscripts, soliciting their help in finding a publisher. Not only had they failed to give him a leg up, they had rubbed salt in the wound by stealing his ideas and using them in their own books. The conspiracy outlined in the flyer was daft enough to catch the attention of the seriously paranoid, but as a motive for serial murder, it seemed a little thin, Duvall thought. It never ceased to amaze her how little it took to tip some people over the edge from common or garden nutters to homicidal maniacs. No doubt Fiona Cameron would have a technical term for it.

In the anteroom, away from the clamour, the DC shook his head. 'What the hell was that all about?' he demanded. 'How did that lunatic get in there?'

Duvall shrugged out of her jacket and inspected the damage with pursed lips. Let the DC slug it out with the media creep; she wasn't about to get into that particular war.

'He must have had some sort of press credentials,' the Press Liaison Chief stammered defensively. 'Otherwise he wouldn't have been allowed in.'

The DC waved a hand as if seeing off a troublesome wasp. 'Never mind that. Who the hell is he?'

Duvall looked up from her torn jacket and took a deep

breath. 'According to the leaflet, which the world's press are now in possession of, he's called Charles Redford and he's a wannabe thriller writer who thinks the victims stole his plots.'

'Is he for real?' The DC looked bemused.

'That's what I plan to find out right now. I told them to take him straight down to the custody suite. I'm going to arrest him on suspicion of murder and take it from there.'

'Do we need to arrest him at this point? He could be nothing more than a time-wasting attention-seeker.'

It was, Duvall thought, a long time since the DC had done policing without the politics. 'I want this by the book, sir. If he is the killer, I don't want the slightest chance of it falling down in court on some procedural glitch. I want him under arrest, I want him legally represented and I want him on the record all the way.'

To her surprise, the DCS from Dorset weighed in on her side. 'I think DCI Duvall's quite right,' he said, the edge of a country burr in his voice adding unexpected authority to his quiet bass. 'I'd want the same thing in her shoes. And I'd very much appreciate being able to sit in on the interview.'

'I don't think we can accommodate that,' the DC said dubiously. 'A matter of jurisdiction, you know?'

'We've got one interview suite with an observation room,' Duvall pointed out. 'Surely there would be no problem with our colleague using that facility? I think it could be helpful, sir. Another pair of eyes, another pair of ears.' She didn't for a moment think the provincial DCS would spot anything that wasn't obvious to her, but she knew she was still going to need cooperation from Dorset in putting her case together. It would cost her nothing to keep their senior officer happy.

'Fine.' The DC nodded and drew her to one side. 'But

that's as far as it goes, Duvall,' he added in an undertone. 'This one's ours.'

Maybe not if he killed her in Dorset, Duvall thought. But if there was a name to be made here, she was determined it was going to be hers. He'd confessed on her patch. He was going to stay hers if it was humanly possible. 'I'll get down to the custody suite, then,' she said.

The two men watched her swing her ruined jacket over her shoulder and stride off confidently down the corridor.

'God help him if he's wasting her time,' the Dorset man said.

'She's going to have her work cut out,' the DC said.

'How do you mean?'

'How do we usually weed out false confessions? We catch them out on the details that haven't been made public. Only, this killer has been using previously published material as his blueprint. He's going to know all the answers, whether he killed them or not.'

The Dorset DCS drew his breath in sharply. 'Oh shit,' he said.

'And I'm not sure if DCI Duvall has worked that one out yet,' the DC added, pursing his lips in a superior smile.

Fiona closed her eyes, blotting out the e-mail on the screen in front of her. Confirmation of what she had been dreading was the last thing she wanted in her face. Eventually, she forced herself to reread Kit's e-mail. This wasn't the time for self-indulgence. He needed her support, not for her to whimper in the corner like a scared bunny. She composed herself and hit the <reply> button.

From: Fiona Cameron
          <fcameron@psych.ulon.ac.uk>
To: Kit Martin <KMWriter@trashnet.com>
Subject: Re: Bad as it gets

My darling Kit,
I'm so, so sorry about Georgia. You must be
hurting, my love, and I wish I could do something
to take the pain away.
I fear I can be of little use on this particular case,
even supposing DCI Duvall wanted my help. It's
already clear to anyone with half a brain that these
cases are connected, and you know I don't get into
the touchy-feely <wet the bed when he was 9 and
tortured the neighbour's cat> stuff. So what could I
give them? Not much except common sense.
So, my love, it is important that you take extreme
care of yourself. I'll be home at the usual time, or
earlier if I can manage it.
I love you.
F.

Chapter 42

Charles Cavendish Redford was adamant that he did not want legal representation. He insisted that he knew more about the criminal law than the average duty solicitor and was perfectly capable of withstanding a police interrogation without someone to hold his hand.

It was a decision that pleased Duvall. She knew that even the most newly qualified duty solicitor would caution Redford to say nothing further. But if he wanted to damn himself from his own mouth, that was fine by her. Lacking a solicitor would simply mean there were fewer interruptions to the flow of what Redford wanted to reveal. And if one thing was clear, it was that Redford was a man who was eager to have his say. She'd had to keep shutting him up when the custody sergeant was processing him; the last thing she wanted was for him to get it all out of his system then clam up once they were in the interview room and on the official record.

As soon as he'd been formally arrested, Duvall sent a team of officers to search his house. Another team were given the task of finding out as much as was humanly possible about the life and times of Charles Redford, self-styled pre-published writer. Then Duvall escaped to her office for ten minutes. She tossed her wrecked coat in the bottom of her locker and replaced it with a lightweight black wool jacket that lived there on permanent stand-by. She shot a mist of her favourite perfume into the air and walked through the miasma, feeling its coolness on her skin. Then she sat down with notepad and pencil, sketching out the main points she needed.

Finally, about an hour after the commotion in the press conference, Duvall found herself facing her self-confessed serial murderer across a Formica-topped table. The room was claustrophobically small, the large mirror on one wall seeming to shrink the space rather than to increase it. The normal scents of stale sweat, smoke and fear were overlaid with a layer of her Versace Red Jeans. No Hannibal Lecter, Redford didn't so much as twitch his nose.

'At last,' he said impatiently. 'Well, go on, get the tape running.'

Duvall's sergeant reached out and switched on both tape decks. For the record, he dictated date and time and details of those present. The DCS from Dorset, ensconced behind the mirror with his own sound feed, was not on the list.

Duvall sized up Redford. Medium height, medium build. His hair and beard were neatly trimmed, his complexion the pasty-white of someone who spends little time out of doors. His eyes were a dark grey-blue, watchful and deep-set. His tweed jacket looked as if it had been expensive when new, but that had been a long time ago. It fitted him well enough to have been tailored for him, but that meant nothing in these days of charity shops sprouting in every high street like mushrooms. The collar of his tattersall check shirt was a little frayed on the inside edge. His long fingers restlessly intertwined in an endless, meaningless sequence. The impression was one of intensity behind a mask of genteel poverty.

'You'll have sent a team out to search my flat,' he stated, a smirk quirking one corner of his mouth. 'What a waste of time. You're not going to find anything there except old newspapers. The sort of thing anyone might have who was a bit remiss about going to the recycling bank.'

'We'll see,' Duvall said.

'You'll see nothing, Detective Chief Inspector Duvall,' he said, almost chewing the words of her title. 'What's your first name? Something pretty and girly that you hate, I bet. Well, Detective Chief Inspector, I am your worst nightmare.'

Duvall allowed herself an indulgent smile. 'I don't think so, Mr Redford.'

'Oh, but I am. You see, I committed these murders. I'm freely admitting to that. And I'll tell you how I did them and what I did. But only up to a point. I'm not going to lead you to any physical evidence, I'm not going to tell you places to look for witnesses. Do you have any idea how many tourist beds there are in Edinburgh? That should keep your opposite number in Lothian and Borders amused for a while. No, all you're going to have is what I admit to, Detective Chief Inspector.' He grinned, showing small even incisors like a child's milk teeth. 'You're going to have so much fun with the Crown Prosecution Service. No evidence except a confession. Oh, dear me.'

Duvall looked bored. 'Fine. So can we get on with the confession?'

Redford looked momentarily hurt. Then he brightened again. 'I see what you're up to,' he said triumphantly. 'You're trying to wind me up by making me feel dismissed. Well, let me tell you, I've read enough and seen enough to understand all your tricks, DCI Duvall. You're not going to put one over on me. Now, I consider myself to be a storyteller, so let's start at the beginning.'

'No,' Duvall interrupted incisively. 'Let's try a more radical approach to narrative. Let's pretend we're Martin Amis or Margaret Atwood. Let's start at the end, with Georgia Lester.'

'My.' Redford let out a long drawl of admiration. 'A literate cop. I shall have to watch my story structure here. But don't you want to hear why I've taken against thriller writers in such a big way?'

Duvall produced his flyer from her plain black no-nonsense handbag. 'I am showing Mr Redford one of the leaflets he distributed at a police press conference earlier this afternoon,' she said for the benefit of the tape. 'I presume your reasons are outlined here? You sent them your novels, hoping they'd help you. But not only did they ignore you, you believe that they stole your plots and plagiarized your writing. An accurate summary?' Her tone was brisk. He was so filled with confidence, the best she could hope for was to unsettle him, and she was going flat out for that. She could feel the adrenaline coursing through her, creative tension holding her tight as a bowstring. It was so seldom that an interrogation proved anything approaching a challenge, and Duvall relished the confrontation.

'Well, yes,' he said, an edge of dissatisfaction in his voice. 'But I thought you'd want to know more about that. It's why I started. You should be interested.'

She shrugged. 'Motive is much overrated in detective fiction, Mr Redford. Remember that GP in Manchester? Harold Shipman? Convicted of killing fifteen elderly patients with morphine overdoses. Nobody really knows why he did it, but it didn't stop a jury putting him away. I'll leave the motive to the lawyers. I'm interested in the mechanics of what you did and how you did it. And let's stick to Georgia Lester, eh? You'll have plenty of opportunity to talk about your other alleged crimes with officers from other jurisdictions in due course. If, that is, you can convince me that you had anything to do with Georgia Lester's murder.'

Redford sat back and steepled his fingers in the manner of a patronizing academic. 'I knew she had a cottage in Dorset,' he began expansively.

'How did you know?' Duvall shot back. She was determined not to let him relax into his tale.

'*Hello!* magazine did a feature on her last year. There were interior and exterior photographs. The article said the cottage was seven miles from Lyme Regis. It wasn't that hard to find. So I tracked down the cottage, and then I laid my plans. I made sure I knew what her schedule was—'

'How did you find that out?' Duvall demanded.

'It's on her website. All her public engagements. I knew she went down to Dorset most weekends, and it was easy to work out when she'd be due back in London from the events listing on the web page. Must you keep interrupting?' he demanded peevishly.

'I thought you'd welcome my questions,' Duvall said smoothly. 'You say you want me to believe you. You should be grateful that I'm trying to confirm your story with all these details.'

His eyes flashed a momentary anger. 'You think you're clever, don't you, Duvall? But you're no match for me. I killed them, and you're going to have to charge me with Georgia Lester's murder.'

'Either that or with perverting the course of justice, Mr Redford. So, you stalked Georgia. What a pathetic little crime that is. How did you capture her?'

An hour later, Duvall left the interview room. She felt drained and frustrated. In spite of her constant hammering of questions, she hadn't been able to extract a single fact from Redford that hadn't either been published in the press or couldn't have been gleaned from a studious reading of Georgia Lester's text. She let herself into the observation room where the DCS from Dorset was sitting with a notepad on his knee. 'What do you think?' she asked.

He looked up and pulled a face. 'I think you need something concrete from your search, something that isn't already in the public domain. He's given you nothing that a good brief won't demolish for a jury. He wants his day in court, but he doesn't want to be convicted, that's how I see it. And he thinks he's cleverer than you.'

Duvall leaned against the wall and folded her arms across her chest. 'And that might just be where I can trip him up. Reading that flyer, I was struck by how similar some of the language is to the threatening letters that have been sent to some of the crime writers. With the right expert witness, I think I can tie him to the letters, whether or not we find the originals on his computer. And if we can tie the letters to the murders, then we've got a way in. It's going to be a bastard to make it stick, though.'

'Do you think it really is him?'

Duvall pushed herself off from the wall and crossed to the one-way mirror. Redford was gazing up as if he could see her, a confident smirk on his face. 'That's what I keep wondering.'

The DCS tapped his pen on his pad. 'It strikes me, reading that flyer, that he'd do just about anything to get his books published.'

Duvall sighed. He had expressed a notion that had already crossed her mind. 'You think he'd go as far as murder?'

'I think he'd certainly go as far as *confessing* to murder.' He shook his head. 'I tell you something, DCI Duvall. I'm not going to fight you over who gets this collar.'

*   *   *

399

Fiona found Kit upstairs in the living room, stretched out full-length on the sofa. On the floor beside him, a bottle held about two inches of red wine. The glass balanced on his chest contained another inch. There was an Australian soap on the TV. His eyes were looking at the screen, but she knew he wasn't watching it.

'I'll get another bottle,' she said.

'That'd be a good idea,' he agreed, no trace of the drink in his voice.

When Fiona returned, she sat down cross-legged on the floor beside him and tipped the remains of the bottle into her glass. 'I'm more sorry than I can say about Georgia.'

'Me too,' Kit said, shifting his position so he was half sitting, leaning against the arm of the sofa. 'I'm also scared. There's somebody out there killing people like me, and it's hard to escape the idea that I could be next on his list.'

'I know.' Fiona drained her glass and started on the second bottle. 'And there's nothing I can say or do that will change that. God, how I hate that feeling.' She reached up and gripped his hand.

The silence between them was filled with the inane chatter of the soap's teenage love interest. More than she had ever wished anything, Fiona wished she could wave a magic wand and remove the sense of threat that clung to them both like a sticky spider's web, blinding them to everything except its presence. 'It was kind of Steve to come and tell you himself,' she said finally. 'Especially given the way we left things.'

'He loves you too much to be petty.'

Fiona gave him a quick glance of surprise. She had always thought the burden of Steve's love was her private secret. It had never been mentioned between them before, and she had assumed Kit had accepted her version of their relationship; a long-standing defiance of the theory that friendship between heterosexual men and women was inherently impossible.

Kit shook his head, a tired smile creeping over his face. 'You think I never noticed?'

'I suppose so. I presumed because you never objected to him that you took it at face value,' she admitted.

Kit reached for the bottle and topped up his glass. 'Why should I have minded? It's not as if he's ever been any kind of threat. I've always known you didn't love him. Well, you do love him, obviously, but like a friend. And he's never tried to tell me how I should be treating you. So why should there be a problem?'

Fiona laid her head against his thigh. 'You never cease to surprise me.'

'Good. I'd hate to think you had me sussed.' He released her hand and stroked her hair. 'You're a very good reason for staying alive, you know. I'm not going to take any chances.'

Fiona grasped the offered opportunity. 'So first thing in the morning, we're going to call a security firm and get you fixed up with a minder.'

'Are you serious?' His tone was a mixture of incredulity and outrage.

'Never more so. You can't live like a hermit, Kit. You know it'll drive you stir crazy within a couple of days. You'll get frustrated and bad-tempered, you won't be able to work and then you'll do something that you think is safe, like going for a walk on the Heath. You'll expose yourself.' As he started to argue with her, Fiona held up her hand in an adamant gesture. 'I'm not going to argue, Kit. Your safety's the most important consideration, but you've still got to be able to live.'

'Fair enough. But a minder? I'll feel like a complete plonker.'

'It's better than the alternative.'

Before Kit could say more, the final credits of the soap faded and the familiar urgency of the *Six o'Clock News* theme swelled from the TV. Fiona swivelled round to watch the screen. 'Let's see what they're saying about Georgia,' she said.

The newscaster gave his trademark sombre smile and launched into the news. 'Good evening. The remains of missing mystery writer Georgia Lester have been discovered in a freezer in London's Smithfield Market. And in a dramatic development, a man has confessed to her murder at a police press conference.'

The rest of the headlines were lost on Fiona and Kit. 'What the fuck?' Kit breathed.

They didn't have long to wait. Georgia was the first item in the main bulletin. 'City of London Police called a press conference this afternoon to announce that a search of Smithfield Market had ended with the discovery of Georgia Lester's remains. Their grisly find came in the early hours of this morning as police worked through the night following a new line of inquiry. Ms Lester went missing somewhere between her cottage in Dorset and her London home ten days ago. Since then, concern has been voiced for her safety.

'But the revelation was overshadowed by the events of the press conference itself. Over now to our reporter Gabrielle Gershon.'

A solemn-faced thirty-something with fashionable glasses gazed into the camera. 'Police were giving little away at the press conference. They admitted only that Georgia Lester's dismembered body had been found in a freezer at Smithfield Market, but refused to be drawn into speculation as to whether there was any connection between the bestselling crime author's death and the recent murders of fellow thriller writers Drew Shand and Jane Elias.

'But as the press conference drew to a close, a man pushed his way through the crowd of reporters, claiming to be responsible for all three deaths. He then distributed leaflets alleging that all three of the murdered authors had stolen his work and that he had killed them in revenge for their plagiarism.

'For legal reasons, we cannot show the footage of this dramatic event. However, the man has been taken into police custody and within the last ten minutes, police have admitted that he has been arrested on suspicion of murder.'

The newsreader's voice interrupted. 'Did the police appear to be taken by surprise by this extraordinary intervention, Gabrielle?' he asked.

'Yes, Don, it threw them into complete confusion. Up to that point, they'd given no indication that they had any suspects whatsoever in Georgia Lester's murder.'

'It's a remarkable turn of events. I can't recall anything quite like it ever happening before,' Don the newsreader said as the screen returned to a view of the studio. 'Thanks, Gabrielle. We'll come back to you if there are any further developments.' He looked seriously at the camera. 'Later in the programme, we'll be bringing you an appreciation of Georgia Lester's life and work. But now, the other main stories tonight.'

Fiona reached for the remote control and flicked the mute button. 'Unbelievable,' she said wonderingly. 'He confessed in front of a room full of journalists?'

'Now there's a man who doesn't need a publicist.'

'Pass the phone,' Fiona said.

Kit stretched and grabbed the cordless handset. 'Who're you going to call?'

'Wood Street. I want to find out if this is the real thing or the local neighbourhood nutter.'

403

'You think they'll tell you?'

Fiona gave him her disapproving tutor's stare. 'You think they won't?'

Ten minutes later, she put the phone down. Sarah Duvall had, inevitably, been unavailable. But once Fiona had explained her connection to the case to a slightly wary sergeant in the incident room, she had been rewarded with the assurance that yes, the murder squad was treating the confessor seriously. And, strictly off the record, he was likely to be charged with something by morning. Maybe not murder, not quite yet. But something serious.

It was, she thought, like the moment when you realize the dental anaesthetic has worn off. She felt tension seep from her shoulders like a liquid flow. Her initial response of scepticism had been dispelled by the CID sergeant's stolid reassurance that someone as sharp as Sarah Duvall was taking this seriously. And if the confessor had been one of the usual suspects who came out of the woodwork whenever there was a major crime in the headlines, the police would have known. She smiled up into Kit's anxious eyes. 'They seem to think he's kosher,' she said, letting out a long breath. She hastily moved from the floor to the sofa and wrapped her arms round him. 'I hope they're right,' she said softly. 'Oh God, I hope it's finished.'

Chapter 43

The air in the room was redolent with the heavy fragrances of ylang-ylang, sandalwood and rose. The flicker of a pair of candles took the chill off the clinical white of the walls and transformed Steve's bedroom from a monastic cell to a place where romance was possible. The massage oil and the candles were Terry's contribution to the atmosphere; after the first night when urgency had been everything, she wanted to give their love-making a more sensual framework.

They lay in a languid tangle of limbs, a pair of champagne flutes within reach but for the moment disregarded as they gave each other the history lessons of their past. As he listened to Terry's tale of her childhood, Steve luxuriated in the sense of having been swept out of the mundanity of his life.

When the shrill note of his mobile phone cut through Terry's gentle ironies, it was a dislocating wrench back into his former life. 'Shit,' he swore savagely, even as he was disentangling himself from her.

She chuckled. 'Ignore it. You're off duty.'

'I can't,' he said angrily, crossing the room in a handful of long strides and abruptly grabbing the phone from the dressing table. 'There's too much on. Bloody thing.' He hit a button and barked, 'Preston here.'

'Steve? This is Sarah Duvall.'

Steve stifled his exasperation and backed up to the edge of the bed, where he flopped down. 'What can I do for you, Sarah?'

'Have I caught you at a bad moment?'

'No, it's fine.'

Duvall registered his clipped tones, knew it wasn't fine, but pressed on regardless. She wasn't about to allow Steve Preston's convenience to come between her and her objective. 'I wanted to ask if you thought Dr Cameron would be open to a formal approach from us to liaise on the Lester murder.'

Steve glanced uneasily at Terry. He felt faintly uncomfortable talking about Fiona in front of her. It felt almost incestuous. 'I don't see why not. The problem is with the Met, not in general. What was it you were after, specifically?'

'As you know, we've got a confessor in custody. But I'm having peculiar problems with checking out his authenticity because so much of the detail of the crime comes from Lester's book. However, I think he could be tied to the letters. What I want to try for is linking him to the letters, then linking the three murders, especially if we can establish that Shand and Elias also had letters. I thought Dr Cameron could look specifically at the letters and the flyer he distributed at the press conference, then she could review the evidence in the other two cases to see if there's linkage. With three cases to go at, we've got more chance of turning up some witness evidence, or something else that would either tie in the confessor or eliminate him.'

'I'd have thought it was worth trying,' Steve said cautiously. 'And there's no better person for that kind of job.'

'I don't want to wait till morning,' Duvall said. 'Have you got a home number for her?'

'I think you'd get a better response face to face than over the phone.' This wasn't the time to tell Duvall that her phone manner wouldn't ingratiate her with a woman who was already predisposed to dislike her because of Duvall's reluctance to provide protection for Kit and his fellows.

'A home address, then?'

Steve cast a quick glance at Terry, who was curled on one side, watching him with a smile. For a brief moment, he considered going through to the other room to avoid any chance of Terry recognizing her supervisor's details. The instinct to confidentiality was bred in the bone, but he realized that if he was going to stand any chance of making this relationship work, he had to let her into his life. He took a deep breath and recited the familiar address. Terry's eyebrows rose and her expression changed to one of curiosity. Steve ended the call and tossed the phone back on the dressing table.

'I won't pry if you'd rather I didn't, but I couldn't help recognizing Fiona's address,' she said.

Steve got back into bed and stretched out his arm to pull her into his embrace. 'You heard about the guy who confessed to Georgia Lester's murder at the press conference?'

'I saw it on the news, yes.'

'Well, City of London want to consult with Fiona about it. They think he's a strong suspect.'

'And they want to establish linkage with the other two crime-writer killings, is that it?' Terry's interest was piqued and she shifted so she could prop herself up on one elbow.

'That's right. She'll jump at the chance. Apart from anything else, it might reassure her that they've got the right person and she can stop worrying that Kit might be next on the hit list.'

'Of *course*. That's why she's been right off the planet the last couple of days.'

'It didn't occur to you that Kit might be a target?'

'What can I say? I'd sort of forgotten about Kit. I've only

407

met him once. Plus, Fiona never talks about her home life. And really, nobody's been talking the serial killer angle up much. The papers all made out that there was no connection between Drew Shand and Jane what's-her-name.' She shook her head crossly. 'God, how could I be such a dummy? She must have been off her head with worry.'

Steve sighed. 'She's been as near as Fiona ever gets to frantic. We had a row over it yesterday. She was angry because she was the one who actually came up with the idea of searching Smithfield, but neither City nor the Met could commit to protecting Kit.'

Terry frowned. 'Oh Steve, that's bad. Torn between the personal and the professional. What a shit of a time you and Fiona must have been having. Worried stiff about Kit and ending up going head to head with each other.'

'It's not been easy,' he acknowledged. 'At least it looks as if Kit is safe now, for which I am profoundly grateful. The guy's my best mate, and if anything had happened to him, I don't know how I would have coped. The only thing is, I'm afraid it's really screwed things between me and Fiona. She's not a woman who forgives easily.'

'She'll come round in time,' Terry said with breezy confidence. 'Especially if you do a bit of serious grovelling. She always responds well to a good grovel, in my experience.'

Steve shook his head. 'It's going to take more than that this time, I think.'

Terry cuddled into him. 'All my hard work, getting you relaxed, and now you're wound up like a spring again.' She reached for the bottle of massage oil. 'There's nothing for it. You're just going to have to put Kit and Fiona out of your mind and lie down and take your medicine like a man.'

Steve managed a smile as he shuffled on to his stomach,

feeling his muscles fluttering as she straddled him. 'Whatever you say, Doctor.'

'I'm not a doctor yet,' she said. 'Just think how much better I'll be when I'm qualified . . .'

He groaned as her hands, slick with oil, began to massage his shoulders. 'I don't know if I'm strong enough for that.'

'We'll work up to it gradually, soldier.' Her strong fingers kneaded the powerful muscles of his back, erasing all thoughts of Sarah Duvall and even Fiona Cameron from his mind.

Fiona was in the kitchen making coffee when the doorbell rang. Frowning at the unexpected interruption, she walked down the hall to check the spyhole in the door. The chances were it was some hack who had decided that he needed to try Kit for a juicy quote for the morning's paper. If it were, Fiona would take great pleasure in blowing him off. One thing was certain. No friend would have called round this evening without checking ahead by phone first.

To her surprise, Fiona recognized the person on the doorstep, though what Detective Chief Inspector Sarah Duvall was doing there was beyond her. Muttering, 'Hell and damnation,' under her breath, Fiona opened the door. 'DCI Duvall,' she said.

'I'm sorry to interrupt your evening,' Duvall said stiffly, as if apology were a stranger in her mouth. 'But I hoped you could spare me some time.'

Fiona stepped back and indicated that Duvall should enter. 'Second left, the kitchen. We'll talk in there.'

Duvall walked down the hall, taking it all in as she went. Good-quality wooden flooring, expensive oriental rugs, a couple of dramatic landscapes in oils on the walls. At the turn of the stairs, a man she recognized as Kit Martin appeared, looking curiously at her.

'It's work, Kit,' Fiona called. 'I need to have a word with DCI Duvall.'

'Can't wait till morning, eh? No problem,' he said, turning and vanishing back upstairs.

'I saw on the news that you've got someone in custody,' Fiona said as she followed Duvall into the kitchen. 'Please, have a seat.'

Duvall pulled out a chair and sat, crossing her legs precisely.

'I was making coffee. Would you like a cup?'

'Thank you.'

'Black, wasn't it?' Fiona didn't wait for a response, reaching for a second mug and filling it up from the cafetiere. She put milk in her own mug and brought them both to the table, where she settled down opposite Duvall. Carefully keeping her face blank to match the police officer's, she said, 'So, what brings you to my door?'

'As you said, we have someone in custody. We had little choice, given the very public nature of his confession,' Duvall said, an ironic note in her voice. 'But the position is far from clear-cut. His name is Charles Redford and he's admitting the killings, but he's giving us nothing that isn't already accessible to anyone who has studied newspaper reports and the Georgia Lester novel that the murder appears to be based on. A search of his flat produced nothing conclusive. He had copies of the three crucial books by Shand, Elias and Lester on his desk. There was a stack of newspapers containing stories about the three murders, but so far, nothing for forensics to have a serious go at.

'We have had one break, in that his phone bill shows that he made calls to both Shand and Lester's numbers within the last three months. And an agent has given us a statement saying that Redford threatened her. She had been considering taking him on, but she'd decided against it. When he got her letter of rejection, he turned up at her office and barged past the receptionist. He got into her inner office and shouted abuse at her. He snatched a paperknife that was lying on the desk and waved it in front of her face, telling her she should be careful who she insulted. Then he threw the knife at the wall and stormed out.'

Fiona sipped her coffee and said nothing, merely raising her eyebrows slightly. Her earlier encounter with Duvall had left her with no desire to make this any easier for her.

Duvall cleared her throat and continued. 'She says she decided not to call the police because she was flying out to New York the following morning and she didn't have time for the, quote, "hassle".' Her expression was of grim disapproval. 'We also took a look at his computer, but so far we haven't found any trace of the threatening letters. I'm hopeful that the computer specialists will be able to find something when they examine the hard disk more closely, but I'm not prepared to pin my hopes to that.' She lifted her slim briefcase on to her lap and opened it. 'I've brought with me copies of the letters and also a copy of the flyer he distributed at the press conference this afternoon.' She extracted a handful of transparent plastic envelopes, each of which contained a photocopied sheet of paper. She closed her briefcase, replaced it at her feet and placed the envelopes on the table. 'I believe the language is distinctive enough to demonstrate they were all written by the same person. I intend to place these with a linguistics expert, in the hope we can demonstrate that.' Duvall met Fiona's eyes. There was no help there, but she continued regardless. 'What I hoped was that you could look at them from the point of view of a psychologist and tell me what you think.'

'What I think about what?'

Duvall pursed her lips. She hadn't been expecting an easy ride. Open hostility she would have handled easily. But Fiona's stubborn failure to give anything back was too similar to her own style for her to understand how to get round it. 'Whether the same person wrote all these. Whether that person is capable of escalating from letters to action. Whether there are clues in this material to indicate a connection to the crimes. Whatever you find there, I'm interested in.'

Fiona held her mug in both hands and looked steadily at Duvall. 'Do you think he's the killer?'

Duvall pushed the bridge of her glasses against her nose. 'Does that matter?'

'I'm curious. I have something at stake here, if you remember,' Fiona said coldly.

Duvall uncrossed her legs. 'I'm not someone who operates on instinct. I work on evidence and experience. Based on that, I'd say he's more likely the killer than not. He's arrogant and overconfident. He's vain, very vain. He's convinced that he has been ripped off. I think he's planned this very carefully, so that he'll be charged and tried and found not guilty. Then he'll finally get his chance to show off to his heart's content. I think your partner is safe, Dr Cameron.'

Fiona had heard what she needed to hear. 'I'll do it,' she said.

Duvall placed a hand on the envelopes. 'There's something else,' she said.

Fiona didn't like the way Duvall worked. There was a cold calculation to everything the detective did and said that made her feel used. If it hadn't been for her personal connection to this case, she would never have gone as far as she had. But she was irritated by the assumption that having gone this far, she could be pushed further. 'It's late, Chief Inspector,' she said, her voice cold. 'Let's cut to the chase.'

Duvall blinked. 'I'm not here to waste time, Doctor. Yours, or mine. I'm well aware of your work on crime linkage. If we are to get this case into court, I believe it's important that we make a convincing case for connecting the three murders. I've already spoken to my colleagues in Edinburgh and Ireland and they're willing to let you review their evidence with a view to formulating a tenable theory that we can take to court that the three murders are the work of the same person.'

Fiona shook her head, an expression of disbelief on her face. 'You took for granted that I would agree to this?' she said.

Duvall shook her head impatiently. 'I hoped you would. If you say no, I'll find someone else. But I'm told you're the best. And, as you pointed out to me, you have had something personal at stake in this case.'

Fiona stared at Duvall, a mixture of reactions battling inside her. She was outraged at the woman's presumption, angry that she had been outmanoeuvred, flattered in spite of herself, and intrigued as she always was by the prospect of a professional challenge. This wasn't one she wanted to hand over to someone else, she admitted to herself. But the knowledge that Duvall would see her agreement as some kind of triumph smarted. 'The circumstances of these murders are very different,' she said, determined not to give Duvall what she wanted right away. 'It's unlikely that I'm going to be able to come up with the sort of concrete connection that juries like.'

Duvall gave her small, tight smile. 'We both believe that the same person killed Drew Shand, Jane Elias and Georgia Lester. We both know if that is the case, they have to have left their signature on each crime. You know how to read the invisible ink. I know how to translate that into hard evidence. Are you in or out?'

The two women stared at each other across the kitchen table. It was, Fiona knew, time to put up or shut up. And this case was too close to home for her to bear the thought of leaving it up to someone else. She reached out for the envelopes. 'I'm in,' she said.

Charles Cavendish Redford leaned against the cold wall of his cell. He knew there was no point in trying to get some sleep. They'd be watching him through the peephole in the door and they'd simply wait till he nodded off, then wake him up to take him back to the interview room, hoping he'd be disorientated enough to let his guard drop and give them something only the killer could know. He wasn't going to fall for that. The beauty of having read so many detective novels and true crime was that he knew all the tricks of the trade. He was going to stay awake and alert, fuelled by adrenaline. There was a strict time limit on how long they could keep him without charge. Whatever they did then would suit him fine. Charged or released, he'd still be within the plans he'd made so carefully.

It was all going beautifully. That policewoman was a godsend. He could wind her up, and the more antagonism that built between them, the more likely she was to charge him with Georgia Lester's murder. He would have his hour in the sun.

He wasn't afraid of being found guilty. He was far too clever for that. One way or another, he would walk out of this a free man. And then publishers would be falling over themselves for his work.

He shifted on the thin mattress, making sure he didn't get too comfortable. He smiled inwardly. For far too long,

Charles Cavendish Redford had put up with being slighted, robbed and cheated. Soon, however, that would be history. Soon he would be a household name. Just like Drew Shand, Jane Elias and Georgia Lester.

Chapter 44

Fiona leaned against the doorjamb of the living room. 'Duvall wants to send someone round tomorrow to interview you,' she said. 'To see if you remember a bloke called Charles Redford sending you any manuscripts or letters.'

'That's not why she came round though, is it?' Kit said from his prone position on the sofa.

'No. That was incidental.' She walked into the room and chose the armchair that gave her a view of Kit's face.

'Charles Redford. He's the man they have in custody?' he asked. He knew she'd tell him the point of the visit when she was ready. Till then, he was happy to let the conversation go where it was comfortable.

'That's right. Do you know him?'

Kit's brow furrowed as he trawled his memory. 'I've got a feeling he sent me a manuscript a couple of years ago.'

'What did you do with it?'

'What I always do with unsolicited manuscripts. Sent it back with a polite letter saying unfortunately I don't have the time or the expertise to critique other people's work and suggested he get an agent.' Kit yawned. 'I don't remember hearing any more from him.'

'You didn't read it?'

'Life's too short.' He reached for his glass and tipped

the dregs of his wine into his mouth. He waited for Fiona to get round to the real purpose of DCI Duvall's visit.

'I'm going to Edinburgh in the morning,' Fiona said.

'Drew Shand?' Kit asked.

'Duvall seems to think there's some value in trying to establish linkage between the three murders. I'm not sure I see the point. They occurred in three different jurisdictions, and as far as I understand the legal principles, you can only try each case in its own jurisdiction. And I'm not sure to what extent each court would allow evidence of the other crimes. But the other police forces involved have agreed to cooperate with the attempt, so they must think there's some value in it, if only to clear their own books. Duvall appears to reckon she'll have more chance of nailing him for Georgia's murder if she can demonstrate a pattern of behaviour.'

Kit elbowed himself upright. 'So the info we got earlier was spot on? They've got the right man.'

'Duvall thinks he's a strong suspect. And she's the person on the ground. There's certainly little doubt he's the letter-writer. Duvall says the language is practically identical. And, embarrassingly for me, she reminded me of a case I read about in the US where someone who wrote threatening letters went on to kill half a dozen people. I hold my hand up. I was wrong when I said I didn't think this letter-writer would escalate into murder.'

Kit grinned. 'Can I have that in writing?' Fiona met childish with childish, sticking her tongue out at him. 'So when are you leaving?'

'There's a flight just after nine.'

'I'm glad you're going. I liked Drew. And Jane. I don't like to think that whoever killed them is going to get away with it. If anyone can build strong enough linkage to convince a jury, it's you.'

Fiona sighed. 'I wish I shared your confidence. It's going to be a hard one to stand up.' She looked away. 'I'd like it if you came with me.'

'Why? There's no need, not now they've got what's-his-name behind bars.'

Fiona, who couldn't quite articulate what was bothering her, shrugged. 'I know. I'd just rather you were with me, that's all.'

'I've got a book to finish,' he protested.

'You can work just as easily in Edinburgh. You can sit in the hotel room and write all day.'

'It's not that simple, Fiona. I'm all over the place. This business with Georgia, it's doing my head in. It's all I can do to get the words on the page right now. And that's sitting in my own office with my own music and my own things around me. There's no way I'm going to be able to concentrate in a strange place, with chambermaids bombing in and out and nothing to filter out the background shit except daytime TV. I'm not coming, and that's that.' His jaw jutted defiantly, daring her to disagree.

Fiona ran a hand through her hair in a gesture of frustration. 'I don't want to leave you here on your own. Not when you're so upset. I can't give you the support you need if I'm four hundred miles away.'

They stared at each other across the room, each uncompromising in their resolution. Eventually, Kit shook his head. 'Can't do it. I want to be inside my cocoon. Where I belong. Besides, my friends are down here. We're going to need to get together and raise a glass to Georgia. It's a rite of passage, Fiona. I need to be here to be part of it.' He stretched a hand out towards her, appeal in his eyes. 'You gotta see my point.'

'Point taken,' Fiona conceded. 'I was thinking of myself as

much as you, I suppose. I've been so scared for you, I just want to keep you close, remind myself that everything's OK again.' They shared a rueful smile, each conscious of the tendency of their work to interfere with the shape they wanted their lives to have.

'How long are you going to be away for?' Kit eventually asked.

'I'm not sure. I'll probably fly straight on to Dublin and do the Irish end as soon as I'm finished in Edinburgh. Tomorrow's Friday. I should be in Ireland by Sunday, maybe home Monday night? Any more than that and I'm going to have serious problems covering my teaching commitments.'

'I'll cook something special for Monday night, then,' he said. 'We'll have a romantic dinner. Turn off the phones, take the battery out of the doorbell and remind ourselves what's so devilishly attractive about each other.'

Fiona grinned. 'Do we have to wait till Monday?'

Fiona stepped off the plane into a grey drizzle. Low clouds obscured the Pentlands and the Ochils, while the rain laid an ashen sheen over landscape and buildings alike. The day had started badly, and it didn't seem to be improving. Her mind had been on Georgia as she'd grabbed her laptop to pack it in its case. Preoccupied, she'd let it slip from her grasp and it had crashed to the floor, the case splitting open and dislodging the screen. 'Oh, fuck!' she'd exploded. There had been no time to deal with it then. Furious with her carelessness, Fiona had opened the cupboard in her desk and pulled out the folder that contained the CD-ROMs and floppy disks she needed to run her programs. She'd shoved them into her briefcase and run downstairs.

Kit had looked up from the morning paper. 'What's wrong?' he'd said.

'I just smashed my laptop casing,' she'd said. 'I can't believe I did that. Can I borrow yours to take to Edinburgh?'

He'd been back in moments, zipping up the laptop bag, far calmer than she'd have been in the circumstances. It was a measure of the toll the previous days' anxieties had taken that so small an accident had ruffled her so thoroughly.

But at least she had a laptop to work with. She'd already used it on the flight, to record her comparisons of the death threat letters and the flyer Redford had distributed at the press conference. There was no question in her mind that the same person had composed all the documents. And she could not rule out the possibility that the letter-writer had become sufficiently obsessed with his grievances to turn his words into action. If it came to it, she would so testify in court.

Now she walked briskly from the small plane to the terminal across tarmac greasy with damp. Inside, she shook her head to free the sparkles of raindrops from her hair and followed the exit signs. The walk from the gate to the arrivals hall seemed interminable, endless corridors turning back on themselves in the kind of maze that experimental rats were better at solving than frazzled commuters.

Eventually, she emerged into the bustle of the airport. She looked around and saw a man carrying a piece of white card with CAMERON neatly inscribed on it. He was a wiry, dark-haired whippet of a man whose sharp suit hung from his shoulders as if it was still on the hanger. With his foot tapping impatiently and his restless eyes flicking across the concourse, he looked more like a villain expecting a tug than a police officer. Fiona crossed to him, put down her overnight bag and touched his elbow. 'I'm Fiona Cameron,' she said. 'Are you waiting for me?'

The man ducked his head. 'Aye, that's right.' He folded

the card and stuffed it in his jacket pocket, then extended a hand to her. 'I'm Detective Sergeant Murray. Dougie Murray. Pleased to meet you.' He pumped her hand vigorously. 'I've got the car outside.' He released her hand and walked off.

Fiona adjusted the strap of the laptop on her shoulder, picked up her bag and followed. Outside the door was an unmarked saloon car. Murray gave a wave to the traffic warden patrolling the kerb and made for the driver's door. Fiona opened the back door of the car and deposited her bags, then got in beside him in the front. He was already gunning the engine. 'The Super sends his apologies. Meeting came up that he couldnae give the body-swerve. I'm to take you to St Leonard's. That's the Divisional HQ where the investigation's based. The Super'll meet you there. Is that OK?'

'I'd like to go to my hotel on the way,' Fiona said firmly. 'Only to check in and drop my bags off. I don't want to be lugging my overnight bag around all day,' she added pointedly.

'No, right, 'course you don't. We've put you in Channings, so we'll have to make a wee detour.' He spoke in a tone of satisfaction, as if it had made his day to have to plan something more creative than a straight run back into town.

They swung off the ring road at the art deco Stakis casino, cutting through a chunk of green belt to join Queensferry Road. Fiona stared at the traffic without registering anything, her thoughts occupied with Kit. He'd be sitting at his desk working, the CD player loaded with whatever was the flavour of the moment. REM and Radiohead would certainly be in the stack somewhere. Maybe The Fall, maybe the Manics. He'd be alternating between bashing the keyboard and staring out of the window, choosing work to keep his personal demons at bay. But now she had to put him out of her mind and concentrate on what she'd come here to do.

421

The bungalows suddenly gave way to tall sandstone terraces set back from the main road, elegant Victorian family homes now mostly divided into flats with huge windows and high ceilings to swallow heat. They made an abrupt left turn on to granite setts, the car wheels rumbling as Murray swung it round the next corner. 'Here we go,' he announced, double-parking outside a blond sandstone building with a canopy and a pair of ornamental lampposts. 'I'll wait in the car,' he said. Fiona wasn't surprised.

The elegance inside matched the sandblasted facade. She checked in and followed a youth up an elegant staircase. Her room was on the first floor, looking out over the wide gardens that divided the street. Through the smirr of rain, she could see the steely ribbon of the Firth of Forth. Over on her left, a vast looming Gothic pile with twin towers dominated the streets spread below her. 'What's that building?' she asked the porter just as he was leaving.

'That's Fettes College,' he said. 'You know? Where Tony Blair went.'

It explained a lot, she thought.

Fiona unpacked her case and made her way downstairs. Ten minutes later they'd cleared the Georgian New Town, dipped down to cross the Cowgate and zipped up The Pleasance to a modern building that housed A Division of Lothian and Borders Police. She followed Murray indoors and along a corridor. He opened a door with a flourish and said, 'I'll tell the Super you've arrived. You'll be working in here, so you might as well get yourself settled in.'

As he turned away, Fiona decided it was time to start asserting herself. 'A cup of coffee would be nice,' she said without a smile.

'Aye, right. Milk? Sugar?'

'Milk, no sugar, please.'

He turned on his heel and marched off, jacket flapping with the speed of his stride. Fiona turned into the room. It was surprisingly pleasant, if small. There was a pale wooden table with a desk chair in front of it. Two standard armless upholstered chairs sat against one wall. There was a small side table with a phone, a jug of water and two clean glasses. Best of all, there was a window. She could see across the car park and, beyond the wall and the rooftops, a slice of Salisbury Crag just about hanging on to its green tones through the rain.

Fiona dumped the laptop on the desk and got down on her knees to find the phone point. She was just plugging in the adapter for her modem cable when the door opened. A pair of stocky legs in trousers that strained over the thighs came towards her. Fiona leaned back so she could see the man over the desk. The sight jolted her memory. A picture formed in her mind like an image on photographic paper swimming into definition in the developer bath. A stocky man with startling red hair and a freckled face ruddy with the East Coast winds. Pale-blue eyes fringed with unusually dark lashes. A button nose and a pinched cherub's mouth. Detective Sergeant Alexander Galloway of Fife Police. Instantly she was transported back a dozen years to a dark and dreary pub in St Andrews where he'd agreed to meet for a drink so she could pick his brains about Lesley's murder. He hadn't been involved with the case initially, but when it had come up for review six months after the event, he'd been one of the officers assigned to it. He'd been able to tell her nothing new.

Now she gaped in shock. She hadn't made the connection when Duvall had explained that Detective Superintendent Sandy Galloway was the officer in charge of the inquiry into Drew Shand's murder. But there could be no doubt. The red hair had faded to a dull gingerish grey, and his flushed face had developed a purplish tinge that would worry his GP, had he ever found time to visit the surgery. But the eyes were the same pale blue, outlined with those remarkable dark lashes. The snub nose was a Jackson Pollock of red veins, and the mouth looked more crimped with disapproval than she remembered. But then, that's what a dozen years at the sharp end of policing would do to a man, she thought. He looked down at her and gave a little smile. 'No, no, Doctor, you've got it all wrong. It's us that are on our knees to you this time,' he said genially.

Fiona scrambled to her feet. 'I had no idea ... I was just looking for the phone point.'

Galloway tutted. 'Murray should have sorted you out.'

'I don't think Murray does sorting out,' Fiona said wryly. 'At least, not for older women. I'm still waiting for my coffee.'

Galloway threw his head back in a soundless laugh. 'By, you've got sharper over the years.'

'Professional observation, that's all. I'm taken aback to see you again, though.' Fiona extended a hand. Galloway's grip was dry and firm.

'I mentioned to DCI Duvall that we'd met before. I thought she would have told you.'

'I think DCI Duvall likes to keep us all on our toes,' Fiona said, her voice as neutral as she could manage.

'Aye, well. I was sorry, you know? That we never got anybody for your sister's murder.'

Fiona looked away. 'I won't pretend I wasn't angry at the time. But these days, I understand better how hard it is to find a serial offender.' She met his eyes again. 'I don't harbour any grudges. You did your best.'

Galloway rubbed the side of his nose with his index finger. 'Aye, well. I learned a valuable lesson from you, you know.'

'You did?'

'Aye. Never forget that murdered folk have families that need to know what happened. It doesnae hurt to keep that at the front of your mind.' He cleared his throat. 'Anyway, it's good of you to come at such short notice. What I've done is I've got one of my officers bringing down the murder file. Is there anything else you want to see?'

Fiona unzipped the laptop case. 'I want to spend some time in Drew Shand's flat.'

'It's been searched thoroughly, you know.' He leaned forward, fists on the desk, frowning. It should have been an aggressive pose, but somehow Galloway made it merely eager.

She looked him straight in the eye. 'I'd just like to get a feel for it. And I want to double-check that there's nothing there to connect Drew Shand with Charles Redford.'

Right on cue, there was a knock on the door and a uniformed PC wheeled in a trolley stacked with files. He brought them over to the desk. 'Will that be everything, sir?' he asked.

Galloway looked a question at Fiona. 'Coffee,' she said. 'Either point me in the direction of the best coffee in the building, or have somebody bring me a cup every hour.'

'You heard her, Constable,' Galloway said. 'Away up to my office and bring down the tray with my filter machine and the coffee.' He smiled at Fiona. 'I can always come down here for a cup if I get desperate. Now, I'm just going to leave you to it. If you need anything, or you want to discuss anything with me, just pick up the phone and ask the switchboard to find me. And when you're ready to go over to the flat, just let me know and I'll organize a car for you.'

'Thanks. Looking at this lot, I'm going to be pretty busy for the rest of the day,' Fiona said. 'I'll probably be ready to go over there late afternoon, but I'll call you when I can see light at the end of the tunnel.'

Left to her own devices, she loaded her software on to Kit's computer. Before she began the work, she sent him a quick e-mail to say she'd arrived safely. Then, making sure her mobile was switched on, she set about the task. She was familiar with police files by now, and although she skipped nothing, she had learned how to skim for material of interest.

What she was looking for were factors common to all three murders that, taken individually, were insignificant but which, taken together, built to form a conclusion that was inescapable. Fiona suspected that in this case, there was little she could achieve that any intelligent police officer couldn't do equally well. But the advantage for the police in having her do the work was that she could testify as an independent expert witness who was an acknowledged authority in the field of crime linkage.

For once, she had something firm to hang her analysis on. It was clear that each of the three murders had been modelled on an episode from a book written by the victim. The Irish Police's arrest of a suspect had diverted attention away from that, but Duvall had made it clear to her that the Garda would be reviewing their position in the light of Redford's confession. She had no doubt that their suspect would be freed shortly.

What was clear was that each of the victims must have been stalked. One of the things she'd have to check out over the next few days was how much information about each of them was readily available in the public domain. With luck, some of that material would be in the murder files already. And of course, the police forces involved would be trawling for fresh witnesses now they had a suspect whose photograph they could release.

For Fiona, the task was more subtle. And for once, she could work at her own pace. The chances were, as Kit pointed out, that Duvall was right. This time there was no ticking time bomb of a killer preparing to strike again.

Chapter 45

DC Joanne Gibb walked down the corridor to Steve Preston's office with a bounce in her stride that seemed to deny the hours she'd spent hunched over her computer running criminal-records checks against everyone on the electoral roll in a clutch of streets on the borders of Kentish Town and Tufnell Park.

She'd been practically cross-eyed with fatigue and on the point of tears of frustration at the fruitlessness of her task when the phone had rung. The previous day, she'd tried to contact the local information collator at the police station serving the area Terry had identified, only to discover the constable who ran their card index was on holiday and not due back until Monday. It had felt like the last straw, but she'd hacked on through her lists, hoping against hope she'd still turn something up.

Then, late morning, the call had come through. The collator, Darren Watson, had dropped by the station to pick something up and he'd seen the message marked 'urgent' from Joanne. At the end of her rope and almost without hope, Joanne had outlined what she was looking for.

'Right,' Darren had said. 'A couple of likely lads spring to mind. Why don't you come over and we'll have a look?'

'Now?' Joanne could hardly believe her luck. In her experience, police on their day off would do almost anything to avoid being dragged on duty.

'Sure. I've just come back from a week in a cottage in Cornwall with my other half, and frankly, anything that keeps me out of the house for an hour or two would be a bonus. Get yourself over here and we'll see what we can dig out.'

Joanne didn't need asking twice. She'd practically run downstairs to her car and invited several outbreaks of road rage on her way to the North London police station where Darren Watson might just have the answer to her prayers. Local Information Officers were responsible for maintaining the informal intelligence of the station. As well as keeping a card index file of every known villain on the patch with details of their convictions, a good collator recorded associates, suspicions and gossip. There were sound reasons why much of what they had tucked away was never entered into a computer. A card could always be conveniently misplaced, whereas even deleted computer records left traces. Omniscience coupled with deniability was the hallmark of a good collator. Joanne hoped that was what she was going to find.

Darren was in a small subterranean office that had the atmosphere of a wartime command bunker. One wall was covered with large-scale maps of the area, with pins in a variety of colours marking specific locations. Another was lined with filing cabinets. Shelving along a third wall sagged under the weight of box files piled along its length. Darren was sitting on the edge of the desk that occupied most of the fourth wall, dressed in his civvies: a navy fleece over a white T-shirt, blue jeans and brilliant-white trainers. Joanne's first thought was that if his appearance was anything to go by, Darren's files would be immaculate. Joanne was acutely aware that the attrition of the day's work on top of too little sleep had left her a long way behind the collator in the grooming stakes.

They introduced themselves and Joanne came straight to the point. 'Like I told you, I'm trying to develop a suspect in a series of rapes. We have reason to believe he might be on your patch. I've done a trawl through electoral records, but I've come up with a blank. We think he might have a record for minor sexual offences, maybe even attempted rape. What we're looking for is an offender who works out of doors, who targets white women, usually blonde. He may ride a bike in his getaways and he uses a knife in his attacks. It's possible that some of his attacks may have been witnessed by small children.'

Darren pushed off from the desk and headed for his filing cabinets. 'I've been giving it some thought and I've come up with two names.' He hauled open one of the card index drawers and flicked through. 'There we go.' He took out a small bundle of cards held together with an elastic band. 'Gordon Harold Armstrong.' He handed the cards over to Joanne and moved to another drawer.

Gordon Harold Armstrong was twenty-five, unemployed, and had been in and out of prison for burglary and indecent assault. His technique was to grab women on their way home from work, fondle their breasts and expose himself. He had threatened three of his victims with a knife. There was no mention of a bike. But for Joanne, the crucial disqualifying factor was that Gordon Harold Armstrong was black. And based on both Fiona's analysis of Susan Blanchard's murder and the evidence of the rape victims, the man she was looking for was white.

Darren turned to her with a single card. 'Any joy, do you think?'

Joanne shook her head. 'I think I'm looking for an IC1.'

Darren proffered the card. 'Try this one.'

Gerard Patrick Coyne, twenty-seven years old. New Zealand-born, he had arrived in the UK as an eighteen-year-old student. Which explained his absence from the voters' roll, Joanne realized. Having graduated from Kent University with a social sciences degree, he had worked for various market research companies as a data analyst ever since. His first arrest had come four years previously after a woman had complained he had attacked her in a local park. He had pushed her to the ground and tried to have sex with her. But she'd struggled and got away from him. The charges were later dropped on the grounds of insufficient evidence. He'd been arrested for the second time a few months later. A foot patrol had found him lurking in the bushes of another park, this time carrying a knife. He'd been charged with possession of an offensive weapon and had been given two years' probation. According to the notes on the back of the card, Coyne had been a suspect in two other sexual assaults. In one case, the victim had been too traumatized to take part in an identification parade. In the other, the woman had been unable to pick Coyne out of the line-up.

Coyne, not surprisingly for a sex offender, had no known criminal associates. What he did have was a bike. Darren Watson's scrupulous notes revealed that he was a member of a local cycling club and had won several road races.

Joanne allowed a slow smile to spread across her face. 'Darren, you are a star,' she said, waving the card like a winning lottery ticket.

'You like our Mr Coyne, do you?'

'Like him? I love him.' As she spoke, Joanne pulled her notebook out of her handbag and began to copy down Coyne's details. Address, date of birth, date of arrests and his conviction for the offensive weapon charge. And the name of his cycling club.

As she knocked on Steve Preston's door half an hour later, Joanne was convinced her boss was also going to love the prospect of Gerard Patrick Coyne. She walked into his office, a grin spread across her face. 'Have I got news for you!' she began, sitting down opposite her boss without waiting to be invited. She flicked open her notes and read out Coyne's details. She looked up. 'I've run his CRO. Looks like we've got a suspect at last, guv.' She sorted through the bundle of computer printouts, collating a set to give to her boss.

'And nothing to tie him in to Susan Blanchard,' Steve reminded her. 'Nothing except informed speculation and a bit of computer analysis.' He took the sheaf of paper and stared at the top sheet, which included Coyne's photos. 'Wait a minute,' he said, an edge of excitement creeping into his voice.

'What is it, guv?' Joanne leaned forward in her eagerness, as if she would somehow see whatever it was that Steve had latched on to.

'I know that face. I've seen him.' He closed his eyes and frowned in concentration. When they opened, his whole face was alight with excitement. 'He was at the Bailey the day Blake was set free! I know it was him, I noticed him particularly because he was in cycling clothes. Carrying a helmet. It was him, Joanne, I know it was him.'

'Are you sure?' It was as if she dared not hope.

'I'm sure. I was paying attention to the public gallery crowd, because I still had it at the back of my mind that we'd brought the wrong man to court. I was checking out the faces. Just in case I saw anybody that rang a bell.' Steve jumped to his feet and started pacing. 'What we've got to do . . . Joanne, I want you to get me the video footage we shot at Susan Blanchard's funeral. We had full cover, all angles. And see what you can get from the press. Whatever pix and footage

432

they took outside the Bailey. And the magistrates' court, see if you can find anything from there. You'll have to be discreet, you know how they get on their high horse if they think we're trying to come the heavy hand with them. Go and talk to the press office, see what they can do for you.'

'What about Coyne? Are we going to pull him in?'

Steve spread his hands in frustration. 'I haven't got the bodies for this, Jo. Let me see . . .' He was talking half to himself, doodling on his desk pad. 'John's relieving Neil at Blake's place at six . . . Maybe Neil could go over to the suspect's address then, keep on him till midnight . . .' He looked up at Joanne. 'Any chance you can come in tomorrow at seven and pick Coyne up for the day?'

Joanne nodded, enthusiasm overcoming weariness. 'Of course. This could be the break we've been waiting for. But . . . if you don't mind me asking . . . Why are we still surveilling Blake when we've got Coyne to go at?'

Steve gave a resigned nod. 'Good point, Jo. I suppose I've got a thing about Blake. Oh, I know he's not the killer. But if Fiona Cameron's right, and he did see what happened on the Heath that morning, I'd love to get something on him. For all we know, he's in contact with Coyne. I'd like to stay on him for as long as we can manage it. But Blake's not what you should be concentrating on now. Leave it with me, I'll make the arrangements. Just get yourself to Coyne's place for seven tomorrow and stay on him.'

She got to her feet. 'If that's all, I'm going to clock off now and catch up on some sleep.'

'You deserve it. Great job, Jo. Well done.' He smiled. 'Our luck's on the turn. I've got a good feeling about this.'

Before the door had even closed, Steve was on the phone. Within fifteen minutes, he had everything in place. Neil had agreed to take on the extra surveillance, and another CID

433

officer was lined up to cover Blake the following day while Steve's core team were elsewhere. It was far from satisfactory, but it was the best he could manage at such short notice. And given the way things had started to run in his favour, he couldn't help feeling optimistic. Maybe they'd finally get their hands on the real killer of Susan Blanchard. Nothing would make him happier.

Then he remembered Terry Fowler and amended the thought.

Now everything was in place. It didn't matter that the van he'd hired using one of his false driving licences had no logo on the side; courier companies often hired anonymous white vans when their own fleet was overstretched. Anyway, it was only a minor prop. The key vehicle, the four-wheel-drive Toyota, was already parked in the narrow lane that ran behind the row of houses where his target lived.

All it had needed was patience. He'd cruised by the target's house a couple of times earlier in the day. No surprises there. If there had been any kind of protection in place, it had disappeared in the smoke and mirrors of the previous day's confession. He couldn't believe his luck when he'd switched on the TV the night before. Just when he thought things were going to get even harder for him, the police had fallen for a faker. Now nobody would be expecting him, least of all his target.

Everything was in place. Even the weather was working in his favour. A grey drizzly afternoon meant empty streets and poor visibility. He turned the key in the ignition and flicked the indicator down. *Ready or not, here I come.*

Kit stared at the screen without seeing the words. Time had drifted past without him noticing, engrossed as he was in the process of grieving for his friend. He replayed Georgia in his mind like a series of videotapes, recalling her gestures, her facial expressions, the way she laughed. Whole chunks of conversation dropped out of his memory and reverberated round his head. So many times they'd stayed up late in hotel bars, talking about their work, their colleagues, the publishing business and gradually moving on to more personal issues. She'd talked fondly of Anthony, lasciviously about her lovers. He'd confided the whole process of falling in love with Fiona to Georgia, and right up to the end he'd still shared more of their relationship with Georgia than anybody else.

It wasn't that they lived in each other's pockets. Weeks could go past without them meeting, but theirs was the sort of friendship that always picked up where they'd last left off. He missed her already, a dull pain like the beginnings of hunger. He wished Fiona were with him. She understood the mechanism of loss; she could be his guide through the uncharted terrain of grief.

He shook his head, like a dog worried by a fly, and opened his e-mail program. He downloaded Fiona's message and read it. Words at a distance, but still they soothed.

Kit glanced at the clock and was surprised to see how late it was. The detective from the City of London Police was due to take his statement in half an hour. Not that he had much to say. His vague recollection of being sent a manuscript by Redford wouldn't advance their case much, he suspected. He wondered if Georgia had also been on the receiving end of one of Redford's unsolicited offerings. If so, there would probably be a record somewhere. Unlike Kit, Georgia had employed a part-time secretary to deal with her correspondence. Somewhere, there would doubtless be a copy of any covering letter that had accompanied the manuscript on its return journey.

The creak of the gate interrupted his meandering thoughts and he looked out of the window. A courier was struggling up the path with a large cardboard box, the sort that contained author copies of books. A clipboard was balanced on top of the box.

Kit got to his feet and walked out into the hall. He opened the front door before the courier had even managed to ring the bell.

'Parcel for Martin,' the man said, peering over the top of the box.

Kit reached out to take the box. It was as heavy as he'd expected and he stepped back so he could turn round and put it on the floor clear of the door. Out of the corner of his eye, he saw something move. He half turned as the courier's arm came down in a savage arc. He saw the blow coming, half raised his arm to ward it off. He knew as soon as the impact hit his skull that he was too late. Red and white pain bloomed behind his eyes. Then everything faded to black.

The courier walked back down the path, swinging his clipboard. He climbed into his van and drove off. Two streets away, he found a parking space. He pulled off the tight uniform jacket and replaced it with black leather. He climbed into the back of the van and stripped off the coarse blue trousers, pulling on a pair of black jeans in their stead. Then he locked up the van and walked back to the lane that ran behind Kit Martin's back garden.

He pushed open the garden gate he'd left unbolted a few minutes earlier, then, in the gathering dusk, he made his way past the bare branches of the plum trees and across the patio through the french windows he'd unlocked. Handy of Kit to have left the key in the lock. Across the kitchen and into the hall. Nice place, if you liked that sort of thing. Himself, he preferred the more traditional, farmhouse kitchen to all this stark modernity.

And there he was. Victim number four. Trussed up like a chicken, cuffed hand and foot with those convenient plastic restraints. Mouth stopped with a wide strip of elastoplast that would allow him to breathe even if his nose got bunged up. He didn't want him dead yet. Not by a long chalk. Not so powerful now, Mr Kit Martin, creator of false gods. Destroyer of lives.

Time for him to face his own destruction.

But first, more patience was needed. Darkness was what was required. It wouldn't do for the neighbours to see their friendly neighbourhood celebrity rolled down the garden path like a lumpy carpet and dumped in the back of a four-wheel-drive.

He checked his watch. Half an hour should do it. Then they'd be on the road for the long journey home.

Chapter 46

The video viewing room was as high-tech as anything a broadcasting company could have provided. Steve wasn't quite sure how the techies had managed to swing the budget for such a sophisticated suite, but for once he felt it was worth every penny taken away from more direct forms of policing. He was sitting beside a technician who was taking him through the videos of Susan Blanchard's funeral.

It had been a sparkling, sunny day, which had doubtless felt grotesquely inappropriate for the grieving family and friends, but which had made the police camera operators' job easier. Three video cameras had been set up at a discreet distance from the graveside, taking advantage of the aged yew trees that ringed the churchyard. They had filmed the mourners arriving at the church, then assembling at the graveside for the interment. Then, as the crowd had dispersed, one camera had remained to film the grave itself for the remainder of the afternoon.

Steve's eyes were glued to the screen as the video played out before him in slow motion. Every now and again, he asked for a freeze-frame and zoom so he could take a closer look at individual mourners. The first tape had yielded nothing concrete, although there were a couple of rear views that could have been Coyne.

By the time they were halfway through the second tape,

his eyes had begun to feel gritty and tired. 'I need a break,' he told the technician, pushing back his chair and stretching. 'Give me ten minutes.'

He left the video suite and climbed the two flights of stairs to his office. On his desk there was a thick brown envelope with, 'Urgent. FAO Detective Superintendent Steve Preston,' scrawled across it in black felt-tip. He ripped it open and pulled out half a dozen black and white photographs. A compliment slip fluttered to the desktop and he saw it had come from the picture editor of a national daily, a man he'd shared a drink and a few jokes with at one of Teflon's ghastly cocktail parties the previous Christmas. Nothing could beat personal contact for results in that grey area of press and police cooperation.

The photographs had all been taken outside the Old Bailey on the day of Francis Blake's acquittal. Steve rummaged in his top drawer for his magnifying glass and began to study the prints methodically. As he worked his way across the third picture, he let out a sigh of relief. His memory hadn't been playing tricks on him. On the fringe of the crowd surrounding Blake was the unmistakable face of Gerard Coyne. Steve scanned the remaining photos and found Coyne on two others. In one, he was full-face to the camera, in the other two he was in profile. But there was no possibility of error.

The man who had been identified by Terry's geographic profile had been there at the trial of Susan Blanchard's putative killer.

Fired with fresh enthusiasm, Steve ran down the stairs to the video suite. 'Let's roll,' he said. 'He's here somewhere, I know it.'

His patience was rewarded a mere ten minutes later. The second tape had picked up Coyne emerging from the trees at the side of the graveyard. He was wearing a dark suit, with collar and tie, appropriate to the occasion. He had hung back from the main body of mourners round the grave, staying on the fringes. A significant number of people had respected the family's grief and stayed well back while Susan's twins had thrown roses on their mother's coffin and watched it lowered into the ground. But they had all dispersed fairly quickly after the ceremony was over. Coyne, conversely, had melted back into the trees then, when the last of the congregation was long gone, he had re-emerged and crossed to the path that led to Susan Blanchard's grave.

Steve felt his pulse quicken as Coyne moved in slow motion down the path. As he drew level with the open grave, he didn't so much as glance sideways. Instead, he continued along the path. Two graves along from Susan Blanchard, he stopped abruptly and turned to face that headstone. 'Damn,' Steve swore softly. 'We can't see his face. I bet he's looking at her grave. I'd put money on it.'

Coyne stood, head slightly bowed, for a couple of minutes, then he turned and went back the way he had come. There was nothing in his behaviour to suggest anything untoward. He could, if pressed, have claimed he'd delayed his planned visit to the grave near Susan's because there was a funeral in progress. But taken in conjunction with his presence at the Old Bailey and the geographic profile, it was another brick in a circumstantial case that might yet prove sufficient to put him behind bars.

'I want you to print me a series of stills from that video,' Steve said. 'The best views of his face. Blow them up so we get the best possible definition. I don't want there to be any doubts about this.'

'No problem,' the techie said. 'I suppose it's urgent?'

'It's urgent.' Steve was already heading for the door. He checked his watch. Teflon had a habit of finding excuses to be out of the office early on Friday afternoons, but he might just catch him.

Commander Telford was actually waiting for the lift that Steve emerged from. 'I'm glad I've caught you, sir. I need to speak with you urgently about the Susan Blanchard case,' he said firmly.

'Can't it wait, Superintendent? I've got an appointment.'

With a large gin and tonic, Steve thought cynically. 'I'm afraid it won't wait, sir. Perhaps you could call ahead and tell them you've been unavoidably delayed?'

Telford pursed his lips and snorted through his nose. 'Oh, very well. But keep it as brief as you can.' He turned on his heel and marched back to his office.

Steve had barely closed the door behind him when Telford said, 'What is it that's so important, then?'

'We have a viable suspect in the Blanchard case, sir. It's my intention to bring him in for questioning and search his premises. I thought you'd want to be kept informed.' He crossed to the visitor's chair and sat down, ignoring the fact that Telford was still standing.

'Where has this come from?' Telford said, unable to hide his scepticism.

'If you remember, sir, you authorized a crime linkage and geographic profile based on cases with similar components. Using the results of that, my officers did a trawl of criminal records and we emerged with a likely name.'

'That's it?' Telford interrupted. 'You think that'll stand up in court as a reasonable excuse for pulling someone in and turning over his home?'

'There is more, sir,' Steve said, biting back his frustration. 'The suspect is a member of a cycling club and we have two witnesses who put a cyclist at the scene of the crime. Even more significantly, when I saw the suspect's photograph, I recognized him. I had seen him before, sir. He was present at the Old Bailey when Francis Blake was in court. I've verified that from photographs taken there that day. And I've since examined the videos we took at Susan Blanchard's funeral. He was there too. After the funeral, he walked past her grave. In my opinion, sir, we have enough circumstantial evidence to arrest him on suspicion of murder. And to conduct a search under Section Eighteen of PACE.' He held Telford's eyes, willing him to agree. He knew his strength should be more than Telford's weakness could withstand, but he'd never tested it in a head-to-head before. Maybe he should have done it months ago, when Telford had pushed through the decision to dump Fiona and use Horsforth. But he had backed down then, and the price had been too high for him to be comfortable with the idea that the same cost might be extracted again.

'It's thin,' Telford complained. 'And you've already come a cropper with this case. I don't want another disaster on my hands.'

'We can keep the lid on it, sir. There's no need to make any kind of announcement until we're ready to charge him. Nobody need know about the arrest and search. I can keep it really tight – just me and my immediate team.'

Telford shook his head. 'You make a convincing case. But I want to run it past the AC Crime before we go any further.'

'But the AC's on leave,' Steve protested. He could see his case slipping out of his grasp and he felt powerless to stop it.

'He's due back on Monday morning. I suggest we have a meeting with him first thing. Until then, nothing must be done to alert the suspect.' Telford's smile was genial. He'd found a way to pass the awkward buck, and he was

442

happy. 'We've waited long enough. Another couple of days won't hurt.'

'That's not good enough.' Steve could feel his cheeks flush with anger as Telford's smile changed to a frown. 'My team have worked all the hours God sends on this and I am not about to sacrifice our momentum. I propose leaving a message on the AC's home phone so he can contact me for a briefing as soon as he gets back.'

'How dare you threaten to go over my head? You are out of order, Superintendent,' Telford shouted with all the bluster of a man who knows he is out of his depth.

Steve got to his feet. 'That may be, sir. But this is my investigation and I will not jeopardize it. I'm prepared to take full responsibility.'

Faced with an implacability he could not shake, Telford immediately back-pedalled. 'If you think it's necessary, then do it. But you'd better be very sure of your ground if you're going to disrupt the AC's leave.'

'Thank you, sir,' Steve said, his tone bordering on the insolent. He left the room before his temper escaped his control, even managing not to slam the door. It wasn't the result he'd hoped for, but at least he had side-stepped Teflon. The Assistant Commissioner for Crime wouldn't be thrilled to come home from whatever foreign parts he was visiting to find an urgent message on his answering machine. But although he knew how to play politics as well as any other senior manager, the AC had been a far more courageous detective than Telford had ever managed. He would understand what was driving Steve. And, he felt sure, the AC would give him the go-ahead. Till then, he would have to keep the surveillance as low-key as possible.

Nothing, he thought as he walked back to his office, was ever as straightforward as it seemed.

*   *   *

It was a sentiment Fiona would probably have agreed with. She had ploughed through the murder file on Drew Shand, which had proved to be a singularly unproductive activity from the point of view of developing strong points of linkage. Among the few things she could say so far was that in spite of careful staging, there was no indication of the sexual motivation of the fictional killings being replicated in the real murders, which was significant in itself. It meant that there was clearly some other motive behind the deaths of Georgia and Drew. They had both been stalked; they had both been abducted; neither had been killed in their own homes, but at some unspecified site; and they were both award-winning writers of serial killer thrillers which had successfully been adapted by other media. All of this was in the realm of the psychology of the act, however. There was little of a concrete nature from which further evidence could be developed.

What had struck Fiona was that the killer was prepared to deviate from his template. In each case, there was a significant alteration between the events outlined in the book and the path the murderer had taken. With Drew Shand, the body dump was different. Although there were sites nearby that would have better matched the precise description in the book, his body had been displayed somewhere else, presumably because it was less exposed and the killer could drive right up to the location. With Jane Elias, the torture that had been carried out on a live victim had been translated into the mutilation of a body already dead. Either the killer had misjudged his initial attack or he hadn't had the stomach for that degree of sadistic experiment. Fiona inclined to the latter view because it conformed to the element of expediency in the earlier variation.

In Georgia's case, the crucial difference was the discovery of the head accompanying the victim. Furthermore, according to Duvall, there was no sign that the killer had slavishly stuck to the book; there was no indication that he had had sex with the severed head. Again, a mixture of squeamishness and expediency had come into play. For the killer to be certain that his actions would be identified, he had to make sure that the meat in the freezer was clearly the remains of Georgia Lester. So he had made changes.

It wasn't exactly a signature, but it was a pattern. With this new realization in the front of her mind, Fiona approached Drew's flat with more optimism than she had felt earlier. Perhaps there really was new material to be had there.

Late in the afternoon, Murray had been despatched to navigate her through the rush-hour traffic to Drew Shand's New Town flat. He had let her in, then left her to it, with instructions to her to lock up after her and bring the keys back to St Leonard's in the morning.

It was a beautiful flat, she thought. The rooms were elegantly proportioned, with elaborate plaster friezes in the living room and main bedroom, which looked west across a large communal garden, grass and mature trees enclosed behind iron railings and separated from the surrounding houses by the road. The flat had been expensively fitted out, with heavy curtains and comfortable furniture. Framed film *noir* posters adorned the walls, an interest mirrored in the collection of videos that filled an entire bookcase in the living room. In spite of that, and the books that lined the freakishly tidy office, it felt more like a display for a magazine feature than a home. Even the bathroom was preternaturally tidy, with all the normal clutter hidden behind handsome mirror-and-chrome cupboards. Not even a half-squeezed tube of toothpaste disrupted the order.

This much she learned from her first pass through the flat. But Fiona was no behavioural psychologist. It wasn't her business to try to read the crime by reading the victim. In this instance, her primary goal was to find something in Drew Shand's life to connect him to Charles Cavendish Redford. She knew the police had searched the flat thoroughly, but at that point they'd been looking for a connection with the gay S&M world, not a communication from a frustrated writer.

She pulled the desk chair over to the filing cabinet and started going through the files. The bottom drawer was devoted to personal papers – mortgage, accounts, household receipts, car insurance, the general detritus of modern life. The next drawer contained a series of suspension files that seemed to relate to Drew's published work and work in progress. She searched the files quickly, on the off-chance that he really had stolen an idea from Redford. But there was nothing to indicate any source for his material other than his own imagination.

The top drawer was devoted to correspondence. There were files for his agent, his publisher, his publishing contracts and, finally, one marked 'Fan Mail'. It was a surprisingly thick file, Fiona thought as she pulled it out of the drawer. She'd lived with Kit for long enough to have an appreciation of the sort of volume of mail a successful writer would ordinarily receive, but Drew's file exceeded her expectations. The first dozen letters were much as she expected; letters of appreciation for his first novel, enquiries about when the second would be out, requests for signed bookplates, the occasional, slightly embarrassed pointing out of a minor error in the text. There were a couple of letters expressing disgust at the violence of *Copycat*, but nothing that would stir any great feeling of concern in the recipient.

The bulk of the file, however, consisted of letters and

printed-out e-mail from men who expressed an interest in meeting the author of *Copycat* because they found him attractive and were intrigued to know if his personal sexual tastes were reflected in his novel. These were held together with a paperclip. Stuck to the top sheet was a Post-it note that read, 'Saddo file'.

As she flicked through, a single letter dislodged itself from near the back of the sheaf. It was a folded sheet of A4. Fiona unfolded it, and let out a long sigh of satisfaction.

> 'Drew Shand,' she read, 'Your career has barely begun, but already it is based on the dangerous ground of theft. You have stolen from me. You know that you have taken my work and passed it off as what you have yourself made. And your lies deprive me of what is rightfully mine.
>
> 'Your work is a feeble reflection of other people's light. You take, you destroy, you are a parasite who lives off the life force of those whose gifts you envy. You know this to be true. Search your pathetic grimy soul and you will not be able to deny what you have deprived me of.
>
> 'The time has come for you to pay. You deserve nothing from me but my contempt and my hatred. If killing you is what it takes to grant what is rightfully mine, then so be it. It is a fair price for stealing my soul.
>
> 'The hour and the day will be of my choosing. I trust you will not sleep easy; you do not deserve so to do. I will enjoy your funeral. From your ashes, I will rise like a phoenix.'

There were differences between this letter and the ones she had already seen. But the similarities were overwhelming. There was no doubt in her mind that Drew Shand had received a letter from the same person who had written to Georgia and Kit, and who had also composed the flyer distributed to the press conference where he had admitted his guilt.

447

It was hard to find an argument to contradict what Fiona was now beginning to accept was the case. The coincidences were piling too high. Whoever had killed Georgia had also killed Drew. And it looked as if that person really was Charles Cavendish Redford.

Chapter 47

Her flat was like her, Steve thought. Light, bright and smart. Stylish and bold. Terry lived on the top floor of an old brick building off City Road. The three floors below her were occupied by a graphic design business, a leather-goods workshop and a company providing post-production facilities to independent film makers. The label by the third-floor button in the goods lift read simply, *Fowler Storage.* Steve suspected there was no planning permission for residential use for the top storey. He also suspected that Terry didn't give a toss.

Her living space consisted of a large open room around forty feet by fifty feet. A door at the far end gave on to a narrow bathroom and a shower cubicle. The main area was whitewashed, the floor painted a dark glossy terracotta. There was a sleeping area with a brass bed and brass rails for hanging clothes, a sitting area with half a dozen beanbags and a mini stereo system, a work area with a desk, a computer and floor-to-ceiling bookshelves. A kitchen area was squeezed into a corner by the windows, complete with a round pine table and six folding chairs. A portable TV and video on a trolley were stowed in one corner. The walls were decorated with framed Keith Haring prints, their bright splashes the main source of colour.

She'd opened the door with a flourish, imitating a trumpet fanfare through pursed lips. He'd stood on the threshold, appraising the room with a professional eye. He nodded. 'Great views,' he said. 'I like it.'

Then he was through the door and in her arms, their hungry mouths searching for satisfaction. No time to undress, just the urgent fumbling aside of whatever clothes got in the way, desire sweeping everything away except the consciousness of each other's body.

Afterwards, they lay in untidy array, breath mingling, both for once entirely lacking in self-consciousness. 'So, what's the main course?' Steve asked.

Terry giggled and snuggled her hands under his shirt. 'That wasn't even the starter. Think of it as an *amuse-bouche*.'

'Consider me amused.'

Terry freed herself from his arms and stood up, lithe movements that he followed with his eyes. 'Let's get comfortable,' she said, pulling her dress over her head and kicking off her shoes.

'Sounds good to me,' he agreed, getting to his feet. He scooped his mobile phone and pager out of his pockets and crossed to the desk, where he put them down next to the keyboard. He shrugged out of his clothes, throwing them over the desk chair. 'Bathroom?' he asked.

Terry pointed. 'Down there.'

'Don't go away,' he said.

'As if.' As soon as the bathroom door closed behind him, she jumped to her feet and moved purposefully to the desk. She stared down at the phone and pager. The mood had been shattered the previous evening by a phone call that hadn't even been his case, bringing to the surface all his worries and fears for his friend. And, even worse, thrusting Fiona Cameron into the space between them. She wasn't sure what the past history there was, but all her instincts told her there was more to it than mere friendship. His body language changed whenever Fiona's name cropped up, betraying something lurking beneath the surface. Tonight, she didn't want Fiona in bed with them. Impulsive as always, Terry reached out. It was the work of a moment to switch off both phone and pager. Besides, she reasoned as she crossed to the bed, tonight was Friday night and the end of the working week. If she was going to have a relationship with this man, Terry knew she would have to change his workaholic ways. And there was no time like the present.

Sarah Duvall stood under the feeble spray from the shower head and wondered why every police station she'd served in had had crappy showers. She'd spent the last hour in the computer room where the officers on her squad were patiently entering the results of all the Smithfield interviews that had been conducted already and were still going on all over Greater London. While the interviews with Redford remained so unproductive, she'd decided to crack the whip in other areas of the investigation. She'd only walked away from the computers when she realized that the lines of print on the screen were wavering before her eyes as if through the lens of a swimming pool. If she had any more caffeine, her system would probably go into cardiac crisis, so she'd headed for the women's showers in the hope that a cascade of cool water would restore her brain to something approaching working order.

The first twenty-four hours were crucial to a murder investigation. Unfortunately for Duvall, those essential hours had passed over a week ago. And she was left picking over a very cold trail. So far as she could tell, not a single witness statement apart from that of the literary agent had anything approaching a positive lead that would tie Redford more strongly into the crime. And that only spoke to motivation, not direct connection to the murder. The only concrete thing they had was a sighting of a metallic-grey four-wheel-drive, possibly a Toyota or a Mitsubishi, seen by a passing motorist parked behind Georgia Lester's Jaguar on the day of her disappearance. The driver hadn't seen either Georgia or the occupant of the 4x4. But there was no record of Charles Redford possessing such a vehicle. She already had someone checking with car hire firms to see if he'd hired one recently.

Duvall turned off the trickle of water and stepped out of the cubicle. She towelled herself dry and climbed into the only clean clothes in her locker – a pair of blue jeans and a Chicago PD sweatshirt. Not exactly ideal, but better than the crumpled outfit she'd been wearing for the past thirty-six hours. The clean material against her skin made her feel more refreshed than the shower had. A cursory glance in the mirror, and she was ready to roll again.

When she walked back into the operations room, she instantly plugged in to the fresh sense of excitement that buzzed under the hum of the computers. She was two steps into the room when one of her sergeants bounded up to her. 'We've got something in from Dorset,' he said, unable to keep his face solemn.

Duvall felt her tired face trying a smile on for size. 'Tell me more,' she said, pulling out the nearest chair and sitting down.

'There's an outhouse at the bottom of a field at the back of the property. They didn't realize it belonged to the cottage, which is why they haven't searched it before now. Anyway, it turns out the husband mentioned it to one of their officers, so they broke in there a couple of hours ago and that's where he butchered her. It's got stone benches along one wall, and there are bloodstains all over them. Even better, he left his tools behind. Knives, hacksaw, chisel, hammer, the lot.'

Duvall nodded. 'Probably thought that was safer than hanging on to them or trying to dispose of them somewhere else. I take it they've got a full forensic team in there now?'

'They're going over it inch by inch.'

'Great. Keep me informed.'

He moved off, glad to have some definite purpose. He had completely missed the troubled look on his boss's face. For the first time since Redford had grandstanded his way into her interview room, something had come up that didn't gel with what he had said. She'd have to double-check. But Duvall was as sure as she could be that he had said he had taken Georgia to, 'a place he'd known about for years, a place they'd never find.' That squared with what the book had said.

It was, however, entirely at odds with the Dorset Police's discovery.

Uneasiness crept through Duvall's weary body, as palpable as nausea. What if her instinct had led her astray? What if Redford was nothing more than an attention-seeker? What if there was still a killer on the loose? She shook her head, unwilling to concede the possibility. It couldn't be. Redford was so right, she felt it in her heart.

But what if she were wrong?'

The pain came first. A desperate localized agony inside his head, red, yellow and white waves behind his eyes. When he tried to groan, Kit found his mouth couldn't move. Then the secondary pains began to take focus. His shoulders ached, his wrists smarted. He tried to shift his position and found himself rolling helplessly from his side on to his back. His hands dug uncomfortably into his spine, and he had to rock his shoulders furiously to get back into the less painful position he'd started off in. Nothing made sense. Opening his eyes was no help. The darkness was more profound than it had been before he'd forced his eyelids apart.

His stomach grumbled. The waves of pain from his head seemed to be directly connected to his gut, producing an uncomfortable queasiness. Slowly, he realized that wherever he was, he was in motion. Now he could hear the low grumble of an engine and the hiss of road noise. Muffled voices separated out and he understood that a radio was playing. It dawned on him that he was inside a moving vehicle and the driver was listening to the radio.

Comprehension brought memory back with bewildering swiftness. The courier at the door with the box of books. The movement out of the corner of his eye. Then nothing, till now.

With appalling clarity that momentarily banished pain, Kit recognized the scenario. He was trapped in a nightmare of his own invention. He was living the story of Susannah Tremayne, the second victim of the serial killer he'd dubbed the Blood Painter. The killer had captured her by pretending to be a courier delivering a package. Then he'd loaded her into his van and driven her to the holiday cottage.

Twenty-four hours earlier, it would have been at the front of his mind. He would never have opened the door to a courier, not even one of the ones he was familiar with. But that had been before Charles Redford had been arrested, before Sarah Duvall had told Fiona the killer was in custody and life could return to normal, without the bite of fear cutting into every moment.

They'd been catastrophically wrong. Terror clutched at his heart. He knew exactly what lay in store for him. After all, he'd written the script.

*   *   *

454

Before she let herself out of Drew Shand's flat, Fiona took a look at the Edinburgh street map on his reference shelf and decided to walk back to her hotel. A brisk couple of miles on the city streets might clear her head. She set off through the Georgian streets of the New Town, heading for Queensferry Road, the damp air clinging to her skin and hair. She was almost the only person on the streets. She turned on to the Dean Bridge, enjoying the spectacle of walking above tree-top level, with random blocks of light from the backs of the New Town tenements glowing pale-yellow through the insubstantial mist. It could have felt spooky, she thought, and if someone with the gifts of Kit or Drew had been describing it, it would have crept off the page and made the hair on the back of her neck stand up. As it was, after a day of airports and the enclosed office at St Leonard's, it felt curiously liberating, a brief escape from the concerns of work and love.

When she arrived back at her hotel, she was almost reluctant to go in. The brief time out had refreshed her, leaving her ready for something more enjoyable than thoughts of murder. The only tantalizing prospect the evening had to offer now was the chance of a conversation with Kit.

Fiona checked at reception for messages. Nothing. She'd hoped he would have called, in response to one of her earlier e-mail messages. Never mind, she thought. She'd call home in the hope that he was monitoring the answering machine and would pick up when he heard her voice. She went up to her room and called room service. While she waited, she booted up the laptop and checked her e-mail again. Nothing from Kit. Not like him, she thought. They'd had no contact since she'd left that morning, which was a break in their usual pattern of communication. Glancing at her watch, she saw it was just past nine. He couldn't still be working. He should answer the phone.

Quickly, she dialled the familiar number, her fingers stumbling so she had to abort the call and start again. The phone rang out. Three, four, five rings. Then the answering machine. His recorded voice for once provided no comfort. She waited for the bleep. 'Kit, it's me. If you're there, pick up, please . . . Come on, I need to talk to you . . .' She waited in vain.

While she ate the pasta she'd ordered and sipped a glass of wine, Fiona flicked through the letters again, checking to see if there was anything she'd missed.

When the phone rang she dropped her fork with a clatter. She grabbed the receiver eagerly and said, 'Hello?'

'This is DCI Duvall.'

Fiona felt intense disappointment. 'Oh. Hello. I was expecting someone else.'

'I wondered what progress you'd made,' Duvall said abruptly.

Fiona outlined her day's work in some detail. As she reported her findings, Duvall made no response apart from the occasional noncommittal sound of someone making notes.

When she had finished, Duvall spoke. 'So, you've found nothing to contradict the theory that Redford is the killer?' she asked.

It was, Fiona thought, an odd way to put it. 'Nothing. Why? Has something come up at your end?' A nervous prickle of anxiety crept across her chest.

She felt the hesitation build at the other end of the phone. 'A minor discrepancy, that's all,' Duvall said briskly.

'How minor?' Fiona demanded.

Duvall outlined what the Dorset Police had uncovered, and how it was at odds with the little Redford had said on the subject. 'We'll have more sense of its significance when we get the forensics back from the outhouse.'

'But that could be days,' Fiona protested. 'If you have got the wrong man in custody, then other people could be at risk.' One person in particular, she thought, fear beginning to clench her stomach. 'The killer's going to feel very safe. He'll be confident about striking again.' *And I can't raise Kit.*

'I'm aware of that. We're doing everything we can to corroborate what Redford is saying.'

'I've not heard from Kit all day,' Fiona blurted out.

'One of my team was supposed to interview him this afternoon. I'll check out what he had to say. He may have indicated he had plans for the evening,' Duvall said with a confident authority she didn't feel. 'I'll get back to you.'

'I'll be waiting for your call.' Fiona replaced the phone gently, as if somehow so doing would also keep Kit safe. She was, she recognized, terrified. Suddenly, she bolted for the bathroom, making it just in time. Undigested pasta swilled round in a bilious red sea of tomato sauce and wine. Her stomach kept on emptying itself in a reflex long after there was nothing left to bring up. She leaned back on her heels, a sheen of sweat across her forehead, her breath coming in ragged gasps.

The thought of Sarah Duvall's call forced her to her feet. She flushed the toilet and brushed her teeth. What was taking her so long? She ran her hands through her hair, gazing at herself in the mirror. Her eyes were haunted, her face made gaunt by the inner fears eating her away. 'You look like shit,' she told her reflection. 'Get a grip, Cameron.'

The phone ringing catapulted her out of the bathroom and across the bedroom. 'Yes, Fiona Cameron, hello?'

'We seem to have a slight problem,' Duvall said hesitantly.

Jesus God, no, she screamed silently. 'What sort of a problem?' she forced out.

'Apparently, he wasn't at home when my officer called on him.'

Fiona groaned. 'Something's happened to him.'

'I don't think you should jump to conclusions, Dr Cameron. My officer admitted he was over an hour late in getting to their appointment. Mr Martin may well have given up on him. I understand from Ms Lester's husband that a group of her fellow writers were planning to get together today to hold a sort of wake. That's probably where Mr Martin is right now. Look, Redford's confession checks out in every detail but one. He's been treating his interviews like a game, a battle of wits. It's entirely possible that he was deliberately misleading us because he's determined not to give us anything concrete. He wants to get away with this, I'm sure of it.' Duvall's voice showed not a trace of doubt. 'I'm sure Mr Martin will be in touch. Try not to worry.'

'Easier said than done, DCI Duvall.'

'I still believe we have the right man in custody.'

'You would say that. You've got too much invested in this to say otherwise.'

'If Mr Martin hasn't been in touch by tomorrow morning, call me.'

'Bet on it.' She slammed the phone down. Her hand shook as she removed it from the receiver. 'Oh God,' she breathed. 'Please God, let it not be him.'

She began to pace the room. Six strides, turn, six strides, turn, like a cat in a cage. There was no comfort for her in Duvall's apparent confidence. She knew Kit wouldn't have left her high and dry without a word. 'Think, Fiona, think,' she urged herself.

She grabbed her personal organizer and looked up Jonathan Lewis's number. She didn't have many of Kit's friends' numbers, but Jonathan and his wife Trish had been regular dinner companions over the past couple of years, so they'd made it to her list. Trish answered on the third ring, sounding pleasantly surprised to hear from Fiona. 'Is Jonathan in?' Fiona asked.

'No, he's gone off on this wake they're holding for Georgia. Isn't Kit with them?' Trish answered.

'He must be. I'm up in Edinburgh and I've been trying to get hold of him without success.'

'They were supposed to be meeting at six,' Trish said.

'Do you know where?'

'Jonathan said something about some drinking club in Soho where Adam's a member. But I don't know what it's called. I know he was expecting to see Kit there.'

'You're probably right,' Fiona sighed. 'He's most likely halfway through the second bottle by now. Sorry to bother you, Trish.'

'It's no bother. If it's urgent, you could give Jonathan a ring on his mobile.'

Fiona copied down Jonathan's number and called it as soon as she ended her conversation with Trish. The mobile rang half a dozen times before it was answered. It sounded as if a small riot was going on in the background. 'Hello? Jonathan?' she shouted. 'It's Fiona Cameron. Is Kit with you, by any chance?'

'Hello? Fiona? No, where is the bugger? He's supposed to be here.'

'He's not there?'

'No, that's what I'm saying.'

'He's not been in touch?'

'No, hang on.' Somewhat muffled, she heard him shout, 'Anybody heard anything from Kit? Like why he's not here?' There was a brief pause, then Jonathan came back on to her. 'Nobody's heard from him, Fiona. I don't know what he's playing at, but he's not here.'

Fiona felt her stomach contract again. 'If he turns up, tell him to call me. Please, Jonathan.'

'No problem. Take it easy, Fiona, but take it.' The connection terminated and Fiona was left stranded with fear coursing through her again. She wanted to scream. But she forced herself to take a rational approach to the situation.

If Kit was going to be targeted, the obvious book to copy would be *The Blood Painter*. Because it had been successfully adapted for TV, it fitted the pattern the killer had adopted so far. If the killer was following the pattern of the book, Kit must still be alive. The characteristic of the Blood Painter was that he held his victims prisoner and drained their blood at daily intervals, using it to paint murals in the place where he held them captive. So if Kit was truly the next victim, whoever had him needed to keep him alive for a couple of days at least so he could reproduce the murder in the book as faithfully as possible.

All she had to do was to work out where he was being held.

It had been a while since she'd read the book, but she remembered that the victims of the Blood Painter had all rented remote holiday cottages in the six months before their deaths. When he came to kill them, the Blood Painter rented the same cottage and held them captive there for the week while he slowly bled them to death and created his grotesque paintings.

But she and Kit had never rented a holiday cottage. They'd not had so much as a weekend break in the UK, preferring to take their holidays abroad. Where could he be holding Kit? Where could they be if the killer was truly determined to follow the book?

460

Chapter 48

The M6 was practically empty this far north of Manchester. Most of the Friday evening traffic had peeled off on the M55 to Blackpool or at the first junction leading to the southern end of the Lake District. As the road climbed up Shap, there were only a few cars and a scattering of lorries heading back to Scotland for the weekend.

In the fast lane, a dark-grey metallic Toyota 4x4 cruised at a comfortable eighty-five. Not so fast it would attract the attention of the traffic police, but a good enough speed to eat up the miles between driver and destination. He'd given up on the radio, replacing the civilized voices of the BBC with a talking book. *The Blood Painter*, by Kit Martin. Read by the author. Apart from anything else, it would keep him firmly on track in case he'd slipped up on any details.

He couldn't think of anything that would make the miles pass more quickly.

Detective Superintendent Sandy Galloway was halfway down his postprandial glass of Caol Ila. His teenage twins were upstairs competing to lay waste some distant planet courtesy of their Sony PlayStations and his wife was loading the dishwasher. He'd have to go in to work tomorrow morning, in the light of this London business. But sufficient unto the day, that was his motto. And so he settled down with his whisky to watch a cop drama on TV and savour all the things they got wrong.

When the phone rang, he ignored it. But he couldn't ignore the teenage bellow from upstairs. 'Hey, Dad, it's some Englishwoman for you.'

'Aw, shite,' he muttered, hauling himself out of his chair and through to the hall. He picked up the phone and waited for the click that indicated the upstairs extension had been put down. 'Hello, Sandy Galloway speaking.'

'It's Fiona Cameron. I'm sorry to bother you at home. I got your number from the incident room sergeant. He didn't want to tell me, but I'm afraid I gave him a rather hard time, so don't be angry with him.' It poured out in a breathless rush.

'No bother, Doctor. How can I help you? Or is it you can help us? Have you found some more letters at Drew Shand's?'

There was a pause. He could hear her draw breath. 'This is going to sound like paranoia. You know my partner is Kit Martin, the crime writer?'

'Aye, I knew that.'

'I've been aware since I first formed the theory that there might be a serial killer at work that Kit fitted the victim profile perfectly. I've been worried that he might be a target. When the City Police arrested Redford, we all relaxed. But I've just spoken to DCI Duvall and she says there's a chink in the case against Redford. And I can't get hold of Kit. He's not answering the phone, he's not been in touch via e-mail.'

'Could it not just be that he's working?' Galloway tried to sound calm and unconcerned. If there was a serious crack in the case, Duvall would have let him know.

'He wasn't there when the police were round earlier to take a statement. And I've never known him not respond to e-mail. The thing is, if Kit's a target, the book the killer will be following is *The Blood Painter*. He'll be holding him somewhere till he's ready to kill him.'

He could hear from her voice that she was frantic with worry. 'I understand your concern, Fiona.' He slipped into her first name, hoping it would soothe. 'The trouble is, there's no evidence to suggest that anything's happened to him. He could be spending the evening with friends. Raising a glass to Georgia Lester somewhere.'

'That's exactly where he's supposed to be. But I spoke to one of his friends, and he's not turned up. And anyway, if that's what he had planned, he would have let me know,' Fiona insisted.

'Anything could have happened. He could have bumped into somebody on the way there and gone for a drink with them first. He could have been held up by transport problems. Fiona, if there was any serious problem with the case against Redford, City of London would have been on to us. You can be sure of that.' Galloway genuinely believed she had no grounds for her fears. The police officer in him knew that without any evidence of a crime, there was no way to justify any sort of formal inquiry. And the man in him knew that people didn't always know their partners as well as they thought they did. Not even if they were psychologists. 'Sometimes e-mail doesn't get through,' he pointed out. 'Servers go down. Maybe he thinks he has let you know.'

He heard her exasperated sigh. 'And maybe he's in the hands of a killer. The police should be checking out that possibility.'

Galloway took a deep breath and inched out on a limb. 'If – and it's a very big if – he is, then where should the police be looking?'

'According to *The Blood Painter*, the killer should take him to a holiday home. Only, we've never rented a holiday home in the UK. But Kit's got a bothy up in Sutherland where he goes to write. I think that's where they'll have gone.'

'Whereabouts in Sutherland?'

He felt her hesitation. 'That's the problem. I don't know, exactly. I've never been there, you see. All I know is that it's near Loch Shin.'

'You don't even know the address?'

'No. We only ever communicate by e-mail when he's up there. He's got a satellite phone, but he doesn't use it for voice calls. We both find it harder to get through the time apart if we actually speak to each other, you see? Somehow, e-mail is more bearable when he's away for weeks at a time.' Suddenly realizing that she was wittering, she forced herself back to the practicalities. 'But surely the local police must know where it is? I thought everybody knew everybody up in the Highlands?'

Galloway rubbed his hand over his mouth. Her fear had transmitted itself to him and he had sweat on his upper lip. '"Near Loch Shin" is a hell of a big area, Fiona. The loch itself must be, what, fifteen, seventeen miles long. I doubt very much that there's anything they could do about it tonight, even supposing we could convince them there was any real reason why they should be looking.'

'There must be something we can do! We can't just sit around doing nothing when Kit's life could be at risk.' Now anger had taken over from fear in Fiona's voice.

'Listen, Fiona, the chances are that you're getting yourself worked up over nothing. Now, this fictional killer of Mr Martin's – what does he do with his victims?'

'He keeps them captive for a week and draws their blood and paints murals with it.'

'Well, that suggests that time is not as much of the essence as it would be if this killer gave his victims a swift death, doesn't it? Besides, if you don't know where this bothy is, how would the killer know? Why don't we wait till the morning? It might well be that Mr Martin has turned up by then. But if he hasn't, we'll get Highland Police on to it first thing. That's a promise. Meet me at St Leonard's at half past seven and we'll see what's what. OK?' His voice was reassuring without being patronizing.

'No, it's not OK,' she said bitterly. 'But it'll have to do, won't it?'

'Aye, I'm afraid it's the best I can do. And I will talk to DCI Duvall in the meantime and see if there are any genuine grounds for concern. Try to get some sleep, Fiona. I know you're imagining the worst, but the chances are, Redford's our man and your chap's alive and well and on his way out for a night's drinking with his mates. Coming to terms with Georgia Lester's death. You know yourself that's by far the likeliest scenario. I'll see you in the morning.'

He replaced the phone and stood for a long minute in the hall, pondering. No, he was right. There was no point in trying to get anything moving tonight on something as tenuous as this. Without something more solid than Fiona had, there was no prospect of getting Highland to take this seriously. By morning, he could maybe convince them there were reasonable grounds for action if Kit Martin hadn't shown up safe, sound and hungover in his own bed. And really, there were no good reasons to think otherwise. Convinced that Fiona was overreacting because of what had happened to her sister all those years before, Galloway headed back to his TV show and his whisky.

*   *   *

465

Fiona slumped in her chair. She'd done her best. But some-times, that wasn't enough. After Lesley, she had done her best too. She couldn't change the fact of her sister's death, but she had taken every step she could to make sure the person responsible paid the price. She'd failed then, and she knew the price that failure had exacted. She couldn't give up on Kit now, not just for his sake but for her own. Duvall and Galloway might think she was a hysterical idiot, but she knew Kit and she knew she had grounds for her worries. Galloway had tried to reassure her with his suggestion that the killer couldn't know the location of the bothy. But Fiona knew him to be resourceful; he'd tracked each of his victims so far. She couldn't afford to be complacent.

She reached for the phone and keyed in a number she knew by heart. Three rings, then the machine clicked in. 'This machine takes messages for Steve Preston. Please speak after the tone and your call will be dealt with at the earliest opportunity.' Bleep.

'Steve, it's Fiona. Call me on the mobile whenever you get this message. I need your help.' She ended the call with a finger on the receiver rest and immediately dialled his mobile. Silence. Then the impersonal voice. 'The number you are call-ing has not responded. Please try later. The number you are calling—' She cut the line. 'I don't believe this,' she muttered, reaching for her personal organizer to find his pager number. When the pager service responded, she left a message asking Steve to call her straightaway on her mobile.

There was, she supposed, an outside chance he was still in the office so she dialled his direct line. She let it ring ten times before she gave up. Where the hell was he when she needed him?

It never occurred to her to try Terry's home number.

*　　*　　*

Gerard Coyne's flat could have been made for surveillance. It was on the first floor of a terraced house a couple of streets back from the Holloway Road. Neil assumed from the fact that there were two narrow front doors that there was no back entrance; Coyne's front door would give straight on to a flight of steps leading up to the first floor. What made the flat so perfect for Neil's purpose was the pub opposite. The Pride of Whitby was a typical North London corner pub – cosy, cramped and busy. But the old-fashioned etched glass had been replaced by clear glass windows allowing a perfect view across the street. Neil had arrived just after half past six and had a quiet word with the licensee, impressing on him the need for discretion. He hadn't specified who he was watching or why, only that he didn't want to be pointed out to the locals as a copper.

The landlord had no problem with that. He kept an orderly pub and relied on the local police to turn up on the rare occasions there was trouble. As far as he was concerned, as long as Neil didn't expect free booze, he was welcome to sit by the window for as long as he wanted.

Neil had already established that Coyne was home. There was a smart mountain bike chained up in the front garden. He'd seen lights on in the first-floor flat and, as a double-check, he'd rung Coyne's phone number. When it was answered, Neil had pretended he had a wrong number. Satisfied, he settled down with a copy of the *Evening Standard* and a glass of alcohol-free lager.

At half past seven, he'd ordered lasagne and chips from the bar snacks menu. It arrived at ten to eight. He'd finished eating it by five past. He returned to his paper, making sure the lighted windows of Coyne's flat were in his peripheral vision. If there was any movement, he'd register it, tired though he was.

By half past eight, the place was heaving. Every other seat at Neil's table was taken, the other occupants crowded round with their pint glasses and cigarette packets. Occasionally, one or other of them would try to draw him into conversation, but he kept himself on the fringes, answering in monosyllables and barricading himself behind his paper.

A few minutes before ten, Coyne's light snapped out. Suddenly alert, Neil folded his paper and drained his third drink. He pushed his seat back slightly, on the alert for whatever was going to happen next. A light appeared in the glass panel above Coyne's front door, then the door itself swung open. Neil couldn't see Coyne very well against the light hitting him from behind, only the silhouette of a slim frame of medium height. Neil readied himself for the off.

Coyne pulled the door to behind him and emerged on to the street. Thank God he wasn't taking the bike, Neil thought. Coyne glanced both ways past the parked cars that lined the street, then crossed the road.

Oh shit, Neil thought, he's coming in here. He unfolded the paper and pulled his chair closer to the table. When he looked up again, Coyne was walking towards the bar, greeting a couple of the men standing there with their pints of Guinness.

There was no mistaking those deep-set eyes in the narrow face coupled with the goatee beard and moustache and the slightly prominent teeth. This was the man whose CRO photograph was etched on Neil's memory. As far as he was concerned, the evidence might be circumstantial, but it had convinced him. If he'd been a gambling man, Neil would have staked a year's salary that he was looking at Susan Blanchard's killer.

He fought to hide his excitement and watched as Coyne bought himself a pint of bitter. Neil pushed back his chair, covered himself by saying good night to the others at his table, as if they'd been his drinking companions, and pushed through the crowd to the door.

The cold night air took his breath away after the stuffiness of the pub. But it did nothing to calm the thrill of anticipation that surged through him. It had worked. Good solid policing, helped along with a bit of flair and inspiration, and he was looking at the first serious suspect for Susan Blanchard's murder since Francis Blake. Only this time, they'd got it right. He had a feeling in his bones.

He hurried along the street to where he'd parked his car earlier. It had a view both of the pub door and, at an angle, of Coyne's front door. He dived behind the wheel and pulled out his mobile. Time to report. He stabbed the speed dial buttons to connect him to Steve's mobile. He couldn't believe his ears when he heard, 'The number you are calling has not responded. Please try later.'

'Bugger,' he said, trying Steve's home number. When he got the answering machine, he swore softly. But he knew better than to hang up without leaving a message. 'This is Neil McCartney, guv. I'm outside the suspect's house. He's just gone across the road for a drink in his local. I know I'm supposed to go off duty at midnight, but I'm going to stay on here till Joanne relieves me or until I hear from you. I don't want him to get away from us.'

Finally, Neil left a message on Steve's pager. Surely he'd get that? The boss was never out of touch, especially since they'd been running this operation on a shoestring. He'd known Neil was watching their new suspect, so he'd be expecting a call. Sooner or later, he'd ring back.

Till then, there was nothing more he could do now except watch and wait.

Chapter 49

Waiting was not something Fiona could bear. Not when she feared for Kit's life. Galloway had tried to be reassuring, but it hadn't gone anywhere towards calming the torment. She knew there was no point in trying to follow Galloway's advice to get some sleep. All that would happen if she went to bed was that she'd toss and turn restlessly, riven with anxiety. She might as well stay up and try to figure out a way to help Kit.

If only she knew where his bothy was. Given that whoever had Kit captive would have to drive up from London, the chances were that they were nowhere near Loch Shin yet. If she could find the exact location, it might be possible to head them off before they ever got there.

Whatever Galloway had said about there being plenty of time, Fiona knew she couldn't rely on that. In each murder, the killer had deviated from the template provided by the book when it had suited him better. Keeping Kit alive for a week was clearly a huge risk to take, and from what she had seen of this murderer's work, he was a man who liked to minimize jeopardy. The sooner she could get to Sutherland, the more chance she had of finding Kit alive. Waiting for Galloway to grind into action in the morning was too big a chance to take. She had to do whatever she could as soon as she could. Of course, it was too late now to find anywhere that could sell her an Ordnance Survey map of the Loch Shin area to check out possibilities. Fiona poured another glass of wine and logged on to the Internet. She entered the keywords 'Loch Shin' into her search engine and impatiently scanned the results. There were websites where amateur photographers displayed their photographs of the area; websites for those who believed the Loch Ness Monster had relatives in Loch Shin; websites for holiday cottages with views of the loch; websites that offered advice on fishing; and even a website devoted to the hydroelectric power station. But no large-scale map. The on-line version the Ordnance Survey offered was too small to show any useful detail.

She had even taken time out to torment herself with the ghoulish gossip of *Murder Behind the Headlines*. Fiona knew even as she was logging on to the site that it would give her no peace, but like an itching scab demanding to be picked, she had to see what Georgia's death had provoked.

At last, confirmation from London of what anybody with half a brain already knew. Yes, there's a serial killer out there preying on the weird and the wired who spend their days writing fiction about surprise, surprise, serial killers. Although it sounds a bit like biting the hand that feeds you, it's true!

Even more amazing was the confession that stopped a police press conference in its tracks. As the police revealed to the world that British crime writer Georgia Lester's butchered remains had been found in a disused freezer in London's Smithfield Meat Market, a man claiming to be the killer distributed a FLYER to the waiting hacks that outlined his motives for the series of gruesome killings.

The confessor is a wannabe writer called Charles Cavendish Redford, who alleges that the three writers in question plagiarized manuscripts he had sent them in the hope of winning their support in getting his books published. Redford, 47, once worked as a hospital porter, which may be where he picked up his murderous skills. He's now in custody, under arrest, but so far hasn't been charged.

The discovery of Lester's remains provided incontrovertible evidence of what some of us had already deduced. To paraphrase Oscar Wilde; One – Drew Shand – is unfortunate. Two – Jane Elias – looks remarkably like coincidence. And three – Georgia Lester – is a series . . .

Lester went missing over a week ago. Sceptics said she'd deliberately staged a disappearance as a publicity stunt, as Queen of Crime Agatha Christie did herself back in the 1920s. And it's true that Lester had been complaining that her publishers weren't taking proper care of her. She'd demanded bodyguards for her latest book tour, but had been spurned by publishers with more sense than money – a rarity in itself these days.

But when we read the accounts of her disappearance – the deserted car in the country lane, the apparent lack of any signs of violence, the absence of any witnesses – those of us with a sensibility tuned to these things felt the creep of dread, remembering the fate of the victims in *And Ever More Shall Be So*, Lester's only serial killer novel, which was made into a film.

Word is that the London cops got the tip to search Smithfield from a psychological profiler – one of those legendary Clarice Starlings (and we all know what happened to Clarice, don't we???) who figure out what the bad guys are going to do next. Mind you, it doesn't take a doctorate in psychology to work that one out. All it takes is the ability to read.

Still, there must be a few thriller writers sleeping easier in their beds tonight. Because if Redford hadn't conveniently spilled the beans, you can bet your bottom dollar it would have been a long time and a few more bodies before the police managed to nail him.

REMEMBER YOU READ IT FIRST ON
MURDER BEHIND THE HEADLINES

Angry with herself for succumbing to the insidious nastiness of the website, Fiona disconnected from the Internet. It had taken her almost an hour to get no further forward.

Frustrated, she tried Steve's numbers again. No change. He was still out of reach. Fiona closed her eyes and massaged her temples. Somewhere locked away in her mind, she must know something that would lead her to the bothy. *Think about anything else*, she told herself. *Let your subconscious do the work.* Easier said than done, though, when all she could think of was Kit and the ordeal he could be going through.

A walk, that would do it. A quick turn through the local streets, where she could force herself to look at the details of the houses and gardens. That might just free her mind sufficiently to open the door to the information she knew must be there.

Glad to have something positive to do, Fiona jumped up and grabbed her mac, still lying on the bed in the damp heap where she'd thrown it when she came in. She pulled it on, picked up her mobile and practically ran out of the door and down the stairs into the street.

She turned to her right and started walking along the terrace, looking intently at the houses as she passed, glancing down into basement areas and taking stock of what people had done to make them attractive. She checked out curtains, appreciated a particularly vigorous Russian vine, made a mental note of an elaborate door knocker. Knitting for the brain.

At the end of the street, she turned left and walked down the hill towards Stockbridge, describing the tall sandstone buildings to herself as she passed them. At the bottom of the hill, she stared in the off-licence window, making a mental selection from the bottles on display. She crossed the road and walked back up the hill, never faltering in the catalogue of her surroundings.

She was halfway along the street where her hotel was when her mind released the treasure she'd known was in there. 'Lee Gustafson,' she said out loud in a tone of wonder. Then she was running, racing back to her hotel room to apply the gift she'd just been given.

Oblivious to the appalled stare of the night porter, Fiona sprinted across the reception area and up the stairs. Almost before her door was closed, her mac was thrown into a heap again and she was back in front of the laptop. Lee Gustafson was an American crime writer who wrote ecological thrillers. He shared the same US publisher as Kit. They'd been sent on a promotional tour together a couple of years previously, where they'd drunk their way round the mystery bookshops of the Midwest and forged a friendship that endured through e-mail. Just over a year ago, Kit had lent Lee the bothy so he could do some background research into conservation of rare species in the Highlands. Lee Gustafson must know exactly where the bothy was.

Now all she had to do was find Lee.

Glasgow was an amber gleam over to the west. But Kit knew nothing of that. He'd suffered the agonies of cramp in the arm he'd been leaning on and managed to shift so that he was now lying on his stomach. It had eased the pain in his shoulders and the pins and needles in his leg, but it wasn't helping the dull ache that still occupied his skull.

He had no sense of time. All he knew was that he had been trapped in this moving vehicle for at least two hours. He only knew that because, in an exquisite form of torture, he'd been forced to listen to his own voice spelling out in his own words what he feared was going to be his own fate. By his estimate, there was another hour of the talking book of *The Blood Painter* to go.

He'd tried to tune it out, singing his favourite songs inside his head. But it didn't work. The relentless story kept intruding, forcing itself into his consciousness. Ironic that he was trapped by the power of his own gift.

At least while they were still travelling, there was hope. At some point, his captor would have to stop for fuel. It would be his chance. He could try to kick the tailgate, or the boot, or the back door, whatever it was that was keeping him from rolling out on the road. He cast his mind back. What did he have on his feet?

His heart sank. He'd been in the house all day. Moccasin slippers, that's what he had on his feet. Even with the full power of his legs behind them, the only sound they'd make would be a dull thud. Hardly audible among the throbbing motors of the petrol pumps. And he didn't think anyone as careful as the man who had captured him was going to park up in the middle of a busy service area and leave Kit behind while he went off for a burger and a coffee.

There must be something he could do. After all, he had constructed the trap himself. If there was any escape, he should be able to figure it out.

It would help if he didn't have to listen to his own voice condemning him to death.

Getting Lee Gustafson's phone number had posed no significant problem to Fiona. International directory inquiries had him down as ex-directory, which didn't surprise her. It was only politeness that had made her try that route first. But in reality, she had no compunction about calling one of the handful of crime writers whose numbers were stored in her personal organizer. She told herself it didn't matter that it was getting on for one in the morning. Nevertheless, she deliberately chose Charlie Thompson first. Charlie lived alone and she knew him to be a night owl. Chances were he was lying sprawled in his armchair watching a horror video, cat on his chest, glass of Armagnac to hand. Rather him than someone who would be panicked out of sleep by her call.

The phone was answered on the fourth ring. 'Greetings, earthling,' a deep bass voice rumbled in her ear.

'Hello, Charlie. It's Fiona Cameron.'

'Good Lord. Shouldn't you be a pumpkin at this time of night? Or are you in fact speaking from the fruit and veg department of Tesco's?'

Fiona gritted her teeth and tried not to shout at him. 'I'm

sorry to bother you, Charlie, but Kit's out of town and I need Lee Gustafson's number.'

'Fiona, darling, if you want a man to whisper sweet nothings in your ear when Kit's away, you don't have to pay international call charges. I'd be happy to oblige.' He chuckled.

'I'll bear that in mind, Charlie. Do you have Lee's number?'

'Spurned again, eh? Hang on, Fiona, it's in the other room.' She listened to the sound of furniture groaning, a cat protesting, then heavy footsteps fading off. Charlie, the only man she knew who wore biker's boots round the house. A long minute passed, then the footsteps thudded again. 'You still there? Got a pen?'

'Yes to both.'

He read out Gustafson's number, repeating it to make sure she had it down. 'Enjoy yourself with Lee,' he added. 'But not so much that you forget my heart still burns for you.'

'I could never forget that, Charlie,' she said, forcing herself into the standard flirtatious banter that went with their friendship. 'Thanks again.'

'No problem. And tell that man of yours he owes me an e-mail.'

'Will do. Good night.'

'I'll do my best.' The line went dead and Fiona immediately rang the number Charlie had given her.

The single tone of the American phone system purred in her ear. Once, twice, three times. Then the click of an answering machine. 'Hi. You've reached Lee and Dorothy. And you've missed us. We're out of town till Monday morning. So leave a message and we'll get back to you when we get home.'

Fiona couldn't believe her ears. It was beginning to feel

like the universe was in a massive conspiracy against her and Kit. She had been so convinced that Lee Gustafson was the answer.

In frustration, she dialled into her e-mail program, clutching the last fragile hope that Galloway had been right and Kit had sent an e-mail that had somehow been trapped in cyberspace. Maybe his e-mail provider's server had been down and all the mail had been held up as a result. But of course, there was nothing.

On an impulse, since she was using Kit's laptop and it was set up for his e-mail account, she checked his mailbox. He might possibly have sent her mail to his own box by mistake. She couldn't imagine how that might happen, but she was prepared to clutch at any straw, however frail.

There were a dozen messages waiting for him. Most seemed to be from fellow crime writers, and most seemed to be about Georgia. There was nothing there that could conceivably have come from Kit himself. More worryingly, judging by the timing of the messages in the mailbox, he hadn't picked up his own mail since early that afternoon. And that was as much out of character as his failure to contact Fiona. Instead of consolation, she'd found even more reason to fret.

She broke the connection and carried on staring at the screen. Suddenly, something flickered at the corner of her memory. Just before Lee had visited the bothy, she and Kit had been on holiday in Spain. Kit, as usual, had taken his laptop. He could no more stay out of touch with his e-mail than he could stop breathing. And while they'd been away, he and Lee had been communicating about the bothy.

Eagerly, she opened up the electronic filing cabinet that kept a record of all Kit's e-mail, sent and received. She clicked on the <Copy of Sent Messages> tab. 2539 messages arranged by date. The program offered her the chance to arrange the messages in alphabetical order of the recipient, so she selected that option. She drummed her fingers on the tabletop as she waited for it to complete the task. Then she scrolled down to Lee Gustafson's name and began to check through the mail by date. She knew the month she was looking for, and she soon came to it. Kit had sent Lee nine messages that month. She began at the beginning and worked her way through.

And there it was.

'Take the A839 out of Lairg. About a mile out of the town, you'll see a track on the right signed Sallachy. Carry on up the track (it's pretty rough going, you'll appreciate why I'm lending you the Land Rover) for about five and a half miles. You cross a river gorge, the Allt a' Claon. There's a left turn up ahead, which you take. About half a mile up this track, there's another left turn. The track takes you back across the river ravine on a rope bridge. It's a lot stronger than it looks, but better not go faster than five miles an hour. You cross the river into some trees and the bothy's about a mile ahead of you. I'd say you can't miss it, but you'd probably shoot me.'

Relief coursed through Fiona. She knew where the killer was taking Kit. And now she knew how to get there. Sod Sarah Duvall and her blinkered certainties. Sod Sandy Galloway and his soothing platitudes. And sod Steve, who wasn't there when she really needed him. She'd find Kit, with or without their help.

Chapter 50

Edinburgh might claim to be a twenty-four-hour city during the Festival, but as Fiona soon found out, when it came to hiring a car it was strictly eight till eight. Even at the airport, open round the clock, the car-hire firms went home when the flights stopped arriving.

All professional options exhausted, she was forced back on to the personal. Wearily, Fiona picked up the phone and dialled again. She heard half a dozen distant rings. Then an indistinct mumble. 'Yeah?'

'Caroline?'

'No, it's not. Who is this?' The voice sounded seriously pissed off.

'Ah. Julia. Sorry. It's Fiona Cameron. Can I speak to Caroline?'

'Do you know what time it is?' The hostility level had risen. Fiona knew it was nothing to do with the lateness of the hour.

'Yes. And I'm sorry about that. But I do need to speak to Caroline.'

The phone clattered down. Fiona could hear, as she knew she was meant to, Julia's bad-tempered muttering. 'It's Fiona Cameron. Two o'clock in the fucking morning, I don't know . . .'

Then Caroline's voice, sleepy but alive with concern. 'Fiona? What's the matter?'

'I'm sorry to wake you, but it's really important.'

'Of course it is. So how can I help? What's the problem?'

Fiona took a deep breath. In the background, she could hear an exasperated Julia sighing. Unlike Caroline, Julia did not take the unpredictable in her stride. 'I'm in Edinburgh and I need to be in Inverness. If I wait till the trains start running, it'll be too late.'

'So you want me to drive you there?'

'That won't be necessary, I just need to borrow your car.'

Fiona heard the sounds of movement as Caroline shifted her position. 'Fine. Let me see . . . five minutes to get dressed . . . Probably an hour to get to you. Where are you in Edinburgh?'

'I'm staying at a hotel called Channings. But the thing is, Caroline, time's really vital. Is there somewhere we could meet halfway? Somewhere I could get a taxi to take me to?'

There was a pause. Fiona could hear Caroline moving around now, as if she was assembling her clothes. 'There's some services on the M90,' Caroline said. 'A few miles over the bridge. Halbeath, I think, something like that. It's the turnoff for Dunfermline and Kirkcaldy, just after the big Hyundai plant. Get the taxi to take you there. I'll be there in about . . . thirty-five, forty minutes. OK?'

'Thank you, Caroline. Believe me, I appreciate this.'

'No bother. Fill me in when we meet.' Then the line went dead. Fiona smiled for the first time in hours. At last, she was dealing with somebody who took her on trust, who didn't assume she was overreacting. Steve would have done the same. But Steve was out of reach. And she didn't have time to wait to be proved right.

While she waited for the taxi, she scribbled a quick fax to Galloway, telling him where she'd gone and when she'd left. She gave the night porter instructions to transmit it to the number Galloway had given her for his personal fax at St Leonard's. At least if she needed back-up, they would know where to find her.

Twenty-five minutes later, the taxi dropped her off at Halbeath services, just off the M90 heading north. The drizzle that had turned Edinburgh gloomy all day had grown into full-scale rain, gusting across the parking area. Fiona took shelter in the doorway of the restaurant and stared through the rain at the bright neon of the petrol station while she planned out what she had to do.

Ten minutes later, headlights cut through the darkness on the approach road and she stepped forward expectantly. The service area lights revealed a Honda saloon that splashed to a halt yards from her. The driver's door opened and Caroline jumped out, dashing across to her and enveloping her in a hug. 'Here comes the cavalry,' Caroline said.

'I've never been more glad to see you.'

'What's going on? Why the urgency?' Caroline let her go and stepped back into the shelter of the doorway.

'Have you seen the news?' Fiona asked.

'Is this to do with that murdered crime writer?' Caroline had never been slow to grasp connections. 'I thought they'd got someone for that?'

'Yes. But I think there's a possibility that the person in custody is a fake confessor. An attention-seeker. If I'm right, there's still a serial killer out there. And I'm afraid he's got Kit.'

'Oh my God! And they're heading for Inverness?' For the first time, Caroline sounded shaken.

'Kit owns a bothy out in Sutherland. I think that's where the killer is planning to take him. Kit keeps a Land Rover at a garage in Inverness. I need to get there and pick up the Land Rover and try to head them off before they get to the bothy.'

Caroline frowned. 'Forgive me if I'm being naive here, but isn't this one of those things the police should be dealing with?'

'Yes. But they think the man in custody is the killer. They're not even halfway convinced that Kit's actually missing. They think he's gone off on the razzle with his mates, drowning his sorrows over Georgia.'

'But you know different?'

Fiona spread her hands. 'I know Kit.'

Caroline nodded, as if satisfied. 'Fine. Jump in. I'll drive you.'

'Honestly, there's no need. I can drive myself. I just needed to borrow the car.'

Caroline reached out and grasped Fiona's wrist gently. It was a curiously intimate gesture. 'I said, I'll drive you. Besides, how am I going to get back to St Andrews at this time of night?'

'No, Caro, it's not your fight. Call a taxi. I'll pay for it. Just give me the car keys, Caro, please?'

Caroline shook her head. 'No way. You've always been there for me. I'm not leaving you.' She turned on her heel and marched back to her car, pulling the driver's door open and getting in. She started the engine and wound down the window. 'I thought you were in a hurry, Fiona?'

As they shot up the motorway towards Perth, Caroline broke the silence. 'Tell me what's going on with Kit.'

So Fiona outlined the whole story, from Drew Shand's murder onwards. 'It could be that I'm being paranoid,' she admitted. 'But that's my risk, and it's one I'm prepared to take. Looking stupid on the shores of Loch Shin would be, in my opinion, the best possible outcome of tonight.'

'But you know in your heart that's not what's happening here,' Caroline said heavily.

Fiona nodded. 'He wouldn't stay out of touch. He's in a state about Georgia, and I'm the only one he opens up to. Of all the times he might ignore me, this is the least likely.' They fell silent then, each lost in her own thoughts as the windscreen wipers slapped the rain away and they drove deeper into the Highlands, the looming bulk of mountains rising around them as Caroline hammered up the road towards Inverness to the late-night sound of the Cowboy Junkies. At that time of night, there was little traffic to vary the endless ribbon of the A9 spooling out ahead of them.

Somewhere near Kingussie, Fiona closed her eyes and leaned her elbow on the window ledge. With no need for Caroline to stop for petrol (and nowhere to make a stop, even if she'd needed it), Fiona drifted in an edgy doze until they made it to the outskirts of Inverness just after half past six.

Fiona was already two and a half hours later than she would have needed to be to hit the wilderness ahead of Kit.

Joanne Gibb drove cautiously down the street where Gerard Coyne lived. Thankfully, nobody seemed to be stirring. But then, that's pretty much what she'd have expected in this part of North London so early on a Saturday morning. She hoped it would stay like that for a little bit longer. She needed to identify the house then find a parking space somewhere she could keep an eye on the place. It wouldn't do to lose him because she couldn't find somewhere to sit unobtrusively. It helped having a VW Golf with black-tinted windows. Impossible for passers-by to see inside, and with the added bonus that any local likely lads would probably leave it alone on the general principle that anybody who owned such a mean-looking machine would probably be considerably more well hard than they were.

On her first pass, she identified the house. She couldn't immediately see a place to park, so she drove to the corner, turned round and cruised slowly back. About a dozen yards past Coyne's house, a set of headlights flashed at her. Her first reaction was that someone had noticed her predicament and was indicating they were about to move out of their space. Then she recognized Neil's Ford, a car almost as scruffy as its owner. She drew level and they dropped their windows simultaneously. Joanne's nose twitched as the stale aroma of unwashed male rolled out towards her.

'What are you doing here?' she asked. 'You were supposed to go off at midnight and leave chummy to his own devices.'

Neil yawned. 'I couldn't do it. I tried to clear it with the boss but I haven't been able to raise him. I can't get through on the mobile, his home phone's on the answering machine and he's not responding to his pager. I can't believe it. He's never out of touch. And last night, of all nights, when he knew we were starting a fresh surveillance. It just doesn't make sense. So I decided to stay till you got here, just in case.'

Joanne gave a sly smile. 'I bet I know where he is.'

'Where?'

'He's birding it,' she said.

'Bollocks,' Neil scoffed. 'He's like a monk, the guv'nor. He's forgotten what it's for.'

'You lot never forget what it's for,' Joanne said. 'He came back from seeing that lecturer the other day with a real spring in his step. *And* he asked me for a restaurant recommendation.'

'God, he must have been desperate.'

'Thank you, Neil. Anyway, I reckon he's gone off to her place and decided that for once he's going to forget about the sodding job and have a good time.'

Neil shook his head. 'He'd never turn his pager off.'

'That's what *you* think. So, what are you going to do now?'

Neil reached down and turned the key in his ignition. 'I'm going to piss off back to the Yard and get my head down for a couple of hours until he gets in. Wherever he is, he'll be in this morning to see what's what, I bet you any money.'

'That would be a mug's bet. Hang on till I turn round again and I'll slot into your space, OK?' Joanne drove off. By the time she'd swung round, Neil was edging out, leaving room for her to pick up the surveillance. She waved him off and settled down. She only hoped Gerard Coyne wasn't planning on a bike ride this morning.

Chapter 51

Caroline pulled up at a roundabout on the edge of Inverness and killed the stereo. 'Where to now?' she asked.

Fiona yawned and scrubbed her eyes with the edge of her fists. She had that empty nauseous feeling that comes with too little sleep and too much adrenaline. The rain had stopped and there was a thin grey mist hanging in the air, leaving Inverness looking even more like a ghost town than the hour itself. 'I don't know,' she admitted. 'All I know is that the guy who owns the garage where Kit keeps the Land Rover is called Lachlan Fraser.'

Caroline snorted. 'Like that really narrows it down.'

'I take it Fraser's a pretty common name hereabouts, then?'

'You could say that. The ancestral seat of the clan chief is about half a dozen miles up the road. Fraser is about as common a name round Inverness as Smith would be in London.' She put the car in gear and cruised towards the centre.

'Where are you going?' Fiona asked.

'When in doubt, ask a policeman.' Caroline headed on down the main road. 'We'll either find the police station, or we'll find some night-shift woolly suits in a patrol car sneaking a fly bacon butty at the all-night snack bar.'

'You think Inverness runs to an all-night snack bar?' Fiona said, the professional sceptic.

Caroline flashed her a dark grin. 'Don't make the mistake of falling for the tourist board propaganda. Inverness is a lot more *Morvern Callar* than it is *Local Hero*.'

'Does that mean you know where to score me a wrap of speed?'

Caroline's eyebrows rose. 'I suspect you're either too early in the morning or too late at night for any action like that round here. I take it that was a joke?'

Fiona's grin was savage. 'Only technically. Jokes are supposed to be funny, and the way I'm feeling right now is anything but. Better make do with the all-night snack bar and a shot of caffeine. If I do end up in the arms of the law, the last thing I need is for them to discover I'm pumped full of amphetamines.'

'Hang on, there we go.' Caroline was off on a tangent, waving over to her left where a DIY superstore occupied most of the horizon. Its vast car park contained a fish and chip van, a police car and the business end of an articulated lorry. She veered into the slip road and cruised across to the police car.

'You get the directions. You've got the right accent. I'll get the breakfast,' Fiona instructed, clambering out of the car and stretching. Desperate as she was to get to the bothy, she needed food and drink more than the five minutes she might save by not stopping now. She leaned on the high counter, smelling the rancid agglomeration of stale fat, cheap vinegar, fried onions and diesel. The menu was written in magic marker on what had once been a whiteboard. Describing its present colour was beyond Fiona's vocabulary. Old men's underwear was about the closest she could come to it. The board offered fish, chips, burgers, sausages, rolls and pies. Another sign announced the availability of 'Tea, coffee, asorted skoosh'. Fiona smiled at the large man behind the counter. Judging by his pallor, he lived off his own cooking.

'Two chip rolls, please,' Fiona said. It was probably the safest option. Besides, all that complex carbohydrate would keep her going for a few hours. 'And two teas,' she added.

'Aye, right,' the lard mountain said. He turned away and tended his hissing fryer. Fiona turned to see how Caroline was getting on with the police officers. She was bent over, leaning into an open window, her face all cheerful openness. Would she and Lesley have made it, Fiona wondered? Probably not. First love seldom did. And then she'd almost certainly have lost Caroline as a friend. With a sense of dawning amazement, Fiona reached the complex realization that Lesley's death had actually given her a gift. She scratched her head, deciding to file away the thought for another time, when she could consider it properly. Right now, she was struggling to hang on to any sense of reality in what was increasingly resembling a nightmare.

Caroline straightened up with a nod and a smile and set off back towards the car. Catching Fiona watching her, she gave the thumbs-up sign. 'There you go, darlin',' the chip van man said, plonking down two overstuffed bread rolls on a pair of paper napkins. Fiona handed over a fiver and waved away the change, concentrating instead on juggling the two chip rolls and the two polystyrene beakers of tea.

Back in the car, they fell on the food and drink. Between mouthfuls of surprisingly tasty chip butty, Caroline explained where they were heading. 'Lachlan Fraser's place is out towards the airport. The bobbies knew him, right enough. Not for any bad reasons, you understand. Just because . . . well, they know these things.' She drove intently, sandwich in one hand, tea between her thighs, careful on the corners not to spill her drink.

490

The streets started to waken as they drove, yellow oblongs of light suddenly breaking the grey facades of houses. Now the occasional car or milk float hummed past them, and the first blurring of light in the east started to leak into the night sky. Fiona wondered where Kit was. Whether she'd be in time, or whether she was already too late. Whether the killer would stick to the plot, or settle for an approximation.

If she had allowed her imagination to run away with her instead of forcing what she knew from *The Blood Painter* into a locked box in the back of her mind, she could probably have conjured up a reasonable approximation of what was happening right then a couple of hours' drive away.

Kit was groggily struggling back to consciousness, a woozy giddiness shot through with flashes of excoriating pain. He'd taken a second strike to the head, his long containment in darkness leaving him unequal to avoiding the blow that fell as soon as the tailgate of the Toyota was opened.

Apart from pain, the first sensation he was aware of was cold. He was freezing. He managed to open his eyes and found himself in the middle of a scene that felt like the worst sort of *déjà vu*. He knew this place because it was his; he knew this situation because he had created it. He was sitting naked on the toilet, both arms handcuffed to steel eyes that had been bolted into the wall. His legs were chained together, the chain passing round the back of the toilet bowl, rendering him almost incapable of movement.

He was alone. But he didn't expect that to last.

He knew what was coming next.

Caroline pulled up outside an old two-storey stone building with a peeling red and white sign that read 'Fraser's Garage'. It looked as if it had been there long before the existence of the internal combustion engine. Most of the facade was taken up by a pair of wide wooden doors with a Judas gate cut into one. To one side, there was a plain wooden door with the number thirty-one on it. On the upper storey, a light shone from behind a frosted-glass window. Fiona leaned across to hug Caroline. 'Thank you,' she said. 'I owe you big time.'

'Hey, it's not over till it's over,' Caroline said. 'You don't think I'm pulling out now, do you?'

Fiona leaned back in her seat. 'Don't, Caroline. You have to go home now.'

Caroline shook her head. 'No way. I've not come this far to turn my back and leave you to it. You can't bring me all this way and then send me home when the trouble really starts.'

'This isn't a game, Caro. If I'm right, the man who's got Kit has already killed three people. Without compunction. He won't think twice about killing anyone who stands between him and what he wants to achieve. I won't put you in that place.' Fiona's resolve was clear in her voice as well as her face.

'Since he's that ruthless, you need to even up the odds a bit.'

'No. I know what I'm doing. I can't take the chance of ending up with your blood on my hands. I can't live with that.' Fiona undid her seatbelt and opened the door. 'Please, Caro. Go home. I'll call you later, I promise. I'm getting out of the car now, and I'm not going any further till I see you turn around and drive away.' She pushed the door wide and climbed out, then leaned back in. 'I mean it.' She closed the door gently and stepped back.

Caroline smacked the flat of her hand against the steering wheel in a gesture of frustration, then put the car in gear and moved off. Fiona watched as she did a three-point turn and headed back in the direction they'd come from. As the taillights of the Honda disappeared round the corner, she turned to face the small door. She took a deep breath and pressed the doorbell.

There was a long moment of silence, then heavy feet thundered down a flight of stairs. The door opened to reveal a man in his late twenties dressed in work boots, jeans and a padded tartan shirt hanging loose over a grey T-shirt. In one hand, he held a mug of tea. His expression revealed a mild and friendly curiosity.

'Lachlan Fraser?' Fiona asked.

He nodded. 'Aye, that's me.'

'I'm sorry to disturb you so early . . .'

He grinned. 'It's not that early. And I'm not disturbed. How can I help you?'

'My name is Fiona Cameron –'

His grin widened as he interrupted her. 'You're Kit's bidie-in. Of course! I should have recognized you from that picture Kit's got up in the bothy. Hey, it's great to meet you at last.' He looked past her. 'The man himself isnae with you, then?'

'No, I got a lift up with a friend of mine. I'm meeting up with Kit later. I'm supposed to pick up the Land Rover. Is that OK?'

'Aye, fine, nae bother.' Lachlan fished in his pocket and shooed her forward. 'I'll just get the keys.' He passed her and unlocked the Judas gate. 'They're in here. I'll no' be a minute.' He disappeared indoors and a light came on. He emerged moments later with a bunch of keys. 'Follow me. It's round the back. It's got a full tank, and the jerry cans for the generator are all dieselled up,' he added over his shoulder as he led the way down a narrow alley to an area of wasteground behind the garage. Half a dozen elderly vehicles appeared to be parked at random. Lachlan headed towards a Land Rover that looked like a relic from some forgotten war.

'There you go,' he said, unlocking the driver's door and standing back to allow Fiona to climb up into the driver's seat. 'You driven one of these before?'

She shook her head. 'I've never had that pleasure,' she said ironically.

Lachlan took her through the vagaries of the Land Rover, explaining the four-wheel-drive, then waited while she manoeuvred it out of its parking space and into the mouth of the alley. Then he waved cheerfully as she headed out into the grey morning.

In the area under the jurisdiction of the City of London Police, there are three hundred and eighty-five separate closed-circuit camera systems. Together, they employ one thousand, two hundred and eighty cameras. Smithfield Market is well served by their system, with almost every nook and cranny covered by one camera or another. Inevitably, some of the cameras produce better images than others, given the variation in lighting and lines of sight.

One of the first steps Detective Chief Inspector Sarah Duvall had taken was to bring every available videotape from the previous ten days to the City police station in Snow Hill, where she had set up her incident room. All through the night, detectives had been scanning the hours of videotape, trying not to lose concentration as they searched for Charles Cavendish Redford.

Duvall herself had managed four hours' sleep. They had persuaded a magistrate to allow an extension to Redford's custody, then she had snatched her nap. She hadn't bothered going home to her riverside flat in the Isle of Dogs, just made her way to her own office and curled up on the two-seater sofa she'd had installed for precisely that purpose. Four hours was a lot less than her body craved, but it was enough to function on. Probably.

She was back in the incident room just after seven, eagerly scanning the overnight reports to see if anything confirming Redford's involvement had turned up yet. When she had confronted him with the discrepancy between his statement and the discovery of the outhouse, there had been no flicker of discomfort. He had simply shrugged and said, 'Isn't that what you wanted? To catch me out in a lie? Isn't that what criminals are supposed to do?' It went some way towards confirming her belief that he intended to give them nothing that could corroborate his confession.

Sooner or later, either one of her own team or one of the Dorset detectives was going to come up with that crucial piece of information that would tie Redford indisputably to Georgia Lester's brutal murder. Anything would do, she thought bleakly. Anything at all, since all they had right now was a big fat zero.

As she flicked through what seemed to be a large pile of nothing, one of the officers called her name. She looked up to see him holding a phone. 'Yes?'

'Can you pop down to the video room, ma'am? One of the lads there says he's got something he wants you to take a look at.'

Duvall was out of the door before the phone was back in its cradle. Her long strides swallowed the corridor leading to the room where her officers were scanning the CCTV videos from the market. She'd scarcely crossed the threshold when one of the detective constables started speaking. 'I need you to have a look at this, ma'am,' he said, his voice high and eager.

'What is it, Harvey?' Duvall stood behind him, looking over his shoulder at the screen. 'Have you found him?'

'I've been looking at the tapes of the corridor you have to go down to get to the maintenance area. It doesn't show the door itself, but you can't get there any other way. Anyway, this is from the Friday, two days after Georgia Lester went missing.' He pressed play. With the jerky movement of time-lapse photography, a man came into view, seen from the rear. He was dressed in a white coat and dark trousers, with the jaunty-brimmed trilby-style hat worn by all the butchers for hygiene reasons. He appeared to be carrying a large plastic tray of packaged meat. Harvey pointed to the screen. 'It caught my attention because you can see there's something wrapped in black plastic in the tray. Just there, see what I mean?'

'I see it,' Duvall said cautiously. 'But that's not Redford. The body shape's all wrong. Do we get him coming back?'

'That's what I wanted you to see.' He pressed the fast forward button and the scene jerked into movement. Suddenly, a man came back into view. Harvey froze the frame when the man was about ten feet from the camera. 'That's the best view we get of his face.'

Duvall frowned. There was something familiar about the image on the screen in front of her, but she couldn't place it.

Harvey looked up at her expectantly.

She peered into the screen, willing the image to become clearer. Then suddenly, something clicked in the recesses of her memory. It made no sense, but she was sure she was right. The implications of that were almost too terrible to contemplate. She straightened up. 'Let's get this enhanced, soon as possible. I'm going to get right on to the Met about this. I'll be in my office. Well spotted, Harvey.'

Chapter 52

As Fiona drove north out of Inverness, the weather slowly began to clear. She'd found road maps and Ordnance Survey sheets in the glove box of the car, and she headed up the A9 with the map spread over the seat next to her. Over the spectacular bridge that carried the road above the mingling of waters of the Beauly Firth and the Moray Firth, across the richly fertile farming land of the Black Isle, the sky gradually shifted from grey to blue, the morning mist burning off under the weak warmth of the autumn sun.

She checked the settlements against the map as she drove on along the quiet road. Not that there was much possibility of going wrong. Up here, there were scarcely enough major roads to allow a wrong turning. Alness. Invergordon. Then the bridge across the Dornoch Firth, the dun sands spread wet below her, before the turn inland to Bonar Bridge, leaving behind the low flatlands of the coastal region for the high hill country ahead.

Then she was driving along the narrow inlet of the Kyle of Sutherland, the dark water lined with heavy conifer forests, making somehow sinister the sunlit route into the wilderness that spread out ahead of her. As she turned up the River Shin towards Lairg, she could see she was entering the north-west Highlands proper, with sudden vistas opening ahead of rounded hills brown with heather, their rocky outcroppings grey and random. Scattered in the landscape were the ruined walls of croft houses, often just a pair of battered gable ends left standing. This was the landscape of the Highland Clearances, that brutal depopulation of the countryside where crofters had been driven off their land by rich landowners eager to make the easier money that came with rearing Cheviot sheep. Now the fragments of their homes were the only sign that this land had been the starting point for the Highland diaspora that had colonized the British Empire.

Fiona had never walked this side of the watershed, although the Assynt region in the west of Sutherland had been her destination on a couple of walking holidays in the past. She knew the springy feel of heather beneath her feet, the treacherous pull of peat hags, and the hard clatter of ancient stratified rock beneath her boots. If she was going to venture into the back country where Kit's bothy was, she'd have to make a stop in Lairg. The light shoes and town clothes she had with her would be no match for this terrain.

Lairg was coming to life as she drove down the main street. Shops were opening up, a handful of people were out and about, making the most of the thin warmth of the morning. She found a parking space across the road from a mountain sports shop and jumped out of the Land Rover. Before she headed for the shop, she checked the storage area behind the seats. As well as three five-gallon cans of diesel, there was a lightweight fleece and a waxed jacket. Fiona picked up the fleece and held it to her face, drinking in Kit's familiar smell. *Please God, let him be all right,* she said to herself.

Reluctantly, she replaced the fleece and jacket. They would be far too big for her, but they'd do, she decided. Then she crossed to the shop. Fifteen minutes later, she emerged, wearing fleece-lined Gore-Tex trousers, a lightweight thermal polo-neck shirt, a dark-brown fleece hat, hiking socks with cushioned soles and a pair of summer walking boots that had been reduced for a quick sale. They weren't designed for this time of the year, but they were so flexible they wouldn't need the breaking in that a heavier pair of boots would take. It was a reasonable trade-off, since she didn't envisage having to travel far in them. She would be comfortable if she had to do any walking or scrambling, and that was the main thing. She'd also bought a handful of high energy emergency rations, instant heat packs and a first-aid kit. She had a good idea what might lie ahead of her, and she wanted to be prepared for all eventualities.

Back at the Land Rover, Fiona added Kit's fleece and jacket to her ensemble, tossing her discarded work clothes into the storage space. There was one last thing she had to do. The time had come to recall *The Blood Painter* in all its details. She needed to be equipped for what she might find. She bought a pair of bolt cutters, a chisel and a lump hammer from the hardware shop. As an afterthought, she also added a craft knife with a retractable blade to her shopping basket.

Walking back to the Land Rover, she saw it was no longer alone. Parked behind it was a familiar Honda saloon. Leaning against the bonnet, Caroline stood, arms folded, a stubborn smile on her face. Fiona closed her eyes in frustration. When she came close enough to speak, she said, 'This is not funny, Caro.'

'I know. That's why I'm here. If you won't let me come with you, at least let me cover your back. Let me be there to make sure you come out of this alive. Please?'

Fiona opened the back of the Land Rover and stowed her purchases. When she turned back, she said, 'Have you got a mobile?'

Caroline grinned. 'You think there's any chance of a decent

signal up here?' she asked, gesturing at the hills rising round the town.

Fiona managed a rueful smile. 'Silly question. OK. Here's what we do. You follow me up to the point where I turn off. It's a mile or so out of town. There's no point in you trying to go any further. According to Kit, the road's too bad for anything other than a four-wheel-drive. You give me an hour.' She opened her bag and took out a notepad and pen. She opened the pad and scribbled down Sandy Galloway's office and home numbers. 'If I don't come back inside that hour, it means I'm probably in need of help or else I've managed to get through to the police on Kit's satellite phone. Either way, you call this number and ask for Superintendent Galloway. You tell him where I am and what I'm doing. I did send him a fax, but he might not think it was that urgent. Just a minute, I'll give you the directions.' She opened the driver's door and reached under the map for the e-mail she'd printed off what felt like half a lifetime ago. She held the sheet of paper out to Caroline, then snatched it back. 'Hang on,' she said. 'You have to promise that, no matter what, you will not attempt to come in there after me.'

Caroline gave a reluctant nod of agreement. 'I promise. OK?'

'Mean it.'

Caroline held Fiona's eyes for a long moment. 'I swear on Lesley's life.'

Fiona ducked her head in acknowledgement. 'That'll do me. Like I said, I should be able to call for help myself if I need it, but it might be that I can't figure out how to work the sat phone. You're my back-up.' She handed over the directions and took a deep breath. 'Wagons roll.' She climbed into the Land Rover and started the engine. Her hands were sweating on the wheel, her stomach a tight clench. She knew the odds were stacked against her. They'd had a head start on her. They could have made it to the bothy an hour or more ago. She already knew the killer wasn't totally committed to verisimilitude. Maybe he would drain Kit's blood in one swift act rather than torture him for days, with all the attendant risks.

Maybe she was already too late.

The smell of coffee woke Steve. He blinked for a moment, rubbing the sleep out of his eyes, suffering the dislocation of waking in an unfamiliar place. He pushed himself upright and saw Terry sitting at the table, a mug in her hands. 'I was beginning to wonder if last night was too much for you and you'd slipped into a coma,' she teased.

'What time is it?' he asked, unaware as to how late he'd slept.

'Twenty past nine.'

Steve swung his legs to the floor and jumped to his feet. 'You're kidding,' he exclaimed, sounding more shaken than delighted.

'It's Saturday, Steve. People sleep late.' She grinned. 'Even coppers.'

'I can't believe nobody's phoned. The surveillance . . . Neil should have called to say he was going off for the night,' he said, talking more to himself than to her. 'And the AC, his plane's supposed to have been on the ground two hours ago.' He crossed to his phone and pager. He stared dumbfounded at the blank displays. 'What's wrong?' he said, grabbing his phone and frowning at it.

Terry came up behind him and put her arms round his waist. 'I switched them off. You need to let go, Steve.'

He pulled away and swung round, his face a mixture of

anger and incredulity. 'You did *what*?' he shouted. His mouth opened and closed, words for once failing him.

'The world won't end if you're out of reach for a night,' Terry said, a note of uncertainty in her voice.

'I'm in the middle of a major operation,' he yelled. 'I've got a team on a murder suspect. Jesus, Terry, anything could have happened. How could you do something so fucking irresponsible?' As he spoke, he was reaching for his clothes, pulling on boxer shorts and trousers.

'You didn't tell me,' she blazed back at him. 'How was I supposed to know? Last time we were interrupted, it wasn't even your case. You gave me no indication that you had anything important on the go.'

Steve paused halfway through buttoning his shirt and gave her a livid glare. 'It's confidential, that's why I didn't say. I don't talk about my work to civilians.'

His words cut like a whip. But rather than making Terry flinch, they sharpened her response. 'Unless they're Fiona Cameron?' she raged.

'Is that what this is about? You're jealous of Fiona?' Steve couldn't believe what he was hearing.

Terry's voice dropped and she stared evenly at him. 'No, it's about trust, Steve. It's about openness. It's about not treating me as if I'm a child. All you had to do was mention at some point that you had something going on that might just interrupt our time together. Fucking hell,' she exploded again. 'What about common courtesy?'

Steve thrust his arms into his jacket and grabbed his coat. 'I'm a senior police officer. People need to contact me out of hours.'

'Mr Indispensable. You don't want a lover, Steve. You want an audience.'

He shoved phone and pager into his jacket pocket and

made for the door, shaking his head. 'I don't fucking believe this.'

'You should have told me, dickhead,' she shouted, her anger directed as much at her own impulsiveness as his taciturnity.

His only reply was the slam of the door as he walked out. By the time he got to his car, his hands were still trembling with the adrenaline surge of pure rage. 'Fucking unbelievable,' he muttered under his breath as he threw himself into the driver's seat. He switched on his pager. Five messages. Steve cursed under his breath as he scrolled through. Two from Fiona from late last night. One from Neil just before eleven. One from Neil a few minutes after six. 'Shit, shit, shit,' he said, as the last message revealed itself. The Assistant Commissioner had paged him over an hour ago.

He turned on his phone and called his home number, then keyed in the combination that would release his messages from the answering machine. Fiona again, requesting an urgent call back. Neil, announcing he'd decided to stay on Coyne all night, just in case. Neil again, reporting that he'd handed over to Joanne and would be at the Yard if he was needed for an arrest and search. And a message from the AC, saying he was expecting Steve's call.

He rubbed his hands over his face, trying to calm down to the point where he could make his case for the arrest of Gerard Coyne. After a minute of deep breathing, he decided he was as ready as he'd ever be. He'd just have to lie and say his pager battery had died without him noticing. The hour he'd lost probably hadn't made much difference. But it could have done.

As he dialled the AC's number, he felt a pang of regret. He'd had such high hopes for him and Terry. And, as usual, it had crashed and burned.

He could only hope he'd have better luck with Coyne.

Four hundred miles away, Sandy Galloway was picking at a bacon roll in the canteen at St Leonard's. He'd been waiting for Fiona Cameron for almost two hours, and he wasn't best pleased. The woman had been at panic stations when she'd rung him the previous evening, but now she couldn't even be bothered to make their appointment on time. She hadn't even left a message for him, either with force control or at the reception desk of her hotel. The hotel that his budget was paying for, he reminded himself crossly.

He'd spoken to Sarah Duvall, as he'd promised. He'd watched the end of his cop show, then called her at Wood Street. She was a bright lassie, that one. She'd gone through the discrepancy between Redford's statement and what the Dorset police had found in some detail. She'd explained why she'd initially been uneasy, then ran through the reasoning she'd gone through since. It had clearly stilled her qualms, and he was inclined to think she had jumped the right way.

Which meant, of course, that Fiona Cameron was barking up the wrong tree altogether. Galloway was just fed up that she hadn't bothered to keep him informed of her plans.

It had never occurred to him to check the fax machine that sat behind the secretary's desk in his outer office.

Chapter 53

The directions were carved in her memory like a grave inscription. 'Take the A839 out of Lairg.' Back out of the town centre, across the narrows of the River Shin before it opened out into one of the two inlets at the bottom of the loch. Down the river bank for a short distance, then a turn west, a rounded hillock on her right. Fiona checked in her rear-view mirror that Caroline was still behind her.

'About a mile out of the town, you'll see a track on the right signed Sallachy.' Yes, there was the metalled track. Conveniently, there was a phone box on the other side of the road. Fiona pulled up and pointed exaggeratedly to the kiosk. Caroline gave her the thumbs-up and gestured at her watch, overtaking Fiona, to park right by the phone. Fiona checked the time. 9.37. She had an hour. Moving off, she swung hard right to make the turn.

'Carry on up the track (it's pretty rough going, you'll appreciate why I'm lending you the Land Rover) for about five and a half miles.' She did as instructed. The road, which soon became a rough track of loose stones and hard core, ran about forty feet above the loch side, with scatterings of trees on the steep shore. On her left, a conifer plantation lined the road, stretching up the hill until the flattening of the ridge stole the horizon. But Fiona, now completely focused on the task ahead, had no eye for the beauties of the landscape around her. She passed a handful of cottages as the plantation came to an end in exposed heather-covered hillside. There was no sign of life, other than a thin thread of peaty smoke emerging from a chimney.

After a mile or so, the road began to climb and the trees began again. But this time, instead of regimented rows of conifers, there was a mix of trees. Rowans, birches, alders and tall clumps of contorted Scots pine grew in the apparently random chaos of a well-managed wood that was cut off from the road by a high deer fence with occasional tall wooden stiles.

Abruptly, the trees ended on a bend. Ahead was a ravine, crossed by a sturdy-looking wooden bridge with tubular steel rails on either side. 'You cross a river gorge, the Allt a' Claon.' No mistaking it, she was on the right track. Halfway across the bridge, Fiona slowed to a crawl and looked down fifty feet of craggy rock to the river's rough and tumble below. It was flowing fast through the channel it had cut itself, bursting into white foam as it hit the boulders that had fallen into its path. Cut off from the sparkle of sunlight by the high walls of its gorge, it gleamed the dark cloudy brown of unpolished amber.

Fiona let in the clutch and carried on, the tension in her body transferring itself to the hands that gripped the steering wheel like claws. 'There's a left turn up ahead, which you take.' She took it, wrestling the wheel as the Land Rover protested at the loose shale under its wheels. Time to move into four-wheel-drive, she thought, carrying out the operation Lachlan had demonstrated. The Land Rover juddered slightly, then the wheels gripped more tightly and she was moving forward easily over the rough surface.

'About half a mile up this track, there's another left turn. The track takes you back across the river ravine on a rope bridge. It's a lot stronger than it looks, but better not go faster than five miles an hour.' Fiona made the turn and approached the bridge, a construction of narrow wooden planks suspended on rope cables anchored to thick poles on either side of the gorge. Her heart pounded. It looked far too fragile a construction to bear the weight of the Land Rover. She had to trust Kit's words, however. She rolled to a halt by the start of the bridge and carefully engaged first gear. Then, at little more than a walking pace, she edged forward. The bridge creaked ominously as it took the full weight of the vehicle, but although she felt its sway beneath her, it held firm as she slowly advanced over the thirty-yard width of the gorge.

When she regained solid ground, she let out the breath she hadn't even been conscious of holding. She took her clammy hands off the steering wheel and wiped them on her thighs. 'Fuck, I hope I'm right about this,' she said out loud. 'And I hope I'm in time.'

'You cross the river into some trees and the bothy's about a mile ahead of you.' The end was almost in sight. She drove on into the belt of trees that crowded the track. A couple of hundred yards further on, she rounded a bend and, to her astonishment, almost ran over a man who was walking down the track towards her, a long-handled axe over his shoulder and a bundle of sticks under one arm. She skidded to a halt and wound down the window. The man, who was muffled up in anorak and close-fitting woollen hat, a scarf wrapped tightly round his neck and chin, raised a hand in greeting. 'I'm looking for Kit Martin's bothy,' she said. 'Am I on the right road?'

His dark brows furrowed. 'The writer? Yes, it's about a mile up the track.' Judging by his accent, he wasn't local born and bred, but he obviously knew the area. No doubt one of the incomers who, like Kit, had snapped up many of the properties that came on the market, tempted by the low prices and the peace of a rural lifestyle.

'Thanks,' she said. 'You've not seen him today, I suppose?'

The man shook his head. 'I've just come out for some wood.'

Fiona waved and drove on. Soon she emerged from the trees on to open hillside. The wiry brown stems of heather in its winter plumage stretched up the hill, broken up by rocky outcroppings that varied from a single boulder to uneven patches stretching for as much as thirty yards. Ahead there was another clump of trees. She guessed that was the windbreak for Kit's bothy and pulled over to the side of the road before she reached the woodland.

This was it. There was no turning back now. Fiona felt sick with fear and anticipation, but she had to go on. She grabbed the carrier bag containing her purchases from the mountaineering shop and the hardware store and shoved it inside the waxed jacket. Taking a deep, shuddering breath, she opened the door and clambered out on to the roadside.

Fiona knew she couldn't approach the bothy head on. If the killer was there with Kit, he'd doubtless be watching the road in. She studied the lie of the land and made her decision. She struck off into the woods at an angle to the road, pushing through the young saplings and tramping down the brambles that obstructed her path. It was hard going, especially since she was conscious of trying to make as little noise as possible.

After about ten minutes, the trees ended abruptly in a wide clearing. At the centre was a single-storey stone building with a slate roof. She was facing the end wall, which had no windows. Perfect for her plans. She glanced to either side, disconcerted by the absence of a vehicle. If the killer was there with Kit, they had to have arrived in something. What if she was already too late? What if he'd done what he intended and killed Kit already? She'd never felt so scared. Or so alone.

'Don't overreact,' she muttered under her breath. At worst, they only had a couple of hours start on her. It was important to the killer that he complete the murder ritual as it was outlined in the book. There hadn't been enough time for him to have exsanguinated Kit and painted the walls. Either they weren't there yet or the killer had driven off into Lairg for supplies.

Or else she had guessed completely wrong.

Refusing to allow that thought to settle, Fiona opted for action. Adrenaline pumping, she ran in a low crouch from the trees to the shelter of the gable end, grateful for the flexibility of the lightweight boots. Then, with infinite care, she inched along the wall to the rear of the bothy. At the end, she chanced a quick look round the back. No sign of life. There were three windows in the wall, she noted. She wiped a sheen of sweat from her forehead and boldly turned the corner.

Fiona could feel the thud of her heart in her chest as she tiptoed to the edge of the first window and looked carefully round the edge of the frame. The room spread before her was obviously Kit's bedroom. There was no sign of activity. It was a curious sensation to look in on a life so familiar and yet so strange. A surge of emotion swelled in her chest, making her catch her breath.

She swallowed hard and swiftly crossed the window, slowing again as she approached the second window. This looked like a later addition, having a markedly different size and shape to the other two. As she drew nearer, she could see it was completely obscured by a blind. This was almost certainly the bathroom. If she was right, this was where Kit would be held prisoner. She moved her head through various angles to try to catch a glimpse inside round the edges of the blind, but she could see nothing.

Frustrated, she moved on to the third window. Again, a quick glance confirmed there was no movement inside the room. Seeing no one, Fiona took a long look at the interior. It contained a large table, a couple of armchairs on either side of a wood-burning stove, a small galley kitchen area and a couple of cupboards that ran the full height of the room. A narrow metal cabinet stood open, its door obscuring the contents, and on the floor near the door were a couple of Waitrose carrier bags. They didn't look as if they'd been there for long, being apparently free of dust. She also knew there wasn't a Waitrose within three hundred miles. A tiny piece of evidence, but enough to convince her she'd come to all the right conclusions.

Then she spotted something that confirmed her worst fears and made her stomach churn painfully. In the far corner, half hidden by the angle of the chimney breast, was a small table leaning at an angle. On the floor beside it was a tangle of smashed plastic and metal. It was unmistakably the remains of a satellite phone.

So they were here. And judging by the absence of a vehicle, the killer was temporarily absent. He was obviously a careful operator, the destruction of the phone a clear sign that he accepted the remote possibility that his prisoner might break free. She wondered momentarily about the man she'd seen in the woods. But he'd looked perfectly innocent, with his bundle of wood and his axe. And besides, he'd been on foot. She wished she'd thought to ask him if he'd seen any unfamiliar vehicles around.

But thinking was wasting time. Fiona moved away from the window and ran round the far corner. She passed a small stone shelter that contained a diesel generator, then turned down the front of the house. The double wooden doors were shut and locked, she soon discovered. She pushed with her shoulder, but they didn't budge.

She was going to have to break in, and at the rear was the best place to do it. She ran back to the bedroom window and tugged at the bottom of the frame. Locked. Fiona pulled the lump hammer out of the bag tucked inside her jacket and hefted it in her hand. No point in just breaking the glass. She'd have to smash the wooden strut that ran up the middle of the lower sash. She breathed in, drew her arm back and swung the hammer round in a sharp arc. The wood splintered and the glass on both sides shattered explosively. On the quiet hillside, it sounded remarkably loud. A pair of jays started out of the wood behind her, their hoarse cries making her jump.

As quickly as she could, Fiona broke off the window spar then cleared the glass from the frame to avoid cutting herself as she went through. Gingerly, she put one leg through the gap, hoisting herself over the sill and into the bedroom. The house was quiet, though it lacked the indefinable stillness that usually accompanies emptiness. Fiona stood motionless for a moment, listening for any sign of danger.

Cautiously, she crossed the room and pulled the door wide open. To her left, in the gloom of the hallway, the bathroom door was closed. She reached a tentative hand to the doorknob, almost too afraid of what might lie behind it. She screwed her eyes shut, steeling herself for action, then clenched her fingers round the knob, turning it and throwing the door open in one motion.

Chapter 54

Six hundred miles away in London, Steve Preston had congratulated himself on persuading the Assistant Commissioner that he had enough evidence to go through with his plan. Now all that was left to do was to brief the team who would back up Joanne and Neil when they brought in Gerard, and the forensic squad who would assist in the search of Coyne's flat.

'I've given this a lot of thought. I don't want to arrest him in his flat, because, as you all know, that means that under PACE, we can only do a Section Thirty-two search, with all the restrictions that implies. What I want to do is to wait until he leaves the flat then pick him up in the open. We'll bring him in to the Yard and arrest him on suspicion of murder, and then we can do a Section Eighteen search, which gives us a lot more scope. To make sure he doesn't get out of our grasp, I'm detailing one of you to be on a bike and another on a motorbike. He's a keen cyclist, there's every chance that when he does leave, he'll be on two wheels.'

He forced his face into a serious expression, battening the hatches on his feelings of exultation. 'I want him back here in one piece,' he said forcefully. 'No accidents, nobody falling down the stairs, no unexplained cuts, bruises or broken bones. I want him handled as if he was fine china.

'As soon as we get him back here, I want Coyne arrested

on suspicion of murder. Let's put the shits up him right away. But no delays over letting him call his brief. I want this done by the book. Nothing that anyone can pick on afterwards and say, "Hang on a minute, you didn't follow PACE here, mate." Anybody got any questions?'

A young DC raised a hand. 'What exactly are we looking for in Coyne's flat?'

'Good question,' Steve said. 'Anything that could tie him in to Susan Blanchard's murder, or the North London rapes. So that means newspaper cuttings, any maps with crime scenes marked on them, diaries, photographs. And I want every knife in the place. Also any clothing that matches the descriptions of the cycle gear that the cyclist on the Heath or the rapist was wearing. I know, after all this time, we're probably clutching at straws. But I want Coyne, and together we're going to nail him and lay Susan Blanchard to rest at last.'

He looked around the room. No more questions. He turned to the pinboard behind him and pointed to a photograph of Susan's twin sons. 'I don't want justice for me. I don't even want justice for the Met. I want justice for those two. Now go out there and get it for them.' He hated the cheap emotional shot, but they needed to be gung ho, and he knew exactly how to get them there.

Steve watched the officers file out of the room, wondering how much time he had before they brought their prisoner back. He needed to find out what the hell Fiona was up to. He'd tried her mobile several times since he'd got back to the Yard, but all he'd had was a recorded message telling him that it was not possible to connect his call. Thanks to Sarah Duvall, he knew she'd gone to Scotland to review the evidence in the Drew Shand case. A call to the officer in charge was probably as good a place to start as any.

He picked up the nearest phone and asked the switchboard

to connect him to Lothian and Borders Police. It took little time to discover that the man he needed to speak to was Superintendent Sandy Galloway. But Galloway wasn't in the building. Frustrated, Steve arranged for them to pass on a message asking Galloway to call him back as soon as possible.

What on earth was Fiona playing at, leaving messages he couldn't return? Given the terms they'd been on when last they met, it had to be something serious. It might be worth trying Kit, he thought. But dialling their home number simply connected him to another answering machine.

There was nothing more he could do. Now he had to clear his mind and concentrate on how he would handle Gerard Coyne. This was too important to allow anything to distract him.

It was worse, far worse than the corresponding scene in the TV adaptation. Worse, infinitely worse than her imagination had prepared her for. Her first thought was that he was dead. Kit slumped naked on the toilet, his arms chained to the walls, his legs hobbled round the toilet. His skin was white, his head sunk on his chest. He was only held upright by his bonds. She could see no sign of breath or pulse. In the vein of his left arm, there was a shunt. And on the walls around him, amateurish daubs of trees and flowers, gruesome in shades from dark-carmine to rust-brown. About half of the walls of the compact bathroom were covered. She had no way of estimating how much blood that had required. Her chest contracted in an agony of fear and distress.

With a wordless moan that was closer to a sob, Fiona rushed forward, falling to her knees and throwing her arms around his chill flesh. Her eyes were already brimming with tears. To her amazement, she felt a flicker of movement against her face. Then a breath like a soft groan tickled her ear.

'Kit?' she stammered. 'Kit? Can you hear me?' She put a hand to his neck and felt a weak and irregular pulse. She took his head between her hands and gently raised it level with hers. His eyelids flickered, the whites of his eyes showing through the lashes. 'I'm here, Kit. It's me, Fiona. It's going to be all right.'

His eyes opened a crack and he groaned. She held him close, desperate to transfer her warmth to him. Shock, that's what it was. Loss of blood and the cold had sent him into shock. The first thing she had to do was get him warm. Fiona gently moved away from him and ran through to the bedroom. She grabbed a sleeping bag, a couple of flannel shirts and a pair of jeans, then hurried back to the bathroom. She draped the sleeping bag over his shoulders, keeping up a constant flow of reassuring words. Then she pulled the carrier bag out of her jacket and took out the bolt cutters. It took all her strength, but she managed to snap through the chain that fettered his legs and unwrap it from his ankles. His legs were stiff and cold in her hands, but she pulled them round to the front of the toilet and fed his feet through the legs of his jeans, pulling them up to his knees.

Next she took the chisel and the lump hammer and attacked the shackles holding him to the wall. Beginning with his right arm, a couple of blows were all it took to rip the metal eye out of the wall. His arm fell uselessly to his side and he groaned again.

Fiona moved round to the other side and considered. She didn't want to disturb the shunt in his arm, afraid that if she took it out, he'd start bleeding again. She took a roll of elastoplast out of the first-aid kit and carefully wound it round the shunt, holding it firmly in place. Then she repeated the procedure with the hammer and chisel, freeing his left arm. He fell forward, a dead weight collapsed over his knees. Somehow, struggling against the mass of his torso, Fiona managed to dress him in the shirts, cutting the sleeves to get them over the chains and handcuffs.

Then, grunting with the effort, she hauled him to his feet, propping him against the wall so she could pull up his trousers. It was all taking too long, she thought with a surge of panic. His captor couldn't be far away. Surely he wouldn't take the risk of leaving Kit alone for too long.

Fiona let Kit slump back on to the toilet. She took out the heat packs, flexed them to activate the chemical reaction that would produce life-saving warmth and tucked them inside the shirts next to his skin. Then she went back to the bedroom and searched till she found a pair of thick socks and some battered trainers.

Her next stop was the living room. Inside one of the cupboards she found a couple of cans of Coke. Perfect. Fluid, and sugar. The caffeine probably wouldn't be a problem for a man who routinely consumed as much coffee as Kit did. As she turned back, the narrow metal cabinet caught her eye. Where there should have been the shotgun that Kit used to pot rabbits, there was an empty space. A box of cartridges lay open, half-empty. Fresh panic seized her. Wherever he was, Kit's abductor had a double-barrelled shotgun. What was already a desperate situation had suddenly become worse.

Hurrying back to the bathroom, she thrust Kit's feet into socks and trainers. Then she pulled him upright from his slumped position. 'Come on, Kit. I need you conscious, my darling, I need you able to function.'

The warmth had begun to do its work. With a shivering tremor, Kit's eyes opened properly. He looked at her with puzzlement. 'Fiona,' he croaked.

'Yes, it's me, you're not hallucinating. I found you, sweetheart. Now, I need you to drink this.' She held the can of Coke to his lips and forced herself to be patient while he sipped it through dry and cracked lips. 'We're going to get you out of here, I promise,' she said.

'Where's Blake?' he said, his voice cracked and strange, his consonants slurred.

'Blake?' Fiona asked, wondering from what delirious corner of his mind he'd dredged that name.

'Francis Blake,' he insisted. 'He brought me here. He did this to me.'

It shouldn't have made sense, but suddenly, it did. The man she'd passed on the way to the bothy. Memory jolted into place. She'd never met Blake, but she'd heard his voice on TV. The aural recollection triggered a visual image. She hadn't seen much of the stranger's face, but now she had a template to set it against, she knew it was him. Francis Blake was the man with the axe. But even as her mind accepted the identification, her intelligence balked at it. Why on earth would Francis Blake have kidnapped Kit? How could he be this particular serial killer? It was meaningless, absurd.

It was also something she couldn't afford the time to consider now. 'He's gone,' she said with a confidence she didn't feel. But where was Blake, and what was he doing? Judging by the axe, he'd gone for firewood. Either that or it was simply an elaborate way to disguise the shotgun, constructing a hide of sticks around it. Obviously, he must have been heading back to the bothy, having hidden his vehicle somewhere else. But he'd heard her approach. Even if he didn't know who she was, he knew she was heading for the only habitation on that particular track and so he must have turned round, to make it look as if he was walking away.

A simple enough ruse, but it had worked. She hadn't felt

a moment's suspicion. And now he knew she was there. He couldn't just let them go, could he? It was inconceivable.

Fiona shook her head in an attempt to clear her thoughts. 'I'm going to get the Land Rover,' she said, keeping her voice brisk in an attempt to hide the fear twisting her guts. 'I want you to stay here. If you can drink the rest of the Coke, that would be good. But don't worry if your fingers don't work yet. The circulation will take a while to come back. Do you know how much blood you've lost?'

'More than a pint,' he sighed, his voice still sounding like a drunk. 'I passed out then. I suppose he must have stopped.' He blinked and focused properly on his surroundings for the first time, shuddering at the bloodwork on the walls. 'Fuck,' he said with a laugh that turned into a cough. 'He's a fucking terrible painter.'

Fiona stood up and hugged his head to her chest. 'I'll be as quick as I can.' She let him go, and took the craft knife out of the bag, sliding the blade out an inch then putting it carefully in her jacket pocket. Leaving him behind was the hardest thing she had ever done, but the only way out for them was in the Land Rover. She couldn't afford to wait for Caroline to summon the cavalry, not now she knew Blake had a gun.

She crossed to the front door and inched it open. She stared across the clearing down the track through the trees. Nothing stirred. Her flesh prickled with apprehension. He could be anywhere in those trees, sighting her down the barrel of a gun. He could be lurking behind the Land Rover, axe ready to swing down on her head. The prospect made her stomach cramp. Cautiously, she opened the door further, her free hand slipping into her pocket and gripping the knife handle. Still nothing stirred. If he was watching her with the gun at his shoulder, she'd be a harder target moving than standing still dithering, she told herself firmly. *Now or never.*

From a standing start, she sprinted across the clearing and down the track. She reached the Land Rover with a rapidity that surprised her, having forgotten how much more direct this route was than the initial approach she'd taken to the bothy. She yanked the door open and jumped inside, then leaned her head on the steering wheel for a moment, a sob of relief escaping from her gasping mouth. *Get a grip,* she chastised herself, straightening up.

Thrusting the keys into the ignition, she had a moment's panic. What if Blake had disabled the engine? Quickly, she turned the keys and almost wept with relief when the starter motor turned over and caught first time. She slammed it into gear and roared up the remainder of the track, hauling on the heavy steering as she entered the clearing to swing the vehicle round in a circle so the tailgate faced the cottage door.

Leaving the engine running, she opened the rear door of the Land Rover, then hurried back inside. Kit was more upright now, leaning back against the toilet cistern. He was still deathly pale, but his eyes were open and he seemed more alert. Fiona scrabbled around in the bedroom, unearthing a couple of blankets and a pillow. She grabbed the rest of Kit's shirts and took her bundle out to the Land Rover, adding the sleeping bag on a second trip. She made a sort of bed on the floor, then returned for Kit.

'I'm going to need some help from you,' she said. 'I can't carry you.'

Kit nodded. 'I think I can just about stand up now. There's a walking stick in the living room. That might help.' His voice was cracked and barely audible.

Fiona found it propped up in a corner. It was a modern

aluminium stick, spring-loaded to absorb impact, and telescopic. She extended it slightly, so that Kit could use it as a shepherd would a crook.

Back in the bathroom, she pushed Kit's hand through the fabric loop and helped him clasp the handgrip. 'Pins and needles,' he muttered.

'Trust me, that's a good sign,' Fiona said. She slipped under his other arm and between them, they got him to his feet.

'Christ, I've got cramp,' he moaned, his right leg buckling as it took his weight.

It felt like an eternity before he was able to put one foot in front of the other. Fiona could feel the sweat of fear pooling in the small of her back. Slowly, they stumbled the few yards to the front door. Then they were at the Land Rover. Fiona manoeuvred him so that he was sitting on the tailgate. Then she swung his legs on board and settled him as comfortably as possible. 'Are you OK?' she asked.

He managed a wan smile. 'Compared to what? My head's splitting, everything's spinning, and I feel sick as a dog.'

'It's only dehydration and low blood pressure. Trust me, Kit.'

A tremendous wave of euphoria flooded Fiona as she finally closed the door and put the Land Rover in gear. She'd made it. Against all the odds, she'd found him in time. They were going to make it! She moved off, almost feeling like singing. Into the woods, then out into the open. She could see the belt of conifers ahead that hid the final approach to the bridge.

As they drew nearer to the trees, Kit's voice came faintly from the back. 'He's not going to let us go this easy, Fiona,' he said weakly. 'Pull up.'

Much as it ran against her instincts – to get out as fast as possible – she did as he asked. She squirmed round in her seat to face him. 'What's wrong, Kit?'

'If the bridge is down, we're stuck,' he said. 'In the glove box – binoculars. Go and have a look up ahead. Please.'

'He's got your gun. Kit. He could be watching us right now.'

'He'd have shot us already. Please?'

Fiona thought for a moment. There was sense in what Kit had said. If Blake had been on this side of the ravine, he could have picked them off easily when they were getting into the Land Rover. And at least she had the conifers for cover. In Kit's state of shock, she wasn't prepared to take unnecessary risks. She climbed out and, sticking close to the edge of the trees, walked to the curve in the road that brought the bridge into view. As she rounded the bend, taking cover behind some closely planted spruce, she smiled at the sight of the bridge still in place. Kit's fears had been groundless, she thought happily.

But, because he'd made her take the binoculars, she decided to check anyway. It wouldn't hurt just to make certain there was no loose planking. She raised the glasses to her eyes and focused on the bridge. At first, everything seemed to be fine. Then her heart leapt in panic. She lowered the binoculars, took a deep breath and looked again. She could have wept.

On the far side of the bridge, both ropes had been cut part way through, the fraying obvious through the powerful field glasses.

There was no way out. The bridge had changed from a lifeline to a deathtrap.

Chapter 55

Caroline double-checked the number Fiona had given her, and nervously checked her watch again. Sixty-one minutes had passed since she'd waved goodbye to Fiona. Whatever had been waiting at the end of her friend's journey, it clearly hadn't been straightforward. Caroline was angry with herself for letting Fiona face the danger alone, but she recognized the sense in what she'd been instructed to do. If Fiona couldn't deal with it on her own, the chances were that Caroline would have been more of a liability than a help. That knowledge assuaged neither her guilt nor her fear.

Hastily, she shovelled all her change into the coin box of the phone and keyed in the number. The phone on the other end rang three times, then she heard the choked-off ring of a call being diverted to another phone. This time, it was answered on the second ring. 'CID, DC Mullen,' a husky male voice grunted.

'I need to speak to Superintendent Sandy Galloway,' Caroline said.

'He's not available just now. Can I help you?'

Where to begin? 'Are you working on the Drew Shand case?' she asked.

'Have you some information pertaining to the inquiry, madam? Can I take your name?'

'No, I don't have information, as such. I'm calling on

behalf of Dr Fiona Cameron. She's been consulting with Superintendent Galloway on the case. Look, it's vital that I speak to him.'

'I'm afraid he's not on duty. Can I pass on a message?'

Exasperated, Caroline struggled to find a quick way to tell the detective what was going on, conscious that her credit was dribbling away by the second. 'She's following a lead, she thought she might be heading into a dangerous situation. She thinks the killer's still on the loose, you see. And she asked me to call Superintendent Galloway if she hadn't come back within the hour,' she gabbled, aware that she wasn't explaining the situation well. 'I think she needs back-up.'

'Back-up for what?' He sounded bemused.

'She thinks the killer's holed up with his next victim. Nobody would listen to her, she's gone after him on her own.'

'Look, miss, I think you're under a misapprehension here. We believe that Drew Shand's killer is in custody. Where are you calling from?'

'Just outside Lairg. On the shores of Loch Shin.'

'Lairg? I'm afraid you're a wee bit off our patch,' he said, sounding amused. He'd clearly decided to consign her to the drawer marked 'crank'. 'Maybe you should be talking to Highland Police?'

'Wait, don't hang up!' Caroline shouted. 'I know this sounds crazy, but I'm not some kind of nutter. Fiona Cameron's in danger. I need help here.'

'Talk to the police at Lairg. They're the men on the spot. They'll be able to help you. Either that or leave a message with me for Superintendent Galloway.'

'You'll get it to him right away?' Caroline demanded.

'I'll make sure he gets it.'

'OK. Tell him Fiona's at Kit Martin's bothy. It's near the

Allt a' Claon on the shores of Loch Shin.' She spelled out the name of the river gorge for him. 'She sent him a fax, but I don't know if he got it. Please, tell him we need help, urgently.' An electronic voice in her ear told her she had ten seconds left. 'It's really important,' she stressed as the line went dead.

Caroline slammed the phone down. 'Bugger!' she shouted in frustration. 'You really fucked that up, you moron.' She smashed the flat of her hand into the glass wall of the box. She'd blown her one chance with the Edinburgh Police, and every minute that ticked past might put Fiona's life at even more risk.

She had a horrible feeling that the local police were going to be even less inclined to take her seriously. But there was nothing else for it. She'd have to go back to Lairg anyway for more change to make phone calls.

Still cursing her incompetence, Caroline made for her car, all the time praying that Fiona was still in one piece. 'No thanks to you if she is, fuckwit,' she said out loud as she threw the car into a U-turn and headed back into town.

When Gerard Coyne emerged from his flat that morning, Joanne let out a sigh of relief. 'He's not taking the bike,' she said, peering into the rear-view mirror.

'Thank Christ for that,' Neil said. He watched in the carefully angled wing mirror as Coyne drew level with their car and continued on up the street. Before he reached the corner, two detectives were on his tail, one on either side of the street. Joanne started the car and pulled out of the parking spot. The brief was clear. Wait until Coyne was stationary, then close in. The two officers on foot were each shadowed by another back-up, with Joanne and Neil in the car ready to join in the endgame.

Coyne cut through the maze of narrow streets and emerged on Caledonian Road near its junction with Holloway Road. As he approached a bike shop with its wares covering most of the pavement outside, his pace slowed and he came to a halt, studying a racing bike. 'Time to make a move?' Neil asked Joanne as they crawled towards the shop.

'I think so,' she said, braking to a halt and flicking on the hazard lights.

Neil spoke into the radio set. 'Alpha Tango to all units. Move in on suspect now.' He jumped out of the car and strode across the pavement. The other officers had surrounded Coyne, who was standing with his back to the bike display, his eyes wide with astonishment.

'Gerard Patrick Coyne?' Neil said.

'Yeah, who wants to know?' Coyne demanded, trying for cool and missing by a mile.

'I am Detective Constable Neil McCartney of the Metropolitan Police and I would like you to accompany me to a police station to help with my inquiries into a serious matter.'

Coyne shook his head. 'You must be mistaken, mate. I've done nothing.' His eyes were darting from side to side, as if seeking a way out. But his path was blocked by the police officers, as well as the pedestrians who had stopped to see what was going on.

'In which case, you won't mind answering a few questions, will you, sir?' Neil took a step closer.

'Am I under arrest?' Coyne demanded.

'That's up to you at this point, sir. We'd prefer it if you accompanied us on a voluntary basis.'

'I don't have a lot of choice, do I?' he said, his voice the whine of those who feel victimized.

'I have a car waiting,' was all Neil said.

The officers formed a phalanx around him, and escorted him to the back seat of the car, where he was hemmed in by Neil and another detective. Coyne's narrow face was set in a petulant mask, his arms tightly folded across his chest. 'You're making a big mistake,' he complained.

'You'll have plenty of opportunity to put us right,' Neil said pleasantly. He could afford the courtesy; everything had gone according to plan.

Fiona rested her head on the steering wheel. 'So what do we do now?' she asked. 'I've got back-up – Caroline should have called the cops by now. But they're not going to treat this as a matter of urgency, I just know they're not. Besides, it'll take them forever to get here. You say there's no other way out?'

'Not by road,' Kit said. He'd propped himself up into a sitting position. Now the cramps and the pins and needles had passed, he felt slightly less like someone knocking at heaven's door. His head still felt like he was half-drunk, half-hungover, but he was gradually getting used to that. 'On foot. There is a way on foot. It's about six miles across the hill. I don't think I can make it. But you could hike out and get help.'

'I can't leave you here,' Fiona protested, her voice muffled as she spoke into her chest. 'There's nothing to stop Blake coming back for you. We don't know that he's left. If I was him, I'd be in the woods on the other side of the ravine waiting for us to plunge to our deaths. And if time passes and we don't do that, he'll probably look at the map and figure out what we're doing. So he'll come back for you. Even if he has to hike back down the road to the bridge by the loch side and back up again through the woods, he'll still get to you before I can make it to the main road.'

'What other choice is there? Apart from waiting for your back-up?'

'You need to get to a hospital, Kit. And besides, what's going to happen when they roll up? Either they're going to spot what's happened to the bridge and they'll be stuck that side of the ravine. Or else they won't and they'll end up crashing into the gorge like we're supposed to have done.'

There was a long pause. Then Kit said, 'There is something that might work. But it's a very long shot . . .'

'A long shot's better than no shot at all.'

'You might not think that once you've heard it.'

Steve was generous in his praise of his team. 'You did a great job. Like clockwork, and by the book. Not a thing that the defence could pick on. Well done. The drinks are on me tonight. He's been formally arrested now, has he?'

Neil nodded. 'On suspicion of murder. He looked completely gobsmacked. But he knows what he's about. The only thing he said was that he wanted his lawyer.'

Steve picked up a sheet of paper from his desk. 'Right. I've drawn up the authorization for a Section Eighteen search. I want you to take charge of that, Neil. You know what we're looking for. Now, I want John and Joanne to start the interview. I'm going to be watching from the observation room. John, I want Joanne to take the lead. This guy has a problem with women. I want to wind him up, and Joanne coming on the macho cop will do just that. OK with that, Joanne?'

She smiled grimly. 'It'll be a pleasure, guv.'

Before he could say more, Steve's phone rang. He grabbed it and said, 'DS Preston.'

'Steve? It's Sarah Duvall. I wonder, is there any chance you could drop round to Snow Hill? There's something I'd like you to see.'

'Sarah, I'm up to my arse in alligators right now. Can it wait?'

'I'm not sure it can, actually. Let me just explain. I've had a team checking the Smithfield videos and we think we've found the man who deposited Georgia Lester's remains in the freezer.'

'That sounds like good news. But why are you calling me?' Steve said impatiently.

'We think it's Francis Blake.'

'What?' Steve couldn't believe what he was hearing.

'I've looked at it myself. I've compared it with Blake's mugshots. I don't think there's any doubt about it.'

Confused, Steve said, 'But what about Redford?'

There was a pause before Duvall spoke. 'We might be wrong about Redford.'

There was a strange ringing in his ears. If Redford wasn't the killer, how could it be Francis Blake?

More importantly, if Redford wasn't the killer, where were Kit and Fiona?

'So, can you come over and take a look?' he heard Duvall say, as if from a very great distance.

'I've just ... no, I'm about to ... Sarah, can you bike it over?'

There was a long pause. 'This is an active murder investigation, sir. Can't you spare me half an hour?' The reproach was in the tone as much as the words.

'We've just arrested someone for Susan Blanchard,' Steve said stonily. 'I can't leave the Yard. Hang on a second.' He covered the mouthpiece and waved his free hand towards the door. 'Give me five minutes. I'll see you in the CID room.' As they filed out, he turned his attention back to Sarah Duvall. 'Look, you should be aware that Fiona Cameron seems to have vanished off the face of the earth. She was supposed to meet Superintendent Galloway this morning and she didn't show. Now, he tells me that she had a bee in her bonnet last night about Redford not being the man. She was convinced that the killer was still on the loose. And she was also convinced that he'd kidnapped Kit Martin. I can't raise either Fiona or Kit. I think we've got a serious problem on our hands here.'

'I couldn't agree more,' Duvall said.

'But I don't see how it can be Blake. According to my surveillance reports, Blake didn't leave his flat at all yesterday.'

'It's Blake, Steve. I'd stake my life on it.'

What worried Steve was that it wasn't Duvall's life that was at stake. 'You need to talk to Galloway,' he said.

But Duvall had her own priorities. 'The person I need to talk to is Francis Blake.'

From his vantage point in the trees beyond the ravine, Francis Blake stared at the track emerging from the trees. What was keeping them? She must have managed to get him free by now. There was a box of tools in the generator shed, he knew. That's where he'd found the axe that he'd used to smash the padlock on the gun cupboard.

He couldn't believe his bad luck. He'd only gone out to move his 4x4 to the far side of the gorge. But some inner caution had made him take the gun, hidden in a bundle of firewood. Luckily he'd heard her approach in the Land Rover and he'd had the sense to turn around and make it look as if he was walking out of the woods. A bit more warning and he could have been ready and waiting for the bitch. OK, it would have meant breaking the pattern, but to have killed Fiona Cameron at close quarters would just have been the icing on the cake.

He propped the shotgun against a tree and tucked his

hands into his pockets for warmth. The sun might be shining, but it was October, and here under the canopy of the trees, it was like midwinter. But it would be worth the wait when the pair of them plunged into the ravine. That would finish them off, no messing.

Then he'd be free and clear, either to kill again or to leave it alone. He didn't think he was under any threat from the police. Fiona Cameron was acting alone, he felt sure of that. She hadn't been able to convince her cronies in the force to back up what could only have been a hunch. After all, they had that lunatic Redford in custody. They must be pretty sure they had their killer under wraps. Otherwise, given the clout she had with the police, they'd have turned up mob-handed if they'd thought there was any serious chance of laying hands on a serial killer of his calibre. There was a kind of sweet irony in that, too. It was psychological profilers like her who had destroyed his life and he'd set out to destroy the people who had turned profilers into gods. Now, the profiler herself couldn't get anyone to believe her. Maybe that meant he'd made his point?

Blake took his hand out of his pocket and chewed the skin on the side of his thumb. Fucking profilers. They'd set him up to prove how clever they were. But he'd outsmarted them. He'd turned the tables and now nobody could touch him.

He'd had plenty of time to lay his plans. He'd always known he would get off when his case came to court, and he'd spent his time on remand brooding on the injustice that had been done to him. It would have been too obvious to go for the cops and the psychologist who had concocted the campaign against him. Besides, they'd never suffer enough to make up for what they'd done to him. He'd lost his home, his job, his girlfriend and his reputation. They'd only lose their lives.

No, somebody else had to pay. Who was responsible for

making the world believe that psychological profilers had all the answers? Simple. Thriller writers. Especially the ones whose books had been turned into films and TV shows that millions of people had watched. They were the ones who were really responsible for what had happened to Francis Blake. And they were the ones who would pay.

It had been easy to get hold of their books while he'd still been in prison, and relatively easy to find out about their lives. They were always talking to journalists. Plus the British ones all featured in a book of detailed interviews that some sad anorak had just published. Then when he got out, there had been the Internet. It hadn't taken long to put it all together. The hardest thing to find out had been the precise whereabouts of Kit Martin's bothy. He'd known the rough location, thanks to various interviews, but a search of the Land Registry had given him a precise address, and the Ordnance Survey map had done the rest.

Nobody had been watching him while he'd been in Spain, he'd made sure of that. And from Spain, it was easy enough to drive across the land borders in Europe and pick up ferry crossings from there. And eluding the pathetic Met surveillance on him once he'd returned couldn't have been easier. As long as he showed his face every other day and made it look like he was living the life of a recluse, they'd looked no further, leaving him forty-eight-hour spans free to do what he had to do in Dorset and, later, in Sutherland. He wouldn't mind betting they hadn't even figured out there was a back way out of his flat into the vanway behind the shops.

One thing they'd never understand, and that was how his life had changed after what he'd seen on Hampstead Heath. Then, he'd understood how easy it was to take a life away. Doing it himself had turned into a piece of piss, really.

Until Fiona Cameron came along and fucked up his

neatly laid plans. Well, she'd get her come-uppance soon enough.

He ran over the getaway in his mind once more. He'd moved the Toyota away from the bothy as soon as he'd unloaded Kit and locked him up tight. It would cause much less comment if a local spotted it on the access road up beyond the turning to the bothy than if they noticed it sitting outside. It was parked about five minutes away from his present position, facing down the hill towards the loch. He'd be on the road south in no time at all.

Then he heard the Land Rover again, its engine revving out of sight. It rounded the bend and slowed down to a crawl. He could see the outline of two figures through the windscreen. Then it began to roll forward towards the bridge, the engine complaining at such high revs in first gear.

As soon as the front wheels hit the bridge, the ropes snapped. In a crash of wood and metal, the Land Rover kept on coming, plunging downwards in a tangle of planks and rope. There was a fragmentary moment of stillness, then a terrible rending crash as timber and steel hit the rocks below.

Blake struggled through the undergrowth and emerged near the lip of the ravine. He edged forward, nervous of slipping and joining his victims. He looked down, hoping to see the broken bodies among the wreckage.

The tumble down the gorge had ripped the roof from the Land Rover, leaving its mangled base exposed to the rushing river. But where he'd expected to see Kit Martin and Fiona Cameron, there was nothing but strewn clothing and what looked like a couple of saucepans.

Blake swore fluently. The bastards thought they could

outwit him, did they? Well, they could forget that. Furious, he ran back to the Toyota and pulled the Ordnance Survey map out of the glove box. One way or another, he would have their blood on his hands by the end of the day.

Chapter 56

Caroline looked at the police constable behind the counter in the Lairg police station and despaired. He looked about twelve. A gawky, awkward twelve at that. He had dark-blond hair that had been cut by someone with no feeling for the job. His face was a pale moonscape of lumps – a bumpy forehead, prominent cheekbones, a thin nose with an angular bridge and a curiously round tip, jawbones like chestnuts, a sharp jut of chin and an Adam's apple the size of a ripe fig. He'd actually blushed when she walked in and said she needed his help.

'This is going to sound kind of strange,' she said. 'But it's a matter of life and death.' *Oh fuck, I already sound like a nutter.*

He picked up a pen and said, 'Name, please.'

'Dr Caroline Matthews.' Sometimes, having a title helped. Sometimes, even the wrong assumption that went with it helped. 'Look, I don't want to be difficult about this, but can we leave the form-filling for now? My friend's life may be in danger, and I think you need to deal with that as a matter of urgency.'

His mouth set in a stubborn line, but five seconds of Caroline's cold blue glare reduced him to submission. 'Aye. Right. What seems to be the problem, Doctor?'

There was, she realized, no point in attempting the whole

story. 'A friend of mine has a cottage locally. Kit Martin? The thriller writer?'

The young policeman's face lit up in a smile. 'Oh, aye, out at Allt a' Claon.'

'The thing is, he's been receiving threatening letters and his partner was worried about him because she couldn't make contact. She's afraid he's got a stalker and that something must have happened to him. Anyway, she went out there about an hour and a quarter ago. She said if she wasn't back in an hour, I was to go to the police.' She gave him her warmest smile. 'So here I am. And I really think you should head out there and see what's what.'

He looked doubtful. 'I'm going to need to go and talk to somebody about this,' he said, in the tone of voice that indicated he was suggesting something monumentally difficult.

What's keeping you, then? Caroline wanted to scream. 'Make it quick. Please?'

He scratched his forehead with the end of his pen. 'I'll go and talk to somebody, then.' He unfolded his long, thin body and crossed to a door in the far wall. 'You just wait there, I'll be back.'

Caroline closed her eyes. She could have wept. With every passing moment, her dread grew. *Please God, keep her safe,* she prayed to a deity she had never believed in. He hadn't kept Lesley safe; deep in her heart, she knew he'd be no use to Fiona either.

But there was nothing else she could do.

The news from the team searching Gerard Coyne's flat was distinctly encouraging. Steve began to feel slightly less anxious as he listened to the preliminary report from the officer in charge.

Underneath the bathroom carpet, they'd found an area of floorboarding that had been cut and glued to allow a section to be lifted clear of the rest. Inside the cavity, they had found a plastic ziplock bag stuffed full of newspaper cuttings. The stories covered every one of the rapes Terry had identified as being part of the cluster, as well as a couple of general pieces in North London freesheets about the prevalence of sexual attacks in the area. Even more significantly, there was a thick wedge of clippings relating to Susan Blanchard's murder. There were no other crime reports in the bag.

Also in the cavity was a Sabatier kitchen knife with a sharply honed blade. It was already on its way to the Home Office labs where it would be exhaustively tested for the slightest trace of Susan Blanchard's blood. 'I can't believe he held on to the knife,' Steve had said, still capable of being astonished by the stupidity – or arrogance – of offenders.

'We don't know yet that it is *the* knife,' his colleague cautioned. 'It might be the one he used on the rapes. It's not necessarily the same one he used on Susan Blanchard.'

Among Coyne's clothes, they had found several lycra cycling garments, all of which had been bagged up and sent for analysis.

They also found several trophies and certificates for cycling races that Coyne had won. There was no question that he could have been the cyclist hammering down the paths of Hampstead Heath that morning. He had both the skill and the stamina to have carried it off without even breaking sweat.

Steve walked into the observation room and settled down to watch the two officers he'd chosen to interrogate Gerard Patrick Coyne begin their work. The questioning had just begun when the call came through from Sarah Duvall.

Looking at the map, Blake could see only one possibility. No way they'd head down to the loch side road. They knew he had wheels at his disposal and they'd have no chance of avoiding him. The only other option was to hike out across the shoulder of the hill. That way they'd hit the road into Lairg near some cottages where, presumably, somebody would have a phone.

He couldn't believe that Martin had the stamina or the strength to make it that far. She'd probably leave him at the bothy and set off to find help. That would suit him perfectly, he thought with satisfaction. If he drove round to the end of her escape route, he could climb higher up the hill and find a vantage point where he could take her out with the shotgun. There were plenty of places to hide a body in a landscape as wild as this.

Then he could make his way back across the hill to the bothy and finish what he'd started. It would be a bonus, allowing him to get back to *The Blood Painter*. Much more satisfying than if they'd perished in the ravine.

It looked like the gods had decided to reward him for his patience. He deserved it, but it wasn't often in this life that people got what they deserved. He'd been changing that lately, and it was nice to see the universe joining in on his side.

Blake turned the key in the ignition and smiled with satisfaction as he set off back down the hill towards the dark waters of Loch Shin.

Few of the officers who worked with Steve Preston had ever seen his temper. But there was no doubting the towering anger that had him in its grip as the hapless officers who had been responsible for the surveillance on Francis Blake stood before him. Joanne and John, pulled off the interrogation of Coyne before it had even begun, and Neil, summoned back from the suspect's flat before the search was complete, were in no doubt that they had not so much fallen down on the job as collapsed in a disintegrating heap.

'It's beyond belief,' Steve raged, his face pale apart from two spots of high colour on his cheekbones. 'You're supposed to have had this man under tight surveillance, yet according to the City Police, he's been in and out of his flat at will, without any of you knowing. You have no idea what he's really been up to, have you?'

'Nobody told us about the bike,' John said stubbornly.

'All this time, Blake's had a ten-speed racing bike in the back yard, a key to the back door, access to the vanway that runs along the back of the row of houses. In all the time you were supposed to be watching him, did none of you think to take a look at the back of the premises?'

Neil stared at the floor. Joanne shrugged helplessly. 'We didn't realize you could access the back door from Blake's flat, sir,' she tried.

'You're supposed to be detectives,' he spat, his voice heavy with contempt. 'A uniformed probationer would have had more nous than the three of you put together. As it is, City think we're a complete bunch of tossers.' He slammed the flat of his hand on the desk. 'Does anyone have any idea where Francis Blake is right now?'

No one responded. Steve closed his eyes and clenched his fists. He needed this like a hole in the head. Kit appeared to be on the missing list, Fiona was God knew where in the Scottish Highlands doing God knew what, and he couldn't do anything about it because the Susan Blanchard case was suddenly alive and kicking again. It was his worst nightmare. He opened his eyes and growled, 'When was the last time any of you logged him in or out of his flat?'

'He went to the paper shop on Friday morning,' Neil said.

'It was a miserable day, so when he didn't come out again, I wasn't too surprised. The light was on in the flat all day.'

'It could have been on a timer switch, couldn't it?' Steve snapped. 'So the bottom line is, we have no idea where Blake has been since yesterday morning? And we have no idea when he'll be back?'

Again, none of them replied.

'Has anyone *any* idea where he's gone?'

They exchanged looks. No one spoke.

'Brilliant.' Steve took a deep breath, trying to get a grip on his anger. He took a cigar from his desk drawer, unwrapped it and lit it. The nicotine hit seemed to go straight to his very soul, calming him with its familiarity. 'Neil, I want you round at Blake's flat. Talk to the neighbours, see if you can get anything out of them that City have missed. And you two – go and have a coffee, get your heads on straight and get back here in twenty minutes. We've got a suspect to interrogate, even if City don't.'

As they filed out, his shoulders slumped. This was rapidly turning into the worst day of his life. And it could get a lot worse before it got better.

Fiona rounded the outcropping of rock where she'd left Kit fifteen minutes earlier. He was sitting on a flat stone, leaning against the boulder, sipping a can of Coke. His face was still ghostly pale, but he appeared more alert than when she'd helped him the few yards from the Land Rover to his resting place.

'How did it go?' he asked.

Fiona rubbed her shoulder where she'd landed awkwardly. 'Let's just say it looks a lot easier in the movies,' she said.

'But it worked?'

She nodded. 'I left the driver's door open, I put it in first

539

gear, wedged the rock halfway on the gas pedal and jumped. And as you predicted, the door shut behind me and the Land Rover carried on in a straight line. On to the bridge and down into the gorge. I don't think he can have seen a thing.'

Kit managed a wan smile. 'You did well, Fiona.'

'It was fucking scary, let me tell you.'

'Are you hurt?'

She pulled a face. 'Shoulder. I caught it on a rock as I rolled. Nothing serious, I don't think, but I'll have a hell of a bruise. Now, we need to start making tracks.'

'I don't know if I can do this,' Kit said. 'I'm still so dizzy.'

'I don't know if you can either,' Fiona said. 'But I'm not leaving you here. If Blake has rumbled our little ploy, he's going to come after us. And I'm not leaving you alone and vulnerable. Let's get as far along the hill as we can. And if you can't go on, we'll find somewhere safe where you can lie up and wait till I fetch help. But this is far too near the bothy. We've got to put some distance between us and Blake.'

She folded out the Ordnance Survey map and together they studied it. After she had spotted the problem with the bridge, Fiona had driven the Land Rover back to the bothy, then as far as she could across the rough ground behind it, where she'd unloaded Kit. According to him, it was possible to walk from here to the main road near where she'd left Caroline. It was a distance of between five and six miles, she reckoned. On her own, it would take her a little over two hours. With Kit in his present state, it could be more like four or five. But they had to make the effort. At least he didn't seem significantly concussed, which would have put the whole idea out of the question.

She got him to explain the route to her, then went over it again for her own benefit. For the largest part of the trek, they would be more or less level, staying on the contour line above the forestry plantations. According to Kit, there was a rough path – little more than a sheep track – most of the way.

'OK, let's do it,' Fiona said, stripping off the wax jacket and helping Kit into it. It would help conserve his body heat, and she suspected she'd soon have no need of the extra warmth. She tucked herself under Kit's right shoulder and heaved him to his feet. With the stick in his left hand, he slowly started to drag himself along the track. Fiona walked on the heather by the side of the narrow path, her eyes on her feet to avoid loose rocks and treacherous roots. At least the weather was on their side, she thought. In Kit's condition, a cold wind and even a shower of rain could be fatal. But the sky was more or less clear, the sun shining still, and hardly a breath of wind disturbed the cool air.

The rasp of Kit's laboured breathing was all she could hear, the weight of his body against her all she could feel, and the low thrum of his anxious fear all she could sense. They wasted no energy on speech, concentrating simply on putting one foot in front of the other.

After half an hour, she called a halt at the first suitable point, a long low escarpment of striated schist a dozen shades of grey against the heather's brown. She lowered Kit into a sitting position, then sat down beside him. 'Five minutes,' she said. 'There's some high-energy bars in your jacket. Can you manage to eat one?'

Kit nodded, too tired for speech. He fumbled a bar out of his pocket, but his numbed fingers still couldn't manage the unwrapping, so Fiona took it from him and opened it. 'You'll be OK,' she reassured him. 'It's just that nothing's working properly yet. It's the shock to the system.'

He ate slowly, munching every mouthful carefully before he swallowed. He offered the bar to Fiona but she shook her head. When he'd finished, she got to her feet. Time to make a move. By her reckoning, they'd covered about a mile, and it wasn't enough.

Again they plodded on, Fiona taking as much of his weight as she could bear. The ability of the human body to respond to crisis was amazing, she reminded herself. What a fabulous drug adrenaline was. She knew she'd crash and burn when all of this was over, but she also knew that until then, her capacity for endurance would be more than she could have imagined possible.

Another half-hour, another break. She could see he was tiring fast, and knew that there was no way he could manage another four miles of such rough going. If she could get him another mile or so along the way, Fiona decided she would seek out a hiding place where she could leave him. Under her own steam, she could cover the remaining three miles in half an hour to forty minutes if she pushed herself. Help couldn't be far away then, so near to Lairg. With luck, Caroline would have persuaded Sandy Galloway to mobilize some sort of local response. They could do the rest for her.

She got Kit to his feet and urged him on. The landscape was changing now, the heather hillside giving way to rock. The path had more or less disappeared and they had to pick their way more carefully. The route was still clear, but it was rougher going, with patches of loose scree that threatened to send them flying. After about twenty minutes, Kit said, 'I need to stop. I just can't . . .'

'No problem.' Fiona looked around for a suitable perch. A few yards ahead there was a pair of flat boulders that would do for a seat. She steered Kit towards them and helped him to settle. His breath was coming fast and shallow and a sheen of sweat glistened on his face. It wasn't looking good. Fiona took deep breaths and tried to stay calm. They must be close to the halfway point, she thought. Time to start thinking about finding Kit a bolthole. She leaned back against the rock and stared at the hillside ahead of them.

Suddenly, something caught her eye. About half a mile away, maybe seventy feet above them on the hill, what looked like a pipe kept bobbing into sight above the machair. It dawned on her with appalling clarity that it was the barrel of a gun. Blake was no countryman; he clearly didn't realize that although he was keeping low, the gun barrel was as obvious as a mastiff in a crowd of dachshunds. 'Kit,' she said. 'I don't want to worry you. But I think there's somebody up there ahead of us. On the hill. Is it likely to be somebody local? Or a hillwalker?'

'Where?' he said lethargically.

'I don't want to point in case it's Blake. But it's round about where a reasonably fit man would be if he'd driven back to the main road and started hiking in from this end. Over to the left, maybe seventy feet above us. There's a shoulder of the ridge behind him. He's maybe forty or fifty yards to the right of it.'

'I can't see anything,' he said. His voice was slurring again, Fiona noticed with anxiety.

'I saw what looked like a gun barrel bobbing up and down. Could it be a local?'

'I don't think so. There's no reason for them to be up here. There's nothing to shoot.'

'Fuck,' Fiona breathed, getting a better view. 'He's coming after us. Let's move on a bit and see what he does.'

Wearily, they dragged themselves to their feet and laboured on to the next place where it was possible to sit down, a stagger of about five minutes.

'Has he moved?' Kit asked.

Fiona angled her head so it looked as if she was staring

543

straight up the mountain. But out of the corner of her eye, she was scanning the area where she had seen the barrel. 'I've got him,' she breathed. 'I can actually see the blur of his face. I don't think he's moved.'

'Good,' Kit said. 'About five minutes ahead, there's a sort of crevasse. It's about four feet wide, but from up there, it just looks like a dark line in the rock. It's about half a mile before it opens out again. He won't be able to see us in there. Leave me and go on, you'll have a head start. It's not that far to the road, you can get away.'

'And what about you?'

Kit sighed. 'There's no way I'm going to make it out of here. I'm practically on my knees now. I can't go much further. He doesn't have to get both of us. Please, Fiona. Leave me.'

She shook her head. 'I'm not leaving you, Kit. I can't. Not after Lesley. Dying would be easier, believe me. But I don't have any plans to die either. Give me the map.'

Kit pulled the map out of his pocket and she spread it across her knees. 'Right. We must be about here?' She pointed.

'No, not quite that far along.' He corrected her, jabbing the map clumsily with his finger.

'There's a stream runs down across this track,' she said. 'How far is that from the end of the defile?'

'A few yards. Maybe a dozen?'

'How deep are the banks?'

'I suppose a couple of feet deep . . .' His voice began to trail away as his energy ebbed.

Fiona nodded. 'So if I can get up the stream bed without him seeing me, I should be able to come up above and behind him. I can jump him. Hit him with a rock or something. Deal with him, anyway.'

'You can't do that. He's a big strong bloke,' Kit protested. 'And he's got a gun.'

'Yeah. But I'd put money on my will to live being a damn sight stronger than his. And that, my love, is a professional opinion.'

'You're crazy. He'll kill you.'

Fiona put her hand in the pocket of her fleece and took out the craft knife. 'I'm not exactly unarmed. And I'm willing to use it. It's our only chance, Kit. I'm not going to sit here and wait to be killed.'

Kit put his hand over hers. 'Be careful.' He frowned at the inadequacy of his words. 'I love you, Fiona.'

She leaned into him and kissed his cheek. The cold clamminess of his skin reminded her there wasn't time to delay. She checked that Blake was still in position. Then she stood up. 'Let's do it.'

Chapter 57

Caroline checked her watch. It felt as if half a lifetime had passed while she'd been sitting in the reception area of the police station. Whatever was going on, it was taking long enough.

At last, the door in the far wall opened again and the PC returned, followed by a man who looked as grey and monolithic as some of the rocky outcroppings on the nearby mountain. His light-grey suit was creased in all the places it should have been smooth and he showed no sign of pleasure at Caroline's presence. 'I'm Sergeant Lovat,' he said. 'You're lucky I'm here. I only popped round with a message for Sammy here.'

'Has he explained the situation?'

'Well, he's told me what you told him, which doesnae sound like much of an explanation to me.' He leaned against the counter and cocked his head, as if assessing her and not much liking what he saw.

Caroline was conscious that she was not at her most prepossessing. Her hair was a mess and she knew she was probably almost as crumpled as Sergeant Lovat. Nevertheless, she needed to make an impression. 'I've never been more serious in my life, Sergeant,' she said. 'I really do think something untoward has happened to Fiona Cameron.'

'Untoward, eh?' Lovat said, chewing the word as if it were spearmint gum.

'Look, I know it sounds like a bizarre tale, but Dr Cameron is not a woman who wastes police time. She's worked as a consultant with the Metropolitan Police for years and I don't think they'd be . . .' Her voice tailed off as a possible solution to her dilemma presented itself. She'd been so busy worrying about getting her message across, she'd lost sight of the obvious lateral route. She took a deep breath and smiled at Lovat.

'Detective Superintendent Steve Preston,' she announced. 'New Scotland Yard. Please, call him. Tell him what I've told you. He'll know this isn't some wind-up.'

Lovat looked faintly amused. 'You want me to call Scotland Yard on your say-so?'

'It won't take you more than a few minutes. And it could save at least one life. Please, Sergeant Lovat.' She forced a cool smile. 'It would be so much better coming from you than from me. But if you won't make the call, I'll have to.'

Lovat looked at the PC and raised his eyebrows. 'What are you waiting for, Sammy? This should be a good one.'

The rock walls closed around them, about a dozen feet tall, producing a narrow channel that twisted away to the left. As soon as they were inside the sheltering defile, Kit urged Fiona ahead. 'Go, now. Just leave me. I'll find a place to sit down.'

She threw her arms round him in a quick hug. 'I love you,' she said. Then she was gone, moving swiftly along the base of the passage. Sure-footed and driven, Fiona moved with the easy confidence of a regular traveller in the rough terrain of hill and mountain. Within minutes, she could see the defile start to widen out, opening into a rocky slope with patches of heather and bracken pushing through. She paused, checking out the lie of the land.

The stream cut its own channel through the peat hag, its banks a rich, dark chocolate-brown fringed with the yellow of rough upland grasses and the cinnamon of bracken. It was, as Kit had said, about a dozen yards from the final cover of the low cliff. There was no way of checking whether Blake had figured out where they would eventually emerge or if he was just scanning the hillside in frustration, wondering where they'd disappeared to.

She considered for a moment. If she ran across to the stream, the very speed of her movement might attract attention. The fleece was a bright scarlet. But the thermal polo neck was mid-grey, her trousers a dark olive-green. If she shed the fleece, she would be pretty well camouflaged against the rock. It was worth a try.

Fiona pulled the fleece over her head and tossed it to the ground. Then she remembered her knife and retrieved it, making sure the blade was retracted before she put it in her trouser pocket. She dropped to her knees, then spreadeagled herself against the rock. In an agonizingly slow commando crawl, feeling hideously exposed, she crossed the dozen yards to the stream, crabbing round as she reached the bank so she dropped in feet first. The water was so cold it took her breath away for an instant. She crouched in water that came up to the middle of her calves, her head barely above the bank. She scanned the hillside, looking for Blake's vantage point.

'Gotcha,' she said softly. From this side, he was entirely unprotected. She could see the outline of his body against the hillside, the gun barrel protruding like an obscene prosthesis. He had a hand up to his eyes, as if he was looking through binoculars. Fiona made a rough calculation of where she needed to be so that she'd emerge above and behind him. The burn took a sharp left bend a few yards beyond where she wanted to be. Taking that as her marker, Fiona ducked down below the banks and started up the burn.

It was a treacherous ascent, the stones of the stream bed slippery with algae and too uneven to make her passage anything other than slow and awkward. More than once, Fiona lost her footing altogether and sprawled full length in the chilly waters. After the third or fourth ducking, she decided she couldn't get any wetter and started using her hands and arms to move her along faster, scrabbling up the burn like a chimpanzee.

So fiercely was she concentrating on her progress that the bend in the burn was upon her before she realized how far she'd come. She squatted on her haunches, trying to get her breath back. No chance of a stealthy approach if she was panting like a dog on a summer's day.

Slowly, cautiously, Fiona peered over the lip of the bank. She frowned. She was pretty sure she was looking in the right direction. But there was no sign of Blake. She sighted down the burn, to make certain she'd come far enough up. There was no doubt about it. She was exactly where she'd planned to be, which meant Blake should have been about a hundred yards away from her, maybe fifteen feet down the mountain. But he wasn't.

The tight hand of panic gripped Fiona's chest. She stood up, scanning the mountainside. There was no sign of her quarry. 'Fuck,' she moaned, scrambling out of the water course and on to the rocky side of the bank. Even with this higher vantage point, there was no mistake. Blake had vanished from the landscape.

That could only mean one thing, she thought. He'd panicked when they disappeared and made his way down to the last place he'd seen them. Where Kit was lying, vulnerable and weak as the runt of the litter.

Fiona took off like a mountain hare. Heedless of her safety, she hurtled across the steep slope at an angle she hoped would bring her to the beginning of the channel in the rock where she'd left Kit. Her wet boots squelched, skidded and slipped as she ran, and only the sharpest of reflexes stopped her pitching headlong down the slope.

As she raced down the hillside, what had started as a dark line in the rock gradually defined itself as the gap. From this angle, it looked like a giant split in a massive slab of stone. The closer she approached, the more Fiona realized she had misjudged her line. She was actually going to hit the edge about halfway along. She adjusted her course slightly, but the going was too steep now for it to be possible to make much of a correction.

She slowed to a walk, stepping sideways until she was at the edge of the drop into the defile. She looked back towards the beginning, but the angle of the bend was too sharp for her to see all the way to where she'd left Kit. Without the concentration of the downhill run to protect her, fear coursed through her like electricity.

Fiona forced herself to breathe deeply and started the treacherous scramble back along the rock. Halfway to her destination, she came to an abrupt halt. She could hear a man's voice raised in anger. She inched forward so she could see over the edge again.

What she saw made her stomach clench in pure terror. Down below, about fifteen feet away, Kit was sprawled on the ground, half sitting, propped against the rock wall. With his back to her, Francis Blake stood above him, hefting the shotgun in his hands. She couldn't make out his words, but his intent was clear. He took a step back and started to raise the gun.

Without pause for thought, Fiona sprang into action. She

took a short run up along the edge of the defile and launched herself through the air.

As the gun levelled out, Fiona crashed on top of Francis Blake, the momentum carrying them both in a heap on top of Kit.

The crack of a gunshot split the mountain air.

Chapter 58

The city glittered below her in a tawdry galaxy, zirconium to the diamond sparkles of the stars blotted out by the light pollution. It was, Fiona thought, probably all she deserved. She'd come up to her favourite vantage point on the Heath in spite of the frosty night air because she wanted to be as alone as it was possible to be in the heart of the city.

She pulled the letter out of her pocket, fumbling it through her gloves. There was barely enough light to make out the letterhead, but she needed to check its reality. The Procurator Fiscal had decided she was not to be prosecuted for culpable homicide. There were to be no formal repercussions for that single minute of chaos when the gun had gone off, taking most of Francis Blake's head with it. They had finally accepted that there had been nothing calculated in her actions; a few seconds either way and the outcome would have been quite different. Earlier, and Fiona might not have won a struggle for the gun. Later, and Blake would have fired and destroyed Kit utterly. Somehow, miraculously, she had landed at precisely the right moment. The gun had jerked back, Blake's finger on the trigger, and suddenly it was all over.

Both Fiona and Kit had been injured too, which was probably what had made the police believe her story that she had had no intention of killing Blake when she jumped from the edge of the defile on to his back. It would, she thought, have been much less credible if they hadn't taken some collateral damage.

She couldn't really blame the police for their incredulous reaction. She must have presented a bizarre sight, staggering off the hill covered in mud and blood, soaked to the skin. Reeling from the shock of what had happened, she had been cold-hearted enough to strip Francis Blake's body of his padded jacket and use it to make Kit as comfortable as she could. Then she'd torn herself away from him and covered the last few miles to the road in a blur of fear and pain, every stride sending a sickening wave of agony through the shoulder that had taken a blast of shot in the fatal moment.

Only adrenaline had kept her going all the way to the road. When she finally emerged from the last belt of trees, the phone box where she'd left Caroline had shimmered like a mirage through the miasma of her exhaustion. She'd staggered over to it and dialled the emergency services. Her relief when she was connected to a police officer almost made her buckle at the knees.

A squad car had been with her within minutes. Somehow, she'd managed to string her story together. And because Caroline had made the police talk to Steve, they took her seriously. But suspiciously.

And at least they'd mobilized an emergency helicopter to get Kit to hospital. She'd had no time to luxuriate in her relief; while paramedics extracted lead shot from her shoulder, the police had hovered, grim-faced and unsympathetic, waiting to pick holes in her story.

But she had been believed eventually. Everyone, from Steve to Sandy Galloway, had assured her there was no chance of her facing charges, but it had taken anxious weeks for the official notice to reach her.

She wasn't sure what she felt. Part of her believed she

deserved some sort of punishment for taking the life of another human being. But her rational self kept telling her how foolish it was to imagine that anything formal could assuage that particular guilt. And she couldn't deny that she felt a sense of remission that she wouldn't have to relive those terrible seconds when she had to make a life and death decision that, ultimately, had been no choice at all.

It was ironic that the only person who would ever appear in a courtroom in connection with Francis Blake's murders was the false confessor, Charles Redford. He was languishing in prison awaiting trial, charged with perverting the course of justice, threats to kill and offences under the Protection from Harassment Act. On the same wing as Gerard Patrick Coyne, due to face a jury for the murder of Susan Blanchard. The proximity of the two men who linked the crimes of Francis Blake provided a satisfying symmetry to Fiona.

The sound of footsteps on the path broke into her thoughts. She turned her head and saw a familiar figure approaching. Fiona looked back across the city lights, unwilling to appear eager for company.

Steve cleared his throat. 'I thought I'd find you here. Kit said you'd gone out for a walk.' He stood by the bench, uncertainty on his face.

'Did he also mention I didn't want company?'

Steve looked embarrassed. 'His actual words were, "You're taking your life in your hands, mate. She's off doing a Greta Garbo."'

She sighed. 'Now you're here, you'd better sit down.' They'd rebuilt most of their bridges over the previous weeks, but the sense that Steve had somehow betrayed her still lurked in Fiona's heart. That was something else she wanted to disappear from her consciousness, along with the memory of killing Blake.

Steve sat down beside her, keeping his physical distance. 'Kit also told me the news.'

'You didn't know already? I assumed that's why you came,' Fiona said.

'No. I came because I finally managed to get Sarah Duvall to give me a copy of Blake's journal. He started it while he was in prison, and kept it right up until a couple of days before his death. It was written in code, but it was pretty simple, and Sarah got it transcribed. I thought you'd be interested in seeing it.'

Fiona nodded. 'Thanks.'

'It covers all the practical stuff of how he laid his plans and carried them out. How he gave the Spanish police the slip when he was supposedly over there in Fuengirola. It turns out he has a cousin who lives in Spain. This cousin lent Blake his car, and simply stayed at the villa when Blake was over in the UK and Ireland, killing Drew Shand and Jane Elias. They looked similar, and as long as the Spanish cops saw someone answering Blake's description when they cruised past the place a couple of times a day, it never occurred to them that it wasn't him.'

Fiona nodded listlessly. 'I see.'

'He was able to enter the UK and Ireland by ferry without a problem because, of course, there was no general alert out for him. He'd got all the background information he needed from the Internet and from published material about his targets. He even managed to track down Kit's bothy via Land Registry records. He was a clever bastard. He covered all his bases. The only mistake he made was not taking account of the CCTVs in Smithfield.'

'That's fascinating, Steve. But does this journal answer the important question?'

'You mean, the motive?'

'What else?' Attempting to understand had kept her awake more nights than she could count. She knew there had to be some coherent motivation in Blake's actions, even if it only appeared reasonable to him. But why he should want to take revenge on thriller writers for what had happened to him had eluded her so far.

'It's twisted, but it makes a kind of sense,' Steve said.

'Don't they always?' Fiona said ironically. 'So, what's the story?'

'Blake was eaten up with the desire for revenge for what happened to him. But he knew if he took direct vengeance, he'd never get away with it. The more he brooded, the more he realized that there were people other than the police he could blame.'

'Thriller writers?' Fiona protested. 'I still don't see it.'

'He reckoned that if the police had never called in a psychological profiler, he'd never have had his life destroyed. But he also decided that the main reason profilers get taken seriously is because they've been turned into infallible heroes. And who turned them into heroes?'

Fiona sighed deeply. 'His victims all wrote novels where the profiler was responsible for tracking down the killer. And their work inspired films and TV that took the idea to a much wider audience. So, ultimately, they were the ones to blame.'

'That's about the size of it,' Steve agreed.

'And seeing Susan Blanchard's murder had made him realize it wasn't such a hard taboo to break,' Fiona said, half to herself. She looked up at Steve. 'Does he talk about her murder?'

'Endlessly. How much it excited him. How it made him understand that killing was the most powerful thing one person could do to another.'

'It always comes down to power,' she said softly. Fiona got to her feet. 'Thanks, Steve. I needed to know that.'

'That's what I figured.'

'Would you like to come back for dinner? I'm sure Kit's half expecting you.'

Steve stood up. 'I'd love to, but I can't.' He stared down at the ground, then looked up to meet her quizzical look. 'I said I'd meet Terry for a drink.'

Fiona's smile was one of genuine pleasure. 'Not before time,' she said, stepping forward and hugging him. 'I was getting really bored with telling the pair of you how much you'd misunderstood each other.'

'Yeah, well. I'm not saying I forgive her for what she did. But we both reckon we should at least listen to what the other has to say, now the dust has settled.'

Fiona looked out over the Heath. 'Is that what's happened?'

'Isn't that always what happens after the world gets turned upside down?' Steve said. 'Even if it takes a while, the dust always settles.'

Epilogue

Dear Lesley,
I'm writing to say goodbye.

If you'd still been around, you'd know that I turned into the kind of psychologist who doesn't really believe in this kind of therapeutic device, but since I agreed that I'd have post-traumatic stress counselling, I feel honour bound to do what the professional recommends, no matter how foolish and self-conscious it makes me feel.

It's amazing how little we understand of what provokes our responses. Even trained professionals like me lack insight when we're dealing with our own motivations. But what I've come to realize is that your death and the manner of it has never left me, no matter how hard I've tried to pretend otherwise. Its legacy has been one of pain and guilt. I felt guilty because I encouraged you to go to St Andrews instead of joining me in London. I felt guilty because I survived and you didn't. I was your older sister and I was supposed to protect you, and I failed. I felt guilty because I didn't manage to push the police into uncovering your killer. And I felt guilty because I couldn't stop what happened to Dad after you died.

As well as that, there has been the pain of loss. At every milestone in my life, I am conscious of your absence; I wonder what you would have achieved and how your life would have been. I watch Caroline changing and growing, making mistakes and getting things wonderfully right and I think about how you would have handled them differently.

Sometimes I look at Kit and wish more than anything that you two could have known each other. I know you'd have liked each other. The two people I love best in the world. How could you not? I can feel the time together we've missed, the happiness lost to us, and it tears me up. I miss you so much, Lesley. So many of my best memories have you in the centre of the picture. You were the one with the gift of optimism, the giver of grace. I was so proud of you, and I never told you. I loved you so very, very much, and I never told you. You died without knowing how much you were cherished, and that's another bitter regret for me. Because the guilt and pain have been so strong for so long, I'd lost any sense of the blessing you were while you were alive. What I'm trying to do now is to take the good things from the recesses of my memory and put them in the foreground, in the hope that they'll gradually swamp the hurt and stop it shaping the way I view the world.

What I also have to accept is that the other legacy of your murder has been my professional life. Because of you, I chose to move in a particular direction. It was as if I felt that, having failed you, I had to try to do what I could to stop something similar happening to anybody else. I suppose I was looking for a kind of redemption.

So I have to acknowledge that when Kit went missing, my subconscious probably grasped at this as an opportunity for finding my own salvation by saving him. In hindsight, I could have, should have done more to force the police into action. But at some level, I accept now that I almost wanted them to reject me, so that I would have to walk the high wire.

I did not expect that it would leave me with blood on my own hands and a different kind of guilt.

And when I saw the man I love staring death in the face, none of those considerations came into play. I simply acted without thought or hesitation and did the only thing it was possible for me to do.

But I still wake up at night to the sound of a gunshot and the nightmare memory of Francis Blake's head exploding in my face.

The one outstanding item, according to my therapist, is my need to reconcile myself with you. That's what this letter is meant to be about. I suppose what I have had to come to terms with is that it is impossible for me to change the past. I have had to accept that what happened to you and to us as a family is not my responsibility but rather the responsibility of the man who took your life.

I guess I was afraid that if I admitted that to myself, I would have no reason to carry on doing what I do so well. I was wrong. What I do is worth doing for its own sake. I probably would never have chosen it if you had not died as and when you did. But that should not be a millstone around my neck. It is, like my friendship with Caroline, a gift your death gave me.

Understanding that and accepting it are two different things, of course. But one will almost certainly lead to the other, and this letter is a step in that journey.

And so, I take my leave of you. I will never forget you or stop loving you. What I hope is that I will stop feeling that I owe you something I can never pay.

With love,
Your sister
Fiona.

A Place of Execution

Val McDermid

'Compelling and atmospheric . . . a tour de force'

MINETTE WALTERS

Winter 1963: two children have disappeared in Manchester; the murderous careers of Myra Hindley and Ian Brady have begun. On a freezing day in December, another child goes missing: thirteen-year-old Alison Carter vanishes from an isolated Derbyshire hamlet. For the young George Bennett, a newly promoted inspector, it is the beginning of his most harrowing case: a murder with no body, an investigation filled with dead ends and closed faces, an outcome that reverberates down the years.

Decades later he finally tells his story to Catherine Heathcote, but just when her book is to be published, Bennett unaccountably tries to pull the plug. He has new information which he refuses to divulge, information that threatens the foundations of his existence. Catherine is forced to reinvestigate the past, with results that turn the world upside down.

A taut psychological suspense thriller that explores, exposes and explodes the border between reality and illusion.

'A terrific and original novel, brilliantly executed'

Daily Mirror

ISBN 0 00 651263 1

The Wire in the Blood
Val McDermid

Young girls are disappearing around the country, and there is nothing to connect them to one another, let alone the killer whose charming manner hides a warped and sick mind.

Nobody gets inside the messy heads of serial killers like Dr Tony Hill. Now heading up a National Profiling Task Force, he sets his team an exercise: they are given the details of missing teenagers and asked to discover whether there is a sinister link between any of the cases. Only one officer, Shaz Bowman, comes up with a concrete theory – a theory that is ridiculed by the group . . . until one of their number is murdered and mutilated.

Could Bowman's outrageous suspicion possibly be true? For Tony Hill, the murder of one of his team becomes a matter of personal revenge, and, joined again by colleague Carol Jordan, he embarks on a campaign of psychological terrorism – a game where hunter and hunted can all too easily be reversed.

'Stunningly exciting, horrifyingly good'

RUTH RENDELL

ISBN 0 00 649983 X

The Mermaids Singing

Val McDermid

You always remember the first time. Isn't that what they say about sex? How much more true it is of murder . . .

Up till now, the only serial killers Tony Hill had encountered were safely behind bars. This one's different – this one's on the loose.

In the northern town of Bradfield four men have been found mutilated and tortured. Fear grips the city; no man feels safe. Clinical psychologist Tony Hill is brought in to profile the killer. A man with more than enough sexual problems of his own, Tony himself becomes the unsuspecting target of a battle of wits and wills where he has to use every ounce of his professional skill and personal nerve to survive.

A tense, brilliantly written psychological thriller, *The Mermaids Singing* explores the tormented mind of serial killer unlike any the world of fiction has ever seen.

Winner of the 1995 CWA Award for Best Crime Novel of the Year

'Truly, horribly good'   *Mail on Sunday*

ISBN 0 00 649358 0